SEVEN COWS:

Pandemic, Resilience and Hope

Eaton Rapids Joe

Auctoritas Publishing LLC
Springfield, Missouri

This is a work of fiction. Any resemblance between persons living or dead is a coincidence.

The following images are by contract with Shutterstock: "Bling Heels", "Plain Sneakers", "Caution: Giant Hogweed", "Puppies!" and "Ms Sheridan".

Front cover art by Tina Garceau
Back cover art and images (c) Turning Records Entertainment LLC

First Publication May 2020
2 1
Paperback ISBN: 978-1-7350191-0-9
Digital ISBN : 978-0-9858017-9-3
Published by Auctoritas Publishing LLC
Springfield, Missouri
www.auctoritaspublishing.org

DEDICATION

This book is dedicated to the tens of millions of quiet heroes who do the right thing, especially when nobody is watching.

Special thanks go to my parents who got me started. Thanks to Dennis Dezendorf who is my "Blogging Godfather" and Jim Curtis (aka Old-NFO) who is my "Writing Godfather".

A special tip-of-the-hat to my editor, Anita Bailey; without her there would be no book. And another tip of the fedora to Tina Garceau who cheerfully provided over forty versions of the cover art before it was perfect.

But most of all, this book is dedicated to you: The people who are raising kids, going to work everyday and giving every job your best effort. I salute you as you volunteer in your communities as coaches, Sunday School teachers, board members, and cutting the lawns of little-old-ladies. The list of what you do is endless.

Prelude

And it came to pass at the end of two full years, that Pharaoh dreamed that he stood by the river. Out of the river came seven fat cows and they fed in a meadow. Then seven more cows came out of the river, ill favoured and leanfleshed; and stood by the fat cows upon the brink of the river. The skinny cows killed and ate the seven well favoured and fat cows. So Pharaoh awoke.

Genesis 41:1-5 NEV

PART 1

SEVEN FAT COWS

CHAPTER ONE

The bulletin boards and forums were on fire with rumors of Ebola having made land-fall in the continental US.

The original posts cited videos that had been quickly yanked off the internet. A typical video was of a middle school basketball game where one of the players suddenly collapsed and started vomiting bloody fluid.

The CDC felt compelled to issue a statement that the seasonal flu sometimes exhibited those symptoms and to not panic. The CDC claimed to have everything under control.

Rick Salazar had plenty of time to track the progress of the phantom epidemic. He worked the gig economy and was currently in a lull. Also, the middle of January was a slow time on the farm. On nice days he might cut a little bit of firewood but other than that all he did was walk the dogs.

Rick was one of those people who could walk up to a group of ten men anywhere in the Western Hemisphere and instantly blend in. He was a little shorter and a little darker of complexion than the average US citizen. He was reasonably fit and about sixty years old, give or take five years. If he had one quirk it was that he tended to dress a wee bit more casually than average, one of the advantages of working from home.

What was distressing to him was that the videos seemed to all originate in San Diego, California and St. Paul, Minnesota.

If the CDC's story was true then the videos should be originating in a semi-random fashion that was roughly proportional to population density.

It only took a few minutes of internet research to learn that San Diego and St. Paul were epicenters for refugees from Uganda and its neighboring countries. IF Ebola was going to show up in the US then it was more likely to show up in those two cities than just about anywhere else.

Rick logged off his computer and took a stroll around the property. He did not like what he saw.

There was nothing wrong with the forty acres. It was fifteen miles from "the city" of 200,000 and roughly five miles from two cities of five thousand each. Nope, the problem was not the property. It was the house and its proximity to the roads.

The house was a scant 150 feet from the road and another road pretty much "T" ed into the front yard. The house was indefensible.

Rick rode his mountain bike on the frozen but snow-free roads around the two square miles that contained his forty acres. After that he rode a couple of miles up the road that Teed into the road he lived on.

What he saw was that the landscape rolled and undulated and there was a high point about every quarter mile. In some places the vertical distance between the peak and the valley was fifty feet. In other places it was five. The only places where the land was perfectly flat were the muck fields.

He also saw the reason why the road department decided to end the one road at the T. The two square miles were bisected the long way by extensive muck bottomed marshes. Rick had heard one neighbor say that some of those muck deposits went down thirty feet. Not a desirable roadbed by any stretch of the imagination.

The only conceivable defense against the Golden Horde, the lawless mob of desperate people who were expected to decamp the cities in the event of massive, civil strife involved posting sentries on the road at the hill tops and to have a means of communication. That was going to take some thinking.

Rick also counted mailboxes. The pieces he rode varied between thirty mail boxes per mile down to two mailboxes per mile. Figuring three people per house he passed 360 people and he did not see a single soul who was not in a motorized vehicle.

Getting back to his study he did a quick study of passive, infrared sensors. He ordered twenty of them from an online vendor. Even if this plague were just a hoax, he would have a lot of fun playing with them. Who knows, maybe it would help him get his next gig.

After placing the order Rick started organizing his junk. He had once been an avid prepper but his interests had changed.

Hand tools went into one outbuilding. "Chemicals", motor oil and such went into another. Motors, pumps and the like were moved into the yard where it would be convenient to cover them with a tarp. Building supplies and fencing were assembled into piles.

Rick was exhausted when Kate came home from her volunteer work. It was the deep weariness that forebode of several painful mornings to come.

The Property

Rick spent the second day doing inventory. It is of no value to have "stuff" if you cannot find the tool you need in five minutes.

Rick had three fence post drivers, a dozen hammers, more

screwdrivers than were worth counting etc., ad nauseam.

That is when he made a fundamental decision. Rather than grouping items by what they were, he grouped them by task. One fence post driver went into the pile for pasture fencing. One went into the pile for gardening. The third went into the pile for "back-up". To make them easy to find he painted them white and made a mental note to paint over the white with a fluorescent orange...if he had time.

A distressing number of items were junk. He started a burn pile and covered the pile with "natural" wood. The township was pretty easy-going with regard to the ordinance against burning "manufactured products" but he knew better than to rub their noses in the fact that sometimes the occasional broken shovel handle ended up on the bonfire.

The inventory revealed that he had enough pesticides to last for a decade but he was woefully short of fertilizer and certain kinds of seeds. There were lots of bicycles and twice as many flat tires. Enough high-end 2-stroke oil to mix 120 gallons of gas for his chainsaw but only 2 gallons of oil for the chainsaw bar...when he would need 60 gallons to match the gas.

He leased twenty of his forty acres to a local farmer who grew the traditional corn-beans-wheat rotation. The last rotation had been wheat and consequently the fields were fallow in late December. If events wobbled the very worst possible way the farmer would not be planting corn the following spring. More likely he would get them planted but the prices would be so low come November it would not pay to harvest. Or maybe nothing would happen.

Rick and Kate had a horse that Kate occasionally rode. And when they had a bunch of kids at home, they typically raised a couple of beef animals each year. They ran those animals together on about three acres of pasture behind the house.

The house sat on two acres along with the garden and orchard.

There were ten acres at the back of the property that Rick had never done much with. It was low and swampy and filled with "gopher wood", that is, wood that burned so fast you threw a load into the woodstove and immediately went to get another.. Over the last few years Rick had cut all the dead ash out of the woods as it died off from the emerald ash borer. He had also been scattering walnuts and acorns at the edge of the swamp in hopes of up-grading the stock and improving the hunting but so far those trees were very young.

The last five acres were along the west edge of the property. Rick had dedicated that to a wildlife travel corridor. While the trees were a little bit of everything, he had planted clumps of Black Locust such that 25% of the trees were that species. Not only was Black Locust great firewood, it made durable fence posts and the nitrogen the trees fixed help their neighbors grow better.

When Kate came home Rick said, "I have been thinking on this Ebola issue. I don't know if it is for real but I want to move up some of the improvements we have been talking about."

Kate sighed. There had been a scare five years ago and Rick had done the same thing, although to his credit he had lived like a pauper until the pre-spending had been paid for.

They fed the stored grain to meat chickens and kept the entire, extended family in meat for two years.

"How much and what do you think we should spend it on?" Kate asked.

The Shopping List

Rick said "I think we can get most of what we need for about five thousand."

Kate winced.

Kate did not like spending money. In her early-sixties, Kate was famous for gently using clothing and making them last for decades. Due to her extremely fair complexion Kate had to wear full-brimmed hats and long sleeve shirts when outside. Her favorite fedora was twenty-five years old.

“We are good on firearms and ammo. In fact, we have more than we need and we should probably feel out our neighbors to see who can be trusted with them,” Rick said.

In addition to the 12-gauge pump shotguns that every rural family had at least one of, Rick had been picking up .22LR semi-automatic rifles and AR clones on sale. Add in 20,000 rounds of .22LR ammo and 5000 5.56mm NATO ammo and "the makings" to reload an additional 10,000 rounds, and Rick thought they were more than squared away.

Rick’s rough list had seeds, grain, large griddles, firewood, wire, calves, deep-cycle lead-acid batteries, 3V laser diodes, oil for two-stroke motors....

“How long do you think we have before we know?” Kate asked.

“Hard to tell,” Rick admitted. “If it doubles every twenty days and there are twenty patients now then it will take ten doublings, say seven months, to hit twenty thousand patients. That is when people will lose faith in the CDC and the economy will shut down. Then another seven months to hit twenty million. That is when there will be a total, blood-in-the-streets shitstorm.”

Kate said, “I am not opposed to pulling the trigger on this stuff but I will be a lot more comfortable if you can show me some confirmation.”

“Meanwhile, let’s use the time to refine the list and find good prices," Kate said.

Rick spent the next several days sorting and inventorying their gear. He also scheduled appointments with the eye doctor and dentist for both he and Kate. He knew that he had an old prescription for his glasses and his dentist had been bugging him to get some of his teeth capped before they split. Now seemed like a good time to get that done.

He also visited a few of the neighbors who he knew kept the long view in mind. It wasn't so much that they would completely buy into Rick's hypothesis about Ebola, but they knew that civilization was fragile and there was always something nibbling at the foundation. It might be an EMP event or war or plague or the shredding of shared social bonds, but the cause was not important because the consequences and actions required to mitigate would be nearly identical.

One neighbor was a Romanian born electrician who lived a half mile closer to one of the main roads. Another was a disabled vet. The third was a skilled tradesman who had retired in his mid-fifties and dabbled with his hobby farm and hunted and fished.

Dmitri, the electrician, took on the problem with the IR sensors. He had experience installing fire alarms and the communication protocols were a walk-in-the-park for him. He would have a working prototype shortly after the mail-order source dropped off the battery carriers, transistors and such.

Tim, the disabled vet, and Rick cruised the neighborhood several times on Tim's utility vehicle and talked through probable "zombie kill zones" and which clusters of dwellings were most defensible and which were write-offs.

Kelly, the tradesman, pointed out that the marsh could be augmented by the simple expedient of plugging the drain tile. Or, if it was desirable, damming the drainage ditch. Kelly also took on the task of mapping out who owned the larger tracts of land. If the owners lived in a different state, then the land would be up-for-grabs whether for squatters or for "common use".

For his part Rick said that he would keep them supplied in food if things shut down. Even if that food was nothing more than cornmeal pancakes. That is when Tim offered the use of his four passenger, gas-powered utility vehicle to help in the delivery. A full-on quarantine would have people starving in their homes. A person can take a lot of cold if they have the clothing and the calories.

Unlike most of their neighbors, Rick and Kate had very few power tools. They had a pickup truck, two chainsaws and a lawn mower but little else. They did not find it limiting because they fiddled around on a small scale and rented out the land for a neighbor to farm.

Confirmation, Sort of

The first partial confirmation came a week later.

There was a small item in the news feed for San Diego that the Navy was diverting ships and planes to bases other than San Diego. The reasons given were that the dry-dock was being overhauled and the other maintenance facilities were being audited for pernicious computer viruses that might infect fire-control and avionics systems.

The article had a few "human interest" tag-alongs where dependents shared their feelings now that their partners were being diverted to Bremerton and Pearl. The hardware and humans who moved them were isolated to facilitate cyber-forensics and that had the dependent's knickers in a knot.

Rick was puzzled that two potential breeches showed up at the same time and appeared to be at the same stage of development. It was just a matter of time that one breech would show up. It was a huge statistical anomaly that two had popped up at the same time...or it was not a random fluke. Said another way, statistics suggested that Ebola's arrival in the US was the result of enemy action and was not an accident.

That got Rick sniffing around Atlanta and DC news feeds. Atlanta and DC were the other primary destinations for refugees from the Horn of Africa. DC was of particular interest because that is where people were most likely to be "in the know".

What he found was that it was impossible to hire somebody in Maryland or Northern Virginia to install retaining walls and/or security fencing...that they were booked six-to-12 months out. When he called one of the security fencing companies and tickled them to see how busy they were, he learned that customers had already paid substantial deposits for those commitments and he could not cut to the front of the line by waving cash.

He also found that many of the communities in and around the Beltway had very strict zoning restrictions that prevented fencing and the wholesale clearing of vegetation. Curiously, nearly all those communities had put those ordinances into abeyance for the time being.

Rick shared this with Kate, Dmitri, Tim and Kelly.

Kate gave the go-ahead to purchase the items on Rick's list. Rick sent the kids an email and told them that he had started the count-down to the zombie apocalypse. "The Zombie Apocalypse" was their code for when friends and neighbors might become potential hostiles and when it became necessary to implement a new rules-of-engagement.

He wrote, "Come when I say come. Keep your gas tanks full and warm stuff in the trunk. I don't know how fast things will get sporty, but I want you to be ready because I cannot promise that we will be able to open our doors to you if you dally."

The girls emailed back. They wanted to know if they could bring a friend when the time came. They also wanted regular emails so they could judge for themselves the urgency of the situation.

Rick and Kate talked over the problem of "friends". They agreed that friends were "OK" as long as they were an asset, i.e. low maintenance and willing to pitch-in and do chores and would cheerfully live in tents or the barn.

After noodling on the issue a bit, Rick started sending out a weekly email update. The first one outline the conditions under which "friends" would be welcome.

Predictably none of the boys responded.

Apple Pies

Not every visit with neighbors went smoothly.

Rick visited one of the larger landowners in the neighborhood, one who actually lived on his property.

Rick had just hit a garage sale next door to Carson Duckworth's house when Rick saw Carson poking around in his back yard. Rick strolled over to say "Howdy."

The conversation went into the septic tank almost from the get-go.

Rick knew for a fact that Tim, the disabled vet, was short of firewood so Rick asked "What would it take to have a neighbor come over and cut some of the dead wood in your swamp?"

"Why don't you cut your own?" Carson asked.

"Not for me. For one of our neighbors," Rick said.

"He can kiss my rosy-red ass," Carson spat back.

Later, Rick shared the story with Kelly while they sampled some fine, Kentucky sippin' whiskey. Kelly then told Rick about Davidson, Kelly's dog.

Davidson was a Bluetick Hound and a hunting fool. Davey got out one evening and treed a coon on Carson's property. Kelly went over to collect Davey when Carson came boiling out of his house. Kelly kept his cool and tried to explain what happened.

Carson "brandished" by making sure Kelly could see he was packing. Then Carson was in Kelly's face the whole way off the property, threatening that he would file charges for trespassing.

The threats weren't idle. Kelly found out there was a bench warrant out for him after a cop stopped him for speeding. In addition to the traffic ticket, Kelly lost a day of work and got popped for $350 in court fees to clear up the matter. Kelly was not a fan of Carson.

Rick was just shaking his head. He was trying to get ready for Armageddon and he was trapped in the meat-space equivalent of a Facebook pissing match. Petty politics and gossip were a big reason he chose to leave corporate American and join the gig economy.

Kelly changed the topic. "I'd like you to do me a favor," he said.

"Whaddya need?" Rick said.

"I want to borrow one of your .22s... whatever model you have most of," Kelly said.

Rick frowned. He knew that Kelly had no shortage of firearms.

And then Kelly winked.

There are times when it is not wise to ask questions.

“Sure. No problem,” Rick said.

Later that evening Rick shared what he learned with Kate. He had not anticipated open hostility when approaching neighbors.

Her reply was succinct. “You need a spoonful of sugar.”

“I beg your pardon?” Rick replied.

“Mary Poppins. ‘Just a spoonful of sugar makes the medicine go down,’ “Kate lilted in her soprano.

“What do you suggest?” Rick asked.

“You could start cleaning out the root cellar. Come April we throw out three-quarters of the apples you put down there. Why don’t you make apple pies and leave them on porches? You can even blame me...tell them that I ‘made you’ do it,” Kate suggested.

That proposal solved a couple of problems and Rick figured it was worth a try. He fiddled around and came up with a cover letter to explain the pies (cleaning out the root cellar) and on his next trip to town he bought a hundred, folding pie boxes.

The next day he figured out how to make four pies at a crack.

CHAPTER TWO

A Lull

Six weeks had gone by since the first tickle and there was no further confirmation. Even Rick was beginning to have doubts. If the hemorrhagic disease was Ebola, the swarm of CDC people were putting the limited supply of vaccine to good effect and were creating air-tight rings around the carriers.

He did not regret the purchases but he would have stretched them out.

Well, that is not entirely true. He had picked up a couple of woodstoves for the cost of scrap metal. Then he had to buy stove pipe. The regular, single walled pipe is dirt cheap and is the pipe of choice for runs that are more than eighteen inches from the wall because it transfers a lot of heat from the exhaust into the heated space. The expensive pipe is the pipe that must be used to pass through walls or ceilings and roofs. That is some fancy, expensive hardware.

Rick was not just buying "stuff", he was installing it. The best place to store a piece of equipment is to install it and tie it in. He improved his fences. He built a large shed to store firewood.

Then he spent the better part of two weeks filling the shed with firewood. He worked four hours a day which was about as much as he could manage and stay safe. It doesn't pay to run a chainsaw when you are ragged out.

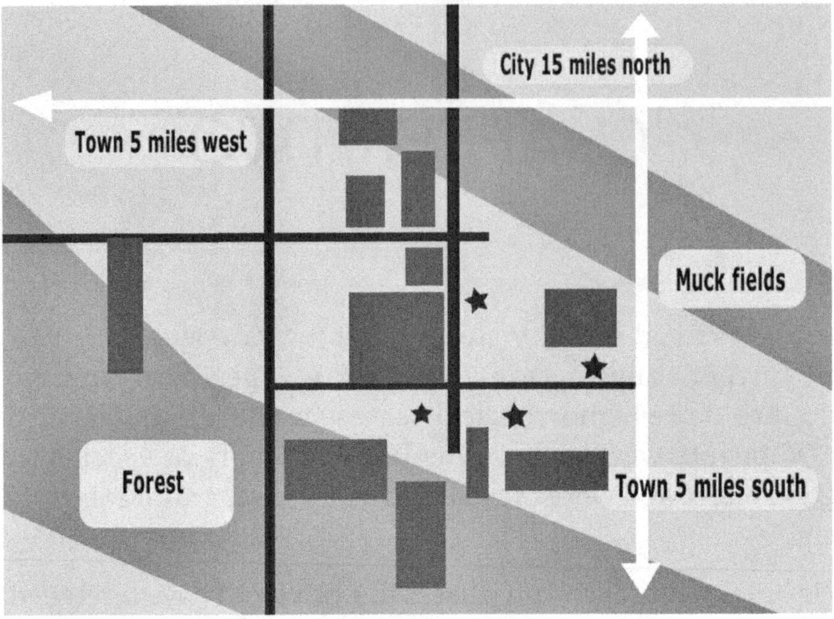

Starting with top star and moving clockwise: Top is Tim's place. Dmitri is at 3:00; next is location of Rick and Kate's property; Kelly and Di are at 7:00. Grea areas are muck fields. Dark grey are forest. Dirt roads are darker and paved roads are lighter.

The pies were a big hit. One of the things that Rick did not comprehend was that there were multiple networks that tied the neighborhood together. Some of the ties were family. Some of the ties were church and social organization. Some of the ties were common places of employment. Many of the ties came through children, their clubs and sports teams and school activities. Parents who sat next to each other in the bleachers and at dance recitals had developed relationships that were invisible to Kate and Rick.

By the second week the neighbors had "patterned" his gifting and the next four recipients generally had a box out on the porch to receive the gift. That confirmed in Rick's mind that one person cannot hope to match intelligence that lives in "the cloud".

The apple pie project forced Rick to think through the natural extent of his neighborhood. His natural inclination was to keep it to within a half mile of his house which would keep it all to "dirt road" people.

Tim, the disabled vet had different ideas.

"Lookit, Rick. I know you read history. Nations are defined by natural boundaries. There are a few exceptions, Canada and the US come to mind, but other than that defensible, natural barriers are the rational places to put frontiers," Tim said.

Sitting in Tim's golf cart, Rick said "Why don't you show me what you are thinking. I do better with something concrete."

Tim drove the cart out onto the paved road a mile from Rick's house. Perched atop a rise Tim said, "We live on a finger of high land that is oriented west-northwest-by-east-southeast. Each finger of land was separated from the fingers to the north and south by peat fields and muck bottomed marsh."

Rick nodded in agreement.

"Those are our natural boundaries," Tim said.

Rick had never thought of those houses on the paved road as being part of "his" neighborhood. For one thing he almost never walked on the busy, paved road. He could see Tim's thinking. The paved road was a natural conduit for the Golden Horde and the best place to defend it was the knot of homes at the southern edge of the peat field. Anybody attempting to approach them would be exposed and leaving the road ran the risk of getting bogged down in drainage ditches or feather-soft ground.

“OK, I see what you are saying,” Rick said. “What else do you want to show me?”

Driving two miles to the west Tim pointed at a bridge to the south. Then he drove to the north to the next intersection and pointed to where the road crossed peat bog. Then, turning east he went a mile and then turned north. A half mile later the road crossed peat fields and you could tell based on the wallows and sinks in the road.

“What is to stop them from coming cross country along the finger of land?" Rick asked.

“Nothing, yet,” Tim admitted. “But roads are the primary lines of drift. Leaving the road is much harder going...takes four times as long, minimum. Gets your shoes wet. More bugs. Ain’t gonna happen unless it is an organized attack with disciplined soldiers,” he finished

"There is one more thing I want you to consider,” Tim said. "I almost didn't bring this up but it is something you need to know."

"Your original plan for boundaries puts my house, and Dmitri's, right on the frontier. That might be right comfortable for you but not so much for me. If the push-and-shove of defending this neighborhood happens, then my house is right on the front lines”, Tim said.

"But SOMEBODY's house will be on the frontier,” Rick said. "Why not somebody who is trained to defend it?"

Tim looked at Rick. It occurred to him that much of what was instinctive to him was opaque to Rick.

"Let's walk this through,” Tim said. "In a set-piece battle the early parts of the contest have a lot of mobility. For one thing, the defenders need to determine if the group pressuring the border is passing through or intent on conquest."

"Once the battle is joined, the defenders need to be able to mount a counter-attack and push the attackers back to a boundary that the defenders can maintain," Tim said.

"There is no terrain that is defensible between my house and yours," Tim said. "You are inviting defeat when you think in terms of arbitrary distances rather than terrain that is inherently defensible."

He continued, "The other thing you need to think about is that there are almost no people living in the muck fields. They are the only place to draw the line where very few people are going to feel like they are being sacrificed for the good of the many."

Rick resigned himself to making a lot more pies.

Rule of Threes

Rick kept bumping into the Rule of Threes:

Three seconds of stupid can get you dead
Three minutes without oxygen will get you dead
Three hours of cold and wet can get you dead
Three days without water can get you dead
Three weeks without food can get you dead

He shared with Kate that he felt he was not focusing on the most important things.

Kate, as always, helped Rick stay grounded.

"How long does it take to grow a forest?" she asked.

"Short rotation, coppice...maybe three or four years to grow wood big enough to be worth burning," Rick replied.

"How long does it take most people to find a five-gallon bucket?" Kate asked.

"Maybe a few minutes. Maybe an hour if they have to borrow one or buy one," Rick replied.

"There you go!" she said.

"But what about the 'stupid' part?" Rick asked. "I am not even sure what I can do to help folks with that."

"'Stupid' can cover a lot of territory," Kate mused. "It can be ignorance. It can be trailing the curve during fast moving events. I am sure it can mean other things as well."

Rick nodded his head in agreement. "Yeah, that is what I am talking about. I need help breaking it down into actions I can take and make a difference on."

"Does anything pop into your mind for 'ignorance, just not knowing'?" Kate asked.

Rick said "Hmmm. You know I once spent a summer at a cottage with no TV. They had a set of 1936 Encyclopedias. I am thinking that those books are more applicable to the life we might be living than Wikipedia, for instance."

"Can you still buy sets of encyclopedias?" Kate wondered.

"I dunno. Pretty easy to find out. All I have to do is tickle the internet," Rick replied.

"That still leaves me without a way to address fast moving events," Rick said with a frown.

"Radios," Kate said.

"Huh?" Rick said. Sometimes Kate could read his mind and she assumed he could read hers.

"Radios. Those little walkie-talkies you used hunting before everybody got cell phones," Kate said.

"How far do they have to transmit?" she asked, rhetorically.

"That is the tough thing. Maybe two-and-a-half miles and it won't be line of sight," Rick said.

"How did they handle that when you worked maintenance

in the factory?" Kate asked. "You weren't all in the same building."

"Well, they used GMRS band radios and they had repeaters in each building. At least that is what the electricians told me," Rick admitted.

"Is there any reason you can't do something like that?" Kate asked.

"Once again, I will have to do some research. But that is something I am pretty good at," Rick said. "One thing I know is that if we put in repeaters, we will need to have batteries and either solar or wind power to keep them going. That costs money."

Kate sighed. EVERYTHING cost money. "Work up a plan and a budget," she said. She would count it as a victory if the money was spent slowly and if the items that were bought performed as advertised.

Di

Rick and Kate were visiting Kelly and his wife Di. They alternated weeks. One-week Rick and Kate would host and Kelly and Di brought the libation. The next week Kelly and Di would host. It was a lot cheaper than going out for entertainment.

Di was showing Kate the paintings she had finished since the last visit. Di liked to stay busy.

About a half dozen acrylics were propped up against the wall in the sparsely furnished, wood floored living room. As might be expected of an artist, the house was abundantly supplied with windows. It only took one glance to see that Di favored large splashes of vivid colors...Brilliant blue skies, parrots, lush meadows and gaudy irises, orchids and sunflowers.

Rick and Kelly were in the sunroom sipping a white wine

from Chile. Rick was overwhelmed by the task of nation-building. There were just too many pieces.

Kelly was giving Rick a pep talk and trying to coach Rick on the art of recruiting others.

Meanwhile, Kate was being drawn out by Di in the living room. Di wasn't in-the-loop but she knew something was afoot.

"So, Rick thinks the flu that has been in the news might destroy civilization?" Di exclaimed. "Is he nuts?"

Kate shrugged. "That is just the way Rick is. He goes off on these jags. 'Full immersion', he calls it. He is super-energetic while he is learning something new and then he kind of mopes when he gets to the end of it. It just seems to be how he learns," Kate said.

The girls helped themselves to goblets of wine and then joined the boys in the sunroom.

Without preamble Di braced Rick. "So what is this about the flu ending civilization? It sounds like a good story." Her inflection on the word 'story' was totally neutral. Her inflection didn't imply she thought it was bullshit nor did it imply that she bought in.

"I am not sure it is the flu," Rick said. "The last outbreak of Ebola in Africa is now endemic in four countries and is in fast-smolder mode. The symptoms of this 'flu' look a lot like Ebola."

"Wouldn't the government tell us it was Ebola?" Di asked.

"Have you looked at the stock market lately? It has been a dead-man walking. The government is doing everything it can to prop it up," Rick said.

"Have you looked at the trade-wars we have going on? Every one of those trading partners is itching for an excuse to slam the doors on American exports. Active cases of Ebola would be just the thing," Rick said. "Nope, I think if it were Ebola...and I am not saying it is, just that it could be...the bureaucracy would do everything in its power to suppress the story in the hope they could contain and extinguish it," Rick concluded.

Di snorted. "Two people can't keep a secret. What makes you think a million government employees can?"

Rick shrugged. "Great question. How many people really need to know it is Ebola? Just tell all the people on the hot end that the meds and vaccine are for the flu and tell them to use universal precautions."

"The list of people in-the-know might be a single lab in Atlanta and a straight chain-of-command up to the President," Rick said. "Many of those labs are run by ex-military and they run a very tight ship."

This was a novel concept for Di. She thought that with everybody on social media, everybody knew what everybody else was doing.

"So, you think this could be Ebola and it could turn into a total shit-storm?" Di questioned.

"It could. On the other hand, it might not be Ebola. Or they could throw an airtight containment ring around the outbreaks and crush the outbreak before it gets legs," Rick admitted.

"Does Ebola kill people or just make them sick? I really don't know anything about Ebola," Di admitted.

"Ebola kills 80% of the people who get it," Rick said. "It blinds and inflicts brain-damage on a significant portion of the people who survive."

Looking for a bright side, Di suggested "Maybe in Africa. But what about the US? Don't we have better immune systems, all those vitamins and protein and stuff?"

"Doesn't help," Rick said. "Ebola targets the immune system and the better your immune system the faster it takes over your body. The other thing is that Ebola kills you by triggering a cytokine storm. Basically, that is a super-immune response that kills your blood vessels by way of collateral damage."

"Is there any good news?" Di asked, barely able to take in the enormity of Ebola.

Rick shrugged. "Some of the evolutionary biologists speculate that Ebola will become less lethal in the future. Killing your host in 14 days limits your ability, as a virus, to spread. Some biologists think that in two human generations Ebola will be just another cold virus or STD as it detunes to optimize spreading. Those same biologists point to syphilis as an example of that happening," Rick said.

Di said, "Well that isn't going to do us any good. It isn't likely any of us will be here forty years from now."

"So, what is your plan to save Western Civilization?" Di asked.

"I don't know if it is possible to save all of Western Civilization. I will be tickled if we can save our four-square mile neighborhood," Rick said.

"Well, what is your plan to save the neighborhood, then?" Di asked.

"To have a fighting chance we need to be able to go into self-quarantine. We need a self-contained economy that isn't dependent on outside inputs. An economy that doesn't depend on the grid, doesn't depend on gasoline or diesel," Rick said.

"You mean we have to live like the Amish," Di said.

"Sort of. But most Amish shop at Walmart just like the rest of us. We need to be able to live like the Amish did in 1910. Oh, and we need to be able to defend ourselves, something the Amish refuse to do," Rick said.

"Count me in if it means horses," Di said.

Kelly snorted. "Horses are just a way to spend money quickly," he said.

A pet horse was one of the on-going discussions that had been running between Kelly and Di ever since they had moved out to the country twenty years ago. Kelly was all for Di raising animals that ended up in the freezer but he thought everything else was a waste of money, ESPECIALLY horses.

Rick perked up. "You are interested in horses?"

"Yeah," Di said. "I am not sure I want to ride them but I think it would be cool to have a buggy." Di was a tiny woman and it would be a feat for her to mount a standard sized horse without a stool.

Kelly was still skeptical. "See, not only do horses cost thousands of dollars, now you want to buy a fancy rig."

"You are putting words in my mouth," Di said. "I bet you could whip up a dandy buggy in your shop. It doesn't have to look like something you see in the movies. I want something I can take the grandkids for a ride and maybe carry groceries in."

And then Kate piped up. "We didn't pay thousands of dollars for my horse, Billy."

"What did your horse cost" Kelly asked.

"Billy is a retired trotter. They are called 'Standardbreds' and there are several Standardbred rescue organizations. We paid about $400 but we had to drive to New Jersey to pick it up," Kate said.

"Trotters? Don't they pull those tiny carts? What are they called?" Di asked.

"Sulkies" Kate said. "And they are not the least bit skittish because they have been racing in front of crowds thirty weeks a year. Most of the rescue horses are geldings and are eight or ten years old."

Di clapped. "Count me in if it means horses," Di said.

Kelly squinted at Di. "You are serious about pulling a cart and not interested in all that 'dressage' stuff?" he asked.

"That is what I want. A simple cart and a horse to pull it," Di affirmed.

"And you would be OK with a cart that I fabricate in the shop?" he asked.

"Yup. Just make it so it doesn't jar the fillings out of my teeth when I hit a pothole and big enough to carry me and the four grandkids," Di said.

Kelly shook his head. They had never gotten far enough in the discussion for him to have a solid picture in his head of what Di wanted.

"In that case," Kelly said "we might as well get two of them. They can keep each other company and the hard part of taking care of animals is waking up on cold mornings to take care of them. Don't see how two of them will be that much more work than just one."

The Buggy

Kelly went over to Zane's salvage yard to see what was available. He had a half-backed plan to salvage the running gear from an automobile and use it beneath Di's buggy.

OK, it was more than a half-baked idea but he was still flexible on what vehicle he was going to strip the undercarriage from.

Zane invited Kelly in for coffee. It was a blisteringly cold morning and Kelly was a valued customer.

The neighborhood's view of Zane was complicated.

One neighbor hated Zane like poison. Zane was dragging a piece of farm equipment to his yard when the neighbor's dog gave chase. After nipping at Zane's rear wheel for fifty yards it turned away from the truck right into the spinning disks.

Zane never even slowed down. He was playing his radio loudly and had never even noticed the dog. The neighbor was sure that Zane swerved to hit his dog because what dog would be stupid enough to turn in front of a piece of equipment that sliced it up like baloney.

Other neighbors looked down on Zane. They automatically equate "salvage" with garbage. They worried about automotive fluids leaking out and polluting ground water. They worried about resale value. They worried about his yard becoming an eyesore.

They did not realize the effort Zane put into draining the vehicles. Heck, it was to his advantage. He had not purchased gasoline in years and his oil burner loved transmission fluid.

Most of the neighbors who disapproved of Zane had moved into the neighborhood recently. Those neighbors who had been there more than ten years had figured out that Zane was way smarter, both in book learning and human nature, than anybody would have guessed.

Zane was always ready to lend a hand cleaning up a yard or a barn. He had pulled more than one young man out of a ditch. Why not, he had a wrecker.

"Whatchya looking for today?" Zane asked. "It must be a pretty hot project because it is colder than a congressman's heart out there."

"Gunna make Di a buggy," Kelly grunted. "She is gunna get a horse and she wants a buggy."

"That could be OK," Zane agreed. "You got a picture in your head?"

"I was thinking of more a wagon than a buggy," Kelly said. "I see a lot of trailers made from the back end of pickup trucks. I was thinking of keeping the frame and all four wheels. Maybe hook up to the horse with something like a tow-bar."

Zane nodded his head sagely as the words painted a picture in his head. "What kind of horse is she getting. A big one?"

Kelly shook his head "No. It's gonna be a retired trotter. I don't know how big they are but I am guessing a thousand pounds."

Zane offered the opinion "A full sized frame might be more than that size horse could handle."

"That's why I was thinking the frame from a small truck" Kelly said.

"Naw, you want to stick with a full-sized truck. The front suspension goes with the frame and you don't have a bunch of stuff sticking way up. You won't have to dick around with McPherson struts and figuring out how to get structure up to them," Zane said.

"But then we are back to the frame being too big," Kelly said.

"Did you ever think about shortening the wheelbase by cutting two or three feet out of the middle and welding it back together?" Zane asked. "Mr. Pepper used to do that to convert mil-surplus trucks to semis 'back in the day'."

After finishing the coffee, the men walked out into the salvage yard. Zane started the tractor with the forks mounted on the front and tipped over a few trucks so Kelly could look them over.

"You know," Zane said "if it were me, I would dump the engine, tranny and gas tank, doors and front-end sheet metal. You might as well keep the cab because you can't beat the hydraulic brakes that are already installed. All you got to do is figure out how to mount the cab. You are probably gonna have to raise it up to get over the rails."

Kelly said, "Di will probably like that, having a cab to keep her out of the weather and being up a little higher."

Kelly and Zane dickered a little while. It was more a matter of form than serious bargaining. After agreeing to a price, Kelly drove his truck over to his new project. He started the generator and then plugged in the air compressor after it had warmed up. Then he got busy with his impact wrench.

He had to stop a few times to warm up but he was able to drag the carcass back to his place later that afternoon.

Kelly hit a bunch of sites to find plans and dimensions for Amish buggies. It came as little surprise that there is very little information on the Amish on the internet. He figured he would just have to wing it. If it was a failure, then he would learn from it and make another.

Rambling Wreck

Kelly was spreading peanut butter on a couple of slices of bread when he announced to Di, who was in the other room painting, "Do you want this buggy to be any particular color?"

Di asked, "What color is it now?"

"Kind of a dingy blue" Kelly said back. They had an open

floor plan and Di's "studio" was separated from the kitchen by a half wall.

"Yellow," Di said. "Yellow with black racing stripes."

"Yellow like a school bus or taxi cab?" Kelly asked.

"Nope," Di said. "Yellow like a Camaro."

"Why yellow?" Kelly asked. He really wasn't surprised that she had chosen a bright color. It was a reflection of her extroversions and her enthusiasm for life.

"My first bicycle was yellow," Di said. "Actually, it was my second bicycle...but it was the first NEW bicycle I ever had."

"Or you could just buy me a Camaro," she added, slyly.

Kelly snorted. Low-slung sports cars are not a good choice for dirt roads that are given to chatter bumps and massive potholes.

"Yellow it is," Kelly said.

He made a call to his nephew, Josh, and Josh agreed to take on the project after hours. He agreed to pay extra for Josh to do the body work, filling in the dents and such.

Then he loaded the cab and box onto the truck and drove them over to Josh's shop.

"Yellow?" was all Josh said. "Must be for Aunt Di, am I right?"

Kelly nodded his head in the affirmative. Di was a favorite aunt in the clan.

Josh called a week later. The body was ready to go back on the frame.

Not only was the sheet metal bright yellow but Josh had enhanced it with bold, black racing stripes. The front of the racing stripe was a fist and the back segued into a vicious looking yellow jacket. Josh had also foamed and formed the front to look like the front of Santa's sleigh.

“Nice graphics,” Kelly said. “What made you think of that?”

Josh shrugged. He was an artist. “I have catalogs. The yellow jacket is a version of Georgia Tech’s mascot but nobody around here will know that. The fist...well, I thought you might be driving it sometime.”

“I guess the Georgia Tech mascot is appropriate. This really will be a ‘rambling wreck’," Kelly said.

By the time Kelly had the buggy all assembled Di had brought the horses back from New Jersey and had spent some quality time bonding with them.

One thing Di did not tell Kelly was how much she had spent on tack and horse care equipment. Di had a fun money account for projects and the folks at the adoption center had been very thorough in walking her through what she needed to care for her two new babies.

Di was also pleased that the center had taken pains to ensure that the two boys (geldings) got along. Horses are like humans and have distinct preferences for who they enjoy hanging around with.

Kelly dragged the buggy out of the barn with his tractor.

If Di was disappointed that it was a wagon rather than a buggy, she did not let it show.

“Oh! WOW!” she said.

Kelly could see every imperfection but Di seemed dazzled.

“It is BEAUTIFUL!” she gushed.

A couple of months later Kelly was driving to Vermontville and saw an Amish buggy clipping along between fifteen and twenty miles per hour. That was three times faster than either horse could pull the yellow wagon.

Slow runners are eaten. Slow runners don't catch dinner. Slow runners do not get to mate with prime females. It is deeply embedded within the "Y" chromosome to not be slow.

Kelly bought a "real" buggy shortly after that. Much to his surprise Di continued to drive the wagon more than the "real" buggy.

She really did like it. It was yellow.

CHAPTER THREE

Rick and Kate's Kids

Rick and Kate had five kids. Three of them were biologically theirs and two of them were foster kids who had joined their household as fifth graders and then "aged out" at eighteen.

The Girls

Gabriella

Gabriella was Rick and Kate's biological daughter and their oldest child. Gabby taught high school English in a suburb of Memphis, Tennessee.

Gabby was married to Guillermo (Bill) Gonzales. Bill drove a delivery truck. Gabby and Bill were both physical fitness nuts.

Gabby was organized and had to work very hard to not be "bossy". Sometimes she was successful in that endeavor.

More than once she had been in a staff meeting where the boss was wasting time, spinning his wheels about how hard some task was going to be to execute. In one case the task was to organize a 5k race to support a local charity. Twenty seconds after the unproductive, hour-long meeting ended, the boss received a "Ding!" of an incoming email. Gabby had collared ten volunteers, purchased the T-shirts, commissioned a design from a local artist and tentatively sourced the printing at the printer who worked for the firm. She had also laid out the course and scheduled the event for the weekend when the closest competing race was fifteen miles away.

That was Gabby on a normal day.

They had no children but they did have a Jack Russel cross (with a beagle?) named Sam.

Janelle

Janelle was removed from her mother when Janelle was seven. Janelle had been in-and-out of her mother's house several times until her mother tested HIV positive. Then the courts placed Janelle into the foster care system where she bounced around until she was about to enter high school. That is when she landed in Rick and Kate's house.

Janelle personified many people's preconceptions of "poor, white, trash."

Janelle was into body art: Piercings, tats...the works. The image she projected was completely the opposite of her personality. It was many years before Kate figured out that the body art was Janelle's armor. She looked tough so bullies picked on other people.

Janelle spent the most of high school taking on-line classes and then after graduation she drifted west. First to Grand Rapids, then to Chicago, then Denver, then Seattle.

Janelle kept in touch with Rick and Kate but was usually pretty thin with details about exactly what she was doing for work and housing. Kate figured that Janelle's situation changed so fast that she didn't know where her next dollar was coming from.

Janelle was willing to work but could be "moody" and was not trustful of others.

Mostly, Janelle simply wanted to be left alone.

Nyssa

Nyssa entered Rick and Kate's house as a twelve-year-old.

Nyssa's mother had moved up to Michigan with her brood of feral children and promptly over-dosed.

If anybody knew anything about Nyssa's mother's history, they kept their mouths shut.

The brood was broken up because their poor behaviors reinforced each other.

In one of those circumstances that make predicting human behavior so aggravating, Nyssa not only thrived with Rick and Kate, she excelled. That is not to imply that life didn't get exciting with Nyssa around.

Nyssa was mixed race, almost six feet tall and muscled like a leopard.

Nyssa was working on her Master's in Nursing at a university affiliated with a very large, urban hospital.

The Boys

Luke

Luke was born two years after Gabriella. He had gotten his growth late in life and that shaped him.

Luke had cultivated the fine art of invisibility. Luke worked third shift in a warehouse.

If Luke had a social life, he did not share it with his parents.

Mark

Mark was the middle boy and was Rick and Kate's youngest biological children. Where Luke was quiet Mark was brash.

Everybody knew when Mark entered a room.

Mark had been a wrestler in high school. Like Rick, he was of medium height and had dark, brown hair.

Mark joined the Coast Guard after high school and had been stationed in New England. He met a a local girl named Betsy and got married. They made two babies in quick succession and were living in picket-fence perfection Portsmouth, New Hampshire.

Mark sold cars, trucks and SUVs and was financially doing very well.

All five kids could prepare a meal all the way from digging the potatoes out of the ground and killing the chicken to setting a fancy table to torching the crème Brule to washing the dishes. Shooting a scoped .22 rifle offhand they could hit a soup can at fifty yards as often as not. They knew how to pick a decent camping site and set up a tent and start a fire in the rain. They had all changed oil in an engine and changed a flat tire.

Trial Run

Rick jollied Kate into making a two day "trial run" of their preps.

Kate was onboard with the wood heat but opted out of the diet. She did agree, however, to document the experiment.

The trial run was a fiasco from the start.

The cistern pump that Rick had purchased on-line was not able to pull water from the well. If Rick had researched a bit more, he would have learned that "sucker pumps" can only pull water up twenty-five feet or so. The water in his well was a good forty feet below the surface. Even pulling from a spigot in his basement left him trying to pull too much.

Then he found that getting water from the nearest source of open water, Kelly's pond, left much to be desired in the winter time. He had to spud a hole through the ice and lift it out with a scoop. Then carry the five-gallon buckets to the truck.

Half the water sloshed out on the way back. Kate asked what the plan was when the gasoline ran out. Rick did not have a good answer. Kate made notes in her spiral notebook.

Rick boiled the water on the stove. The stove used LP gas. Kate asked what his plan was when the LP ran out. Rick did not have a good answer. Kate added to her notes.

Then Rick started a fire in the fireplace. Once it started going, he turned on the blower. Kate looked up, "I thought the grid was down?"

Rick turned off the blower. Almost no heat entered the living space. Kate donned a parka and mittens. That, as much as anything, aggravated Rick. Kate's exact age was privileged information, it was sixty give-or-take something, but Rick still found her attractive and was perplexed that she was looking like the Michelin man.

On Saturday, Rick broke open one of their oldest five-gallon, food storage buckets. It contained white rice, split peas and vegetable oil. The air seal on the bucket had broken and pantry moths had gotten in. Rick washed the insect remains out of a couple handfuls of the rice and boiled it for breakfast. Kate looked the other way when he drank a cup of coffee from the pot she had brewed. Rick was a bear when he did not get his caffeine.

Rick's lunch was white rice with green-pea gravy as was his dinner. He was going to add vegetable oil to the green-pea slurry but the oil had turned rancid in its plastic bottle.

By noon Sunday Rick was constipated and had no energy. His lethargy left him cold. It was all he could do to pry himself off the couch and drag in more firewood... firewood that wouldn't provide any heat.

He was also bored out of his mind. He was used to getting on-line. He had a few favorite TV shows. It was like an itch he could not quite reach far enough to scratch.

The postmortem was enlightening.

The rule-of-three puts water at three days. Clearly, something had to be done. After batting about several ideas, Rick and Kate decided on a roof-top collection system for spring-summer-fall and a solar powered, immersible pump for winter.

The solar powered pump could irrigate the garden and orchard during the summer.

The issue of heating raised a bit of a quandary. Kate wanted things to look nice. She was not ready to jump right to a wood stove. She thought most of them were hideously ugly.

Rick had to do some research before he found a wood stove that had glass that wrapped around the fire. Kate bought into that kind of stove but did not want it in the center of the room.

United Nations level negotiation ended up with the wood stove 24 inches in front of the old fireplace and spun thirty degrees from square. That was so the heat radiating from the back of the stove reflected off the back wall and into the room rather than heating up the wall behind it.

The stove pipe ran up parallel to the fireplace chimney to within 12" of the ceiling and then "Teed" horizontally through the wall. Rich had learned that much of the heat thrown off by a wood stove is actually radiated from the stovepipe. The "tees" made it easy to clean the pipe.

The lethargy was a bit of a mystery until Rick was watching one of his TV shows, *Live Below Zero*. It was the episode when several of the characters affirmed that absolute need for fat in cold weather. It was a light bulb going off for Rick.

The soybean oil in plastic bottles was removed and replaced with "creamy", partially hydrogenated vegetable oil packed in glass whiskey bottles scrounged from a willing bar owner. Partially hydrogenated oils have very low linolenic acid (18:3) content, the component that goes rancid the most quickly.

The other revelation was the food buckets. Rick had packed them with the intention of having them last one adult for one month. Extrapolating, it was far more realistic to plan on having them last 20 days and to include instant coffee or tea, bran, salt-and-pepper, vitamin tablets, a deck of cards, a paperback mystery and a minimum of three liters of oil.

Pride Goeth Before Fall

The joint CDC-FEMA teams who had been playing whack-a-mole with the Ebola outbreaks in Minneapolis and San Diego were justifiably proud of the job they had been doing. Not only had the contained the outbreak but they had kept the news out of the public eye. It had not come cheaply. They had burned through 85% of the vaccine in the western hemisphere.

***

Clara waited for the city bus outside the Section 8 block where she lived. She carried two infants in a shawl and held the hand of a small boy with a runny nose.

Her name was really not “Clara” but her given name was incomprehensible to anybody who was not from her tribe in Somalia. She happily traded her name for a better life in Minneapolis.

The boy was six and small for his age. He had a deep, hacking, liquid cough that welled up from deep in his gut. Clara was worried because tribal lore was that his condition nearly always ended in death. But this was America, land of miracles.

The trip across town was a major expedition for Clara. She had seventeen children in her apartment. Eight of the children were her biological children. Seven belonged to her sister who had been raped and murdered in the refugee camp. The extra two were her grandchildren. Most of the kids went to school or Head Start. Clara had parceled out the youngest ones across several Somali families.

Not being very familiar with the bus system, Clara was not able to choose the most efficient path. She took her children to the downtown transfer center and it took her an hour to figure out which one went to the clinic that she thought would best be able to handle the problem.

Workers and University students streamed around her and her coughing child. Like most things in Minnesota in the winter, the bus depot was inside.

After figuring out which bus she needed, she boarded a bus crowded with the morning shift heading to the hospital.

The triage nurse tried to send Clara home. The nurse took an IR temperature read and the child barely had a temperature. The nurse dismissed it as a common cold. Clara would not be dissuaded. She mentioned her concern but the staff did not recognize the tribal term as anything alarming.

Cases deemed to be more critical than her son were queued in front of her as she and her three charges waited

More than seventy "John Does," homeless men, shuffled back out through the waiting room. They had spent the night in the hospital to get out of the cold. It was trash and recycling day on the south-west side of town and like migratory possum they followed the trash. They would not be back to this particular hospital for three days.

The City Mission did not allow people with alcohol on their breath into the facility but hospitals had to take them. If anybody had bothered to chart the number of homeless in any given hospital, they would have found it tracked trash pickup and free church dinner nights.

Medical students new to the Emergency Room would badger them about their symptoms. The nurses would roll their eyes. They would learn soon enough. The nurses privately called the homeless men "dirty-ankles" or DAs.

The dirty-ankles knew what symptoms forced the hospitals to hold them. Sharp pain on the lower right side of abdomen. Chest pains. Shortness of breath. If the doctor persisted after running expensive diagnostics and tried to discharge the patient the dirty-ankle simply dredged up another symptom. A dirty-ankle could easily rack up $100,000 of unbillable tests in a night.

The newbies quickly learned to simply put the dirty-ankles on a gurney, give them a blanket and a baby aspirin and a cup-of-soup and they would miraculously be cured in the morning. If there was something actually wrong with them, they would be hollering bloody murder.

Miracles-B-Us

The six-year-old boy "coded" in the Emergency Waiting Room after a particularly violent, racking cough. The small boy's aorta had split longitudinally and he bled out internally within seconds.

That smugness of the CDC-FEMA team evaporated after the labs on the six-year-old were finally run and confirmed. The results were what nobody wanted to hear. Unfortunately, the results were communicated twenty minutes after the first shift had left for the day and that vastly complicated the response.

That is also when the last 15% of the Ebola vaccine that was not staged in Minnesota and San Diego was flown to Washington D.C. and administered to the highest level government functionaries.

The joint CDC-FEMA quick response team had a very strict set of protocols for this scenario.

The Emergency Room was closed to new patients due to “a sewage line leak”.

Patients that were still in the pipeline were not discharged until after they had been given the vaccine. They were not even told what it was.

Caregivers in the Emergency Room were vaccinated.

Caregivers from the prior shift were told to put their clothing into a plastic garbage bag and take a hot, soapy shower before coming back to the hospital. They were told that their jobs were contingent on doing so. They all came back and were vaccinated from the rapidly dwindling supply of vaccine. Four day’s pay were automatic added to their next paycheck.

Then the tedious task of contacting the ER patients who had cycled through the ER during day-shift began. The patients who had been sitting within one bench of the deceased child were identified from video, chased down and vaccinated.

All this in spite of the fact that everybody knew that Ebola is not airborne.

The problem with the protocols was that they had been created by administrators. Some of them had served in Emergency Medicine but it had been twenty-five years since they were on the sharp end of the stick. They had gotten very good at telling other people what to do and had forgotten many of the details that made execution difficult.

In all, the heavy-lifters did a phenomenal job.

The two details that slipped under the radar was that the child had a cold and was coughing and sneezing, spewing billions of tiny globules of bloody mucus and saliva into the air. The reason Ebola was not spread by air-borne means was because Ebola rarely triggered sneeze-and-coughing reflexes. The same could not be said about the colds that were sweeping through central Minnesota.

The other detail was the seventy-plus John Does that had filed through the ER before fanning out across the city.

Unintended Consequences

Part of the protocol was to have multiple people interview the people closest to the outbreak. The intention of the multiple interviews was to glean as much information as possible.

Clara was interviewed for six hours straight. Four different interviewers were involved. Due to language issues, there was an interpreter.

Clara was intimidated by the interviewers. She knew they were cops. She could see the bulletproof vests and pistols. And they wore face masks. She assumed they were going to rape her. The good news was that they would let her live, otherwise they would not have bothered with the masks.

The interpreter was attempting to impress the officials. He intended to get paid a lot of money. He kept rushing Clara, promising dire consequences if she did not answer with perfect honesty or did not answer them quickly.

The protocol was very clear that some questions were to be asked several times and must be asked verbatim. One of them involved the number of children and other people living in the house.

The interpreter, intent on impressing the officials with his speed and efficiency truncated the question and asked about “her children”. Clara never mentioned her deceased sister’s children.

After the interviews, ambulances queued up outside the Section 8 housing and her biological children were taken, one to an ambulance to be transported to quarantine.

Up until that point Clara had believed the best about Americans. And then she knew: The story of White People draining blood from Blacks to make medicine must be true. She knew her children were dead.

There was nothing left to hold her in St Paul and every reason to leave. She would move in with her cousin and start over.

She gathered up her sister's children from where they been hiding and went down to the Catholic Church. She was close to one of the older men who worked at the Saint Vincent de Paul food bank. She told him that her sister had died (which was true) and that she needed transportation to the funeral (which was not true).

The old man had no family. He had nothing better to do. He went to the ATM and withdrew $500 and threw a mattress into the back of his old, plumber's van. After all, it was a long drive from St. Paul, Minnesota to Bladensburg, Maryland, seven miles from the United States Capitol building.

CHAPTER FOUR

Firewood Planning

Back in Michigan, Rick picked up the event on his news feed. He kept one specifically for winnowing through the blizzard of the 24-7 news items looking for key terms like "Emergency Room". His feed picked up the unfolding events in Minnesota but Rick accepted the explanation that a sewer pipe had broken.

Meanwhile, Rick continued to worry about the availability of firewood.

Rick sincerely believed that energy is the keystone resource. Food is one kind of energy.

Firewood is another.

A rough estimate of the new, larger neighborhood was that it held 150 homes. Most were clustered close to the paved roads, that is, they were biased to the east and in the northwest corner.

The woods were scattered but most of them were oriented through the middle on a north-south axis with heavy concentrations on the southern border.

About half of the 400 acres of woods were on parcels where the owner lived. The other 200 acres were on the property of absentee land-owners or belonged to commercial farmers.

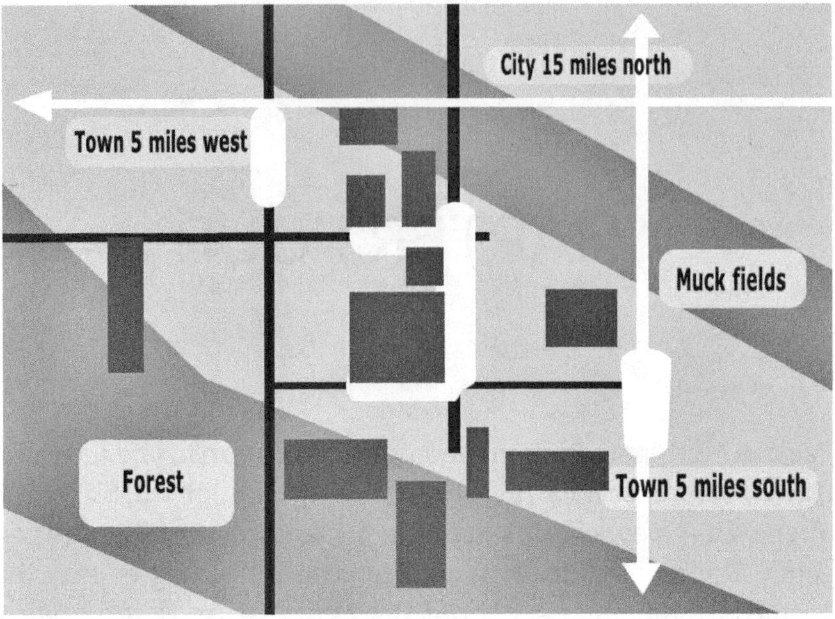

A heat map of the population density and wood resources, with the white oblongs representing population and the dark squares forest.

Looking at the parcels with few standing trees, those 100 or so homes had 200 acres of woods or about 2 acres per home, assuming the farmers were willing to let residents harvest those woods.

Rick and Kelly had done a little bit of 'tresspassin' hunting rabbits in late winter. Afterward, Rick estimated that most of those woods had 100 trees per acre and about 12-to-15 full cords of standing wood per acre. Some was better. Much was worse. After all, it was marginal ground that had been allowed to revert to woods.

Assuming the neighborhood could create a logging industry from nothing, that 2 acres per home would supply enough heat for three years at current rates of consumption.

Rick was on good terms with the farmers. He was pretty sure that they would be more than willing to let neighbors pay them to clean out fence rows and pot-holes in the middle of their crop fields.

The key point was neighbors would need something to use as currency, something the farmers wanted. Rick figured that they would be willing to let some of the neighbors to cut on shares. After all, the two commercial farmers in the neighborhood heated with wood and there would not be much of a market for their corn, beans and wheat if the money economy collapsed.

Rick deduced that he needed a two-pronged approach. He needed to lower expectations to reduce the demand and he needed to boost production.

The standard rule-of-thumb is that a northern woodlot produced between a half to one full cord of wood per year. To make the math in his head easier and to wash out the difference in the heat content of various types of wood, he rounded that to the energy in fifty-to-one-hundred gallons of heating oil and a typical home might burn a thousand gallons of heating oil a winter.

That was the basis for "needing" fifteen acres of woods to heat a home. Twenty-five pounds of air-dried wood has approximately the same amount of heat energy as a gallon of heating oil.

Like all broad generalizations, there were some significant caveats. Younger woodlots of selected "biomass" clones were treated like row crops and produced significantly more wood per year. In some cases, as many BTUs as two or three hundred gallons of heating oil per acre, per year.

Another advantage of these super trees is that they would be large enough for small stove-wood in three years and big stove-wood in eight, they grow well on muck and they can be planted by simply sticking 8" of a 10" cutting into the ground.

Rick decided it was a good time to start a small nursery where he could harvest cuttings in the future. He ended up purchasing a hundred cuttings of two kinds of hybrid poplar (NM-6 and DN-177) and three kinds of hybrid willows (Millbrook, Fabius and Preble). He also bought a couple pounds of Black Locust seeds and thought he would try his hand at growing some of them.

Some of the varieties were patented and propagation was prohibited. If the rule of law went into the septic tank, that would be the last of Rick's concerns.

If events did not go pear-shaped, he could plant the Black Locust around the edges of his ten acres of swamp and the poplar and willow in progressively wetter parts of it. If they did go pear-shaped, he could supply cuttings and seedlings to convert excess crop ground into short rotation firewood production.

Rick's Dilemma

Rick's dilemma was that he did not know very much about managing wood lots and even if he did, he would not have time.

He knew he could count on the two farmers to ride herd on wood cutters. The problem was managing the woods that were growing on the land of absentee owners.

Drinking coffee with a retired forester who lived south of Eaton Rapids filled in some of the gaps on woodlot management. Some trees just need to be cut: Trees with bad form, widow-makers, dead trees, senile trees, trees with low-value wood that are shading out more desirable species.

On the other hand, there are some trees that will continue to grow in value and serve as seed sources for valued species: Oak, Sugar Maple and Walnut with good trunk form, niche players in tough spots and any kind of nut producing tree.

Some species benefit from clear cutting. Many of those species are pioneer species that are not shade tolerant. One of their adaptations is to produce a gazillion, vigorous root sprouts. Selective cutting of these species results in diseased trunks and substandard growth.

The forester's very broad rule-of-thumb was to clear cut sites that are dominated by species with wood that rots quickly. He had seen too many cottonwood, aspen and soft maple that were booby-traps for the unwary. They looked fine on the outside and were hollow on the inside

The only species he considered suitable for allowing to grow beyond 24" diameter were prime black walnuts and oaks in the white oak clade. They had sufficient rot resistance that it was worth the risk to let them continue growing.

Some species thrive on selective cutting. They need a lot of competition to produce tall, limb free trunks but then need more light to gain girth and volume.

The forester also had advice on herding cats.

"You need a contract," Bill said. "You aren't the first guy to run into this and you won't be the last."

Rick asked, "What kind of contract?"

"You have been beating around the bush, but it sounds to me like you have a limited partnership/general partner situation. You have lots of stakeholders and you need one person to run the show," Bill replied.

"What keeps the limited partners from cheating?" Rick asked.

"Ah, that is the easy part. The general partner holds the contract with the mill and the trucking company. The guy who cheats...his logs rot in the woods unless the limited partner wants to do a ton more work," Bill said.

"How do you pick a good general partner?" Rick asked.

"You don't pick them," Bill said with a wintry smile. "It doesn't work if you pick them. It has to be the group of partners. The general has to be somebody they respect. There will be times when they don't like him or what he decides, but they have to respect him."

Things were starting to shape up for Rick. It might be possible to avoid a train wreck if the neighborhood simultaneously ramped up the production of super-trees and "milked" the harvesting of existing timber so existing stocks lasted five years.

He figured the first year would be easiest as dead ash, fence rows and senile trees were harvested. After that, blocks of the lowest value "trash trees" to be cut in a checker-board pattern with a plan to have them last three or four years. Finally, selectively cutting the highest value parcels the last year as the super-trees started reaching stove-wood size.

Woodstoves

Kelly and Zane were touring the salvage yard during an unseasonably mild day in early March.

Kelly said, "You have quite the treasure trove here."

"I don't think I have ever seen so many vehicles on your lot," Kelly continued.

"That is just the way it goes. Prices are low so I hang onto them until the prices go up," Zane said. "When prices are high, I sell them as soon as I have enough vehicles to pay for the crusher to come in."

Looking around there were places where Zane had crushed the roofs flat and stacked one vehicle on top another to get double duty out of the space.

"So, I was wondering," Kelly said "do you get anything extra for separating out materials?"

"Depends. I do get a little bit more but it doesn't pay for the time," Zane said. "I do it when I can get cheap labor. I can see you have something on your mind. Whatchya thinking?"

"I noticed that many of these trucks have enormous mufflers and they hardly have any rust on them," Kelly said.

"Yeah, the factory uses stainless steel. It is all about emissions," Zane said.

"I was thinking," Kelly said, "That those might make decent wood stoves for deer blinds and cabins and such."

"Yeah, I seen small woodstoves made out of ammo boxes at gun shows. I think those mufflers would be way too big for a deer stand but about right for a garage," Zane sort of agreed. He cocked an eyebrow. "You thinking of going into the woodstove business?"

"Depends," Kelly said with a twinkle in his eye. "Di gets a little pissy about my dragging 'junk' home. Would you let me pull them and stash them somewhere on your lot and pay for them as I use them? That way if the idea fizzles you can sell them for the higher price you get for stainless."

Zane knew a good deal when he heard one. He extended his right hand. "It's a deal. Let's shake on it."

Guys who are handy are quick to develop a system. Kelly was one of those handy guys. He figured out how to flatten the roof and roll a truck against another junk vehicle so it was securely half way between standing edgewise and completely upside down. Then he figured out how to make the minimum number of cuts to remove the muffler and the straight runs of pipes.

The catalytic converters had already been pulled.

After a few hours Zane came wandering out where Kelly was

working.

Kelly was ready for a break so he turned off his plasma cutter and generator.

"You know, I got to thinking about your woodstove project," Zane said.

Kelly helped him along "And?"

"I remembered a conversation I had with my Uncle Sid. He was a designer at a firm that engineered boilers and steam generation plants down in Jackson. I asked him where I should add welds to a cheap box woodstove that I had after it developed cracks," Zane said.

"He told me adding welds was the wrong way to go. Said I needed to make it looser, not tighter" Zane said. "That seemed so exactly ass-backwards to me that I asked him to explain."

Kelly nodded. "That is not what I would have guessed."

"Uncle Sid said the problem was something he called 'differential heating'. He said any firebox will tear itself apart unless it can flex or the parts with the most temperature difference can move relative to each other," Zane said.

"So, I asked him what he would have done differently if he had designed that box stove?" Zane said.

"Uncle Sid looked at the box stove for a minute and tapped the sides. Then he said, 'I woulda made a frame of angle iron where these edges and corners are. Then I woulda set loose plates in for the sides, top and bottom and clipped em into place."

"Said he woulda cut two-inch pieces of angle iron for clips and sandwiched the plate between the angle iron frame and the clip with the clip on the inside and tied it all together with a bolt," Zane said.

"Wouldn't the stove leak like a sieve?" Kelly asked as he visualized the stove without welded joints sealing the sides.

"Uncle Sid said the key is to have a tall chimney that pulls a strong draft and is way above the tallest roof line. That way all the leaking will be into the stove instead of out of it," Zane agreed.

Kelly pointed at the stack of mufflers he had been stacking to the side. "Well, it looks like I am screwed."

"Maybe not. That is thin metal that will flex. All you gotta do is be careful when you frame out the door. Maybe use oversized holes and loose-bolt the frame so they can float," Zane opined. "Then make sure the door hinges have some up-down slop and you are good-to-go."

"Yeah, I see what you are saying," Kelly said. "Thanks for the tip."

CHAPTER FIVE

Homeless in Minnesota

Bart was a typical member of the indigent population of St. Paul/Minneapolis.

He had been raised in a small town in northern Iowa. He struggled through school and probably should not have graduated from high school but No Child Left Behind metrics encouraged teachers to pass kids instead of flunking them.

After graduating Bart stayed in town while many of his classmates went to college or left town for jobs. Bart and a few of his buddies picked up a few jobs here-and-there for folding money. They drank a little and smoked a lot of weed.

Things changed in his mid-twenties. Most of his buddies had live-in girlfriends and steady jobs. Bart's stretches of unemployment got longer and his periods of employment got shorter.

Bart had been kicked out of the house when he was twenty. His dad said, "Enough is enough." It is possible that Bart's mental disorders would have been recognized and addressed if his family lived in an affluent suburb or a big city school with lots of free "services." But they lived in a small town a hundred miles from any serious mental healthcare providers.

Bart's behaviors became increasingly over-the-top and the live-in girlfriends were "creeped out". Bart no longer had a couch to sleep on.

He moved to Minneapolis.

Paranoia was one of Bart's personal demons. He would move into a homeless shelter and everything would be fine for a week or two and then he would notice people staring at him. Then he would be back out on the street.

It was a grand life in the late spring, summer and fall. Winters were hard.

As a last resort he would throw a brick through a shop window and wait for the cops to show up and haul him off to a nice, warm jail cell. The major downside of jail, as far as Bart was concerned, is they put him on his meds-of-record and he could not get weed or booze which he was sure worked much better.

At age 42, Bart lived inside the body of an old man. His lungs were shot due to countless infections from heavy smoking, living in packed shelters and aspirating vomit while on benders.

The booze and a bout of hepatitis had trashed his liver.

His diet and poor hygiene resulted in many lost teeth and many episodes of skin rashes.

He was tired. Deathly tired. He chalked it up to getting old.

It was ten days since he had walked through the Emergency Room where Clara's child was coughing. The Ebola virus that had landed in his congested, upper lungs found a cornucopia of monocytes and T-cells to infect.

Bart spent the night in one of the smaller shelters. It was

a church “common room”. Mattresses were pulled out of a storage room and spread out on the floor with barely enough room to walk.

Forty men shared two bathrooms. More than half of them had colds or flu. Bart was not the only person hacking and sneezing throughout the night. Nobody noticed that Bart’s mattress had acquired additional pinkish stains. Bart’s stools were stained red with blood.

Bart left before breakfast. Breakfast was served after chapel and Bart was hungry now. He went to the shopping mall and hung out at the food court. He cadged dollars to buss tables. Of course, he slipped half eaten sausage sandwiches and handfuls of hash-browns into his pockets and ate them in the lulls between waves of diners.

Later, Bart snoozed at benches and couches put out for shopper’s convenience. Security would usually prod him to move along but today Bart was itchy and could not get comfortable. He tried several different benches in various parts of the mall but was unable to get comfortable.

When he went back to the food court at lunch, security would not let him scavenge food. He looked like a freak from a horror show. The left side of his face was a massive hematoma as body fluids leaked into the spaces between his skin and fat and muscles.

He left the mall and walked a block to a fast food restaurant. He would get lunch there. He went to the trash dumpster and started to root around through the bags but he just didn’t have the energy. Thinking he just needed a nap to get his energy back, he went behind the dumpster and spread cardboard on the ground. Then he covered himself with more cardboard for blankets.

The garbage truck that came the next day did not see his corpse. The hydraulic arm reached out and snagged the grab-bar. After emptying the dumpster, it dropped it back into place, crushing Bart's head.

Bart's remains were found when the recyclers came to pick up the cardboard. They called 9-1-1.

The ambulance crew took multiple, digital photos and sent them to the coroner. The coroner was overwhelmed and would do a "drive-by" cause-of-death. He would undoubtedly write "exposure/hypothermia" into the appropriate space.

Bart was cremated in all of this clothing. He did not even have a wallet.

Milo

Nyssa was late getting to the event venue. The line to enter the auditorium was fifty yards long and snaked back-and-forth on itself. Consequently, she was able to hear the spat that happened at the front of the line close to where security people were checking backpacks and wanding attendees.

A gloriously beautiful, platinum-blonde woman who had been walking behind Nyssa got into line immediately behind her. Looking the line over, the blonde recognized a friend. She left the line and walked to the front and said "Hey Milo! What a surprise to see you here!"

Milo was four event-goers from the entrance.

"Oh. Hi Krystal," Milo said. It was clear that he found her dazzlingly beautiful. Any guy would. Her body was sculpted perfection and every asset was perfectly highlighted by a clingy, white sweater, red yoga pants and her rhinestone encrusted Badgley Mischka Tampa heels. She was a walking confection of ice, spun sugar and maraschino cherries.

Nyssa hated her on sight.

It was equally clear that she expected Milo to let her cut into line.

"You know that's unfair to everybody behind me?" he asked.

"Party-pooper," she pouted loudly enough for Nyssa to hear. "I just want to talk to you," she said in a fawning tone as she caressed Milo's forearm.

"Great!" Milo said. He gripped her hand. "Let's go to the back of the line so we can have a good, long time to talk." And he pulled her out of the line, relinquishing his place.

Krystal yanked her hand out of his. "You asshole." When Krystal was angry her voice acquired the warm and endearing harmonics of a dental drill.

Milo got into line behind Nyssa. "Hey, come here. Let's talk," as he beckoned her to join him

Krystal scanned the line and recognized another 'friend'. "Fuck you," she spat out as she stalked over to the next friend.

Nyssa had seen and heard the entire sequence of events.

“Sucks to be you,” Nyssa said with a sympathetic tone.

“No worries,” Milo said. “That is a cheap price to pay to find out what was hiding behind the pretty makeup. It is like loaning somebody $20. If you never see them again it is a cheap price to broom a loser out of your life.”

“Milo is an unusual name,” Nyssa observed. “Were you named after the character in the book Phantom Tollbooth?”

“No, actually I was named after the famous Greek wrestler who was the inspiration for Hercules in mythology,” Milo said.

“My dog is named ‘Hercules’,” Nyssa said.

“What kind of dog?” Milo asked.

“Labrador-Rottweiler cross,” Nyssa said.

Milo nodded. “Those are cool dogs but they huge. They need a lot of room to run,” he said. “Do you keep him in your apartment?” he asked.

“No. My parents have property. I am a student and working. It wouldn’t be fair to have him cooped up all day,” Nyssa said. “I see him on weekends.”

Nyssa noticed that Milo would do a heads-up-and-scan every thirty seconds or so. It wasn’t super obvious but he wasn’t hiding the fact that he was doing it and he was clearly practiced at it.

“Just curious,” Nyssa said, “But what is a cop doing going to the Michigan Cannabis and Hemp Conference?”

Milo shot her a glance. “Didn’t know it showed. I was an MP in the military but am not a cop now. How did you guess?” he asked.

"Situational awareness," she responded. "That, and you aren't dressed like most of the people in this line."

Most of the people in the line were dressed in urban-chic. Just-so footwear, skin-tight pants, color coordinated EVERYTHING.

Milo's clothing was given to muted greens, browns and grays. They were baggy and richly endowed with pockets...very practical considering the early-March chill. He was wearing side-zip tactical boots.

Milo gave Nyssa the once over. "Neither are you," referring to her choice of clothing. Nyssa was wearing her "comfortable" after-shift clothing: sweat pants, zippered fleece top and navy-blue, Chuck Taylor Converse All Stars.

Nyssa blushed. "I am not here for me. I am here because my dad asked me to check some things out."

Milo cocked an eyebrow. "Your dad is a stoner?"

"My dad has hobbies," Nyssa corrected. "His current passion is primitive technologies and ethnobotany."

"Hemp is critical for making rope and different cannabis clones have psycho-chemical activity," Milo finished for her.

Now it was Nyssa's turn to be mystified. "You know what ethnobotany is?"

"Yup. I am not just another pretty face," Milo said loftily. "There is no excuse for anybody with access to the internet to be ignorant."

"You don't look or smell like a stoner yourself," Nyssa said turning the conversation back to him.

"That's because I am not a stoner," Milo said.

"Then why are you here?" she asked.

"I have a buddy who sells grow lights. Nobody sells them for the listed retail price and John wants to do competitive pricing analysis. The problem is that everybody who sells lights know him so they won't give him honest quotes," Milo said.

"So, I am going in, pretending to be a grower, and asking for quotes to help out my buddy," Milo finished.

"You know," Nyssa said, "four eyes are better than two. Wadia say we cruise the conference together? I will keep my eyes peeled for lighting suppliers and you keep your eyes open for hemp as an industrial plant and cannabis clones for medication."

"Sounds great to me!" Milo said. "I think vendors are a lot more likely to accept me as a grower if I have my 'girlfriend' with me."

"Deal!" Nyssa said.

Entering the huge auditorium Nyssa automatically started to turn to the right when Milo engulfed her hand with his and pulled her to the left.

Nyssa was not a tiny woman. She was 5'-11" and 180 pounds and none of her could be classified as "excess to need". Nor did she have small hands.

Yet Milo moved her like she was a pinch of thistle down and his hands were huge and hard. That is when she realized that when Krystal had yanked her hand out of Milo's it was because Milo wanted her to.

Milo said, "Everybody turns to the right or goes straight in. The bargains are to the left."

Nyssa decided that if they were going to act like boyfriend/girlfriend she was going to have to be a little bit closer to him. He put his arm around her and pulled her close. That felt GOOD.

Reciprocating, Nyssa determined that Milo was the antithesis of the millennial soy-boy. "Weight lifter?" Nyssa had given Milo's deltoids a playful squeeze and they were massive.

Milo nodded. "A little bit. Mostly I work out at work."

"What do you do?" Nyssa asked, genuinely curious.

"I install sea-walls," Milo said.

"I woulda thought all that was done with power equipment," Nyssa said.

"Oh, we have power equipment. But somebody has to position materials. Sometimes we use brute strength. Sometimes we use pry poles. Sometime we drift them with mauls," Milo said.

"BFHs?" Nyssa asked.

"The biggest" Milo said with a smile. She talked his lingo.

They leisurely strolled from display-to-display. Few of them were of interest to Milo or Nyssa but when they did find something the proprietor had plenty of time to chat with them and were very eager to make a sale. Milo was right. There was far less traffic on this side of the auditorium.

A couple of times Nyssa caught herself idly massaging Milo's trapezius. She stopped herself. The second time she stopped Milo looked over and smiled. "You can keep doing that. It feels good."

Damn! That is what happens when you grow up with dogs. You pet them without even noticing.

Milo, for his part was delighted to notice that Nyssa was as sleekly muscled as a leopard beneath the baggy sweats. He was fed up with dating anorexic waifs that looked like they would break when he touched them. He remembered an old term he had heard his dad use years ago, "corn fed".

Nyssa saw a flash of white sweater and scarlet yoga pants through the gaps between the booths. Based on their pace "savoring" the displays, there was no doubt in Nyssa's mind that it was inevitable that Krystal would catch them together. The last thing Nyssa wanted was a scene.

Krystal came stalking around the corner. She had ditched the "friend" who she had buddied up with to get into the auditorium.

High heeled shoes are designed to enhance the sashay that women impart to a well-cut skirt. Krystal's high-speed locomotion made her look like a stork on crack.

Milo looked up and saw her.

Milo pre-empted the conversation. Before Krystal could say anything, Milo said, "Krystal! I want to thank you!"

Krystal was taken off stride. "Huh?"

"I want to thank you. If it hadn't been for you, I would have never met Nyssa," Milo said. Milo's hand slid down to rest on the swell of Nyssa's hip and he gently pulled her even closer. It was more of a coax than a command but it was enough for Nyssa to want to lean into Milo.

Krystal looked confused.

"I cannot remember anybody whose company I enjoyed more. Thank you for being you," Milo said as he looked fondly at Nyssa.

Krystal pivoted and fled.

Nyssa said, "That really twisted her nose out-of-joint."

"That is not why I said it," Milo said. "I really have enjoyed your company. I enjoyed our time together more than I can say. I hope you will give me your number so we can go on a proper date," Milo said.

Milo Comes a Courting

Nyssa half expected that Milo would not call. Lots of guys were like that. They would ask for your number as a way to gracefully exit. The thing is that Nyssa got the vibe that Milo liked her.

Nyssa found Milo on social media. It wasn't hard. There are not too many people named Milo Talon in southeast Michigan. She sent a friend request and it was promptly accepted.

What she saw was reassuring. He had about thirty friends. He had been a member for more than seven years. Most of his friends were clearly family. Lots of Talons and the women who did not share the last name showed a clear family resemblance.

She saw that he had been working in Florida through the winter. Unlike some construction tradesmen, he didn't take unemployment through the winter, he went south and kept working.

She wondered how he was able to rent an apartment, being in Michigan eight months of the year. She would ask him the next time she saw him.

Milo called a few days later. After sorting through their schedules Milo suggested that the meet in Livonia for an open mic night at Trinity House Theater. It proved to be a good first date. There was ample time between performers to talk and to share what music they liked and what did not appeal to them

Milo was wearing a light cologne with melon/cucumber top-notes and base notes of sandalwood and oakmoss. It was imperceptible if you were more than eighteen inches away.

The only fragrance Nyssa was wearing was a hand-cream, a necessity with all of the hand washing she had to do on her job.

Neither party was working at buying or selling. They were offering as-is and they were inspecting.

The content of the songs triggered a wide range of conversations.

Afterward they went out for coffee and dessert.

Milo walked her back to her car which she had parked in the well-lit, public parking lot behind the theater. He did not push to get a kiss but told her he enjoyed the evening and asked if she would be willing to go out with him again.

The second date proved harder to pull together. Both of them had busy weeks. Their schedules simply did not align. Finally, in frustration, Nyssa asked if Milo would be willing to go to her Zumba class. To her surprise he accepted.

The Zumba room had a huge mirror behind the leader. Nyssa enjoyed watching Milo break into a sweat. He looked like the Incredible Hulk in a room full of Elasti-girls. Nyssa was a bit concerned that he would be distracted by all of the eye-candy in the room but she caught him looking at her far more than looking at others. That made her feel pretty good.

Afterward they grabbed a snack at the in-facility snack bar. Nyssa had a banana-passion-fruit smoothie. Milo had nachos and an iced-tea. That is when she found out he had put in an eleven-hour day in the sub-freezing weather. She was duly impressed that he was willing to drive almost an hour to her side of town and then do another hour of Zumba just to share time with her.

Their third date was on a Tuesday. They went to a Mardi Gras party in Monroe, Michigan. This was the first time she rode to a date in Milo's truck. She took the precaution of messaging a couple of friends and her mom with her itinerary.

Milo showed up looking like a lumberjack.

Nyssa was dressed as Xena Warrior Princess complete with a Chakram (mock) and a Marble's throwing axe with a sixteen inch handle. She had spray painted the head of the hatchet with bronze paint.

They had an absolute blast.

This was the first time they visited a place where alcohol was served. Nyssa brought a credit card in case she couldn't get an Uber ride home and needed a cab. It would not be the first time she chose to pay for a ride home rather than ride with a drunk driver.

Milo drank two draft beers in the five hours they were at the party, he drank twice as much water as beer. The dinner was buffet and Nyssa was impressed that Milo tried the local delicacy, roast muskrat and seemed to enjoy it.

Nyssa was almost sleep walking through classes the next day. Brittany was one of her study-buddies and they usually sat close together during lectures.

They arrived about five minutes before the lecture started when Brittany asked, "What are you humming?"

Nyssa said. "I am not humming."

Brittany said, "You most certainly are!"

Thinking back, trying to recapture the thought trail as they had walked into the room, she realized she had been thinking of one of the dances she and Milo had shared the night before.

"Maybe I was," Nyssa said.

It had been twelve days since she had first met Milo and he was already a big part of her life. They went together like peas-and-carrots.

CHAPTER SIX

Nyssa Hits the Silk

It was 4 in the afternoon on a cheerful day in early-June. Nyssa sat at Milo's kitchen table as she struggled to write a letter requesting a leave-of-absence from her nursing program.

Nyssa had not moved in with Milo but she had the key to his small house.

Nyssa lived in Ypsilanti and was working a lot at Beaumont Hospital in Royal Oak. It was far easier for her to drive ten miles to the house Milo was renting, take a shower and wait for him than it was to drive forty miles in the opposite direction, shower and then drive fifty miles back, all during rush hour.

She was waiting for him to get home from his current worksite in Algonac. It was going to be brutally hard to tell him she was moving back home.

The events of the last 24 hours had left Nyssa rattled.

Nyssa worked for a temp agency as a nurse. Nyssa had been covering a shortfall at the University hospital. One of the advantages of working as a temp is that she had the freedom to refuse work assignments. That is why she was working in Labor and Delivery and not in the Emergency Room when all hell broke loose.

Two people in the waiting area coded nearly simultaneously. According to one person they melted like slugs sprinkled with salt. Body fluids were everywhere as the patients had seizures as they dissolved. Arterial blood sprayed the walls.

The overwhelmed staff, for the most part, had not read the latest updates on procedures. Those procedures required that the E-Room stop taking admissions, to close all doors between the Emergency Suite and the rest of the hospital and to document that the suite was running negative air pressure. Those actions were not taken until the next shift arrived.

Fortunately, Labor and Delivery where Nyssa was working was in a different wing and three stories higher in the complex.

What really rattled Nyssa were the reactions of the seasoned, Emergency Room staff. Accounts on social media were quickly purged of the reports but not before Nyssa had seen several of them.

As far as Nyssa was concerned, this was the starting gun that her dad asked her to watch for.

Three Weeks Earlier...

Dissatisfaction with the President was running at a fever pitch.

Million Man Marches were run most weekends protesting SOMETHING about how his administration was running the government.

The problem the opposition encountered was finding enough bodies to flesh-out the million-man marches. The only way to get media coverage was to trumpet the number of participants. The demonstrations were anything but spontaneous and the organizers were running into fatigue on the part of their usual cadre of demonstrators. It was getting hard to get even seventy-thousand to show up for each million-man march.

Then one of the organizers had an idea that was pure genius. Bus homeless people and unemployed refugees to populate the marches. Warm meals, hotel rooms and cash money were offered. On the down-low, potential volunteers were told that the price of drugs in the DC area was half of what it was in the upper mid-West.

The street people were also offered the option of being bussed back to any city of their choosing. Mindful of the recent brutal winters in the north, many of the street people were tempted by the opportunity to relocate in Houston, New Orleans, Miami and other balmy, southern locations.

The program was a run-away success. There was no shortage of "volunteers". The program vacuumed up indigents from Fargo-to-Austin, Portland-to-Miami and mixed them all together. It also sucked up indigents from Minneapolis, Chicago and Cleveland where Ebola had been in a fast smolder and created the perfect Petri dish for incubation.

The law of small numbers suggests that progression will not be smoothly monotonic in the early stages of an epidemic. It will stall and waffle, even diminish, as it struggles to get its sea-legs. The law of small numbers also suggests that an unfortunate confluence of events can increase the spread of the disease by several orders of magnitude for short periods.

Some of those conditions are subtle, like a high pollen count increasing the coughing and sneezing of pre-symptomatic carriers while simultaneously increasing the eye and nose rubbing of the yet-to-be infected.

Other contributors are glaringly obvious, like the crowding of tens of thousands of the least monitored and must vulnerable into hermetically sealed, metal cylinders for up to twenty-four hours at a pop.

And that is what had happened.

Nyssa did not know any of that but she had seen the feeder bands of the incoming hurricane and did not like what she saw. Nyssa was hitting the silk.

You Can Go Home Again

Milo came home about 5:30. Nyssa waited until after he had a shower and a quick sandwich. Then she hit him with the news.

"I am going back home."

Milo blinked a couple of times. Then he frowned. "You mean to Eaton Rapids?" he asked.

"Yes," Nyssa said with formal precision. "We had our first Ebola patient today. It is time for me to go."

"I am not arguing with you, but don't nurses have an obligation?" Milo asked. "I never understood how that worked."

"I am a 'temp' worker. Those obligations hold until I am relieved by the next shift and am tagged out. If nobody shows up then I stay until the NEXT shift or until the administration shuffles personnel around and can boot me out," Nyssa said. "If I was a formal employee then there would be other obligations."

"Are you sure it is Ebola?" Milo asked.

"How can anybody be sure? It is not like they will share the test results," Nyssa said.

The news that Nyssa was moving back home hit him pretty hard. They had become very close in the last three months. Nyssa was like none of the other girls he had dated.

"It could be worse," Milo said. "Eaton Rapids is only 90

minutes away. I can still spend weekends with you."

"Well, yes and no," Nyssa responded. "Mom and dad are old fashioned. When Bill and whatshername came up the summer before they were married, they made Bill sleep in the camper."

"Of course, now that they are married, they get their own bedroom," Nyssa said.

"Oh, I think we can work around some of the obstacles," Milo said with a twinkle in his eye. "Besides, the main thing is that I will get to spend time with you. Maybe your dad will stop being such a grump."

Nyssa had to smile. She had taken Milo home three times to meet the family. Milo is the only guy she had brought home since graduating from high school.

Nyssa had been filled with consternation the first time Milo and her dad met. Their reaction seemed cold and distant.

Then her mom commented, "Just a couple of big dogs fluffing up and sniffing butts. They will get over it." That cracked her up. That is EXACTLY what it was. A couple of alpha males taking each other's measure.

Milo and her dad had not spent enough time together to sort out all the alpha stuff but they had clearly been more at ease the last time Milo came visiting. Nyssa thought her mom may have had a talk with her dad.

At least her dad didn't try to arm-wrestle Milo.

The second time they dropped in on her parents it was just before lunch time. Mom was putting a lunch of peanut butter sandwiches and minestrone soup made from leftovers on the table. Milo and Nyssa just popped in without calling ahead. Kate made more sandwiches and heated up more soup.

Milo ate the meal with gusto and was very complimentary, even though it was with the "sawdust" bread that Nyssa had loathed since childhood.

It was a very short visit. Afterward Rick commented "I think you could have served Milo dog-food on crackers and he would have eaten it and said he liked it."

Kate's tart response was "You would rather have Nyssa interested in a high-maintenance snow-flake? Or worse, somebody who treated her, and us by extension, like shit?"

Rick thought it was humorous. Kate did too, but for a different reason. Rick had been exactly the same way after they got "serious."

The third time Nyssa-and-Milo (now said as one word) visited, Rick twisted Milo's arm and gave him a tour of the forty acres. Milo was far more impressed than Rick could know. Milo had grown up in eastern Connecticut and after being discharged from the military had spent most of his time in densely populated, southeast Michigan.

Milo knew at an intellectual level that somebody owned the farmland but he assumed it was corporations. Most of his work was for home owners associations and corporate concerns. The few individuals who put in seawalls were incredibly wealthy and none of them owned more than an acre or two.

To rub elbows with somebody who owned as much land as four city blocks was a revelation.

Rick was delighted to have a new person to show the property. He had been "developing" it for three decades, develop in the sense of adding value to it. It had been by trial-and-error. There were some patches of it that were in the fourth iteration as Rick tried to find some combination of plants and structures that were both useful and minimum effort.

Rick had come to the conclusion that some eroded knobs of exposed sub-soil would only be useful for bird-watching. In time nature might rebuild the top-soil but it wouldn't be in his lifetime.

Milo was VERY comfortable visiting Nyssa's childhood home. The fact that the forty acres had about fifteen secluded coves where romance could be pursued in privacy weighed on his mind.

Milo Gets Laid Off

A week after Nyssa bailed out, the Washington Fence Newspaper ran an article about a woman whose body had been fished out of the Anacostia River.

The cause-of-death was reported to be Ebola.

What was not reported is that the woman had a record for soliciting. The other unusual thing was that she was dressed in traditional, Somali burial robes. Those details were omitted to avoid backlash against the immigrant community.

The difference between this story and the other stories that had been written over the last six months is that the Deep State allowed this one to be published.

The Deep State had no choice. Ebola cases had erupted in a score of communities, like embers dropping into drifts of dry pine needles miles from the main forest fire. By allowing the story to print they hoped to control the message.

The hopes were ill-founded.

In quick succession, the developed nations of the world prohibited US originated vessels and aircraft from docking or landing. Ships bringing critical, high value components from over-seas anchored off-shore waiting instruction from HQ. Planes destined for the US diverted to land in Canada, Mexico or the Caribbean. Hotel rooms in Halifax were going for $1000 per night.

Planes originating from the US were turned back or if they were past the point of no-return landed and were refueled without allowing passengers to deplane. Minimum maintenance was performed and volunteer pilots who wanted to return to the States were allowed to board. Then the planes flew back.

Within minutes of the stock exchanges opening the circuit breakers popped. They were reopened after buy orders had accumulated. The circuit breakers promptly popped again as sell orders swamped buyers. The ride down was both bumpy and violent.

Three days later Milo was pink-slipped with an "indefinite" layoff. They said they would call him if business picked up. Milo was not holding his breath.

After a few hours of weighing his options, Milo called Nyssa and asked her for Rick's phone number.

Milo did not beat around the bush. "Hello Mr. Salazar, I want to rent your camper."

Rick could not resist playing Milo a little bit. "Planning on going camping?" Rick knew perfectly well what was happening to the economy.

"No, actually I want to leave it on your property and live in it," Milo said. He knew what he was asking was presumptuous and it caused him to swallow, hard.

"Why don't you drive out here so we can talk about it, face-to-face," Rick suggested.

A few hours later, Milo's F-150 pulled into the Salazar's drive.

"Let's take a walk, Junior," Rick suggested.

The standard walk was around the block, a distance of four

miles. It took almost an hour-and-a-half if you were not in a hurry and it was the perfect amount of time for a long conversation with no interruptions.

"Why don't you start by telling me the picture in your head," Rick started out.

"The grand-slam home-run would be if you would let me leave it behind the barn and run a power cord out to it to run the fridge, a fan and maybe a TV," Milo said.

"Renting usually means paying rent. Have you given any thought regarding what you would pay me?" Rick said. He had too many buddies who let shirt-tail relatives "rent" trailers and they never saw a penny of rent. That, and the people living in the trailer beat the hell out of it.

"Yessir. I gave that a lot of thought. I am paying $900 a month for my house in Sterling Heights. Utilities cost another $200 a month. I figured I would pay you $1100 a month," Milo said.

"That's a lot of money for a trailer," Rick responded, quite taken aback. The trailer had cost $3000 when he bought it used.

"The way I see it," Milo said "the trailer comes with lots of advantages. It will make it easy for me to see Nyssa and I can't think of a better place to be if this Ebola takes off."

"Location, location, location," Rick mumbled under his breath.

"How are you going to afford $1100 a month if you aren't working?" Rick asked.

"Putting in seawalls paid well. I have $40k in the bank. I am not bragging, just saying that I didn't spend every penny I earned as soon as I got it. That should be good for three years I am pretty sure I will pick up work in the meantime," Milo said confidently.

"Let me tell you what my home-run scenario is," Rick said.

"You give me ten hours of work a week. Log it on a calendar, when you start each day and when you end," Rick said.

"Just doing some rough figuring in my head, that works out to about $30 an hour, after taxes," Rick said. "That is pretty good wages around here."

"You brought up this being a good place to hunker down if Ebola takes off," Rick continued. "I have been looking at that. We have some major shortcomings."

"What would that be?" Milo asked.

"We are going to have a severe labor shortage," Rick said.

Milo looked at him quizzically. "How do you figure?" he asked.

"We have a lot of retired folks in the neighborhood. Some of them struggle to walk the length of their driveways to get the mail," Rick said, ticking off the age groups on his fingers.

"Most of the people in their prime working years will do OK. We have a lot of folks in the building trades, so you will fit right in. But we also have a fair number of people who picked Eaton Rapids because they are on disability and it doesn't cost a lot of money to live here," Rick said.

"Then there are the kids. Most of them are really good at working a TV remote or a Gameboy Controller but don't ask them to push a lawn mower or even walk fifty yards," Rick said.

"If Ebola interrupts fuel deliveries, it is going to get ugly. Real fast. Everywhere, even here," Rick said.

Rick gets Physical Training

"What do you think of the ten hours a week?" Rick asked. "I

think that between the two of us we can find that amount of work."

Milo brooded a little bit and then said, "With all due respect, sir, I want to propose some work that you might be offended by. I think I know where there is a huge hole in your preps."

Rick was surprised. He didn't think Milo knew enough about property management or his particular piece of heaven to make meaningful comments.

"Go ahead," Rick said, not knowing what to expect from the young man's mouth.

"Sir, you are not in good physical shape. These hills are not that steep and you are huffing-and-puffing. I think we should work-out together, maybe three or four hours a week," Milo ventured.

Rick was taken aback. "I am not in bad shape, especially for a guy who is sixty!"

"Yes sir. I agree. You are not in BAD shape. On a scale of one-to-ten, bad shape would be a one or a two. You might be a five or a six for your age, for an American," Milo said. "The thing is that I have been in Shithole-a-stan and life is a lot more physical. It will be even more physical here if the oil shuts off. You can't afford to be a five or a six.

"The other thing is," Milo continued, "That if the shit hits the fan you will be competing with guys in their twenties who are nines-and-tens for their age group. You will never match them physically, but you at least have a fighting chance on your home turf if you are a ten for your age." That was a long speech for Milo.

Rick didn't like what he heard. He shook his head like a hooked tarpon but the hook had sunk deep. He knew the truth when he heard it. He also knew that he had gained fifty pounds since starting to work at home. The office computer was twenty short steps from the refrigerator.

"Let me give it some thought," Rick said.

Then a couple of minutes later, "What would this 'working out' look like?" Rick asked.

"Running and push-ups," Milo answered with great confidence.

"I can't run very far," Rick said.

"Yep, that is why we are doing it," Milo said. "Running builds the foundation of your body. When the foundation is square, everything else builds itself."

Rick was shaking his head.

"No. Really," Milo said. "Think about it. Leg muscles are huge and gobble lots of calories. Running also torques the trunk of your body so it builds core strength. And you have to throw your arms forward, that builds shoulders."

"The push-ups pick up most of the muscle groups running misses," he finished.

"You still haven't answered my question," Rick said. "What would one of these work-outs look like?"

"We start out running from the house. I set the pace. It will be barely faster than a walk...just fast enough that you have to run. You tell me when you need a breather. We jog out for twenty minutes and give ourselves forty minutes to walk back," Milo said.

"OK, what about the push-ups?" Rick said.

"On the way back, we stop every five minutes, put on gloves, drop down and do push-ups," Milo said. "You tell me how many push-ups you think you can do and we make the set half of that. You think you can do a max of ten, we do a set of five."

"How often do you plan on doing this?" Rick asked.

"Doesn't really matter as long as there is at least one recovery day between them," Milo said. "I am fine with Monday, Wednesday, Friday with the weekends off."

"Wednesdays won't work for me. I have meetings. How about Tuesday, Thursday, Saturday?" Rick proposed.

"Not a problem, sir," Milo said.

The first run went well. Milo showed Rick how to stretch for maximum advantage. The internet is a mighty useful thing, it is.

Milo told Rick to take breaks when he needed them. Rick took a break at five minutes and ten minutes. Milo slowed down a little bit each time. After twenty minutes they walked back and did sets of five push-ups.

Rick even felt pretty good the next day.

The day after that, when they were due for another run, Rick felt like warmed over death.

"Your body is lying to you, sir," Milo assured him. "Hydrate, take a couple of ibuprofens and we start in thirty minutes." The temperature was almost ninety.

Oddly enough, the running was no more difficult than not-running. As they neared the turn-around point Milo reached out to "tag" a tall weed.

"Hey! Don't touch that!" Rick shouted emphatically.

"What?" Milo looked baffled.

"That is Giant Hogweed. You don't want to touch that. The juice will burn the skin right off of you," Rick said. "In fact, I better tell Farmer Don so he can hit them with herbicide before they go to seed."

They walked most of the way back to the house when Rick turned up a drive and motioned for Milo to follow him. The drive was a quarter mile long.

Rick knocked on the door and hollered into the house, "Hey, Kelly. Mind if we take a dip in your pond?"

"No problem. Got somebody with you?" Kelly asked.

"A friend of Nyssa's," Rick said.

Milo followed Rick around the house and then another two

hundred yards south. There, Kelly had a small pond scooped out of the gravel bank next to the marsh. It was eighty yards long by twenty yards wide and was fifteen feet deep.

Rick put his shoes, wallet, eyeglasses and pepper-spray into a basket next to the "beach" and then waded in. Milo followed.

A bit later Kelly joined them. He was carrying a small cooler.

"Do you like beer?" Kelly asked.

Rick informed Milo "Kelly is a home brewer. Don't feel like you have to drink. A lot of people can't...or shouldn't."

"No, I am good," Milo said.

Milo took a long pull from the bottle Kelly handed him.

"I got the recipe off the internet," Kelly said. "It is supposed to be a clone of Alaska Pale Golden Ale. I think it turned out well."

Milo agreed.

Milo Gets Work

Rick was floating in the water about fifty feet from shore. His toes were sticking up in the air and the cool bottle of beer was sitting on his chest, steadied by one of his hands.

"Hey, Kelly?" Rick said. "Milo is looking for work. Don't suppose you know somebody who is looking for a hand."

In this part of the world a man might know somebody who is looking for work. And he might know somebody who needs a hand. But he is not going to mention it unless he is making a recommendation in both directions. Bringing it up would put Kelly in an awkward position if Milo turned out to be a slacker. In a similar way, bringing it up would put Milo in an awkward position if Kelly were a bad person to work for.

"Smattera fact I do," Kelly announced. "Di went and bought a bunch of hay. Farmer Ken baled it up. She wants to go get it with her team of horses."

"You might say we had a discussion," Kelly said. "She wants to handle this on her own. But seeing how she weighs 87 pounds dripping wet and somebody needs to handle the horses, that means she needs somebody. Somebody other than me, that is."

Kelly looked over at Milo. "Have you ever been hayin'?" he asked.

"Nope," Milo answered. "What does a bale of hay weigh?"

Kelly said, "They are supposed to weigh forty pounds, but this hay got cut late, so most of it is gunna weigh thirty pounds or so. Thing is, she bought five hunnert bales."

Milo said, "I am looking for work. Sounds like just the thing," as he came out of the water and started to put on his shoes. "Is 'Di' up at the house?"

"Hold onto your horses, young man," Kelly said with a chuckle. "You go back home and put on jeans and a long sleeve shirt. And a hat if you have one."

Milo looked confused. "But it is hotter than hell!" he said.

"Trust me. You want jeans, work boots, long sleeve shirt and a hat. Bring a jug of water too. You are going to need it," Kelly said.

Di was a chatter-box. Milo did not know it at the time, but she was also a world-class interrogator.

She would be chirping away like a song bird on a fence post and she would slip in questions that her target would answer without thought.

Milo struggled at first. He had never put up hay before, nor had he seen it done.

But he was a good worker and familiar with his body. He got

into the rhythm. Throw five or ten or fifteen bales up on the bed. Di would stop. She coached him on how to stack them so they would not fall over. Lather, rinse, repeat.

It got slower as the buggy filled up. There was less room on the floor to stage them. That is when he could only put five up before stopping, climbing into the wagon and stacking them. It was slow work.

It was the same at the unload end. He tossed the bales onto the floor of the barn. Then he lifted into position. As the stack grew, he had to toss them up and arranged them to Di's satisfaction.

Even with the jeans and long-sleeved shirt, the stalks of grass poked through and abraded his skin. He could only imagine how raw he would have been if he had worn shorts and a tee shirt.

It was 10:30 by the time they were done.

He knew, then, that he had lied to Rick. There were many muscles that running and pushups didn't strengthen. And he was sure he would be able to identify every one of them by morning.

As they were heading back to Di's barn with the last load, she asked him, "What do I owe you?"

Milo said, "Why don't we call this a freebie. I am still learning how things work around here."

"No. That is not okay," Di said, sternly.

"OK, then how about you let me swim in your pond every once in a while?" Milo proposed.

"Rick and Kate already have that privilege. And if you are living with them, it extends to you," Di said.

"Ok, then," Milo said. "Tell me something about Nyssa that I don't know."

For the rest of the evening Di told Milo about how Nyssa was a favorite daughter of Eaton Rapids, that she had baby sat for almost everybody in the neighborhood. She told him about the time she had helped her get un-stuck from a snow drift. She told him about the loser boy-friend she had in seventh grade. She told him that he was the first boy she had brought home to show the family.

Milo considered it well worth the effort.

After the hay was unloaded, Di said, "Why don't you go down to the pond and take a dip. You will sleep better."

"But ma-am, I didn't bring a swim suit," Milo said.

"Just use your birthday suit," Di said. "It's dark and I promise I won't look."

Of course, taking one little peek hardly counted as 'looking'.

Kelly came into the room before she had a chance. "Whaddya think of him?" he asked.

Di was highly intuitive. It was a skill she seldom revealed because it freaked folks out. But she let a little bit of it show now. "When they get married, we are going to let them honeymoon at our cottage. And we aren't going to let them pay a dime."

Puppies!!!

Nyssa and Milo were taking their daily walk.

Nyssa was apologizing for her "crazy" papa.

"Don't apologize for him," Milo said. "That is disrespectful.

"I think your dad is a great guy. He is letting me stay here and work off the rent. There are a lot of people who wouldn't do that. They might figure I was out to sue them or something," Milo continued.

"Yeah, but dad is paranoid. He thinks things might spin back to the medieval times, a new 'dark ages'," Nyssa said. "That is just crazy."

Milo looked at her. "You must not think it is totally crazy. You came back.

"Besides," he continued. "It is not really paranoia if there is a material chance it could happen."

"What are the odds?" Nyssa asked.

"I don't think anybody can say. But consider a typical Roman citizen at the height of the empire. They would have said there was zero chance. Yet we know it was just a matter of time," Milo said.

"Just for the sake of argument," Nyssa said, "What would you do if you knew we were about to enter the new dark ages?"

"I would study up on what folks in northern Europe did at the end of the late middle ages," Milo said. "What they did worked. It was the springboard for the Renaissance."

Nyssa had gotten used to Milo knowing a little bit of everything. He was like her dad, that way.

"Well, just off the top of your head, what would you do?" Nyssa pressed.

"I would get a dog," Milo said with certainty. "In fact, I would three or four of them."

Nyssa drew away. "We have a dog. Hercules!"

Milo knew he had stepped on a land-mine. Ooops!

"Let me tell you my thinking," Milo said. "Hercules can't have puppies. Even if he hadn't been fixed, he is a stud, not a dam."

"The other thing is that most of the dogs in the neighborhood don't fit the middle ages," Milo said.

"Whaddya mean?" Nyssa asked. She had never considered what dogs were like in the middle ages.

"They are either too big, like Hercules...the dogs of kings. Or they are too small to function as dogs," Milo said. "What kinds of wild dogs are native around here? Foxes and coyotes?" Milo asked.

"Both," Nyssa said. "But foxes are more like cats than dogs. They eat mice and climb trees."

"Ok, coyotes. What do they weigh?" Milo asked.

"I dunno," Nyssa said. "Siri, what do coyotes weigh?" she asked her phone.

"Western coyotes weigh between fifteen and twenty-five pounds. Eastern coyotes weigh between thirty and forty-five pounds," Siri responded. "Would you like that in kilograms?"

"No, I am good, Siri," Nyssa said.

"And that is my point," Milo said. "The big dogs are Labs and Pitbulls at eighty pounds...twice what a local coyote weighs. The little dogs are Yorkies and Shih Tzus at five or ten pounds which is a third of what coyotes weigh."

"Why do you have a hang-up on coyotes?" Nyssa asked.

"Because coyotes are what God and Darwin says works best in this climate. Anything too far outside 'the envelop' is going to be pushing a rope," Milo said. He desperately wanted her to see what he was trying to say.

"What breed of dogs do you think a typical farmer in medieval times had?" Nyssa asked.

"I don't think they were 'breeds' so much as types. It is not like they had dog shows and AKC. Just shooting from the hip they probably had small dogs to kill rats and varmints. Some of them might have had something like a collie if they herded sheep, or small hounds if there was small game to hunt," Milo said.

Nyssa was a whiz with her smartphone. "Just give me a couple of minutes," she said.

A couple of minutes later she said, "There is a guy up in St Johns with some Brittany spaniel puppies. He thinks the dad was the neighbor's beagle."

"How big do Brittany spaniels get?" Milo asked.

"Gimme a minute," Nyssa said. "Thirty-to-forty pounds."

"How about beagles?" Milo asked.

"Already working on it," Nyssa said. "Between twenty and thirty-five pounds."

"What is he asking?" Milo asked.

"Fifty bucks a pup" Nyssa said. "Why, you wanna go look at them?"

They came home from St Johns with two female pups. Milo

wanted pups that were in the middle of the litter for size and Nyssa wanted the tri-colors because she thought they were pretty.

Nyssa won.

The best news, from Milo's standpoint, was that the sire was definitely a Beagle and the beagle next door was a hunting dog rather than a pet. He was nine years old and still in great shape.

The other thing that Milo was secretly very happy about is that the sire had a bellow that would rip the horse-hide off a baseball. If somebody tried to break into his trailer everybody within a quarter mile was going to know about it.

Milo wanted to pick out a male pup as well but Nyssa told him that her sister Gabriella had an intact Jack Russel terrier. Besides, when a bitch is in heat there is never a problem finding willing DNA donors.

CHAPTER SEVEN

Big Boy Comes to the Rescue

Kelly got the call from Farmer Don at 10:30 at night. Farmer Don was a little bit frantic. He had a record-breaking crop of wheat waiting to be harvested. He figured he had been harvesting ninety, maybe ninety-five bushel to the acre.

It had been a perfect year for growing wheat. He got the seed in late enough to avoid Hessian Fly, then got a warm period that gave him good germination. The spring started out rainy and then warmed up. An inch-and-a-half of rain came through every week until mid-May. Then there was a real ground soaking, 24-hour rain.

Since then, mid-Michigan had seen nothing but sunny weather and mild breezes with the occasional, clement warm rain.

The wheat mined the moisture stored in the soil and the stalks rose tall and the heads grew heavy with grain.

A wide swath of nasty weather was bearing down on Michigan. The storm system stretched from South Dakota to central Texas and was marked by storm cells, wind shears, hail and tornadoes. Farmer Don had less than twenty-four hours to get the 200 acres of his wheat crop off the field or it would be battered into the ground.

He was combining like gang-busters when he hit the woodchuck hole. He did not see it because he was blinded as he rounded a corner and turned into the setting sun. The rear, outside wheel dropped into the hole and the struts that supported it crumpled. The combine was nearly full and the back end of it dropped down and dragged a groove through the sandy soil, lurching to a stop twelve feet past where the wheel had collapsed.

Farmer Don knew that Kelly was a machinist and hoped that maybe, miraculously, Kelly could fix his rig.

Kelly made no promises.

Thinking a minute, Kelly called Milo.

"You busy?" Kelly asked.

As a matter of fact, Milo was. He was watching a romantic comedy with Nyssa and had plans for the evening.

"Whatchya need?" Milo asked, keeping the irritation out of his voice.

"Farmer Don has a crisis on his hands. He wants me to look it over. I could use a second set of eyes and maybe a hand," Kelly said.

Milo knew that working in the dark is inherently dangerous and, depending on the crisis, might require a second strong back. "Yeah, I will be right over," Milo reluctantly agreed to Kelly's suggestion.

Milo hopped into Kelly's truck and Kelly drove the mile-and-a-quarter to Farmer Don's field. Seeing the lights of the crippled farm equipment lurched sideways out in the field, Kelly drove across the wheat stubble.

Kelly parked the truck so his lights were shining on the destroyed rear suspension.

Milo and Kelly took a walk around the combine.

"Whaddya think?" Kelly asked. As far as he was concerned the rig was going to need at least a week in a shop, somewhere, to get it functional again.

"I can fix that," Milo said.

"Be obliged if you tried," Farmer Don said as he slapped his seed cap against his thigh to knock the dust off it. "I am heading up to the house. I'll be callin' shops to see if they can take it, just in case you can't fix it."

Frankly, Farmer Don hoped he could have it back working when he needed to run corn and beans. He was looking at losing $90,000 worth of wheat, but maybe the worst of the storm might miss his field and maybe he could rent a combine and salvage some of it. Might...maybe...salvage, thin reeds of hope.

"Well, Big Boy, why don't you show me what you got," Kelly said. "Let's drive back to my shop and load up what you think we will need to fix it."

Milo did not hear that Kelly had just handed the reins to him. Milo thought Kelly was just being polite. "Sure," Milo said.

Back at Kelly's shop Milo loaded up a generator, klieg lights, angle iron, cold drawn steel tubing, 3/8" and 11-gauge steel plates, grinders, angle cut-off wheels, cutting torches, a MIG welder and a cylinder of 75%-25% Argon-CO2 and a dozen other odds-and-ends. Looking at the full truck, Milo asked "Do you have a trailer?"

Of course Kelly had a trailer. He hooked up the car hauler and then Milo proceeded to fill it with dozens of railroad ties and lumber scraps.

"OK. That looks like a good start," Milo said.

"Mind if I just watch? I wanna see how you do this. Just give a holler when you need another set of hands," Kelly said.

Milo assumed that Kelly was pulling seniority.

Milo's background installing sea-walls was all about moving heavy items on soft, shifting soils...quick sand, sometimes... aligning them and welding them together. 12,000 pounds is not that heavy when you know what you are doing and have the proper tools.

Milo dug shallow trenches beneath the combine. He took great pains to scrape the bottoms of the trenches flat with the shovel. He used Kelly's long carpenter's bubble level to ensure it was square to gravity. Not satisfied, he scraped another inch of soil out of the far end of the trench beneath the body of the combine.

Then he dragged a pair of railroad ties into each trench and rechecked with the level. Satisfied, he shoveled loose dirt into the space between the sides of the trench and the sides of the railroad ties. He used the end of a spud to tamp it down hard, securing the ties in place.

Then Milo dug around in the lumber on the trailer until he found a couple of rough sawn oak. The planks were short...only three feet long... but they were a full three inches thick and ten inches wide. They were also shot through with dozens of pin-knots. He laid one across each set of double railroad ties.

After setting up the ties, Milo took a couple of hydraulic jacks out Kelly's truck and placed them on top of the oak planks. As Milo pumped them up, Kelly could see that Milo had placed the ties beneath the places where reinforcing plates had been welded in the construction of the combine.

As one of the jacks got close to the reinforced clevis plate, Milo stopped and looked it over. He "Tsk, tsk, tsk," clearly not liking what he saw.

"Mind if I temporarily modify the top of this jack?" Milo asked.

Kelly nodded his assent.

Milo cut a notch in one edge of a three-inch angle iron with the cutting grinder. Then he cut a notch through the right angle. Finally, he chopped the three-inch piece off the end of the length of angle iron.

"Mind holding this?" Milo asked.

Kelly could see that Milo had the short piece of angle iron positioned on top of the jack. As Milo unwound the cable for the MIG welder, Kelly deduced that Milo was going to weld the piece to make a "moose antler" on top of the jack to securely engage the clevis protruding from the combine. The notch in the edge was to engage the clevis on the combine and Milo planned to weld through the notch in the angle to secure the detail to the top of the jack.

After the welds cooled, Milo moved the jack back to the railroad ties and ran it back up. This time he grunted in satisfaction.

Going back and forth between the two jacks, Milo gently lifted the ass end of the fifteen thousand pound, fully loaded combine.

Once it was up in the air, Milo set about stuffing railroad ties and lumber pieces beneath it to ensure that it would stay up if one of the jacks shifted. Kelly figured out what Milo was doing pretty quickly and jumped to help him.

"Now what?" Kelly asked.

"Oh, that was the hard part," Milo said. Pointing to the buckled struts. "They failed because they were bending and in compression. All's we gotta do is cut the worst of the bent flanges out and use a length of stout angle and C clamps and hammers to straighten out the piece. Then we weld the angle 'splints' into place."

Put that way, it sounded easy.

When it was all done, Milo and Kelly pulled out the railroad ties and lumber and Milo bled out the valves on the jacks. The combine unceremoniously eased to the ground.

"How do you know it will hold?" Kelly asked.

"Oh, it will hold," Milo assured him. "It is stronger than the day it left the factory, and judging by the chalky paint, it ran good for thirty years. Ought to be good for another thirty if he doesn't hit a pot-hole with the other side."

"Prove it. You might as well unload it," Kelly said, pointing at the nearly empty semi parked beside the road. "And then fill it up again."

"I never drove a combine before," Milo said.

"But you have driven heavy equipment, right?" Kelly asked. "Just take it slow and figure it out as you go. Can't be too hard. They hire high school kids to run these things."

As a matter of fact, the hardest thing about driving the combine was the limited vision in certain direction. With a lot of fiddling back and forth, Milo figured out the mirrors and got the boom over the center of the semi-trailer and then dumped his load.

Then he started harvesting wheat at midnight. What the hell, Nyssa wasn't waiting up.

Farmer Don was disheartened to see the combine was where he had left it the night before and Kelly's truck was nowhere in sight.

It took him a minute to realize that two-thirds of his field was harvested and the semi-trailer was full.

The engine of the combine was idling.

Farmer Don got on his wife on the phone. "Honey, hook a gravity wagon up to the tractor and drive out to the combine. We are back in business."

Interval Training

While Rick and Milo were doing their morning stretches before running Milo commented, "You have been acting pretty peppy. Are you ready for something a little different?"

Rick had been running the same two miles out and walking the two miles back for the last three weeks. The first week was brutal. The second week was OK. The third week he was itching for more distance.

In the meantime, his push-ups had grown from sets of five to sets of ten. Milo was letting Rick manage that himself. But Milo had been holding Rick back for the last week on the running.

"You bet!" Rick said. "How far are we going to run today?"

"Less than you ran last week," Milo said cryptically.

They started out at the same 11-minute mile pace they had been running all along. Then after running ten minutes Milo had Rick stop and stretch again.

"Here is the deal," Milo said. "We can stretch the distance and you will get great at running eleven-minute miles. Or we can add some speed in and you will use different muscles and, if you find yourself needing to sprint, you will not find yourself locked into running slowly."

"But I can't run a mile any faster," Rick protested.

"You aren't going to run a mile. You are going to run faster for a minute and then you are going to walk until you can run again," Milo said.

"How fast should I run?" Rick asked.

"That is the beauty of this stuff. Just keep adding speed until your stride smooths out. If you can't run a minute then run until you are really breathing hard," Milo said.

"The how long do I walk?" Rick asked.

"Walk until you think you can run that faster pace for another minute. It might be thirty seconds. It might be five minutes," Milo said.

"If you take one thing away from today, I want you to figure out how to listen to your body," Milo finished.

Rick started out, still not seeing how it was going to go. He got up to the eleven-minute mile and then slowly started increasing his speed. At first, his stride got choppy as he made his chubby legs move faster. Then, at about the nine-minute mile pace Rick's movement slicked up and his head stopped bobbing up-and-down.

"This good?" Rick gasped out.

"That is GREAT!" Milo said.

After about forty seconds Rick dropped down to a walk.

"Perfect!" Milo said.

Rick nodded, too gassed to speak.

"Keep walking," Milo advised. It will help flush your muscles out and get them reoxygenated."

Two minutes later, Rick broke into a run and got to his target pace more quickly than before. This time he was able to go a full minute.

It took him three minutes to regain his breath and get his pulse rate back down.

Rick and Milo continued running, walking, running for the next mile. The segments of running got shorter and the walking got longer, but that was all to the good. Rick was paying attention to his body.

Walking back, Rick said, "That wasn't so bad."

"Let's see if you say that tomorrow morning," Milo said with a smile.

"Hey, Mr. Salazar, I could use some advice," Milo said. His tone and the use of the formal 'Mr. Salazar' indicated it was a serious matter.

"What's up?" Rick asked.

Milo explained that Farmer Don insisted on paying him for his work. Milo couldn't figure out what to charge him and was inclined to not charge him, being a neighbor and all.

Rick said, "Let him pay you."

Milo asked "Why?"

"A few reasons. One is that he wants to stay on your good side. He might have another piece of equipment break and he wants to ensure that you will come when he needs you," Rick said.

"Another reason is that it will ease his mind. If you give him a bill and he pays it, then it won't be hanging over his head. You won't pop up later and ask him for money...money he might not have," Rick said.

"So, what should I charge him?" Milo asked.

"You might ask him what he would expect to pay in a shop. Then charge him half. If he kicks you can tell him that you don't have to pay for a shop, and heating and lighting bills. I bet he will go for it."

Looking at Milo after finishing a set of push-ups, Rick asked, "Something else bothering you?"

“Yeah,” Milo said. “A few days ago you said that money might not be all that useful if things fall apart. I was wondering if there was a way I could get paid in wheat.”

Rick was surprised. He thought that was a fabulous idea.

“Sure! Great idea. What is your hang-up with that?” Rick asked.

“Where would I put it?” Milo asked.

“Same place Farmer Don keeps it. In the elevator,” Rick said. “Don pays a small fee for them to store it. They keep it dry and bug free.”

He continued, “You give him a bill. He contacts the elevator and has them write some paperwork transferring title to however many bushels of wheat to you. Then you write ‘Paid in full’ on a copy of the bill and mail it to him. Easy-peasy.”

Farmer Don figured it would have cost him $1000. He contacted the elevator and had $650 worth wheat transferred to a new account in the name of Milo Talon.

When Milo mentioned that they had agreed on half, that is $500, Don pointed out that Milo had done the work in the dark. In effect, Milo had to pay for the lights. Don said he would have paid $500 if Milo had done the work in the day.

After that, Milo started getting texts from people he had never met. They came from as far away as Allegan County, ninety miles away. To save driving, Milo learned to ask for pictures of the damaged equipment. Once or twice a week Milo would drive over to Kelly’s shop, load up the back of his truck and the trailer with tools and materials and head out to a job.

Milo Gets an Education

Milo had just finished up rebuilds on several pieces of equipment for a farmer south of Buchanan, Michigan. The case was unusual because the equipment had not broken first. The farmer noticed that corrosion had weakened the metal around several critical reinforcing patches and decided to address it before it broke. Consequently, the work went quickly.

Milo finished up a half hour after noon. Steve, the farmer, must have been watching him. "Why don't you wash up and eat lunch with us?" Steve suggested.

That sounded like a fine idea to Milo. He had been smelling the food cooking as air currents wafted about the shop.

After washing up, Milo followed the smell to the shop's break-room. Steve ran a medium sized operation of about 4 sections. The break-room was filled with aerial images of his operation with the images taken about five years apart. Steve walked in as Milo was inspecting them.

"I look at those a lot. Helps me see the big picture," Steve said.

"What are those?" Milo asked, pointing to what looked, to him, like rows and rows of the kinds of awnings used to shelter carports.

"Solar panels" Steve said. "Farmers harvest solar energy. Usually we use corn or soybean plants. I figured I would diversify. Solar panels don't need rain. Plus, I get a check every month instead of once a year."

Ladling out the soup, Steve informed Milo that there were "sandwich makings" in the fridge.

The soup was a rich and hearty ham and bean soup and had been brewing in the slow cooker all morning. The deli meats were fresh as was the bread and leaf lettuce.

“Did you make the soup?” Milo asked, surprised that he was being treated like visiting royalty.

“Yup. Sure enough,” Steve said. Then he pointed to quart mason jars on the shelf above the slow cooker. They were filled with beans, lentils and other dried ingredients. "Just add a gallon of water, meat, and plug it in. My sister-in-law makes them for us."

“First time I have ever been served lunch by a millionaire,” Milo commented.

“About that:” Steve said “I farm millions of dollars of land and I have millions of dollars flow through my pockets each year, but I have damned little of it stop long enough to say 'Howdy'. It goes in one pocket and flies right out the other.”

“I keep hearing that. How does that work?” Milo asked.

“Not very well!” Steve said, glumly. “Not very well.”

Milo raised his eyebrows in the universal signal *tell me more.*

“Take, for instance, the Federal loan guarantee program. The only way I can borrow money is if the Feds guarantee the loan. Every banker knows farming is risky business,” Steve said. “That means everybody has the dumb farmer by the short and curly ones.”

“My maternal grandma grew up in an old farm house a half mile from this shop. She read ‘A Tree Grows in Brooklyn' as a kid and planted a Tree of Heaven in the back yard,” Steve said.

“Last year, some Federal government weenie I never met before told me that I had to ‘eradicate’ those trees because they are an invasive, alien species,” Steve said. Milo could see Steve’s face was getting red. “Then he tells me that ‘Your loan guarantees are at risk if you don’t comply’.”

“Bastard. I may just be a dumb farmer but I know when I am getting jerked around,” Steve said. “I’d have bulldozed the whole lot fifteen years ago if it hadn't been for granny's trees...and then he tells me I can't take out the other trees because its within five hundred feet of a stream."

"So I had to go in and hand cut Granny's trees and I still have to farm around the lot," Steve said.

“You are still in business,” Milo said. “That is more than a lot of people can say.”

Steve sighed. “Yeah, and some of that is blind, dumb luck.”

Milo pointed to the picture with the solar panels. “And a lot of it isn’t.”

“Would you like to see them?” Steve said. “I figure I can let the help run the place for a couple of hours. They are pretty good. I been training them since they were born,” meaning his kids, of course.

That is how Milo got a tour of Steve’s farm. It wasn’t a showplace in the sense that Martha Stewart would be proud of it. It was a showplace in the sense that everything worked together, supporting a common goal of industry, productivity, and conservation.

Milo was impressed and he said as much.

Then he asked, “Why do farmers keep all of the old equipment? Even progressive farmers like you.” They were sitting in Steve’s UTV looking out over the “scrap yard.”

“You never know when you might need it," Steve said.

Milo pointed at an old tractor. “Why would you keep that?” Milo asked. “Surely, you aren’t going to be able to farm over two-thousand acres with that little thing.”

Steve chewed on his lower lip, trying to decide how much to

tell Milo. Normally he wouldn't have bothered but Milo was an earnest young man with promise.

"My dad escaped from Poland in 1949 and worked his way over here. He told me how things were during WWII and afterward. Nothing was thrown away. What kept him alive was a tractor far more primitive than that one," Steve said.

"What you gotta understand is that all the grown men, including my dad's pa, were taken away by the Soviets to work in the war material factories. They never saw him again," Steve said. "The Soviets also took the horses and mules. It was just an eighty-year old man and woman and my dad's ma trying to work the farm without horse or mules or oxen."

"Did you know they couldn't get petrol to run them tractors? They figured out how to run tractors and cars and trucks on wood and dried cow shit" Steve said. "It's called producer gas."

"They woulda starved or froze if they couldn't run the tractor," Steve said. "Thing is, you probably can't get one of these super-smart, computerized tractors to run on producer gas. That old beast, however, you can start with gas...if you have any...and then flip over to producer gas and it won't miss a beat," Steve said.

Milo was intrigued. "Is producer gas just as good as gasoline?"

"Oh, hell no. If it was everybody would be using it. You only get about half the horsepower and you gotta keep it in low gear and the RPM up. You let the RPM drop and it takes a gentle touch to coax them back up. It is a pain in the ass to start and getting the wood to feed through the generator is a right bitch unless you bust it up," Steve said. "Iffen it was me, I think I would try to run it on corn. Corn is easy to come by and it flows like greased ball-bearings."

Then, as an afterthought, Steve added "But there are a lot of jobs around the farm that it works for. Plowing and pulling, fer instance. You just have to use a lower gear so it takes longer. Just never let those RPM drop or the feed hopper ever get empty."

CHAPTER EIGHT

Bureaucrats Respond

Ebola cases were popping up at all of the DC and Baltimore hospitals. It was a mix of homeless people and members of the immigrant communities with epicenters in Bladensburg and Suitland.

Hospitals were hammered with absenteeism as personnel called in sick and used up personal days.

The only medical facilities that continued to run with anything approaching "normal" efficiency were the military hospitals where iron clad rules about AWOL and Dereliction of Duty kept the hospitals staffed.

The Beltway was in a panic and demanded that the Executive Branch "do something."

A small rider was attached to an otherwise insignificant piece of legislation and rushed through both houses of Congress. The President quietly signed it into law that same afternoon. The rider enhanced the emergency powers act whereby the Executive Branch could press "critical workers" into the military, in effect, draft them.

Word was passed to hospital management to get their house in order or THEY would be drafted and inserted into the military two grades below the rank they would normally hold.

Absenteeism did not improve. The administrations were given orders to report. The majority complied. Bench warrants were issued for those who blew off the orders. When apprehended they were incarcerated in a military prison.

Lawsuits were filed claiming that forced indentures in the military was involuntary servitude. The judges put them on the slow train to no-where. To a person, the judges had loved ones who needed medical services from time-to-time and had no truck for the absenteeism.

Then the union officials were contacted. They were told to get their house in order or their rank-and-file would be inducted into the military.

Absenteeism did not improve. Entire swaths of the medical community from Pennsylvania-to-Central Virginia were inducted into the military. Those who chose to not comply were apprehended and shipped to a tent city in the Arizona desert.

The exercise became the template for the centralization of the US economy. Private sector was "drafted" and assigned a rank two levels below what was normal. Local and state government employees were drafted and assigned a rank one level lower. There was going to be no ambiguity regarding chain-of-command. The very highest levels of government anticipated that enterprises would attempt to conserve human resources at the expense of the mission. Those attempts were anticipated and crushed.

Every rational response within the private sector and local government were seen as a threat in the battle against Ebola. Every threat was treated the same way.

The "Market" locked up under the triple threat of the frozen import/export sector, the credit markets vaporizing, and the threat of Government take-over.

The cascading failures of the markets resulted in the metastasizing of government take-overs and they occurred at an exponentially increasing rate.

A Change of Plans

"I just can't do it," Rick said.

"Can't do what?" Milo asked as he started stretching for the morning run.

"I can't run today," Rick said.

"What's the matter? Are you sick?" Milo asked with concern in his voice.

"Nope. It's not that," Rick said. "I just can't run today. That interval training you started me on is breaking me down."

"You will toughen up," Milo said with the certainty of youth.

"You don't understand. I CANNOT do it today," Rick said. "The thing you don't get about being older is that it takes longer to heal."

"See this cut?" Rick said, thrusting out his left forearm. There was a scabbed over, three-inch-long scratch on his arm.

"Yeah. So?" Milo said.

"I got it two weeks ago. When I was your age it would have been healed in four days," Rick said.

"We either need to dial way back on the intensity of the work-outs or I need longer than one day rest between them. I am sixty, for God's sake," Rick said. He was a little huffy because he didn't like admitting he was getting older and slowing down. Especially admitting it to himself.

Milo's mouth twitched a bit as he thought. "Well, I did tell you to listen to your body. I would rather have you keep working out even if it means making changes to the plan. I am just throwing this out as a starting point for conversation," Milo said. "What if we let you pick the intensity and distance and keep the one-day rest period, except for once a week we do intervals and you take as long as you need to recover?"

"So, you are saying I pick the distance and intensity and dial it in so I am ready to go day-after. But once a week you kick my ass and then I get to lick my wounds," Rick paraphrased.

"More or less," Milo agreed. "I don't want you to take a whole week off as a general thing. But that means I will be paying attention and won't push too hard."

"Thing is, I can't work out today. I am just too sore in too many places," Rick said.

"Can you walk a half mile?" Milo asked.

"Yeah. Why?" Rick asked.

"Got something to show you over at Kelly's place," Milo said.

Rick would have driven but then thought that walking might help him lose some of the stiffness in his muscles.

Once they got over to Kelly's place Milo took him to Kelly's junk piles behind the barns and asked, "What do you think?"

Rick was mystified. "Think about what?" Rick was not intimately familiar with Kelly's personal junk yard.

"The tractor. The farm implements," Milo said.

For all of Rick's redeeming characteristics, he was not an equipment guy. "What am I looking at?" he asked.

"You are looking at a 1972 Massey Ferguson 165 farm tractor with a 2.8-liter, Continental gasoline motor and the farm implements to drag behind it," Milo said.

"It is ENORMOUS!" Rick exclaimed. "What are you going to do with that?"

"Its listed as sixty horsepower but that really means forty horsepower at the drawbar," Milo said. "The guy I bought it from said it can pull three, 16" plows behind it. Of course, he has sandy-loam," Milo said as if that would mean something to Rick.

Rick didn't know much about machinery but he knew tractor tires started at $500 a tire. He walked over and looked at the rubber. "Nice tires," he said. Then he looked at the hoses and belts. "Musta been stored inside," he deduced.

"Got it for $4500," Milo said proudly. "It got a full rebuild at four thousand hours and then the owner parked it in his barn. I took Mr. Pepper shopping with me," he admitted. "He knows a hell of a lot about old tractors and farm machinery." Mr. Pepper was one of the geezers Rick drank coffee with.

In fact, the farmers who Milo did work for were happy to sell him old farm equipment for little more than what they would have gotten at scrap metal prices. Equipment they sold to him for 25 cents a pound they had refused offers of five times as much from a big city antiques dealer. Milo had shopped hard and bought well.

"This is all very impressive," Rick said, meaning it. "But I don't know that I can help you with any of this. It is really outside my 'wheel house'."

Then it was Milo's turn to be apologetic and shuffle a little bit. "I was hoping to ask for a favor," he said. "I was talking to an old Polish farmer a couple of weeks ago. He told me that they used to run tractors on wood and dried cow shit 'back in the old country'," Milo said.

"He said that I should get smart about something he called 'producer gas'," Milo said. "I started to dig into it and quickly figured out that there is too much conflicting information out there on the internet for me to sort out. Some of my problem is that I am looking at stuff on my phone and I don't have a printer.

"Then Nyssa said that you are a total rock-star at researching," Milo said. "So I humbly ask you, hat-in-hand, would you consider researching 'producer gas generators' sized for fifty-to-sixty horsepower motors? Please?" Milo said. "Oh. The other thing the Polish farmer mentioned was using corn for fuel. Don't suppose I could have you look into that, too." He didn't know if he was pushing his luck.

"Flattery will get you almost anything," Rick said, thinking *Nyssa called me a Rock-Star?. Really?*

"Since I am not working out today, what do you want me to research first: Producer gas generators or Corn as fuel?" Rick asked with a smile.

"Sir, if it is not too much trouble, producer gas generators. All we need are plans and some dimensions, then Kelly and I will knock out a prototype and see what happens."

Logistics

"The Heilers are moving to Lansing," Kate said when Rick came through the door.

The Heilers were a sweet elderly couple who were struggling with a multitude of health issues. Being in your eighties isn't for sissies.

"Why are they doing that?" Rick asked. Moving to an urban area seemed like shear insanity when an epidemic is threatening.

"They got a note from the drug store when they picked up their latest batch of prescriptions," Kate said. "I pulled a copy off the internet."

The notice read:

> *In light of recent events there may be temporary disruptions in the distribution of critical drugs. Bright-Lad Pharmacies cannot guarantee delivery of drugs to outlying outlets. If you depend on drugs for life support, make a transportation plan so you can pick them up at outlets in core areas.*

"The Heilers decided to beat the rush. They figured it would be easier to find an apartment now than later," Kate said.

"Whaddya mean?" Rick asked.

Rick was blessed with robust good health and was oblivious to how many people were dependent on drugs.

That is when Nyssa, the nurse, piped up. "Well, you have all the people who are diabetic, you have folks on blood pressure meds and pulse-rate stabilizers. Then there are the asthma and COPD meds and the anti-psychotics."

"That doesn't even count all the drunks and stoners," Nyssa said. "You know we have them out here. If they have to walk into Lansing to get their fix you know they aren't coming back."

"How many do you figure we will lose?" Rick asked, caught completely off-guard.

"Looking at just hard-core alcoholics and druggies you could lose ten percent. Maybe another twenty percent of the people who depend on drugs to stay alive," Nyssa said. "Then there are people who are going to move to Lansing because their spouse moved to Lansing. My guess is you are looking at losing at least 1/3 of the people in the neighborhood if the epidemic keeps tracking."

Rick's first thought was that his labor shortage just got a whole lot worse. His 450 neighbors were going to drop down to 300.

After thinking about it a bit, he realized that the loss of the hard-core substance abusers was likely to be a substantial net benefit. The people who were dependent on drugs to sustain life were primarily elderly and while he would miss them dearly, the fact that they would abandon their houses meant that the demand for firewood would also drop. Rick's tight-rope act of ensuring adequate firewood without totally destroying the woods just got a whole lot easier.

The next surprise was when all of the state workers with rank, i.e. management, were provided with state cars, were inducted into the military and ordered to relocate to the Detroit metro area and Flint and report to FEMA. It was a surprise because high ranking officials figured that as "knowledge workers" they could work from anyplace as long as it had a solid connection to the internet. Unfortunately for them, FEMA is a boots-on-the-ground organization.

The remaining state workers saw that handwriting on the wall and would soon put their homes on the market. That was going to be another ten houses that would not have to be heated.

Kate said, "Rick, I had a thought. I want you and Nyssa to hear me out before you judge."

Rick had never thought of himself as judgmental but he could tell from Kate's voice that this is something she had put a lot of thought into and it was important to her.

Nyssa merely nodded.

"When you first started talking about an Ebola epidemic, I thought you were crazy," Kate said.

Rick said, "I know. You shared that and I thank you for letting me run with it."

"What I see now is that this not only might happen, it seems likely to happen. After all, Bright-Lad would not send out letters like that if they weren't worried," Kate said.

Rick and Nyssa both nodded in agreement.

"What you haven't considered is how you are going to get all of these supplies to the people who need them," Kate said. "I can see the wheels turning in your head, Rick. The next thing you are going to do is to lay in a supply of drugs, if only for pain and hay fever.

"Are you going to go knocking on houses door-to-door? No, I don't think so," Kate continued. "I think we need to start a small, country store and I think I should run it," she said. "We have the small barn near the drive that would make a good, small store. It has lots of shelves and the office can be locked."

The concept had a lot to recommend it. Rick and Kate did not live in the exact, geographic center of "the neighborhood" but they lived within half a mile of the population center-of-gravity. If things came apart at the seams then a two-mile walk without having to leave the neighborhood was a lot more attractive than having to walk six or seven miles.

Rick was quickly learning that there was no way he could be at the center of everything. The only way things were going to fly was if he let people follow their own paths.

"Kate, I know you get tired of hearing this from me, but you are absolutely right on all counts," Rick said. "How can we help?"

Wrong Diagnosis, Wrong Medicine

The economy continued to crater even as Milo had more business than he could handle.

Federal officials attempted to twist arms to open up the US embargo with zero success. They were stunned.

Over drinks, one of the foreign envoys explained it to a mid-level State Department official. "The only people who didn't know about your Ebola problem were your own citizens. Every country from Bangladesh to Vietnam had copies of your internal documents thirty minutes after you generated them," the envoy explained.

"Can you imagine what Ebola would do in a country like Bangladesh?" the envoy asked with a shudder.

"Don't expect any concessions until you extinguish Ebola," the envoy advised. "And given that the number of cases is doubling every three weeks, you have a long way to go." The envoy allowed the State Department official to buy his drinks.

There were other factors in play.

Both sides of the aisle had been hawkish on war. The number of interventions increased from year-to-year and the pretext for each intervention was increasingly flimsy. The best way to distract voters is to turn their attention away from domestic issues. The United States' staunchest allies were not amused.

The final leg that was being kicked out from beneath the American juggernaut was the dethroning of the US dollar as the world's reserve currency. The US dollar was the hydraulic fluid in the world economy.

As the default currency, any growth in the world economy meant a free-pass for United States borrowers. The only way to obtain US dollars was to buy US bonds, essentially 'giving' products to the US consumer.

Losing the status of the world's reserve currency meant that the tide that had been flowing in would flow out just as strongly.

The US economy was on uncharted territory. The last time the United States had not been in the cat-bird's seat was before World War One.

The urge to do "something" was irresistible. Two generations of politicians had cut their teeth on creating demand. They were congenitally unable to recognize any other kind of problem. It was the classic case of the carpenter who only owned a hammer.

The solution, in their eyes, was to increase demand.

Every living person in the United States over the age of twelve was mailed an EBT/SNAP card. The amount per person had been almost doubled to $800 per month. Not only that, but the rules had been changed so half of that amount was now available for spending in restaurants and "hospitality" businesses.

Casinos, restaurants, and massage parlors were swamped.

Kate sent each of her children an email.

To Mark and Gabriella who lived in Portsmouth, NH and Memphis, TN respectively, she sent the following: "If you think you might want to land here in the event Ebola is not contained, please consider mailing one of your EBT cards to us so we can use it to stock durable goods."

To Luke and Janelle who she presumed were still single and somewhere in Lansing and the West Coast: "You might want to start thinking about how you will get here if this Ebola epidemic explodes. I know money might be tight, but it will be a convenience to us if you mail us your EBT card...if you can spare it."

She got two EBT cards from Mark. Gabriella mailed one EBT card and apologetically told her that they had already given one card to their church. Luke and Janelle mailed Kate their

EBT cards.

With her and Rick's card, plus those of her kids, Kate had $5600 a month to stock her store...as long as the tattered economy held together.

Rick and Kate's first trip to the discount club "big-box" was disconcerting. The greeter explained the near total absence of customers, "They are all visiting the high-end boutiques."

At Kate's insistence, both Rick and Kate got dollies. She had a list of items that would be difficult or impossible to manufacture locally. They had corn and wheat in abundance so that meant there was no point in buying anything starchy. Kate's list also took storage life into account. That eliminated most meat products.

Consequently, the carts were loaded with 35-pound jugs of partially hydrogenated soy and peanut oil, bulk tea and instant coffee, aspirin, ibuprofen, acetaminophen, vitamin tablets, iodine, band aids, condoms.

The first time that Rick objected to what Kate loaded onto her cart was when she put 240 butane cigarette lighters onto the pile. "What are you getting those for?" he asked, incredulously.

"Do you remember when we were camping on South Manitou Island?" Kate asked.

Of course Rick remembered. It was the second summer they were married. South Manitou is a wilderness area in the middle of Lake Michigan. They hiked into their campsite and discovered that neither of them had packed matches or a lighter. Fortunately, a passing hiker had a spare lighter.

"Suppose it was thirty-five degrees and raining. How much would a working lighter have been worth to us?" Kate asked.

Rick said, "I suppose it would have been worth every penny

we had in our pockets. Heck, it would be worth a thousand dollars, if we had it."

"That is my point," Kate said. Kate did not tell Rick that she had also invested in a device that refilled butane lighters from 20-pound LP cylinders. Repeat business is a wonderful thing.

Rick started to comment when Kate turned down the aisle that had toilet paper and feminine hygiene products. He carped that there was no way they could store enough toilet paper for their own use, much less supply the neighborhood.

Kate gave him "that look" and Rick shut up. This was Kate's show and Rick not only trusted her but had learned the path to success is to let others "own" the process and outcome.

Ms Sheridan

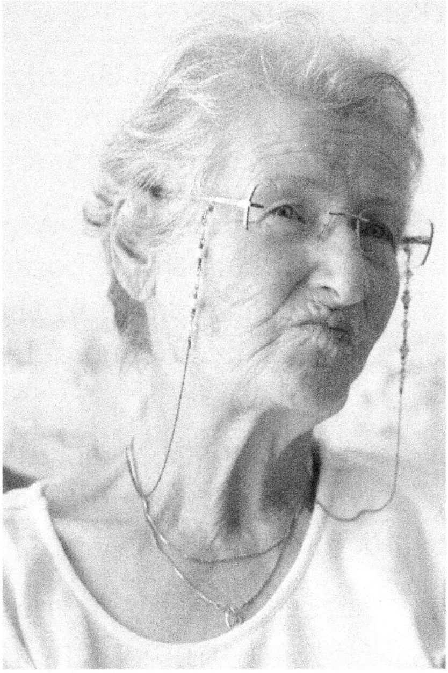

One of the factors that favored Kate's store was the building itself.

It was a pole barn, 48 feet long and 32 feet wide. It was unusual in that it had a gambrel roof with attic trusses, which provided another 800 square feet of under-roof storage area. It also had a small area surrounded by privacy fencing off the northwest corner for additional storage of items that could be out in the weather.

If there was one drawback to the building it was Stacy Sheridan, the neighbor immediately to the west of the Salazars.

Ms Sheridan was a fussy, seventy-year-old woman with a fingernails-on-blackboard voice. Ms Sheridan (never Miss or Mrs) had an accent that Kate could only place as "East coast, BIG city".

In spite of Kate's resolve to be impartial, Ms Sheridan pushed every button in Kate's head.

Ms Sheridan was unfailingly critical. She dismissed the possibility of Ebola getting out of control. She dismissed the possibility of anybody wanting to shop at Kate's.

More to the point, Ms Sheridan was ALWAYS in the store. Kate did not feel like she could throw potential customers out, especially one who lived next door. There was no way to calculate the damage Ms Sheridan could do if she were crossed.

So Kate bit her tongue and tried to be as neighborly as possible. Kate found it extraordinarily difficult to be a good Christian around Stacy Sheridan.

The one thing that hacked Kate off the most was when Ms Sheridan berated Kate for her pricing policies. Kate's formula was simple. Kate required 20% of consignment sales and did a straight fifty percent markup of the goods she had invested in.

Ms Sheridan had the ears of a cat and apparently could do calculations in her head like an adding machine. She was OUTRAGED at the fifty percent markup.

"That is OBSCENE," Ms Sheridan railed. "You are exploiting people. Have you no conscience?"

Kate snapped. "You are free to shop elsewhere," she said.

"Fifty percent markup! That is unheard of!" Ms Sheridan's voice increased ten decibels.

"Actually, it is not. Convenience stores have one-hundred percent markup on candy and ice cream," Kate threw back.

"But people can live without candy and ice-cream," Ms Sheridan shrieked back.

"How dare you?" When Ms Sheridan got excited she pronounced "R"s that were not there and randomly dropped "R"s that were there. She also started pronouncing the "g" in "..ong" and "..ing".

"What is your life worth to you?" Kate shot back. "What is your time worth? Go ahead. Burn an hour out of your life and drive to Lansing. Get Ebola. I. Don't. Care," and Kate stormed out in full fury.

The next day it was as if nothing had happened. Ms Sheridan was no more abrasive than usual. Kate was ashamed of losing her temper and pretended that nothing had happened.

One of the things that saved Kate's sanity was that Sergeant Steve Smith, a retired State Police trooper who offered Defensive Pistol classes for women. Kate suggested that it might be useful for Ms Sheridan to attend. Kate was surprised when Ms Sheridan signed up. That was out of sync with what Kate expected from a liberal, big city woman.

Quite by accident Kate stumbled upon a way of diluting Ms Sheridan's negativity.

Kate absent-mindedly asked Ms Sheridan to put 500 tablet bottles of aspirin in mason jars, add a desiccant pouch and oxygen absorbers and then seal them. Ms Sheridan was all smiles and questions.

Kate told her that the shelf-life of many drugs can be extended by excluding light, oxygen and moisture. Some drugs, like acetaminophen tablets have a thirty-year shelf life without special treatment. Others, like aspirin, need to be protected from agents that degrade them.

Ms Sheridan pointed out that mason jars are glass and the contents are exposed to light.

Kate said, "I was planning on storing them in a root cellar where it is dark. But you are right, there is no downside to blocking out the light except I won't be able to see what is in it just by looking."

With that, Ms Sheridan fastidiously wrapped the sides of the mason jars with a double layer of brown paper and then secured it with blue masking tape. Then she carefully lettering the contents on both the sides and the lid of the jar.

Ms Sheridan became a chatter-box when she was doing the simple, repetitive work of repacking merchandise. Kate was treated to a running monologue of Ms Sheridan's life.

Married at age 29. Divorced at 48. Her husband filed on Gawd-forsaken Eaton County rather than a civilized jurisdiction where she would not have been screwed.

Kate thought, "Why would he choose to file in a place where it would be to his disadvantage?" She kept her counsel. Kate found Ms Sheridan's monologue less grinding than being the subject of her criticisms.

The judge gave her the house. That is, she received $25,000 in equity and $1000 a month house payment. Her husband got his vehicle and a young girl-friend out of the deal.

The judge had not been sympathetic when Ms Sheridan had objected to his settlement. He had explained...of course it was a man...that the court was not responsible for financial decisions the couple had made regarding the remortgaging of the property as it appreciated.

And, in the absence of minor children and with Ms Sheridan's educational level being higher than Mr. Sheridan's, there was no need for child support or alimony.

Since then, life had been a constant struggle for money.

Kate pointed to Ms Sheridan's voluminous, cross-body tote bag. "But you have enough for designer clothes?" she pointed out.

"It's a Salvatore Ferragamo," Ms Sheridan said with pride. "It retails for $1900."

"You can't be doing too badly if you can afford something like that," Kate persisted.

"That just shows how stupid people in Michigan are. I paid $5 for it at the Goodwill store in Charlotte," Ms Sheridan said with bitterness. "You and me are probably the only two people in Eaton County who know how much this bag is really worth."

Kate's inner voice spoke, "Yup, it is worth exactly $5."

Even though it was a flashy looking bag with exotic, leather side panels, it had seen years of use. Kate did not consider it to be nearly as functional as the $10 nylon "camera" style bag she used as a purse.

After that Kate made a point of asking Ms Sheridan's opinion on various types of bulk products. Kate brought back small samples and they would have tasting sessions. Ms Sheridan ALWAYS had an opinion. It was just as easy to buy Ms Sheridan's preferences as not. Caffeine was caffeine, detergent was detergent in Kate's eyes. If things got tough folks would not be choosy.

CHAPTER NINE

Gasifiers

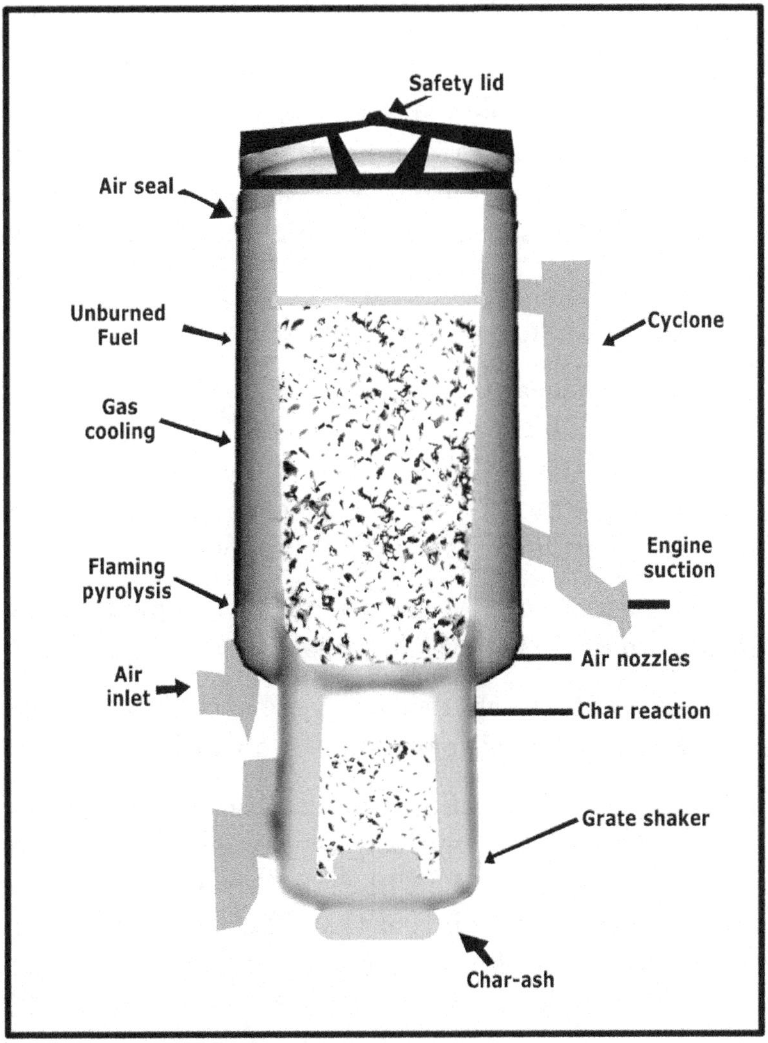

“I have some good news and I have some bad news,” Rick said to Kelly and Milo.

They were in Kelly’s shop and Rick was “reporting out” on what he had learned about producer gas generators.

“Start with the good news," Milo said. “We could use some.”

“The good news is that you can use almost anything organic in your generator as long as it is dry enough. There are even documented cases of folks using peat in them,” Rick said.

“Peat, like the muck out in the marsh?” Kelly asked.

“Yeah, the muck in the marsh that will turn into coal in a million years. You can burn muck if you dry it down,” Rick said. “But that takes a lot of drying and it is a pain to handle. That is why most folks use wood scraps. They are easy to dry.”

“So, it should be a snap to burn corn,” Milo said.

“It’s not quite that easy” Rick said. “All the plans on the internet are for wood scraps. And the reputable sources are very clear that you have to dial in the geometry to the size of your engine and the exact fuel you will use, otherwise you will gum up your engine or lose a bunch of power.”

“That just means we may have to make a few prototypes to figure out what works best,” Kelly said.

“What did you learn about these generators?” Kelly asked. “Maybe we can get a leg up on what we are doing.”

“There is no point in talking about all of the generators,” Rick said. “Everybody who had anything on the ball were using Imbert designs. The difference between the Imbert and the FEMA generator is that the Imbert feeds air directly to the reaction chamber rather than pulling it through the hopper. The simpler designs need constant adjustment because the air flow characteristics change as the fuel in the hopper burns down. Another problem with the simpler designs is that you can get a run-away burn."

Rick pulled some drawings out of his folder.

"As you can see, the reaction chamber looks like a length of stove pipe with grating on the bottom and air inlet ports in the side," Rick said. "Many of the reaction chambers have a choke point, called a 'throat', kind of like the venturi of a carb."

"So, what needs to be tuned in?" Kelly asked.

"The diameter of the reaction chamber and the total area of the air inlet ports need to be tuned into the size of the engine and the distance between the air inlet ports and the grating need to be dialed into the fuel," Rick said.

"Since you know the tractor is rated at 60 horsepower, the throat of the reactor needs to be between eight and nine inches in diameter and it needs seven, three-quarter inch holes evenly spaced around the 'stove-pipe'," Rick said.

"How high above the throat?" Kelly asked.

"That, I cannot tell you," Rick said. "That is something you guys are going to have to figure out."

By the next day Kelly and Milo had kludged together a test system near the big door to Kelly's shop. The feed hopper was a barrel. The reaction chamber was doubled up stove-pipe. They knew the pipe would not last long but they only needed it to last until they collected the data.

The gas was plumbed through a five-gallon bucket half filled with water to cool and filter it and thence to Milo's tractor which was parked in the doorway. Milo had it hooked up to a brush-hog to provide "load".

One of Kelly's innovations was to cut three-quarter inch

holes in the section of reaction vessel above the throat. The holes were five, nine and thirteen inches above the grating.

Then he fashioned a collar that slid over that section of reaction vessel that had oversized holes that were three inches apart vertically. If he started at the mid position, Kelly could use the Vernier effect and change the air inlet height by four inches up-or-down simply by sliding the outer sleeve one inch up-or-down.

They cheated on lighting it. They loaded the bottom of the reaction vessel with charcoal briquettes and lit it with a propane torch. Then, after the charcoal was burning well, they added a hundred pounds of dried corn.

Milo started the tractor and engaged the PTO.

Then they were like boys playing in a sandbox. Kelly knew from experience that he would get distracted and stop taking notes so he recorded the entire thing on video.

Gasifiers: When Theory Collides With Reality

Kelly and Milo were stumped. There was no reason that corn shouldn't work. In fact, it should be the ideal fuel.

They started the experiment with the test platform in the midrange. That is, with the air inlet holes nine inches above the reactor grate. The 60-horsepower motor of the tractor sputtered and barely kept running, much less having enough power to run the brush hog.

Attempts to run the test platform with the air inlet holes five inches above the reactor grate caused the motor to promptly stall out.

At thirteen inches the gasifier barely kept the motor running when the PTO was engaged and the brush hog running. That was with no load on the brush hog other than friction and the air blowing through it.

It was a puzzler.

Kelly, who had more experience with "primitive" engines, meaning engines with carburetors, said "It acts like it is starved for fuel."

They took a break and drank some coffee as they watched the tractor struggle to run at the thirteen-inch setup.

"I got an idea" Milo said. He walked over to Kelly's steel rack and pulled out a six-foot-long piece of fence top-rail. The pipe was almost one-and-a-half inches in diameter.

Milo made a couple of short, longitudinal cuts in one end of the pipe and bent out 'petals'.

Milo wrapped some window screen around the modified end and secured it with a radiator hose clamp and the petals gave the clamps something to grip.

He held the pipe against the side of the barrel and put a wrap of tape around it to provide a sense of scale.

Then he cracked the lid to the hopper feeding corn to the reactor and started pushing the piece of pipe down, toward the reactor. The densely packed corn resisted the effort and Milo had to twist the pipe to drill down through.

"Whatchya thinking?" Kelly said.

"I think air flows through wood chips a lot more easily than through corn," Milo said.

"I wonder if six holes are enough. And even if they are enough, how is that air going to get to the corn in the center of the reactor?" Milo said.

When Milo judged the buried end of the pipe was at the same level as the other air inlet holes, he stopped pushing it in. Then he walked back to his coffee cup to see what happened.

The motor's operation started to smooth up in about a minute. Then it picked up speed and sounded healthy.

"You know, the hell of it is that you can make an adjustment to the gasifier and you won't know if what you did is correct for a few minutes while the generator adjusts," Kelly noted.

"Yeah, I can see why that old farmer said you didn't want to do a lot of shifting, just run it flat out in low gear," Milo said. "It takes too long to tweak the generator into what the engine wants."

Kelly was scratching his head. "I think we need another prototype."

"I think we should try fourteen inches, eighteen inches and twenty inches. I also think we should use your idea of inserting a lance but make it bigger, maybe two-inch diameter pipe. We can always throttle it back," Kelly said.

"Sounds like a plan," Milo said as he turned off the tractor.

Then he pulled out the lance and put the air-tight cover over the hopper. It would take a while for it to cool down enough that it wouldn't spontaneously restart.

Then Kelly and Milo started work on the second prototype.

Kate's Store, Details

Kate quickly settled on the concept of selling small quantities from bulk containers. She would put a five hundred tablet bottle of ibuprofen on the shelf but would sell it by the tablet or gram.

The same way with commodities like corn meal and flour. She would have one of "the boys" grind up what she thought she would sell in the coming week and sell it by the pound with a maximum of seven pounds per person in the household. If requested she would grind grain or coffee beans to order. Visitors found the grinder entertaining and would purchase goods just to watch the grinder run.

She had salt and veterinary supplies. She had 8d and 16d nails and decking screws. Fly ribbon, worming medicine, topical ointments for mange, ticks and fleas.

She had one-pound rolls of #69 polyester thread in basic white and black.

She had scores of zippers in three lengths any color you wanted as long as it was black. She had hundreds of hand needles and thousands of safety pins.

She had the most basic of garden seeds: green beans, sugar-snap peas, sweet corn, storing onion, tomatoes (cherry, slicing, and paste), turnip-rutabaga-and-kale seeds. She also had sacks of seed potatoes in back.

She had #110 and #220 body-grip traps for rent. She had .22LR, 9mm and .223, 12 and 20 shotgun shells. She set a maximum of twenty rounds per week per family and gave a discount if they brought back the spent hulls or brass. She also made exceptions if the buyer regularly brought her meat or hides to sell.

There was also a charging station for batteries and customers were allowed to charge batteries for free as long as they were shopping. That was not a big draw but Kate saw that it would be if the grid got shaky.

A quarter of the store was set up for seasonal produce to be sold on-consignment. The contents of the room changed with the seasons. Spring had greens, rhubarb and mushrooms. Early summer had berries and green onions. Late summer had tomatoes, summer squash and cucumbers. Fall had all of the above, hickory and lots of walnuts and the first meats as the weather turned cooler. Winter had root vegetables and meat.

One part of the consignment area had 'crafts' like soap and

knitted goods. Items needing repair could be left and the seamstress would repair it for a price.

Kate didn't restrict what people placed on consignment but if it spoiled the sellers had to come RIGHT NOW to clean it out. Families that were slow to clean up or hogged prime space were banned for a period of time. That generally caused them to straighten out.

Kate was more than happy to provide floor-space if there was demand. Kate knew that the store was an evolution. The merchandise and prices would evolve as the needs of the neighborhood and as the availability of goods changed.

Kate kept an old-fashioned chalk board where she listed items she was looking for. Customers were encouraged to add items to the board. She also kept a bulletin board for folks to pin business cards.

Kate kept an overly large supply of what she called "traffic builders."

She sold candy bars for less than what the convenience store in town sold them for. She also sold cigarettes, soda pop, Slim-Jims and jerky, toilet paper, feminine hygiene products, tooth-brushes and the like.

Her steadiest customers were the kids old enough to ride a bike. She sold a lot of candy bars. The kids also helped her figure out one of the best ways to spread the word about her merchandise.

She played "I spy" with them. She would name some obscure type of merchandise she carried and then reward the first kid who found it with a FREE candy bar. Size 8 fish-hooks? Bam! Silicon caulk? Bam! Canning lids, mouse traps, fly ribbon? Bam, bam, bam!

Many times, she would ask the kids about an item that was near the item from the time before. She might ask about kerosene heaters one day and then wicks the next. The kids who had not memorized the entire shelf from the last time felt stupid. They rarely made that mistake again.

Traffic was too slow to keep the store open all the time. Kate adopted a sliding schedule where she kept the store open for four hours each day but it was a different start-and-stop time to give folks with differing schedules the option of visiting.

Kate Wants a Radio Station

Coming back from yet another foray at the mega discount store, Kate shared her desire to have a radio station associated with her store.

Rick thought she was insane and shared as much. Not the best way to start a dialog.

Kate persisted.

"You are the one who keeps saying that capitalism and the markets work because of the free flow of information, right?" Kate threw the challenge back.

In fact, Rick frequently said as much.

"So how will information move when the grid is down? When the internet is down? When there is no paper or ink?" Kate asked.

"More to the point, how will people know that I have a store? I need to be able to contact suppliers and customers. I need to let suppliers know what I am buying and I need to let customers know what I have in abundance and am having sales on," Kate said.

It is a bitter pill when your wife uses your exact words to win an argument. But Rick was man enough to surrender when he knew he was going to lose.

"So, what is the picture in your head?" Rick said. "Do you

want something that just broadcasts over the neighbor-hood? We can do that with hand-helds."

"Nope. I want more than that," Kate said. "I need to be able to reach out to Eaton Rapids, Charlotte and Dimondale."

Rick cogitated on what Kate wanted and a half mile from home he pulled off the road and parked the truck and trailer. "Are you super busy?" he asked Kate.

"No" Kate said, baffled.

"Good. We are going to pay Dmitri and Allaina a visit," Rick said. "If we don't do it now it isn't going to get done."

Rick was 99% certain that the very tall antenna in their back yard indicated that Dmitri was into ham radio.

Rick rummaged around in one of the boxes in the bed of the truck and pulled out a bottle of Chopin Vodka.

Dmitri was smoking a cigarette and wearing a "wife-beater" tee shirt when he answered the door. "To what do I owe the honor?" he asked.

Rick was never able to tell when Dmitri was being sardonic. He attributed it to Dmitri's heavy accent. In truth, Dmitri was always sardonic, it was genetic.

"Kate wants a pirate radio station," Rick announced as he held up the bottle and wiggled it. "Can we come in and visit?"

"Sure. Any friend of Chopin is a friend of mine," Dmitri said.

The TV in the corner was tuned into a Central European news station. Dmitri was disdainful of US news outlets. *Cheerleaders* he called them, dismissively.

"Tell me about this station you want," Dimitri said as he sat down and turned off the TV.

Allaina came out from the bedroom speaking Romanian. She was in a bathrobe and drying her hair. She pivoted and went back to the bedrooms.

Kate gave Rick a poisonous look. That is why people are supposed to CALL before dropping in. The look bounced off Rick.

"Tell me about this radio station you want" Dmitri commanded, again.

When Kate did not pipe up, Rick said, "She wants to be able to transmit ten miles in every direction."

Dmitri nodded. "That is not technically difficult. It is illegal and it costs money, but other than that it is not hard."

"Do you want AM or FM?" Dmitri asked.

Before Rick could answer for her, Kate said. "I want both. How much would it cost to do both?"

Dmitri said, "Let me think."

Then as his thoughts came together, he started making notes on a spiral pad.

"You need a good microphone and a couple of transmitters. Ten Watts will work if you have good antennas. You might have $700 in the in-studio equipment," Dmitri said. "You can buy it on DeNile or fleaBait or any of the on-line auction sites."

"You might have trouble finding AM equipment at that power level so we will have to buy an amplifier." Dmitri did not notice that he has switched pronouns, although Allaina who had reentered the room a few minutes ago noticed immediately.

"That doesn't sound too bad!" Kate said.

Dmitri harrumphed. "I was not done."

"And you will need antennas. The money for your project is in the antennas. The FM is easy. Do you have a frequency picked out?" Dmitri asked.

"I want 104.3 for the FM and 1086 for the AM," Kate said, surprising Rick. He had no idea she had given the project this much thought.

"Why them?" Rick asked.

"Cop codes: 10-43 is Information and 10-86 is Officer-on-duty," Kate said.

"We have to look to see if you will be stepping on any existing stations," Dmitri said.

"I already swept the dial with our Sony and they were pretty empty," Kate said.

"So, if there are no other problems with 104.3 FM you will need an antenna that is.." Dmitri said while tapping on his calculator, "....4.3 meters long if we go with a 3/2 wave antenna."

"What is that in feet?" Kate asked.

A little more tapping on the calculator: "Fourteen feet, one inches," Dmitri said.

"That isn't bad. I don't see why that will be very expensive," Kate said.

"It isn't the antenna that costs the most money. It is the structure you need to put it twenty meters in the air," Dmitri said. "And the surge protectors you will need to protect your equipment."

"And the FM is the easy one," Dmitri said.

"What will it take for the AM?" Kate asked.

“A full wave for 1086 kilohertz is 275 meters long,” Dmitri said.

“So, what is that, like a thousand feet?” Kate asked, flabbergasted.

Dmitri nodded his head in the affirmative.

“Well, there goes that idea,” Rick said.

“Not so fast,” Dmitri said. “There is a kind of antenna called a ‘ground loop’ antenna where the antenna is laid on its side. Do you have some place where you can erect a square of mounting poles about 900 feet on a side?” Dmitri asked.

“Rick. How big is our property?” Kate asked.

“It is forty acres,” Rick said.

“I know that,” Kate said. “What are the dimensions on a side?"

“A quarter mile. That is 1320 feet on a side,” Rick said.

“Would that work?” Kate asked as Allaina served cookies and iced tea.

“It will work fine as long as it is not in the bottom of a canyon,” Dmitri said.

To celebrate, Dmitri opened the bottle and served a round of shots.

Antennas

Milo was working with Dmitri erecting the FM antenna mast.

“This is the first time I ever did this,” Milo said.

The mast was a forty-foot long utility pole. At the top of the pole was an orange, adhesive-bonded fiberglass section that added an additional eighteen feet. The first twelve feet of the fiberglass section was rectangular and fabricated by adhesive bonding two fiberglass channels together. The remainder of the section was a single, fiberglass channel section.

The top of the mast was surmounted with a pulley exactly like you would see on a flag pole. 1/8" nylon rope was run through the pulley in anticipation of running the antenna.

Milo had augured a six-foot-deep hole and by way of meticulous teamwork with Kelly on his tractor they were able to drop the butt end of the pole into the hole and position it vertically.

The hole was back-filled with crushed gravel and the gravel was tamped down. Then the pole was guy-wired at ten and twenty-five feet. The guy lines were run to eye-bolts that were cast into 200-pound blocks of concrete buried in the ground.

"That fiberglass section looks familiar but I just can't place it," Milo said when they were taking a break.

"It was salvaged from a twenty-four-foot fiberglass extension ladder," Dmitri said. Three of the four legs were still good. It was just a matter of stripping off the attaching hardware, sanding off the mold release compound and then epoxying them together," Dmitri said dismissively.

"Why didn't you just use aluminum tubing?" Milo asked.

"Conductive materials would interfere with the antenna," Dmitri said. "Salvage is cheap. A new, 20' length of tubing costs $400. That one cost almost nothing."

"Why the flagpole pulley?" Milo asked, curious.

"To run up the flag that says 'BROADCASTING'. " Dmitri said.

"No, really. Why the pulley," Milo persisted.

"The trouble with Americans is that you love million-dollar solutions to hundred-dollar problems. It is a common quirk in rich countries. Romania is not rich. We look for five-dollar solutions to hundred-dollar problems," Dmitri said.

"Attaching the antenna wire to the flag means that the antenna and electrical equipment are exposed to lightning only while the station is broadcasting," Dmitri said. "The flag is a reminder to lower the antenna."

"That will work because you mother-in-law only plans to broadcast two hours a day. If the weather looks iffy, she won't broadcast," Dmitri said.

"She is not my mother-in-law" Milo said, somewhat sharply.

Dmitri smirked. "Yet."

Like all happily married men, Dmitri recognized a "done-deal" when he saw one. Milo was clearly the last to recognize the situation. It would probably be a while before he wrapped his mind around the idea of marrying. Then a year after getting married he would wonder why he dragged his feet.

"OK, so you lower the antenna to protect it from lightning. But you cannot do that with the AM antenna," Milo said, pointing at the eight-hundred-fifty foot by eight-hundred-fifty-foot antenna sixteen feet above the ground.

Dmitri had insisted that they make the antenna slightly smaller than full-wave dimensions. He said it is easier to increase the antenna's apparent length by adding clip-on ferrite beads at odd-quarter intervals...the current anti-nodes ... than to pull posts and decrease the dimensions. Heck, he could even wrap paper clips around the aluminum antenna wire if he needed that degree of exactitude.

"Yes, the AM antenna," Dmitri said. "That has a three-pole electrical disconnect. One pole is for the antenna. One of the other poles powers the transmitter and amplifier. The third pole powers the "Transmitting Now" sign. Dump the disconnect and the antenna is not connected to the amplifier."

"What is with the fluorescent light tubes?" Milo asked. This electrical stuff was voodoo and witchcraft to a guy who was used to working with stuff he could touch and visualize.

"That is a bit of Russian engineering," Dmitri said. "You remember I just told you that conductors screw up antenna performance?"

Milo nodded his head "Yes."

"Fluorescent tubes are non-conductive until you put 600V across them," Dmitri said. "That fluorescent tube is a non-conductive switch that opens itself when the lightning hits. That prevents the voltage from getting high enough to jump the disconnect in the studio."

"How do you know so much about this stuff?" Milo asked.

"I have a Master's degree in Electrical Engineering from University of Bucharest," Dmitri said.

"So why are you an electrician's helper in Michigan?" Milo pried.

"Because I have a better life in the United States as a common laborer than I would have had in Romania as an Engineer," Dmitri said. "That, and because companies in the United States won't hire an engineer if they graduated from a university that doesn't have a football team."

"You are bullshitting me!" Milo said in disbelief.

"God's own truth," Dmitri said. "They never heard of University of Bucharest; they won't hire me. Now if they had a football team.." he tailed off with a slight pout.

"Their loss is our gain," Milo said as he watched Dmitri attach the heavy rope to the end of the 1/8" nylon rope. The heavy rope would not cut hands when the antenna and flag were raised and lowered in heavy wind.

CHAPTER TEN

Fish or Cut Bait

"So why do you think Nyssa and I will end up married?" Milo asked Dmitri, getting back to Dmitri's comment about Kate being his "mother-in-law".

"Young men are all the same. You cannot see what is in front of your face," Dmitri said. "I was the same way."

"Meaning?" Milo encouraged him.

"How many girls have you taken on dates in your life? Ten? Twenty? Fifty? A hundred?" Dmitri asked. From his tone, Milo knew that it was a rhetorical question.

"How many did you look at and think, 'She might be a nice girl or a fun girl?' but you never got around to asking out. Twice as many? Five times as many?" Dmitri continued.

"Why aren't you with any of those girls now?" Dmitri asked. That was NOT a rhetorical question.

"'Cause none of them worked out," Milo said.

"How long did it take you to figure out they weren't going to 'work out'?" Dmitri asked.

"I dunno. Most of them a couple of weeks. A few took longer," Milo said.

"And you kept dating them?" Dmitri asked.

Milo was a little uncomfortable. "Some of them," he answered.

"Why?" Dmitri asked.

Milo raised one eyebrow rakishly, "Some of them were a lot of fun."

Dmitri laughed. "Fun but crazy, no?"

"Some of them it was just a matter of convenience. I was down in Florida and it was just easier to stay with the one I was with than to go looking for better. Heck, it wasn't like I was going to be there that long," Milo said.

Dmitri asked, "How long have you been with Nyssa?"

Milo counted off the months on his fingers "March, April...September. About seven months."

"Is she crazy? Is she just a convenience to you?" Dmitri asked.

Milo had the good grace to be a bit uncomfortable. "She is fun but she is definitely not crazy. The convenience thing..." Milo's voice trailed away and he couldn't look Dmitri in the eye. "I don't know. How can I be sure? I mean, things are so strange now with Ebola and all."

Dmitri nodded his head sagely. "There is one way to be sure," he said.

"Tell her you have to get your head straight and that you cannot see her for three days. Spend that three days thinking about how your life will be if you never see Nyssa again," Dmitri said. "I guarantee that she will not like it. But you need to man-up."

"Then, seriously, take the three days and do nothing but think about your future life without Nyssa. You might feel relief. You might find you don't care," Dmitri said with a shrug. "Then you will know."

"And this will work?" Milo asked.

"It worked for me. I was getting ready to leave Romania and I wasn't married to Allaina. Her dad told me to do exactly what I told you. I took a camping trip in the Carpathians," Dmitri said.

"I love the mountains and have always found peace there but thinking about life without Allaina made me very restless," Dmitri said. "I toughed it out for two days but I knew that I could not let Allaina get away. A life without Allaina would be very cold and very bleak."

Di won the pool when Milo came back after a day-and-half and proposed to Nyssa. Nobody was surprised when she accepted.

Marriage Prep

Milo formally asked Rick for permission to marry Nyssa.

"You know I was only her father by adoption for five years before she became an adult," Rick said.

"Nyssa says you are her dad. That is all I need to know," Milo said. "May I have your permission to marry your daughter?"

"On one condition, that you and Nyssa talk to Father Theophilus first," Rick said.

It was not difficult to schedule an appointment as Nyssa's and Milo's schedules were flexible. They met in Father Theo's office, a room with many windows, books and natural shades of leather and wood.

Father Theo listened to their plans to get married. And then he spoke.

"The Bishop requires that couples who plan to marry go through a pre-marriage class," Father Theo said. "We start the class by administering a test that will be the basis, a roadmap if you will, for the content of the class."

He held up his hand to forestall the objections that he knew were going to come.

"It is not a pass-fail kind of class. It is not something that will stop your wedding," Father Theo said. "It is just that the Church has figured out that families are more successful if they have a chance to talk about certain kinds of issues before they are in the trenches, so to speak."

"What kinds of 'issues'?" Milo asked.

"Basically, ones where outcomes are likely to be framed as winners and losers," Father Theo said. "One example is 'Where will you spend your holidays?"

"In your case, you will not be able to celebrate Christmas Day as a family in both Michigan and Connecticut," Father Theo said. "That is one of the easier ones because most couples alternate holidays. They might go to one family on Thanksgiving and then spend Christmas with the other. Or they might alternate years. Some issues are much harder," Father Theo said.

"Like what?" Nyssa asked, respectfully.

"I had one couple who hadn't ever talked about children," Father Theo said. "They took the test, which is only intended to point out areas that might merit from discussion, and the woman was very firm that she wanted at least one child while the man did not want any."

"She asked him, 'What happens if I get pregnant? Accidents happen.'" Father Theo said.

"He told her, 'You will get an abortion. Problem solved.' "

"And if I don't?" the woman asked.

"Then I will divorce you," the man said. "It's as simple as that."

“What happened?” Nyssa asked, aghast.

“The woman decided to not marry the man,” Father Theo said.

“Did she ever meet somebody else and marry him? How did it turn out?” Nyssa asked.

“I don’t know if she ever met anybody else. She moved away,” Father Theo said.

“The point of my telling you this is that too often, couples will know at some level there is a ‘deal breaker’ hiding in the weeds and they very carefully don’t talk about it,” Father Theo said.

“So, she just walked away?” Milo asked.

“Not quite,” Father Theo said. “They talked about it a long time. I heard later that she agreed to use contraception... which is not something I was very wild about, but it was their preparation. And she asked again about ‘accidents.' He was adamant. No exceptions. She had to get an abortion, which she found unconscionable.”

“Then she asked, ‘What if my sister dies. She has two kids. We would take them in? Right?”

He said “Nope. There are lots of families that want to adopt healthy, white kids.”

He said “It would have too big of an impact on my lifestyle. That is why I don’t have pets or house plants. I can pick up and go anywhere, any time.”

Nyssa said “Bastard!”

Father Theo pretended to not hear even though he was one-hundred percent in agreement with her assessment.

“That is a horrible story,” Milo said. “Why would anybody

ever want to take that test?"

Nyssa looked over at Milo, "At least she was young enough to start over. She didn't find herself forty years old and chained to a self-centered child."

"That is part of the discernment process," Father Theo said. "It is not about ME. It is about you two, learning how to bravely confront differences and work through them in good faith."

"Before you give us the quiz, Father, one of my friends said this process takes six months. Is that true?" Nyssa asked.

Father Theo looked pensive. "I have had several long discussions with your father about the tumultuous situation the world finds itself in. As you know, I am at risk of contracting Ebola because my mission is to serve the sick and needy.

"The Bishop requires a six-month discernment process. But he also realizes that situations differ. God gave us brains and the Bishop expects us to use them," Father Theo said.

"So, I propose that we meet three times a week for two weeks. I will give you homework assignments and you bring them back the next time we meet. After six meetings we will talk about what we should do next. Can you work with me on that?" Father Theo asked.

That sounded reasonable to Nyssa.

Mr. Ed's Coffee Hour

"Welcome to Mr. Ed's Coffee Hour," Ed Hall said into the microphone with a jovial voice brimming with bonhomie. "Transmitting on FM 104.3 at eight in the morning and 1087AM a half hour before sunset with a tenth of a Watt power. Mr. Ed's Coffee Hour where you will hear the news straight from the horse's mouth. We might make stuff up but it is only for entertainment."

The statement about the transmission power was a flat out lie. Dmitri had the transmission set to one-point-two Watts. He had sent out short "Up periscope" transmissions to determine the power required to reach the farthest corner of the neighborhood, some two miles distant. Dmitri and Milo synchronized watches and then Milo took a cheap, portable radio to the northwest corner of the neighborhood and tuned in as Dmitri stepped up the power one tenth of a Watt every minute.

Ed Hall took a sip of tea.

"First a word from our sponsors. I am transmitting from Kate's Store where the men are men and the women and children can shoot the whiskers off a horsefly at a hundred yards," Ed said.

In fact, Kate had a "Trophy wall" of targets shot by the neighborhood kids. They were labeled with the kid's name and age, date shot and the position they were fired from. Kate took liberties with the distance. She regularly posted twenty-five-yard targets on the fifty-yard wall and fifty-yard targets on the hundred-yard wall.

She even had a kiddy corner. You might be a little bit dismissive of Nash's handwriting until you noticed he was six years old. His dad cocked the pellet gun but the target really was Nash's shooting. Nash shot at seven paces but Kate posted them on the 25-yard wall ... 5-1/2" across the base and five inches tall.

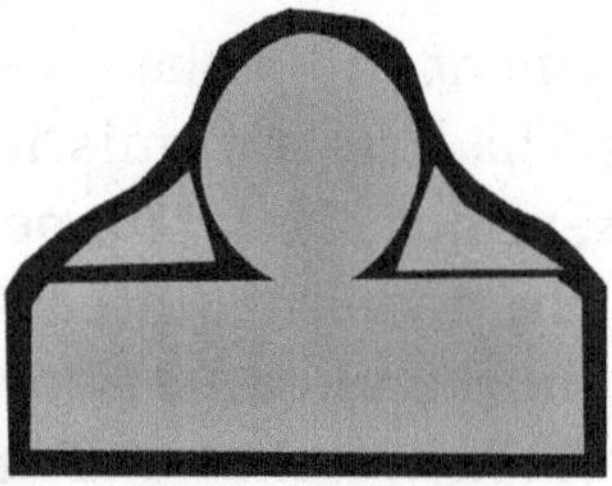

Scaled: 50 meters = 200 actual

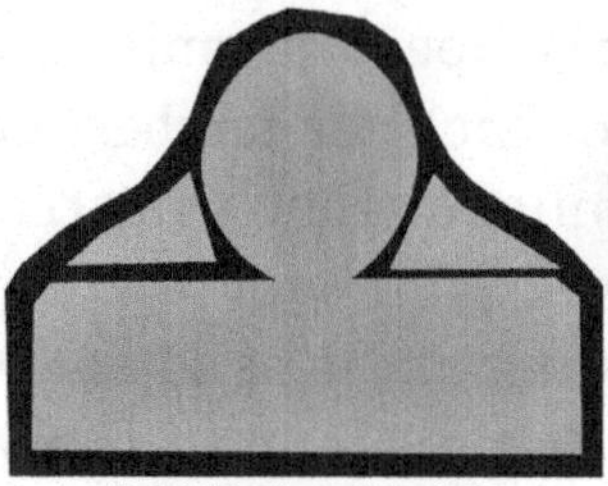

Scaled: 25 meters = 100 actual

Just so folks would get the point, the standard target was a quarter-scale "Target D" simulating a prone shooter as the target. Kate was able to print off two targets on every eight-by-eleven sheet of copy paper. Aim small, miss small.

A little bit of creative misinformation can be a useful tool.

"The Shaw family home-schools and Mrs Shaw is willing to share her educational materials with those parents who decide to keep their kids home from school," Ed said. That would be virtually all of the kids in the neighborhood. "Mrs Shaw asks that the kids put in two hours a week of service time helping senior citizens as repayment."

"In other news, Johnny C. Johnson owner of Stash-ur-Trash on the east end of Eaton Rapids opened up a storage cube yesterday. After auctioning off the contents by-the-piece he still had five mountain bikes and a supply of children's winter clothing left. Johnny plans to open a cube every two weeks for non-payment," Ed said. "You might wanna get ahold of Johnny if you need kid clothes or bikes."

"I know it is early but it is not too early to start thinking about gardening. Peas go in as soon as you can work the ground. Tomato and pepper plants are started inside at the end of March. 'Taters on May first, corn in the middle of May and beans at the end of May, squash and cukes first weekend of June. Lots of folks plant pole beans and cukes under the peas so-as to reuse the trellis," Ed said. "Kate has a supply of seeds but you might want to ask your neighbors if they have something to share."

"On the subject of seeds, Kate would appreciate it if you deer hunters would look through the seeds you have left from last year's food plots. She wants to buy sugar beet seeds and will happily buy any you can spare.

"Ebola is spread by touching body fluids and maybe by coughing and sneezing. Cleanliness is next to Godliness. Wash those hand and cover your mouth," Ed continued. "Doctors say that Ebola spreads at a rate of 1/R-squared where R is the distance we are from other people. That is, doubling the distance will reduce the rate of spread to a quarter its current speed."

"And to help you remember, Ima gonna play a song..." Ed said.

"For those who are interested, today's tipple is strawberry leaf and rose-hip tea. And it is TASTEE," Ed said as he took another slurp of tea.

"Oh, I almost forgot, Sabbath services: Pastor James will deliver a live service Saturday evening at the usual AM broadcast time. Father Theophilus of Charlotte will deliver a recorded service at 8:00 AM Sunday and Pastor Mark will deliver a recorded service at 11:00 AM Sunday," Ed said.

"For those who like to read ahead, Pastor James intends to preach on 1-Peter, Chapter Five. Father Theo will preach on the Big Ten, Deuteronomy Chapter Five and Pastor Mark is on the hook for Matthew Chapter 25.

"I've been hearing about problems with feral dogs. I know it sounds cruel but if they are bothering your chickens or scaring your kids you need to shoot them. Better that than to let them become your neighbor's problem or having them come back and bite your kid," Ed said.

And so, Ed would chatter for the next hour. About half way through he brought in a guest and they talked about events that were of interest to the local population.

"Today we have Kelly Carney of Milo-n-Kelly Cartage," Ed said. "Kelly, you were telling me that you are getting inquiries from folks asking if they can purchase gasifiers. What can you tell me about that?" Ed asked.

"Well, for now we are contracting out cartage. These gasifiers are fussy beasts and a real bear to keep running. We gotta a couple of kids who have a gift for getting the most out of them," Kelly said.

In fact, that was one hundred percent true. Most people struggled to keep them running. An old pilot from 'Nam said it was like flying an old helicopter where you had to increase the throttle while judiciously increasing the pitch of the rotor blades. The throttle moves slightly in advance of the changes in pitch and everything balanced on-the-fly by ear. Most folks can't do it and a rare few are naturals. Milo and Kelly sorted through the neighborhood and found a few drivers who had the knack.

The other thing was that Milo and Kelly had a lot of man-hours invested in perfecting their gasifier. They had perfected a system that could run on either corn or scrap wood. The last thing they wanted was to have a shade-tree mechanic reverse engineer the device. That would be giving away their investment.

"We have a tractor that pulls a hay-wagon or a two-bottom, fourteen-inch plow. We also have a couple of pick-up trucks we converted for pulling trailers," Kelly said.

"You were telling me something interesting about how to get the most out of hiring MNK Cartage," Ed said. "Do you mind repeating that for our audience?"

"Sure, no problem," Kelly said. "The way you get the most out of us is to use three trailers. Let's say you want to haul firewood. You have one trailer a work-crew is loading into. You have full trailer that the other end is unloading. And you have one trailer that the truck or tractor is hooked up to and is dragging from one place to the other."

"That way, the truck never stops working. It drops off the empty trailer and hooks up to the loaded one. Then, on the other end it drops off the full trailer and hooks up to the empty one to take back to the woods," Kelly said.

"Sounds like you better have a lot of workers lined up," Ed observed.

"Yup!" Kelly said. "What we have seen is that you better have at least two people at the load site and one at the unload."

"It is a lot faster to drag or roll wood off a trailer than it is to pry it off the ground and carry it to the trailer," Kelly said by way of explanation.

Ed cheerfully filled the hour with cornball jokes, bits of wisdom and an inexhaustible supply of good humor.

More Intervention

The carnage on Wall Street accelerated.

Market players who had bought on margin were forced to liquidate their holdings when their portfolio of stocks dropped below the value of the funds they had borrowed.

They were forced to put them on the market regardless of the losses it would lock in.

Seeing the tsunami of equities hitting the market, buyers evaporated. Puts were cancelled. Options not exercised.

"Market prices" proved as illusory as the cloud bank that Wile E. Coyote habitually ran onto.

Selling collateral at far less than the amount of the loan vaporized the credit market. The fractional banking system means that each dollar in circulation creates ten or twenty dollars' worth of economic activity. The problem on the back end was that every dollar that was vaporized was like one mountain climber falling off a cliff. Every climber who was roped to him was also doomed.

The complicated financial mechanisms that seemed to cleverly create money and stability out of thin air proved to have lethal side-effects on the downside.

Circuit-breakers, i.e. halts in trading, exacerbated the problem as it gave potential buyers more time to get out from beneath the falling piano.

Attempts by the government to jump-start the market with huge injections of liquidity resulted in buyers pumping that money into European and Asian stock markets.

In terms of the over-all US economy, the agricultural sector was so tiny in dollar amounts that it did not register even as an afterthought.

Prices for commodities like wheat and corn and beans dropped below the cost of harvesting them. Corn sat in the fields. Farmers took a pass on planting winter wheat. Farmers and speculators chose to not sell their grain rather than lock in their losses. They were sure the insanity could not go on much longer and the US would start exporting again.

Beef farmers had a different issue. Prices for beef were at historical highs due to the extremely generous SNAP benefits. Talking with their neighbors who were not planting their fields the beef producers anticipated grain prices were going to go through the roof next year. The rational decision was to sell, sell, sell. They sold fat calves. They sold thin calves. They kept only the youngest brood cows that had proven their fertility. The remaining 80% of their herds were sent to slaughter to take advantage of the historically high prices.

The major food conglomerates found themselves in a pickle. The prices for their most basic raw materials were at historic lows...and they were running into shortages. Consequently, they did not have chips and TV dinners and buns to ship to customers. Shelves started to empty. Fast food restaurants had plenty of burger patties but no buns to put them on.

The government panicked. They notified farmers and grain elevators that they were taking physical possession of the grain even as the farmers retained the electronic title to the grain. When the elevators objected the government pointed to the fine-print on the loan guarantees. Every farmer who stored grain in the elevators owed money to the government and the government had the authority to move the grain.

There are not enough trucks and train cars to move the grain all at once. The grain was moved by bulk trucks and taken to hastily leased space. It was bagged in 100-pound bags and stack two high on pallets. The pallets were then moved into the storage rooms. When the room was full, they closed and locked the door and moved to the next room.

The calmer heads in the room agreed with the plan because unprocessed grain is more compact and easier to handle than finished goods. They foresaw issues with transportation and it made sense to move the grain close to where it would be needed even if there were no facilities for processing it. After all, how hard can it be to process grain? Primitive people who did not even know how to log onto computers could do it.

The majority of the grain was stored in population centers

closest to the final, end-users. Faithful donors to both political parties had refurbed vast expanses of industrial buildings in anticipation of young people gentrifying those neighborhoods. Collectively, they spent billions of dollars bringing them into compliance with Americans with Disabilities Act and local zoning requirements. The mobs of affluent young people never materialized and the buildings sat empty, the payments draining the owner's pockets. The government contracts to store grain were a God send.

Back in Michigan, the local elevator called Milo. "You might want to come and take physical possession of your grain or it will be gone," the clerk in the office said. She had referred more than one local farmer to Milo and had always received rave reviews of his work. Milo made her look like a rock-star.

"Why?" Milo said.

"The Federal Government is sequestering all grain that farmers own. Basically, they are brooming out the elevators. If they take too much, they will sort it out afterward. Maybe. You don't have any Federal ag loans but that might not make any difference in the long run...unless you pick up your grain NOW," the clerk said. "I recommend you hustle so you can get yours before then next bunch of trucks come."

Milo called Farmer Don who loaned him two, 650-bushel gravity wagons. Milo dragged one of them with his MF 165 while Kelly pulled one with his tractor. They made two trips, filling them with wheat at the elevator and then pulling them home to unload into a 40' CONEX that Rick kept for storage.

Across America thousands and thousands of storage sites in urban areas were packed with grain, all of them less than fifty feet from a sewer connection.

What could go wrong? Rat populations are primarily constrained by food availability. Given unlimited food and shelter, the rat population can double in less than a month and increase by a factor of 10,000 over the course of a year.

Ghosts from the Past

Nyssa and Milo went to their second session with Father Theo a couple of days after taking the assessment.

The biggest difference in expectations revolved around careers. In Milo's family a man's worth was measured by the size of the pay-check he put on the dining room table on Friday night. If a man could get a higher pay rate or more hours of work in a different state, they left. Sometimes they sent the pay back home. Other times the family was uprooted and the entire family moved.

Nyssa's expectations were far more conflicted. If you knew her casually you would judge her as imperturbable as a mountain. The discussion regarding deepest values ripped the scar-tissue off and revealed a seething caldera of volcanic anger and insecurities.

Growing up Nyssa had never lived in any one place for more than three months. Her mother invariably did not pay rent or stole from room-mates and they found themselves tossed back out on the streets.

Later, Nyssa's mother took her children to "parties" at hotels and casinos where she turned tricks to pay for her drug habit.

The middle-school years were the worst. Her mother's lifestyle resulted in her looking forty years older than her calendar age. That limited her cash flow. While other girls had slumber parties and went to tournaments in nearby states with their soccer and basketball teams, Nyssa's mother "sweetened the deal" by offering threesomes featuring her older daughters. Yes, even Nyssa.

Nyssa was isolated at school as the other children sensed her strangeness. Nyssa had a feral wariness that kept her from telling them what some of their fathers did on weekends. Even so, it was a very, very hard time for Nyssa.

Her mother died of a stroke in a ratty hotel room in Jackson, Michigan shortly after doing a couple of lines of exceptionally pure "blow." Nyssa was 12. Nyssa thought she had died and gone to heaven when she ended up at Kate and Rick's house. It was like living in that old TV show, Lassie.

Milo had no idea.

After working through the worst of the pain, Milo committed to not chasing jobs. He said he might have to spend a night or two away from home on a big repair job, but he would call or send a text as he wrapped up for the night so she would know he was "OK" and thinking of her.

Milo had never considered that there might be people who did not judge by the size of a paycheck. Milo was, by nature, a creature of habits and considerate. He could work with Nyssa's need for lots of reassurance and gentle touching.

Wedding Bells

Deacon Duncan and his wife Joan were assisting Father Theo in Milo and Nyssa's marriage preparation.

Milo, Duncan and Father Theo were having a meeting. Milo and Duncan had hit it off immediately. After Duncan had spoken a just a few sentences Milo asked, "Military?"

Duncan said, "Air Force. 1968-through-1993. How did you guess?"

Deacon Duncan was a very precise man. His shoes were meticulously shined. His pants were sharply creased. But there are many precise men.

"It was your accent," Milo said. "It is sort of a generic, intermountain West non-accent."

Father Theo looked at Milo quizzically.

Milo said, "Longtime military men speak slowly so even second Lieutenants can understand them. That, and they pick up a blend of American accents that sounds like the intermountain West accent."

Father Theo suggested that Milo tell Deacon Duncan what he was comfortable sharing about Nyssa's past. Father Theo said it was not his to share.

Duncan told Milo that he had a Master's degree in counseling. He had picked it up after the military because he saw the need for counselors who had first-hand experience with Post Traumatic Stress Disorder. Duncan assured Milo that everything he heard was covered by Professional Ethics.

Milo told him everything.

"I am not going to candy-coat this" Duncan said. "Nyssa trusts you and she will follow you through the gates of hell. BUT, and it is a big but, her trust is fragile and you need to be very protective of her trust."

"You will have the best marriage imaginable if you can avoid two marriage-killing mistakes," Duncan said.

"She will always be watching you because she suffered abandonment. She will be watching to see if you are straying," Duncan said. "All women do that to some degree, but Nyssa will be hyper-vigilant."

Milo objected. "I have no intention of two-timing on Nyssa."

"You don't understand," Duncan said. "You cannot give off even have the tiniest whiff of straying."

"You must treat every woman under the age of seventy with the utmost of courtesy and formality, just this side of being cold," Duncan said. "The best thing is to let other women be

Nyssa's friend first and then you are civil with them because of that."

Milo wasn't sure he was willing to write off half of humanity.

"What was the other fatal error?" Milo said.

"She might start testing you," Duncan said.

"Testing?" Milo said.

"Testing. She might start posing hypothetical questions" Duncan said. "She might even troll you through her girlfriends to see if you look at them."

"How would you have me handle that?" Milo asked.

"Tell her to stop testing you," Father Theo said. "That is what Jesus told the devil."

Duncan nodded in agreement. "Tell her that, as a couple, you need to live in the moment. 'Sufficient unto the day is the evil thereof'. You need to tell her that if she keeps testing it is inevitable that you will eventually give her an answer that is not exactly what she is looking for. She will see that as evidence of disloyalty and she will test you even more and she will get more 'wrong' answers."

"That is a path to failure," Duncan said.

"The way to not end up in that trap is to never start down that road," Duncan said.

"Sounds like you are trying to talk me out of marrying Nyssa," Milo said.

"No. Not that at all," Duncan said. "A Marine who wants a successful mission needs a map of the mine-fields."

"You make Nyssa sound like a psycho-chick," Milo said.

Duncan thought for a minute, then he said, "What if somebody offered you a machine where you could put a one-hundred dollar bill into it and it spat out ten crisp, new one-hundred dollar bills. A man would be a fool if he complained that it only took hundred-dollar bills and wanted to trade it in for a machine that could only take one-dollar bills," Duncan said.

"Nyssa only takes one-hundred-dollar bills and she thinks you are man enough to give her that...and I don't mean paychecks. The question is, do YOU think you are man enough?"

***

The wedding was a low-key affair.

Dmitri suggested that it was no longer safe to travel by air since airports are nearly always attached to major metropolitan areas. It was more than cars being vandalized in parking lots; it involved the breakdown of basic infrastructure. Mechanics no longer showed up for their jobs. Fuel availability was spotty. And crowded airports were hotbeds of disease transmission.

Travel by Interstate was also problematic.

Consequently, Milo's elderly mother and father regretfully declined the invitation to attend. They asked that video be posted.

The bride wore an emerald green, A-line, long sleeve midi dress with thick, medium-sized 10k gold, hoop earrings and golden gladiator sandals.

Hanna, the first friend that Nyssa made in Eaton Rapids was the Maid-of-Honor.

The groom wore his best, and only suit. It was a charcoal gray pinstripe in a mid-weight wool-blend.

Dmitri was Best Man.

The newly married couple spent their honeymoon on the

north side of Fremont Lake where Kelly and Di's family had a cabin.

The mid-October walleye fishing was spectacular. Milo and Nyssa motored slowly across the lake before the sun rose. They located the fish with sonar and let the scant, pre-morning breeze slowly drift the boat through the feeding fish. It rarely took long to catch the two fish they would eat that day.

They then motored home after stashing the fish in the live-well. Then they cleaned the fish and put the fillets in the fridge. Afterward they showered together to get the fishy smell from their hands.

Then a nap. Afterward they strolled into town for breakfast at one of the cafes.

Then sight-seeing, lunch, another nap, more sight-seeing.

They visited several orchards and asked the manager if they could pick some of the gourmet varieties that were too tender to ship or too "niche" to be considered commercial.

Most orchards had a row or two of personal favorites that were kept around for sentimental reasons rather than commercial demand. Sweet Sixteen, Keepsake, SpiGold, Spartan, Golden Russet, Mutsu, Melrose and Opalescent were favorites. Dinner was big slabs of fried fish, oven fried potatoes and vegetables, and apple slices.

The evening was a romantic movie and then they turned in for bed.

The last day was spent cleaning. All of the bedding was washed and dried. The bed was remade, floors scrubbed and every speck of dirt cleaned up.

They locked the doors of the cabin when they left, not knowing that they had just left "normal" in the past.

CHAPTER ELEVEN

Feeder Bands

Kate was walking out to the store to open it. It was a Wednesday in early November and she opened the store early in the morning for the convenience of those people who were early risers.

The sun was filling the eastern sky with vivid pinks and salmon colors as it started to peek over the horizon.

As she neared the building, she heard an unexpected rattling sound on the far side where goods were stored outside. Items that were not damaged by the weather were stored in a stall attached to the store. The stall was surrounded by a security fence that used to be a privacy fence around a hot tub. The fence was made of one-by-fours nailed to horizontal, two-by-four stringers. The one-bys alternated sides to allow the free flow of air so water splashed on the deck would dry quickly.

Kate had bags of nuts drying under the eaves and she assumed that squirrels were getting into them. She rounded the corner to scare them away. She had her hand on the latch of the gate when a large man rushed from behind the trunk of a nearby tree. The man's hand engulfed the back of her neck and he banged her face against the gate and he pushed her on through the gate and out of sight.

Her eyes filled with tears.

She was so surprised that she only had time to gasp.

He rushed her across small storage area and crushed her into the far corner. Then he spun her around and crushed her windpipe with his left hand as he repinned her into the corner.

Kate fought back but she had always been fine-boned. The man effortlessly fended off her attempts to repel him. Kate knew that she did not have long because she was not able to draw a breath. Kate later deduced that the man had done this many times before because he anticipated everything she tried.

The door to the stall swung open and Ms Sheridan popped her head in. She was wearing her purple house-dress. Taking in the scene Ms Sheridan said, "Oh. Excuse me. I didn't know you were with a boyfriend. I'll come back later," and then pulled her head back out, shutting the door behind her.

Kate wanted to cry. How could Ms Sheridan be so dense?

Quicker than she could have ever imagined, Kate's vision was dulled by a red mist and she heard a roaring in her ears.

And then the pressure on her throat was released as the man fell away from her.

Looking to her left, she saw the barrel of a small revolver poking through one of the gaps in the fence. The muzzle of the barrel was covered with two incongruous and precisely cut lengths of blue masking tape to keep dirt out of it. One length was across the end of the muzzle and the other length of tape circled the barrel behind the front sight, securing the ends of the other piece.

Then she saw the barrel of the revolver lowered. Time seemed to move in slow motion. She saw the cylinder index and then heard a second roar, and then a third. The barrel of the gun withdrew.

The last two shots were not needed. The first shot had punched the man immediately behind his ear and angled up through his brain. The .22 Magnum had turned his brain to mush and blew a substantial amount of blood and brains out the far side.

Then the gate reopened. A purple clad arm reached in and beckoned her. She saw the backside of a hideously purple house dress. Kate had never been so happy in her life.

Ms Sheridan had her back to the fence and her revolver at low ready. Kate could see that the hammer was cocked and Ms. Sheridan's finger was poised above the trigger guard. It would have been comical under other circumstances but Ms. Sheridan was EXACTLY following Sgt Smith's instructions.

Scan near: Eight o'clock, ten o'clock, twelve o'clock, two o'clock, four o'clock. Don't over focus.

Scan medium: Four o'clock, two o'clock....

Scan near. The one that will get you is the one who is near. Eight o'clock....

Scan far: Four o'clock....

Kate's ears were ringing. She could see Ms Sheridan's lips moving and could not know that Ms Sheridan was mumbling Sgt Smith's mantra.

Ms Sheridan grabbed Kate's arm and dragged her to the front of the store. There, she deposited Kate on the bench.

"We don't know if the store is safe," Ms Sheridan yelled. Ms Sheridan's ears had also been dinged by the .22 Magnum and the revolver's four-inch barrel.

Ms Sheridan would have reloaded but the single action revolver was a pain to reload. Besides, after loading the gun the first time and placing it her purse she had put the bullets away and had no clue where they were. At that instant, she saw the utility of those evil "clips" for reloading defensive handguns as she only had two more shots if things got sporty.

Unfortunately for Kate and Ms Sheridan, the sound of gun shots was a common occurrence and nobody came looking.

About ten minutes later a customer came ambling up to the store.

"Get Rick!" Ms Sheridan commanded in a voice that brooked no argument.

The customer pivoted in mid-stride and trotted up the drive toward the house.

Rick came down the drive a half minute later.

"Please check the store to ensure there are no people in there," Ms Sheridan directed Rick.

Rick's eyes grew wide as he processed the sight of the revolver in Ms Sheridan's hands, Kate's white face and the red marks around her throat.

Rick unholstered the Glock 19 he ALWAYS carried when he was outside and went into the store.

The store was empty.

Ms Sheridan opened the store for the day. Kate went back to the house with Rick. When customers asked "Where is Kate?" Ms Sheridan truthfully informed them that Kate had a sore throat.

Bury Him Before He Starts to Smell

Rick called a friend of his at the sheriff's office. They were running short-handed and were not able to send anybody out.

Rick asked, "What do you want me to do with the evidence?"

"First of all, have you ever seen this guy before?" the deputy asked.

"Nope," Rick said. The man's face was distorted by the shots Ms Sheridan had fired into the man's head but Rick was at least 99% sure he had never seen the man before.

"I want you to get two witnesses. Then I want you to find his ID. Snap a picture of it and send it to me," the deputy said.

Rick was able to collar Ms Sheridan and a customer, who he swore to secrecy. He checked the man's pockets and found a wallet. Rick took pictures of both sides of the driver's license with his smart phone and sent them to his friend.

It took fifteen seconds for the computer to spit out what it knew.

"Hmmm," the deputy said. "Your friend was lucky."

"How so?" Rick asked.

"He has three convictions for fourth degree Criminal Sexual Conduct," the deputy said.

"What does that mean?" Rick said.

"Fourth Degree Criminal Sexual Conduct is a misdemeanor in Michigan. What it really means is that he has a damned good lawyer," the deputy said. "It means he probably raped at least three women and his lawyer plea-bargained the charges down to misdemeanors."

Looking through the history the deputy said, "OK, I remember this piece-of-shit. We popped him by the Lansing Mall. He was stalking a high school girl and she had the situational awareness to notice him."

“Seems like your dead buddy liked to assault famous people. The high school girl was the star of the basketball team that made a run at the State finals. He also assaulted the weather girl from Channel 14 and a few other minor celebrities,” the deputy said.

“Like I said, your friend was lucky. As bad guys go, he wasn’t so bad. He didn’t kill his victims, for instance,” the deputy said. “Most criminals run in packs, or at least teams of two. She would have been toast if it hadn’t been a lone-wolf, sexual predator trying to get his jollies.”

“You have given me a bunch to think about, but it still doesn’t answer the question, ‘What do you want me to do with the body?’”

Rick’s friend in the sheriff’s department said “Nobody is going to miss this creep. I’d be obliged if you buried him. He will start to smell if you don’t.”

Even though the customer had been sworn to secrecy he figured it would not hurt to tell his closest friend...

Sisterhood Welded in Fire

The relationship between Kate and Ms Sheridan underwent a tectonic shift.

Kate was surprised to learn that everything Kate did put Ms Sheridan on high alert. That is, Kate grated on Ms Sheridan every bit as much as Ms. Sheridan annoyed Kate.

“How can that be?” Kate asked.

“I grew up in Providence, Rhode Island,” Ms Sheridan said. “And it wasn’t the tony side of town, either.”

"What you don't know about Providence is that a girl has to defend her bubble,” Ms Sheridan said. "Thugs test you by crowding your space. You are volunteering to be a victim if you don't loudly and vigorously defend your space."

“There is an old joke. Do you know how you can tell you are about to get screwed?” Ms Sheridan said. “You hear the words ‘Trust me.’”

Kate shrugged her shoulders and rotated her hands outward in the universal “No clue” gesture.

“Everything about you screams ‘Trust Me’,” Ms Sheridan said. “You are a walking caricature of the shill saying ‘Trust me.’”

“You had to be phony. That was the only thing that made sense,” Ms Sheridan said. “And if you were a phony then you must think I was pretty stupid to fall for something so obvious. And there is one thing I cannot abide,” Ms Sheridan said. “That is people who look down on me or think I am stupid.”

"Every time you said something kind or smiled, I clenched inside,” Ms Sheridan said. "I kept waiting for the other shoe to fall."

“It has taken me a long time, too long, to realize that you are the real deal.”

The change in attitude toward Ms Sheridan in the larger community were more subtle.

The conservatives who had kept her at arm’s length re-evaluated. She had been tested in fire and had acquitted herself with honor and distinction. She was no longer “other” in their eyes. Stacy Sheridan had proven that when it mattered, she was a force to be reckoned with.

The reactions among the more liberal elements of the neighborhood were more nuanced.

The most liberal, many of them women, found themselves deeply conflicted. They identified with Stacy Sheridan and were deeply suspicious of traditional, cis-male, norms in general and violence in particular.

They struggled to reconcile that Stacy Sheridan, intellectually brilliant and stridently verbal woman that she was, found herself in a situation where she needed to shoot somebody. Not just shoot him but kill him deader than King Tut.

The most liberal elements thought Rick and Kate were curiosities. For one thing, Kate was a social worker and a conservative. That is as common as a flying fish or a penguin. The other thing that put Rick and Kate on everybody's radar were the apple pies. Even liberals love apple pies and had posted many pictures on social media about this "quaint" new custom.

Although they loathed Rick and Kate's politics they found the couple to be very likable. For one thing the liberals who had lived in the neighborhood the longest time knew that the couple had fostered and adopted several needy kids. They didn't grok Rick and Kate's reasons for doing it but the act itself scored points with the liberals.

The biggest thing to come of the attack is that even the hardest core liberal started to have conversations that times might be changing. Stacy Sheridan was an uber-liberal. She weighed about eighty-five pounds dripping wet. And Stacy Sheridan had used a gun to save an innocent woman from a human predator. After the fact, the cops had been unable to send somebody even after a person had been killed so it seems likely that they would not have been able to intervene when the attack was happening.

The uber-liberals did not make a peep when some wag posted signs on the paved roads leading to the neighborhood.

Times were changing.

Come Home

Three days later, Rick sent out the email he hoped to never

have to send.

"It is time. Come home."

He sent it to Janelle who he assumed was on the west coast. He sent it to Rick in New England, Gabriella in Memphis. He also sent a courtesy copy to Luke.

It was time.

Crises come slowly. They gain traction and barriers are breached. Once they reached a critical mass they exploded upon the unwary.

Luke

Luke lived a scant twenty-five miles away. He could walk in if he had to. The others, not so much.

Janelle

Janelle was the first to arrive. Rick got a call at ten in the evening. Janelle sounded whipped.

"Dad, I am in Hudsonville. Can you pick me up?" she said.

"Where in Hudsonville?" Rick asked.

"I am west of town on M-121 at the old celery warehouse. I dropped off a load of apples from Spokane," Janelle said.

Rick had been hording gas but picking up family definitely rated raiding the emergency cache.

He picked her up three hours later. It took a little bit longer because Rick stuck to back-roads. He had been hearing stories about vehicles getting mobbed in cities and even on freeways.

It turned out that Janelle had a Class A CDL license. It was an honorable way to make money when other ways failed.

Janelle told Rick that she had bummed rides to Spokane where she knew a lot of trucks traveled east. She asked around until she found one headed toward Michigan and offered to drive halvsies for just the cost of food. The other trucker jumped at the chance.

Janelle called as soon as the truck hit the dock. She came with the clothes on her back and nothing more.

Rick asked many questions. Janelle said they had taken the northern route. Everything was fine until you hit Minnesota. The guys on the CB said to avoid Minneapolis, Madison, and Chicago.

They left I-94 at St Cloud and headed east, picking up Wisconsin 8 at the state line.

They took Wisconsin 8 to the Michigan line and then followed the north shore of Lake Michigan to the Mackinaw Bridge. Then they drove south to Hudsonville.

Gabby

Gabby said that things were still pretty calm in the mid-South. The school announced that it was going to suspend operations at the Christmas break in light of "issues" in New Orleans, Miami, and Houston.

Gabby said they had a trailer packed and would see them at Christmas...or sooner if it got sporty.

Rick reminded her to be sure to avoid large cities and to have multiple routes preprogrammed.

Mark

Mark was making money hand-over-fist selling vehicles.

Everybody wanted to buy a tricked-out SUV. They called them Bug-out vehicles or G-O-O-D (Get Out of Dodge) vehicles. Customers were fighting over stock on the showroom floor. They were bidding above list.

Then they were dropping thousands of dollars on custom, extended fuel tank options. The commission Mark got on options was almost obscene.

Mark emailed back that he was keeping an eye on things. He wasn't.

***

Janelle's re-integration into the family was rocky.

From the moment she walked in, Nyssa and Janelle were at each other's throats.

Janelle treated Nyssa like the kid she left at home seven years ago.

Nyssa thought of Janelle as an under-achieving loser and it showed.

Kate put her foot down. "Treat each other like adults. You treat total strangers with more courtesy than you treat each other," Kate said. "If you expect to stay in this house then you must treat each other in a civil manner."

For the next week Janelle and Nyssa's relationship was frosty. Sometimes one or the other would slip and earn a death-glare from Kate.

One point of friction was food. Kate put them into a rotation planning and preparing dinner. Nyssa was a meat-and-potatoes girl. Give her pasta and she was happy. Janelle's diet was more eclectic. The only reason Nyssa didn't attempt to strangle Janelle was because there were no sources of seaweed, tofu or durian in Eaton Rapids any more. But it was a near thing.

Another thing that Rick and Kate had to confront was the incredible, shrinking house. They had never had more than four kids in the house at a time, and now they were looking at the possibility of all six of them, plus spouses and kids. Rick had a strong preference for having the family packed like sardines. Kate did not know how that was going to be possible.

By Rick's calculations, the camper could hold Nyssa and Milo. Rick and Kate slept together in the master bedroom. Two bedrooms were earmarked for Gabby and her husband and the other for Mark and his family. That left Janelle and Luke fighting over the last bedroom. Somebody was going to have to sleep in the basement or out in Kate's store.

Kate was worried about competition for bathrooms. Rick did not have the heart to tell her that they were probably going to have to transition to an outhouse. While they could continue to use the toilets and manually flush them with buckets of water, the septic tank would not be able to handle corncobs or newsprint. That, and there would be nobody to pump out the septic tank when that day came.

The nice thing about outdoor toilets is that users seldom dallied.

CHAPTER TWELVE

Mr Ed's Coffee Hour Dec 15

"Welcome to Mr. Ed's Coffee Hour," Ed Hall said into the microphone. "Transmitting on FM 104.3 at eight in the morning and 1086AM a half hour before sunset with a tenth of a Watt power. Mr. Ed's Coffee Hour where you will hear the news straight from the horse's mouth. If we make it up it is only to entertain you."

Ed took a sip of tea to sooth his throat.

"Today's tipple is a big tablespoon of blackberry jam in a cup of hot water. You might be able to tell that I have a sore throat and this is a soothing drink," Ed said.

"First a word from our sponsors. I am transmitting from Kate's Store where the men are men and the women and children can shoot the wings off a blow-fly at a hundred yards," Ed said.

"Folks with chickens are having problems with eggs breaking. The grain elevator closed and now they cannot get special chicken feed or oyster shell grit. Kate is looking for somebody who can supply high calcium, crushed limestone to supplement chicken feed. If anybody has a source, get ahold of Kate."

"Things are happening all over," Ed said.

"I am proud to announce that this show is brought to you by

solar power. Rick just installed 900 Watts of solar panels and that is where our power is coming from today," Ed said.

"He installed the solar panels to power his back-up water pump but he doesn't need all that power.

"In other broadcast news, those of you with CB radios will be happy to learn that Gladys Swartz will be monitoring channel 31. If you run into too much traffic to drill through, they jump up to channel 33. After that the progression is channel 37.... prime numbers if you haven't figured that out already," Ed said.

"Neighbors installed a killer antenna on Gladys' roof and she now has outstanding reception," Ed said.

Gladys was housebound and was delighted to be an active part of the community.

"Things continue to fall apart elsewhere," Ed said.

"You might have seen the orange glow in the northern sky last night. Both lumber yards on Market Drive caught fire early in the evening and then several apartment buildings on Trestlewood Drive caught fire. Delta Township fire department put out a call for mutual aid and nobody came. They were either pinned down with their own fires or were running too short of manpower to respond," Ed said.

"It is not known if the apartments caught fire due to wind-blown embers or whether it is a separate incident.

"Word from the CDC in Atlanta estimates that one-half percent of the US population contracted Ebola. That is pretty close to the one-percent that some experts estimate will totally collapse the economy. We are already seeing shortages of gas and other necessities," Ed said. "Have a plan. If you have a full tank of gas in your vehicle, don't aimlessly drive around. You may need that gas later to cook your food or run a rototiller in your garden.

“I don’t intend to be an alarmist but I do want you to walk around with your eyes open,” Ed said.

“Today’s guest is Sergeant Steve Smith who will be holding another firearms class. The class size is limited to five students. Steve is looking for loaner guns for the new students. Many of his new students have never held a gun, much less owned one. So, Steve, are you an NRA certified instructor?” Ed asked.

“Well, no, Ed I am not. But somebody had to step up. I looked around and decided I am the best guy. I use NRA teaching materials but I have to confess I am not certified by the NRA,” Steve said.

Ed was taken aback but recovered quickly.

“Steve, you were telling me about the three big rules of gun safety.

"I remember taking a Hunter Safety class with Ethan,” Ed said. "I remember that there were Ten Rules."

That surprised Sgt. Smith. "Well," Sgt. Smith said "can you tell me all ten rules?" throwing it back in Ed's lap.

"Hmmm,” Ed said, stalling for time. "Don't put 20-gauge shells in a 12-gauge shotgun?" he guessed.

"That is the problem with ten rules,” Smith said. "You might remember some of them but the ones you remember might not be the most important ones. That is why we boiled it down to three rules and then we hammer those three so you will remember them when you are ninety."

"OK, I see your point. Can you share the Big Three with our listening audience?” Ed said.

“Sure, Ed. No problem,” Sergeant Smith said.

“One: The gun is always loaded.

"Two: Never point the gun toward anything you are not willing to shoot.

"Three: Keep your finger off the trigger until you are ready to shoot."

"You corrected me earlier when I said 'Treat the gun as if the gun is loaded.' Do you want to tell me why?" Ed said.

"You bet. If you load a gun in front of somebody and hand it to them, they treat it differently than if you hand them a gun that they 'know' is unloaded, even if you tell them to treat it as if it were loaded," Steve said.

"When they know it is loaded you can see them thinking about what might be on the other side of a wall or where a potential ricochet might go. They think BEFORE they change where the gun is pointing. You don't see that level of caution after you tell them 'Treat it as if it were loaded.' " Steve said.

"You also told me a story while we were waiting for air time..." Ed said.

"We had a call when I was with the State Police. It was outside of Jackson," Steve said.

"A grandmother was watching her grandkids. She lived in a tough neighborhood and had a shotgun stashed behind the couch. Of course the kids found it.

"Later, we figured out one of the kids had found some shells and they managed to get it loaded. Well, one of the kids got shot. Lost his leg," Steve said.

"If that grandma had been in the mindset that all guns are always loaded, she would have had the gun locked up when the kids came over. It was a completely avoidable accident. It happened because she treated her shotgun AS IF it were loaded," Steve said.

"That is a sobering story," Ed said "Tell me about the other rules."

"Number Two: Never point the gun toward anything you are not willing to shoot," Steve said. "I kind of alluded to the fact that a safe shooter is always thinking about what is behind the target, behind walls and where ricochets might go."

Ed said, "You told me a story about that, too."

"I heard this from a neighbor a few days ago. After you hear the story you will understand why I won't share his name," Steve said.

"He had been hunting with a bolt action rifle but hadn't seen anything. He unloaded the rifle before going into the house. After removing the magazine, he unloaded the chamber but the round did not drop into his hand. There was snow on the ground so he assumed it had missed his hand and fallen into the snow," Steve said.

"After going into the house, he pulled the trigger before disassembling the firearm for cleaning. The gun went off. Because the hunter practiced safe shooting rules, the barrel was pointed at the floor and the bullet lodged in a garbage can filled with dog food in the basement," Steve said. "Embarrassing...but far better than shooting his child or wife who were in the other room watching TV.

"Afterward, the hunter looked at the ammo. It was an inexpensive brand made in Russia. He determined that the groove for the extractor was cut too shallow so he pitched that box of ammo," Steve said.

"Things like that can happen," Steve said. "That is why there are three rules and not just one."

"Number Three: Keep your finger off the trigger until you are ready to shoot," Steve said. "This can actually help you shoot faster and better with a handgun if you point your trigger finger along the frame parallel with the barrel. Then, if you decide to shoot your barrel will naturally be pointing in the same direction as your finger."

Religiously following the Big Three will go a very long way to making you a safe shooter.

Edwards Muck

Shadrack Shaw came into Kate's Store lugging a five-gallon bucket half filled with gray clay.

"Ma-am, Mr. Ed on the radio said you were looking for limestone. I think I can help you out," Shad said.

The Shaw family home-schooled Shad and their other kids and the curriculum was eclectic.

Kate was in the process of cutting Carson Duckworth fifteen feet of 3/16" galvanized steel aircraft cable. Kate looked down, into the bucket and honestly commented, "That doesn't look like limestone."

"That's because it isn't," Shad said. "It's marl. Limestone and marl are both calcium carbonate."

"You sound very sure of yourself," Kate said.

"I did a unit on local soils," Shad said. "Parts of Gruesbeck Drain cut through Edwards Muck."

Kate's face registered lack of understanding.

"Edwards Muck sits on a base of marl. The spoils bank for the drain is topped with marl...pure calcium carbonate," Shad said with the certainty of a fifteen-year-old.

Kate said, "I am certainly no expert on soils but I am more than willing to let local folks try this. They are desperate for something to strengthen their eggshells. For that matter, so am I. I can't sell eggs with broken shells."

"I can work with that," Shad said. "Let me know if it works out and you want me to get any more."

Shad left the bucket.

Kate's customers gave her rave reviews for the marl. Adding five pounds for every hundred pounds of food went through a lot of marl but it also solved the problem with the breaking egg shells. Everybody was happy.

The next time that Shad came into the store, Kate said "We need to talk about what is a fair price for your product."

"Aw, heck Mrs Salazar. I will just give it to you," Shad said.

"That won't work for me for a couple of reasons," Kate said.

"For one, it isn't fair to you. Digging up that marl is cold heavy work and it will get a lot harder once you mine out the spoils bank and have to dig for it," Kate said.

"The other reason is that I need a lot of it. Maybe more than you can dig by yourself. You will need to be able to pay people to work for you," Kate said.

"How much do you think you need?" Shad asked.

"Hard to say. I could probably sell twenty pounds a week but that could go way up if the other neighborhoods can't get limestone. It might go up to a hundred pounds a week...dried marl, not wet," Kate said.

Shad winced. "That is a lot of marl. So, what do you think is a fair price for marl?"

"I have been thinking about that," Kate said. "I get the equivalent of $4.00 for a dozen eggs. That is, ten dozen eggs trades for a face-cord of firewood. That works out to about $2.75 a pound. Seems to me that would be a good starting place for marl, $2.75 a pound. What do you think?"

"Sounds really high," Shad said.

"Maybe so, to you. But think of all the work that goes into raising chickens and making eggs. It all gets wasted if the eggs break when the hen lays them or they break in the basket on the way here," Kate said. "Think of it as selling insurance."

Quite by chance, Carson Duckworth was in the store while this conversation was going on.

It was no big trick for Carson to walk Gruesbeck's drain and see where Shad had been digging. Nor was it a big deal for Carson to throw a bunch of fence posts into the ground and string wire and put up signs declaring it was his property. After all, the drainage ditch cut through "common" property where the legal owners were not in a position to enforce their rights.

Duckworth's audacity created a firestorm within the community.

Duckworth contended that Shad was a kid and did not have the resources to exploit the marl deposit.

He also contended that there needed to be a mechanism for turning "common property" over to private ownership to ensure it was properly looked after.

When families with far less property than Duckworth commented that they were counting on the common property for firewood, he said that they should make their claims. He also said that every adult member of the community should have an equal claim on the commons regardless of whether they were rich or poor.

By his figuring, that meant that every adult was entitled to three acres of "common land". Between him, his wife and Cameron his nineteen-year-old son, they staked claim to the stretch of Gruesbeck drain that cut through the Edwards muck.

The Homesteading Act of Kate's Store

Rick invited representatives from the various parts of the neighborhood to talk about Carson Duckworth's insistence that the commons area be parceled out.

Jonathan O'Brien was from the northwest corner. Jonathan, never John, was very religious and had run his own construction business before the Plague.

Wade Hawk was from the north-central part of the neighborhood. Wade's family had owned much of the land that now made up the neighborhood. Wade knew the land intimately because he had hunted over every square inch of it in his youth. Over the generations bits and pieces had been sold.

Rick tapped Kelly to represent the south-central portion of the neighborhood.

The east end of the neighborhood was tough because that end tended to be more transient, but eventually he settled on Margaret White, a tough old lady who scared the bejeebers out of kids at Halloween.

Rick was number five and only voted when a tie-breaker was needed.

Hawk started out with "Duckworth needs a righteous ass-kicking."

Wade Hawk had been a brawler in his youth. Then he had moved into management and was known for his unyielding adherence to "the rules". Hawk was reputed to be the only man in Eaton Rapids who wore out the seats of his trousers, from the inside.

The Shaw family lived across from his house.

Rick said "That may be so, but Duckworth brought up some issues that need to be addressed. For one thing, are we in favor of private property or are we going to be a hybrid socialist economy," Rick said.

"I don't see why we have to talk about that," Jonathan said.

Kelly piped up at this point. "Either we deal with it now or people are going to get screwed," he said.

"I talked to some of my neighbors and some are for it and others aren't," Jonathan said.

"Same here," Margaret said. "Some want to take ownership of commons property and others don't want to. Seems like the ones who have commons touching a property line are more for it than folks who are hemmed in by private property."

"Lemme throw a stake in the ground," Rick said. "Since we probably can't stop it, let's put some guard rails around it."

"Just for talking purposes, I propose we take the area of the commons area and divide it by the number of adults and set that as the limit of what any one person can claim," Rick said.

"That's not fair," Hawk said. "The few are gonna cherry pick the best pieces and leave the others with total crap, just like that bastard Duckworth is doing."

"Jonathan, I can see you are thinking of something. Is it something you want to share?" Rick asked.

"The Bible has a concept called Jubilee where contracts were dissolved every fifty years. I don't know if fifty years is the right number. I was thinking that maybe it makes sense to allow folks to lease a patch of common land for five or ten years," Jonathan said.

Kelly said, "Leasing makes sense because the land owners might show up, that can be a clause in the lease."

"We are gonna need a deposit. I rented property before and it always comes back wrecked," Hawk said.

Margaret said, "I like the idea of the lease. That way they have to sign a contract. I think five years is too short but ten years might work."

"Wade, you raised the concern that the first people would grab the best pieces. How big should the parcels be to make it fair?" Rick asked.

"First of all, I would take all the wooded land off-the-table. People are going to freeze to death if things keep sliding into the ditch," Hawk said.

Everybody nodded in agreement. That made total sense.

"Second, I think people with parcels must allow easements across their plots. That means that they need to put in at least two gates if they fence it," Hawk said.

"Third, somebody claims a piece of the commons then they give up all claim to the rest of the commons, and that includes the wooded areas," Hawk said.

"Those are all really good points," Rick said. "But it still doesn't answer how big of a parcel we should let people claim."

"I'm getting to that," Hawk said. It was clear he was irritated by Rick's interruption.

"By my figuring there is almost two sections of land that is 'commons'. Call it 1200 acres. How many folks are left in the neighborhood?" Hawk said.

"About three hundred," Rick said.

"OK, so about two hundred adults," Hawk guesstimated. "If it was distributed evenly then it would be six acres per adult. I think it should be half or even a quarter of that."

The discussion went round-and-round after that but they finally settled on two-acre parcels per adult. Adults were defined as fifteen and over so Shadrack Shaw could participate if he wanted to. The rent was three face cords of fire wood a year and the deposit was another three face cords.

The resolution passed unanimously.

To nobody's surprise, Carson, Carson's wife and Cameron, Carson's 19-year-old son latched a hold of three parcels lined out along Gruesbeck's Drain.

They loaded up their truck with fence posts and wire and immediately fenced off the three parcels.

The first time Carson brought a bucket of marl to Kate she refused it. She said "This isn't marl. Its muck."

"It's got marl in it," Carson said. "And you are going to pay me $4 a pound for it or I will sell it to somebody else."

"I can't charge my customers that kind of money for that," Kate said.

"You don't understand, do you? I am the only game in town. You either pay what I tell you or you lose the business," Carson said.

"Knock yourself out," Kate said. She wasn't going to be party to somebody who not only screwed nice kids like Shadrack Shaw, he screwed his own customers.

Limited Partners

Milo asked Nyssa, "What's the big deal about eggs and calcium?"

The neighborhood was in an uproar. It was a constant topic

of conversation at Kate's Store. Kate merely nodded with empathy. It was out of her control.

Carson had not skimmed the top of the spoils heaps like Shad. He, his wife, and Cameron had broken the partially frozen piles into chunks and then shoveled them into the back of his truck and trailer and hauled the entire line of spoils two miles back to his property.

He was charging $4.00 a pound for muck that was only 25% marl. Folks raising eggs were stuck. If they didn't buy from Carson nearly all of their eggs cracked. If they did buy from Carson, they lost money.

The producers bought the muck/marl mix and raised the price of eggs from $4.00 a dozen to $6.00.

Nyssa tried to figure out how to explain the importance of eggs in the new economy.

"Do you notice how we don't have much meat?" Nyssa asked.

"Yeah," Milo said.

"That is because it takes two years to double the number of mama cows and a bit more than one year to increase the number of mama sheep," Nyssa said.

"Pigs reproduce a lot faster but need almost human-quality food. The number of brood sows can increase by factor five in half a year," Nyssa said.

"Laying hens, however, a grower can increase by a factor of thirty in half a year. And they can lay their body-weight in eggs every seven weeks month-after-month-after-month," Nyssa said.

"Not only that, but increasing your laying flock means that half of your chicks growing into roosters that you might as well eat," Nyssa said. "Chickens put more animal protein on the table, quicker than any other animal."

"OK," Milo said. "I get the point about chickens...but what is the deal about calcium."

So, then Nyssa explained that eggshells are pure calcium carbonate and are 10% of the weight of an egg. No eggshell, no eggs.

Milo shook his head. "Carson really is a piece of work, isn't he?" he said.

Nyssa agreed. "The funny thing is he thinks he is getting way ahead. He can't see how he is really pissing people off."

A couple of days later Milo brought up the topic with Kelly.

"Where is Duckworth from?" Milo asked. "His house looks really new."

"I don't know" Kelly said. "They bought a bunch of acreage and moved in about five years ago. He says he is a plumber but nobody ever sees him working a job. He never leaves the house for very long."

"What I don't understand about him," Kelly said, "Is that he seems to be made of money. Everything is top of the line. He has a 30kW generator that had to cost $15k installed, and that is just for back-up power. Made of money and the cheapest guy you will ever meet."

"So, tell me about this limestone stuff. It is a special kind of stone, right," Milo said. "Where does it come from?"

"Limestone is pretty common. It is basically fossilized coral reefs. Nearly all the mid-West was under shallow seas at one time," Kelly said.

"The problem around here is that the glaciers dumped about ninety feet of clay, sand and gravel on top of the bedrock," Kelly said.

"So where is the closest place to find limestone?" Milo asked.

"There might be some places closer but I know there is a limestone quarry in Bellevue," Kelly said.

Milo pointed to the southwest. "That little town southwest of Charlotte?" he said.

"Yup," Kelly said. "The Battle Creek river cut away most of the over-burden."

"So why doesn't somebody just drive down to Bellevue and pick up five yards of it?" Milo asked.

"Maybe you haven't noticed but nobody is going anywhere and nobody is extending credit. Heck, most people aren't even accepting paper money anymore," Kelly said, dryly.

A few days later Milo swung by the Shaw household and asked if he could take Shadrack ice fishing. Since Mr. and Mrs Shaw had a lot of mouths to feed, they thought that was a fine idea.

Teardrop Ice Fishing Jigs

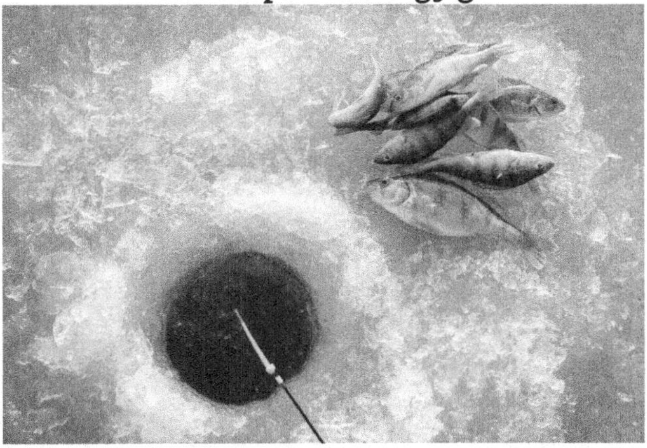

Kelly was already fishing on his pond. The panfish were biting. It was no longer possible to drive to the bait store for mousies and wax-worms but the fish ferociously hit teardrops with little strips of chicken skin for meat.

Milo scooped the new ice out of an existing hole and put a

bucket down for Shad to sit on while he jigged.

Milo cleared another hole for himself.

Kelly told them the magic formula. Drop it down. Bounce it off the bottom a few times to stir up the mud. Then suspend it 8" off the bottom and jiggle it.

The fish hit steadily through the afternoon and the catch started to pile up.

As light started to fade, Milo asked Shad if he knew what a "limited partnership" was.

Shad said, "No."

Milo said, "A limited partnership is where one person supplies all of the management while other partners supply capital. A lot of times, the other partners are anonymous."

Shad chewed on that information for a bit, wondering why Milo brought that up.

As they looked the fish over, Milo suggested that Shad take all of the bluegills while he would take the 'punkin seeds' and perch. There were four bluegills for every punkin seed. "Nyssa and I don't eat as much as your family and she thinks those punkin seeds taste extra buttery," Milo explained as they admired the vivid colors.

"Looks like gold, don't it?" Kelly said.

Events Quicken

The two-vehicle convoy went south to Nye Highway, a minor east-west dirt road. The convoy turned west and went seven miles to Cochran, then south again to Butterfield Highway which became M-78 after crossing the freeway.

The tractor pulling the gravity wagon and the pickup truck pulling a second, smaller wagon with three boys and the gassifier in the back drew attention as they paraded through the village of Bellevue. Just before the river the two vehicles turned left onto Sand Road.

Milo brought a labor crew in case they had to load the wagons by hand.

There they waited, motors idling.

It did not take long for the manager of the quarry to show up. “We ain’t open,” he said.

“We can pay real money,” Milo said.

“We ain’t open,” the man repeated.

Milo wasn’t taking “No” for an answer.

“We can do this two ways," Milo said. “We can break in and load our vehicles or you can open the gates and let us pay you.”

The man was just as stubborn. “That is stealing. Cash ain’t good for nuthin’ round here ‘sept wiping your ass.”

“I didn’t say I was going to pay with dollar bills,” Milo said. He had, in fact, brought paper money just in case the quarry would take it.

“I can pay with silver coins,” Milo said.

That finally got the manager’s attention. “The price is $30 a ton or $50 a yard for ground ag-lime and $10 a ton or $17 a yard for ungraded limestone gravel.”

Milo and the manager got to dickering about the exchange rate. Finally, they settled on twenty-times face which was to the manager’s advantage but then he offered to use the front-end loader to load the gravity wagons. He had no problems burning a little bit of precious diesel when customers were paying with silver.

The manager watched Milo restart the gasifiers. “Don’t suppose you would consider installing one of them on one of my trucks?" the manager asked.

"I thought you were shut down?" Milo said.

"I am for now. Its winter and winter is always slow. Farmers, they ain't spending any money but I think, come spring, a lot of people are going to start gardening and a lot of those gardens are going to need lime," the manager said.

"I will talk to my partner and we will put you on the list," Milo promised.

The two vehicles made it back to the Shaw homestead shortly after midnight as they could not go much faster than five miles an hour with the loaded wagons.

The smaller wagon had three yards of finely ground ag-lime in it. The larger wagon had ten yards of crushed limestone varying between 3/4" and dust.

The manager also gave them a sheet certifying that the limestone was 98% calcium carbonate.

Carson was about to get some competition.

Luke

Luke's supervisor caught up with Luke while he was in the cooler where he was picking carrots for shipment to the Oscar's store in Traverse City.

Oscar's was a large, regional department store that sold groceries.

"Time for you to go home," the supervisor said.

The crew had been told at the start of the shift that the warehouse was going to suspend operation when the security situation became too difficult. Rioters had breached the interior fences at the other end of the warehouse complex where electronics were stored the day before.

Skeleton crews had been working and there was enough room inside the complex, proper, for them to park.

Luke pulled the mule over to the trailer and dropped the load.

Then he punched out.

He drove to this apartment, kissed his roommate good-bye, picked up his cat and drove to Eaton Rapids. His roommate would join him later.

Gabriella

Gabriella taught 6th graders at a private school east of Memphis. Her principal called all staff to the gymnasium after the kids bused out on Friday. There, he pink-slipped them en masse. In the past week the school had three diagnosed cases of Ebola. It was time to pull the plug.

When they asked where to apply for unemployment, he informed him that there would be no benefits, that everything was being handled through FEMA. He would contact them when there was more news or a change of circumstances.

Bill, Gabby's husband, had been laid off two weeks ago.

They had 20 gallons of gas in the small, streamlined trailer they pulled behind their small SUV. They packed up their Jack Russell terrier, warm clothing and a few sentimental items and headed north. They stayed away from Indy and Fort Wayne by jogging east.

Riots

The first documented cases of riots occurred in Cleveland. The FEMA food distribution system was going through growing pains. The temperature was in the twenties and a fierce wind was blowing in off Lake Erie. Most of the people waiting in line were not dressed for the weather.

After waiting two hours to get to the front of the line, Jazzamyn Johnson was handed a small, heavy package of commodities. Jazzamyn said, "What is this shit?" as she dumped it out on the floor

The video recorders on the smart phones started recording.

"This ain't food," she said. "Where are the Hot Pockets? Where are the popcorn chicken? Where be the Coco Puffs? Where be my chock-lic milk? I have babies at home to feed!" With each question her voice got louder.

"I know my rights. You can't make me to eat this shit," Ms. Johnson yelled.

One of the bags split after she kicked it to show her disgust. Split peas scattered across the floor. Then she started kicking the others and dried rice and beans scattered

The Ohio Department of Transportation had been tasked with administering this particular food distribution center. They had not anticipated any issues. They dealt with tens of thousands of citizens every business day. What they failed to anticipate was that people can live (and drive) without a driver's license. The stakes are much higher when you are talking about the food you need to live.

"You be racist," Ms. Johnson said repeatedly as she started turning over tables. Like many grossly overweight people, she carried a lot of muscle.

In the past this had always resulted in the store bending over backwards to mollify her. This time, guards with TASERS started toward her to drag her out.

Other people waiting in line, hearing the ruckus and seeing the kinds of food that were being distributed, became enraged. They hadn't frozen their asses off for two hours to get pig food.

Social media platforms could not stay ahead of the video

of the riots being posted and emailed. In time they stopped trying. They had their own issues with Ebola.

CHAPTER THIRTEEN

Peckerwood

The CB in Kate's store crackled. "Hey, Rick. Got your ears on?"

"Gimme a minute," Kate said into the mic. "Rick is in the back room. Who is this?" Kate asked.

"This is Paul Seraph in Eaton Rapids. I got something I need to talk over with Rick," Paul said.

A minute later Rick picked up the mic and said "Rick Salazar to Paul Seraph in Eaton Rapids. Can you hear me?"

"Yup, you are coming in fine," Paul said.

"What can I do for you?" Rick said.

"We gotta situation with one of your little ducklings," Paul said.

Rick scratched the three-day stubble on his chin. "Don't know which 'little duckling' you are talking about," Rick said.

"I was in City Hall meeting with the new mayor, the chief of police and a handful of concerned citizens when we got a call from the convenience store on the north end of town," Paul said.

"Everybody knows the new chief is a lard-ass and won't move unless he has a car so I volunteered to take care of it,"

Paul said. Paul rode his bike all over town and was known to show up any place, any time.

"I get down there and the guy you sent to pick up gas refused to leave," Paul said.

In his previous life, Paul worked for the Dearborn Heights police department. The department made him an offer too good to refuse after twenty years of service. He and his wife took the retirement and moved to Eaton Rapids where a dollar went much, much farther. Since then, Paul dabbled and had his fingers in multiple business ventures in and around Eaton Rapids.

"Umm, I didn't send anybody to pick up gas," Rick said.

Then, shielding the mic with his hand he asked Kate, "Did you send anybody to town to pick up gas?"

Kate shook her head "No."

"Nobody from Kate's store went to town to pick up gas," Rick said.

"Well, that makes things interesting," Paul said.

"This guy shows up with a white ¾ ton pickup running on fumes and ten, five-gallon gas cans and insists that we fill up his truck and all the cans," Paul said.

"The manager told him he wasn't selling him any gas, that the fuel had been tagged by City Hall for emergency use," Paul said.

"Then the guy started getting shitty," Paul said. "Told the manager that Kate's store and City Hall had an agreement, to put it on the tab for Kate's store and she would handle paying for it later."

"What is the guy's name?" Rick asked.

"Willy Peet," Paul said.

"I don't know anybody named Willy Peet," Rick said. "Can you describe him?"

Of course Paul could describe him.

"About 5'-10". Weight about 180. Maybe 45 or 50. Hair the color of peanut butter. Wearing waffle-stompers and a Carhartt type work coat," Paul said.

"You described about half the population of the neighborhood," Rick said.

"How about his truck?" Rick said.

"Three-quarter ton GMC 2500 dually, white, crew-cab, maybe three years old. The bed has some black dirt in the corners where it didn't get cleaned out. He has the usual Browning buck stickers and... wait, he has a PPU sticker with a couple of crossed pipe wrenches," Paul said.

"Sounds like Carson Duckworth," Rick said. "Ask to see his left wrist. He has a woodpecker tattooed on it."

"Woodpecker? Like Woody Woodpecker?" Paul asked.

"Exactly like Woody Woodpecker except there are flames around it," Rick said.

"If this turns out to be this Carson Duckworth, is he a buddy of yours?" Paul asked.

"Not hardly," Rick said. "Not when he is trying to stick Kate with a bill she did not authorize."

"Thanks. That is all I need to know," Paul said.

Walking back around the convenience store building to where the fuel pumps were, Willy Peet was NOT waiting patiently.

That might have been due to the fact that a couple of locals had shown up and parked immediately fore-and-aft of his truck. The locals were packing heat so there was no way Willy was going to demolition-derby his way out of his parking spot in front of the pumps.

"Pull up your sleeves," Paul said.

"Fuck you," Willy said. "I got rights."

"Pull up your sleeves or you are walking home," Paul said.

Willy pulled them up a half inch.

Paul sighed. "Genuine Carhartt coats might get hard to come by. Be a shame if we had to hold you down and cut this one off of you."

Willy took off his coat and pulled up the sleeves of his flannel shirt.

Woody Woodpecker was vividly tattooed on the inside of his left forearm, just as Rick said it would be.

"Well, CARSON," Paul said. "You are lucky that I am in a generous mood.

"I am going to let you drive your truck back home, mostly because I already have more vehicles than fuel to drive them," Paul said. "I am also not going to throw you in jail because I don't want to feed your worthless ass.

"I am going to confiscate all of your gas cans, however. And I am going to ban you from Eaton Rapids," Paul said.

"If you come into town in the next year, you will be thrown in jail and you won't be fed," Paul said.

"Have I made myself perfectly clear?" Paul said.

Carson nodded "Yes."

"I did not hear you. Do you understand?" Paul said.

Carson mumbled "Yes."

"I am an old man and these two guys holding shotguns do a lot of shooting and their hearing ain't so good. So, Peckerwood, you are going to have to pipe up. I want the MANAGER in the store to hear you," Paul said.

"DO YOU UNDERSTAND?" Paul said.
"Yes, I understand," Carson said. He was rattled that Paul knew the gang affiliation associated with the woodpecker tattoo.

"Another thing I am going to do," Paul said in a more conversational voice, "is talk to my counterparts in Charlotte, Potterville and Dimondale just in case you are tempted to pull this bullshit there."

Paul nodded to the "boys" holding the shotguns. "One of you, grab the gas cans out of the back of this loser's truck. Spread the word around town. I wanna know the second this joker comes back to town, if he ever does."

Salt Rising Bread

"Welcome to Mr. Ed's Coffee Hour," Ed Hall said into the microphone. "Transmitting on FM 104.3 at eight in the morning and 1086 AM a half hour before sunset with a tenth of a Watt power. Mr. Ed's Coffee Hour where you will hear the news straight from the horse's mouth."

Ed Hall took a sip of tea. "Today's tipple is wheatgrass tea. Filled with vitamins and mineral goodness. Oh, and it tastes good, too.

"Now a word from our sponsors. I am transmitting from Kate's Store where the men are men and the women and children can shoot the stinger offen a hornet at a hundred paces," Ed said.

"Kate has calcium back in stock for those of you who have laying hens," Ed said. "Pure calcium, none finer.

"She moved it in the consignment section so Shadrack Shaw can re-coop the cost of fetching it from Cheney's Quarry over in Bellevue," Ed said. "I heard a rumor that he had to pay Kelly and Milo's Trucking with gold. Re-coop, chickens...get it?

"Kate also raised the price a little bit from what she had been charging. This limestone is so pure that even at $3.00 a pound you are getting more calcium than you did when you purchased pure marl from Kate at $2.75," Ed said.

"Don't pay more for inferior imitations. Buy the good stuff from Kate's Store," Ed said. "From what I seen in the Shaw's yard, he has enough to sell to surrounding areas, but first talk to Kate so she can arrange pricing and trucking. Shadrack's ma and pa don't want a lot of strangers visiting.

"Folks heading over to Eaton Rapids or any of the nearby towns are likely to find barricades at the edge of town," Ed said. "You can save a lot of aggravation if you show them ID and tell them where you are going or who you intend to visit.

"I had a conversation with Paul Seraph over in ER. He told me that the rumors about somebody being run out of town with threats of tar-and-feathering are slight exaggerations. Wouldn't of been any problems if the fella in question had been willing to show his Driver's License," Ed said.

"Paul also suggested that we start having conversations about some uncomfortable things," Ed said.

"I ain't ever treated you like kids and I ain't about to start," Ed said. "You can turn off your radio if hard facts cause you stress.

"One conversation we gotta have is about folks who show up from out of our area and want to move in with us," Ed said. "We are sitting pretty compared to most places and folks are going to figure that out.

"We are going to have brothers and sisters, nephews and nieces, cousins and old friends who are going to want to move in," Ed said. "All of them will be coming from places with more Ebola that we have here.

"We gotta talk about quarantine and we gotta talk about what happens when newcomers think it doesn't apply to them," Ed said. "I guarantee it will be a hard fact because nobody likes to be isolated and nobody likes to get Ebola and die.

"Then we gotta figure out where to put them once they are out of isolation," Ed said.

"Another hard thing to talk about is the zombie horde," Ed said. "I am going to be straight up. I got opinions. I think it is a lot smarter to render mutual aid and fight the zombie hordes five or ten miles from our homes rather than to let them into Kate's Store and be afraid of leaving our homes after dark.

"Mutual aid ain't fighting other people's battles for them. Mutual aid is fighting our battle before it gets to our neighborhood.

"Switching topics: Today's guest is Mrs Shaw, Shadrack's mom. May I call you Ardeth?" Ed said.

"Certainly," Mrs Shaw responded.

"Ardeth, you volunteered to come on the show to share a few recipes and tips for cooking with a few basic ingredients. Can you share how you acquired these skills?" Ed asked.

"Sure, Ed," Mrs Shaw said. "I grew up in a prepper tradition. My parents always had at least a year's worth of food in the pantry.

"I came from a large family so money was always tight. Filling the pantry with prepared foods like freeze dried foods or C-Rations was not an option," Ardeth said.

"So my folks bought bulk grains and beans, sugar and shortening," Ardeth said. "Much like the situation we have now."

"What recipe are you going to share with us today?" Ed asked.

"I am going to talk the audience through making 'salt rising bread'," Ardeth said.

"You can make bread using salt instead of yeast or soda?" Ed said, mystified. "And why are you sharing a recipe for bread first?"

"No, salt doesn't make it rise. That is just what it is called," Mrs Shaw said.

"I want to do a recipe for bread first because bread is a comfort food. It is familiar. When times get tough people value foods that remind them of better times. And, for most people, bread is easy to digest. It really is 'the staff of life,'" Mrs Shaw said.

"The key to making salt rising bread is to understand what you are working with," Mrs Shaw said. As a home-schooler of a large brood of children (and several loaners) she easily dropped into 'instruction' mode.

"Salt rising bread doesn't use soda or yeast. It uses a bacteria called Clostridium perfringens. The spores of C.P. are everywhere and are not killed by short exposure to boiling water," Mrs Shaw said.

"Another thing about C.P. is that it loves protein and hates oxygen. So the first thing we do is dry mix some corn meal and flour together and then add double that amount of water that we boiled beans in. The bean-water adds protein. In fact, we want the bean-water boiling hot when we mix it with the flour mix. If you have scalded milk that works even better than bean-water but most folks don't have milk."

"Another thing we need to know about C.P. is that it likes it HOT. Not just warm, but HOT," Mrs Shaw said.

"How hot?" Ed said, more than willing to play the straight man.

"If you have a thermometer, 110F. If you don't have a thermometer, put the pan in your hand and if you can only hold it for ten seconds before it becomes too hot...well, that is about right," Mrs Shaw said. "Make sure you have a lid on your starter. You want to keep the air and dust out."

"We heat with wood so there is always some place near the wood stove that is just-right for getting the starter going," Mrs Shaw said. "Every kitchen is different. It is something you will have to play with, just like I did when we moved here."

"Then what?" Ed asked.

"You will know it is a good starter when it starts bubbling," Mrs Shaw said. "But whatever you do, don't taste the raw starter."

"Why?" Ed asked.

"C.P. can produce toxins. It is a major cause of scours in newborn piglets. In fact, C.P. causes gangrene. Cooking the bread destroys the toxin so you are safe...just don't taste the starter or the bread dough," Mrs Shaw said.

"Many of our listeners don't know what 'scours' are. Can you tell them?" Ed asked.

"Sorry," Mrs Shaw said. "Scours is another name for violent diarrhea in young animals."

"Then what do you do with the starter?" Ed said.

"Mix half of it with your flour and water and kneed to make bread dough. You need to put it in a warm place...110F if you can manage it...to make the dough rise. Let it double, punch it down. Then let it rise again before you bake it the way you would bake normal loaves of bread," Mrs Shaw said.

"The half you save, add more water and flour and put it in a warm place to grow until your next bread-baking," Mrs Shaw said.

The Smell of Skunks

Ed Hall, Dmitri, Wade Hawk and Tim were sitting in Tim's UTV looking north up the paved road that led to Lansing fifteen miles distant. The UTV was crowded but the shared warmth of the bodies was appreciated given the brutal, early-January wind. While others were sleeping off their hang-overs on January first, Ed, Dmitri, Wade and Tim were surveying the defensibility of Kates Store's perimeter.

"So, why did you invite us on this joy ride?" Hawk asked. Tim lived in Hawk's district.

"Mr. Ed said we needed to have some hard conversations. I think it best that we have those conversations out here, looking at where things are going to happen," Tim said.

"You must be talking about the zombie invasion," Ed said.

"Yup," Tim said. "Talking about coming up with a plan. And we might as well be looking at this stretch of road as any other. One stretch of it don't look that much different than any other from here to Dimondale."

"I'm a hunter. You wanna know about bushwhacking deer or kicking brush piles for bunnies, I am your man," Hawk said. "Don't know shit about hunting people."

Dmitri said. "Not that much different. To hunt raiders, you have to know what they think, how they move."

"And what would that be?" Hawk said.

"Ontogeny is the recapitulation of Phylogeny," Dmitri said.

"Speak English," Hawk said, irritated.

"The first zombie raiders won't be sophisticated," Dmitri said. "They will stop at the first house and tear it apart. Then move to the next."

"If there are a lot of them, they might drop off five-or-ten in the first house and the rest keep going. Then, when the first group finishes stripping the house, they might set it on fire and leap-frog to the front of the group to a fresh house," Dmitri said.

"It will be like..." Dmitri said, searching for the term for the picture in his head, "It will be like the caterpillar tread of a bulldozer," he said.

Tim nodded. That is kind of how he had it figured although he hadn't strung it all together.

"So they won't be coming like the army in Mad Max?" Ed said.

"No. They don't have the organizational skills," Dmitri said.

"They also won't be cutting cross-country unless they see a mansion back in the woods."

"There won't be a pitched battle where you can break them down. It will be more like an assembly line delivering zombies to kill," Tim said. "That has disadvantages. If we were dealing with massed troops then we could lay them out with grape-shot."

Dmitri said, "But it also has advantages. They have no logistical support. The first wave will burn out in a couple of weeks if we can stop them."

"I dealt with pricks like this all my life. It won't take much to get them fighting each other, either," Hawk said. He was something of an expert on "pricks".

"How will we be able to tell the zombies from the legitimate refugees?" Ed said.

"Mostly by when they show up and what they are carrying," Dmitri said. "Refugees carry clothing and bedding. Raiders are nearly always young men and will be carrying swag and weapons."

"That. And by when they show up," Tim said. "Refugees will be streaming through our border long before the raiders get here."

"What are we going to do with refugees?" Ed asked.

"If we play this mutual aid idea right, we won't have that many," Tim said. "As soon as the raiders get past Dimondale, we start burning houses down around them at night and shooting them if they make it out of the houses. We can even plant some full whiskey bottles in the house to guarantee they will be spending the night."

"That's pretty cold," Hawk said.

"Killing people always is," Tim said. "But it is better than getting killed."

There was a pause as the men digested that comment.

"Why wait until after they get past Dimondale?" Ed asked.

"Subdivisions," Tim said. "North of Dimondale there are too many ways for them to spill past our containment."

"Distance is our friend if we know how to use it," Tim continued.

"That is one place where we screwed up in the Cold War," Tim said. "Our European allies demanded that we never give up an inch to a Soviet invasion, so we had all of our assets crammed up near the line."

"That was stupid for a few different reasons. For one thing, it put much of it within artillery range. For another, it was provocative. To the Soviets, it looked like we were packing a Jack-in-the-Box to push an offensive into their territory," Tim said. "A defensive configuration will always trade area if it gives the defenders an overwhelming advantage in attrition. Then, the defense can counter attack against the depleted offense and inexpensively regain the original lines."

"What is the picture in your head?" Ed asked.

"Send a team of a couple of scouts up by Vermontville Highway, just south of Dimondale. Have them set up a few hides they can rotate through. Let them use their ears, binoculars and a hand-held CB radio. Swap them out every week," Tim said.

"How long you figure we got?" Ed asked.

Hawk answered. "If it is going to happen, it is gonna start when we smell the first skunks of spring," Hawk shivered in the cold, January wind.

"But when it happens, hang onto your shorts because it is

going to be like the time Toivo cleaned out the vault of the Gogebic high school outhouse with a stick of dynamite. We need everything laid on before the shit starts flying because there won't be much time when we are in the middle of it," Hawk said.

"What are you thinking?" Tim asked.

"Might as well start sorting through the kids. Have them start watching now. Maybe have each kid stay out two nights a week and let them sort out the teams that work best," Hawk said. "That way they will know the territory like the back of their hands when we are playing for keeps."

"They can start looking at rally sites, setting up caches and figure out lines of retreat," Hawk said.

"You really think kids are capable of doing that?" Ed asked.

"They are if you tell them they are designing a video game. Let them use their smart phones. Have 'em take pictures instead of shooting each other. Tell them that if they do a good job and bring back pictures as proof, that they can get out of chores back home," Hawk said. "If they do a piss-poor job, they get to shovel shit."

Booze, Allen Hamilton

Dmitri walked into Kelly's shop the next day and Tim rolled in behind him in a wheel chair. Depending on the weather and how much he had been moving, sometimes Tim used crutches and sometimes the chair was more comfortable.

Kelly put down the tubing he was fitting to a hopper.

"To what do I own the honor, gentlemen?" Kelly asked.

Dmitri said, "Tim and I were discussing who was the best brewer of beer in the State of Michigan and your name came up."

Kelly rolled his eyes. "A little early in the day for a beer but I can spare a few," he said.

"We aren't here to drink your beer. At least not today," Tim said.

"We were talking," Tim said, "That we need to have a distillery."

"It would be pretty hard to lift a chainsaw with a gassifier attached to it. Another thing is that we will soon have a burning need for whiskey," Tim said.

"It shouldn't be too hard to make a little bit of moonshine," Kelly said. "When were you thinking of needing it?"

"How about the end of February?" Dmitri said.

"Well, I have some beer coming along. I could probably distill that, once I cobble together a still," Kelly said.

"How much whiskey would that make?" Tim asked.

"I dunno. Five gallons of beer at seven percent alcohol," Kelly said. Kelly liked to make his beer on the strong side. Less chance of it getting 'off' flavors, he said.

"Should make about a gallon of eighty proof," Kelly said.

"Not enough," Dmitri said.

"How much do you need?" Kelly asked.

"We need two gallons," Tim said.

"Two gallons a day," Dmitri corrected.

"A day. Like for how long?" Kelly asked.

"Dmitri says a couple of weeks but I think he is an optimist. I think for at least a couple of months," Tim said.

Kelly winced.

"And why would anybody need that much alcohol?" Kelly asked.

That is when Dmitri and Tim explained that it was part of the defense plan for when the urban areas came apart and the survivors in the Lansing Metro area exploded outward looking for food. Drunk-on-their ass invaders make more mistakes than sober ones. When possible, help your enemy be stupid; really, really stupid.

"Jesus" Kelly said. "I won't have time to do anything else."

"Can you do it if we get you some folks to help?" Tim asked.

"Don't know if I can do it even if you get me help. But it is sure a lot more likely," Kelly said. "For one thing, we have to keep a wood fire going to make sure the wort is warm enough to ferment, otherwise it just sits there. Cutting and hauling wood and feeding the fire will be a full-time job."

"Anything else?" Tim asked.

"Hell yes," Kelly said. "I need somebody to shovel malt...we will have to use wheat since we don't have any barley. Can't use corn, it just molds when it is cold. And I need people to stir and...."

Two gallons of pure alcohol a day required forty gallons of 5% "beer" to feed the still which in turn required two-thirds of a bushel of corn a day. Kelly was already mentally rounding up. It would be just as easy to size everything to a bushel of corn a day and ferment the wort in every conceivable container, including a 275-gallon bulk container cube. Part of what might save him is that he had a stash of champagne yeast which is very tolerant of cooler temperatures.

"Where you gonna get these warm bodies to help me?" Kelly asked.

"Do you have any objection to Gabby Salazar?" Tim asked.

"Why would I have any objections to her?" Kelly asked.

“For one thing, she is driving Kate to distraction. She is re-arranging the store and trying to boss Kate around,” Tim said. "You might want to think about how you can organize things so she 'owns' the whole distillation end of the business."

“I thought Gabby and Kate got along fine?” Kelly said.

“They do,” Dmitri said. “But you are forgetting it isn’t just Kate and Gabby, Ms Sheridan pretty much lives in the store. Ms Sheridan and Gabby don’t quite see eye-to-eye.”

“So, you are saying that the distillery should be in one of the outbuildings if I value peace and quiet," Kelly said.

“Probably,” Tim said, ruefully agreeing.

“I am not sure she is going to be enough help,” Kelly said.

“Don’t worry about that. If you get Gabby then you also get Bill. She also has a kid she has been bossing around like he is her own, personal property. The amazing thing is, the kid seems to like it,” Tim said. “Think of it as a package deal, three for the price of one.”

“Which kid?” Kelly asked. “I might know him.”

“He is new in the neighborhood. Moved here from Nashville about six months before things blew up. His name is Allen Hamilton,” Dmitri said. “He lives over by me.”

“Are you sure Kate won’t mind?” Kelly asked.

Dmitri rolled his eyes. “You will be preventing a homicide. Maybe two,” he said. “Gabby is like hot chilis, a little bit now and then is fine but not a steady diet.”

“If she is so much like hot chilies, then how does Bill stand her?” Kelly asked.

“Don’t be surprised if Bill is the first to volunteer to go in the woods and cut firewood or drive a truck," Tim said with a smile. "He figured out ways of coping and that means you will get a ton of work out of him."

"And the kid?" Kelly asked.

"If she tells him to stare at a thermometer for three hours then he won't move an inch for three hours. Or if she wants him to sweep a floor three times, one time after the other, he will do it without bitching," Tim said.

"How are you planning on paying for the booze?" Kelly asked. "It ain't like Kate is going to give me the cornmeal."

"That is the beauty of it," Dmitri said. "Tell Gabby what you need. Give her a recipe. Point her at the shed you are going to let her use, the corn field and woodlot, and get out of her way. Make sure you tell her where you want her to put the stuff she cleans out of the shed."

"Where is this corn coming from?" Kelly asked.

"Farmer Ken has 160 acres of corn he didn't pick because prices didn't even pay for the diesel to run the combine," Dmitri said. "Just let him know Gabby and company will be picking corn for a community project and Farmer Ken is fine with that. I am 99% sure Kate will grind it for free."

"How do I pay Gabby, Bill, and the kid?" Kelly asked.

"Tell them they get everything they produce over two gallons a day and they can sell it consignment at Kate's store," Tim said. He seemed to have thought of everything.

"And how about me, what is in it for me?" Kelly asked.

"We won't always need two gallons a day. You will give us what we need each day and the rest is yours," Tim said.

Karma is a Heat-Seeking Missile

It was a memorable day when the Prius pulled into Kate and

Rick's driveway. It was the second week of January and the worst of the weather seemed to be holding off.

Rick and Kate were both in the store but heard the dogs barking. Travel in motorized vehicles had become a rarity. Fuel was hard to find and there was really no place to go.

Walking out the door, Rick recognized the vehicle. The rear end was plastered with bumper stickers *du jure.* He only knew of one vehicle that matched that description: MT's, Kate's sister.

Walking over to the driver's door Rick noticed that she brought his two nieces, Mandy and Dysen. "I thought you decided to weather the storm in Lansing," he said.

In spite of polar opposite political views, they maintained a cordial relationship. Kate demanded it.

MT lived in a neighborhood close to downtown Lansing in an enclave of fellow "woke" residents. Yards were liberally plastered with rainbow flags and "Welcome" signs. MT felt very safe in that neighborhood.

"I thought I had decided that, too," she said.

Rick helped them carry their luggage into the house. There was very little of it. Rick was surprised. His sister-in-law and nieces were not "clothes horses" but they liked nice clothes and had, by his standards, very large wardrobes.

Rick said, "I will cover the store so Kate can come down and help you get settled in."

As good as his word, he told Kate who the visitors were.

"What happened?" Kate asked. She was much better at reading her sister's face than Rick was and knew that SOMETHING had triggered her sister's precipitous flight from her home of twenty years.

MT's face broke up and a sob escaped her. "We had a home invader."

"Are you OK?" Kate asked, immediately rushing over to hug her sister.

"Oh, yeah. We are OK. We were all at the food distribution center," MT said.

The story spilled out of her. To combat fraud, the State required that adults show up in person to collect their food allotment. MT and the girls waited almost three hours in line to collect enough food to last them three days. When they came home, they found the sliding glass doors that led to their deck had been kicked in and the house had been ransacked.

"I tried to call 9-1-1 but the cell service kept dropping out. I finally got through but all I got was a recording," MT said.

"A couple of the neighbors came over but they hadn't seen anything. That is when they told me that my house was not the first in the neighborhood to get hit," MT said.

"They took the safe I keep documents in. They took a gun that Fred left," MT said. Fred was her former, unlamented ex. MT had never even lifted the gun. MT and her daughters were diminutive and the gun was a semi-auto shotgun with a 30" goose barrel. To them, it seemed as long as a telephone pole.

"What did you do then?" Kate asked.

"We threw together some clothes and came out here. I tried to call but the cell phones..." MT's voice trailed off.

"I get that," Kate said. "It seems like nothing is working the way it used to."

Kate was running out of places to put guests.

After thinking about the problem for a bit, Kate texted Mrs

Heiler, the elderly woman whose move to Lansing was the catalyst that crystallized the idea of opening a store in Kate's mind.

"Good Afternoon, Mr. and Mrs Heiler. This is Kate Salazar from Eaton Rapids."

"Hello Kate!" Mary Heiler texted back.

"Do you expect to come back to Eaton Rapids anytime soon?" Kate asked.

"Nope. We are settled in here," Mary Heiler texted.

"I found somebody who wants to house-sit for you. A woman and her two, grown-up daughters," Kate said. "They would make sure the roof didn't leak and the raccoons and possum didn't move in."

"LOL." Mary Heiler texted back. "Are they neat and tidy people?"

"Very neat and tidy," Kate

"Sounds good," Mary Heiler texted back. "The key is under the cranes on the patio."

And just like that the deed was done. MT, Mandy and Dysen were going to quarantine in the Heiler house.

Rick was not sure how MT, Mandy and Dysen would adapt to the Heiler's house. It had been built in the late 1920s. It was a small, one-story house and had inexpensive paneling, wainscoting, worn Formica countertops, linoleum, and icicle plastered ceilings.

MT's house in Lansing was a massive Darius Moon house and had elegant wall treatments, granite countertops, hardwood floors that were so deeply finished that they seemed to glow from within and Italianate plastered ceilings. Rick was not sure how the family was going to adapt to their new surroundings.

Talking with Mandy, MT's 23-year-old daughter a week later when he dropped off their food, he found they had taken to it like ducks to water.

Mandy did not have a clutch between her brain and her mouth. Rick had no doubt that the voluble stream of words gushing from her mouth was the simple, unedited truth...as she saw it.

Both Mandy and Dysen had attended the local Catholic high school. They had gone on mission trips to West Virginia and the Mississippi Delta during their spring breaks. The Heiler house was POSH compared to the trailers and houses they had gutted, wired and re-drywalled on those trips.

Mandy then went on to tell a story of one of the chaperones who planted a large rubber snake in the wall of one of the shotgun shacks they were refurbishing. He tied a length of monofilament fish line to the snake's head and handed a rattle to another student. Then he called the one student who had been a source of misery the entire trip. The chaperone directed the pr!ck-of-misery to reach in and "clean the dirt out of the crack before they sealed it with expanding foam."

For some reason, every person the Richard-head had bruised happened to be within ear-shot.

Mandy's laughter was the shimmery jingle of a hundred silver sleigh bells as she shared how she had always thought the term "crap your pants" was hyperbole, at least that is what she thought until the "snake" rattled and jumped out and bit the nattering nabob of negativity.

Mark Delays

Mark was selling SUVs at the dealership right up until columns of oily, black smoke were rising from downtown Portsmouth. Customers were clamoring for get-out-of-Dodge vehicles, bidding them up to $10k, even $15k over list. Mark could not walk away.

He rushed home and started loading his SUV. He had his necessary stuff staged, sort of. It was a mad rush as he threw stuff into it.

Betsy, his wife objected to the four, long hard-cased packages and the heavy daypack. "Do we really need those?" Mark didn't grunt when he tossed in the daypack but he needed two hands to lift and pitch it in.

"They don't take up that much room," Mark said.

Betsy already had the kid's stuff packed. She was the practical one. The fancy luggage was supplemented with bulky, winter clothing packed in double-up, plastic bags. The pile obstructed the rearview mirror but for once Mark did not object.

The final two items he added were two, five-gallon jugs of gas.

"Oh! Really Mark? Do you realize how dangerous that is? And it will stink up the interior," Betsy said.

Mark took the gas cans out. Somebody would undoubtedly steal them but Betsy was right. The last thing he needed was to be asphyxiated.

Driving, Mark said, "I want you to plot a course on the GPS that keeps us away from towns of 50,000 or more."

"That will take us off the freeway," Betsy said.

"Yeah, I get that," Mark replied tersely. "Look out my side window."

Betsy looked to the east and saw flickering walls of flames where a posh mall used to be.

"How far away from towns?" Betsy asked.

"No closer than twenty miles," Mark said. "Or I want to leave the freeway at the first turn-off for the town and swing wide."

It is a thousand miles from Portsmouth, New Hampshire to Eaton Rapids, Michigan, if you cannot cut across Ontario, Canada. Picking secondary roads added another two-hundred miles and six hours to the drive time.

They gassed up outside of Canandaigua, New York. The SUV was a top-of-the-line Lexus and got great fuel economy but they were bucking the wind and pushing through two inches of snow which kept the all-wheel-drive busy.

The second time they stopped was in Bowling Green, Ohio. They were within two hours of Eaton Rapids but the fuel gage was dinging. Betsy was driving so Mark got out to pump.

Mark saw the men slide out from behind the shrubbery that screened off the back part of the building. He saw their baseball bats and tire irons.

Mark was trying to get a grip on the Glock he was carrying inside his waistband but he was stymied by his heavy, winter clothing.

He started hammering on the side of the SUV. "GO! GO! GO!"

Betsy had been in that zone one gets into when driving for hours and hours and hours. Due to the cold weather and the sleeping kids Betsy had left the motor running. The hammering on the side of the vehicle snapped her out of her tunnel vision.

She looked in her outside, rearview mirrors and saw the men converging on Mark.

Mark's voice brooked no ambivalence about what he wanted her to do.

Betsy might have looked fragile but she was the daughter of old New England. She had grandparents who had farmed granite ribbed hills through the depression. She had French-Canadian cousins named Ouellette who she had played hockey ... without facemasks. She had a bit of Portuguese fisherman in her as well as Greek boat builders. Betsy was made of granite, white oak planking and starch.

She dumped the transmission into Drive and hammered the gas pedal. One of the men tried to jump in front of her. She twitched the wheel at the last second in an attempt to miss him and the Lexus started to fishtail. She drifted into the man and the rear quarter of the Lexus batted him into the berm separating the gas station from the road.

At the "THUMP" her oldest child woke up, looked around and asked, "Where is Daddy?"

Looking back through the rearview mirror she saw the men pummeling Mark with their baseball bats.

She wiped the tears from her eyes and said, "Daddy told us to drive on to Grampaw's. Said he would join us later."

The SUV ran out of gas six miles south of Albion, thirty-five miles short of their destination.

Betsy and Mark

Betsy was able to get the Lexus to the side of the road before the motor stopped sputtering. She knew that it would have been almost impossible for her to muscle over without power steering.

She knew why it had stopped running. The nanny, Bitching Betty, warned her every minute of the low fuel status.

Betsy was not entirely sure where she was. The top-of-the-line SUV had a cloud-based GPS system. She had the GPS coordinates but the map was rudimentary as the internet had been shaky ever since crossing into Ohio four hours earlier.

The kids, Henry, age 9, and Cammi, 6, had awakened as the Lexus slowed and the brush scrubbed the side of the vehicle. "Are we there yet?" Henry asked.

"Not yet," Betsy said. She felt like crying but that would have to come later.

"What are we going to do?" Cammi asked.

"I am going to call Gramma or Grampa and get help," Betsy said.

There was no signal for calls but by standing on a pile of gravel thirty yards east of the road she was able to get one bar for data. She sent Kate and Rick a text. "Car problems. Need help," and she included a snapshot of the GPS coordinates displayed on the vehicles instrument cluster. 42.158112, -84.730938

She walked back to the vehicle and told the kids she needed to wait on the gravel pile for the return message. She told Cammi to get out of her car seat and to sit next to Henry. Then she took the blanket out of the back and tucked it around them. The part of New England she grew up in always had a 'got stuck' kit in back and the habit stayed with her.

Betsy got a return text in ten minutes. "What is the problem? Do you need a tow or is it fixable?"

Betsy texted back. "Ran out of gas."

Back in Eaton Rapids, Rick was perplexed. For one thing, he was a little bit surprised that Betsy was texting him, not Mark. The other thing that baffled him was Mark running out of gas. That was out-of-character. Still, things are what they are.

Rick texted back, "Sit tight. Working on getting help to you."

Then, as an afterthought he added "What is the security situation?"

Betsy replied "Grim. Mark MIA." Betsy was not one to waste words.

That lit a fire under Rick.

He was frantic when he called Kelly on the CB. Kelly calmed him down and said he would be right over.

The plan was a quickly thrown together.

Two trucks, one with a tow-bar. Luke in the bed of the lead truck looking forward. Janelle in the trailing truck keeping an eye aftward. Since both were right-handed, that meant Luke was optimally positioned to suppress threats to the left while Janelle would be best positioned to suppress threats to the right of the direction-of-travel.

They took five gallons of gas, gas which was getting very hard to come by.

It took sixty minutes to cover the thirty miles. Betsy was shivering. They poured in the five gallons of gas and the Lexus started.

The convoy returned to Eaton Rapids with the Lexus sandwiched between the two escort vehicles.

Betsy chivied her children into the safety of their grandparent's home.

Seeing Kate, Betsy dissolved into tears.

***

Mark had wrestled in high-school and the Coast Guard trained him in the manly art of subduing unruly smugglers or drunks. But there is little he could do with three men hitting him with baseball bats and kicking him. The best he could do was to try and roll with the hits.

Even that proved futile when the fourth man joined the attack. A kick to the head left him stunned.

After beating him senseless, the men took his Glock, wallet, cell phone and watch. Then the leader directed one of the men to shoot Mark.

"But don't kill him. None of us want to drag his sorry ass out of sight," the leader said.

Mark was shot with his own handgun.

The man gut-shot Mark. Or so he thought. Mark was lean and fit; his coat was a high-end goose down parka and very fluffy.

The 115-grain hollow point skived a ¾ inch deep groove just below his bottom rib.

Mark grunted. Hunched over, he lurched away from the shooter, around the berm and out of sight.

Nobody followed him. They went back into hiding, waiting for the next vehicle to come into the gas station.

After a hundred yards, Mark's breaths were coming in gasps. He leaned against a wall and blinked to get the tears out of his eyes. He had trouble focusing. Later, he would determine it was due to a concussion.

He knew he was in a world of hurt. He knew, rather he hoped, Betsy would not come back. She needed to get to Eaton Rapids. He would deal with the hand he was dealt.

He straightened up. He tried to look tough. He walked another hundred yards. Damn! His side hurt. It was hard to breath.

Looking around, he saw he was in an area with many strip-mall type buildings. Seeing one that appeared to be a looted convenience store, and thinking, *Why didn't I see this before we pulled into the gas station?*, he stepped through the broken display window and looked for something to bandage himself with.

They say duct tape can fix anything. Mark used some bottled Diet RC cola to repeatedly wash out the gouge in his side. The acidic drink hurt but everything else had been pillaged, even the water. At least the diet pop was sterile. Then Mark put a pad made of coffee filters over the wound and bound it with duct tape.

Mark also repaired the holes in his parka with duct tape. Redneck chic.

Mark's head exploded in pain as he stepped outside, into the light. Eaton Rapids was forty miles west and sixty miles north of where he stood.

He started walking.

~End of Seven Fat Cows~

PART II:

SEVEN SKINNY COWS

CHAPTER ONE

Any Port in a Storm

Mark walked to the west. From his memory, he knew that heading north would take him into Toledo and urban areas. Based on what he had seen he had no desire to go there.

Bowling Green, Ohio, was a college town twenty miles south of Toledo. The town had grown up into seemingly endless rows of townhouses and strip malls. The students were fodder for the greatest wealth extraction scheme since the Conquistadors pillaged the Aztecs. The student's future lifetime earnings were being strip-mined via student loans as they blithely moved into new housing crammed with spas, fitness centers, cable and other amenities that raised the monthly rent to exactly the maximum allowed by the Student Loan Administration.

Mark was in a cold sweat within a mile and was staggering in two more. A trip through another looted convenience store netted him two bottles of Gatorade, a couple small jars of peanut butter and a roll of paper towels.

Just before leaving the built-up area Mark saw a Jo Anne's Fabric and pilfered a bolt of polyester micro-fleece in medium brown.

He spent the night sleeping sitting up in shelter a parent had built near the road for their children to use while waiting for the bus.

Mark had a fever the next day and could only manage another three miles. He was reduced to dipping the now-empty Gatorade bottles into ditches to collect water. That led to Montezuma's Revenge.

Between his shivering and walking he was burning through 5000 Calories a day. Said another way, he was losing a pound-and-a-half of body weight every day and he was only averaging five miles a day.

Seven days later, he hit the wall. He was walking across the flat-as-a-billiards-table farmlands of northwestern Ohio. The weather turned cold and the wind picked up.

He snuck into a hen house to snitch some eggs and passed out.

***

Rosie came back into the house and said, "Gram, there is a man sleeping in the hen house."

Rosie was eight and her parents stashed her with her grandparents for the duration. Gram and Grumpy were glad to have her.

Doreen Cowper (pronounced "Cooper") yelled back into the breakfast nook, "William! Rosie says there is a man sleeping in the hen house. Can you look into that?"

William had just tucked into one of his wife's inordinately large cinnamon rolls, the ones she made by rolling them around slices of Idared apples from the tree out back.

"I'll git to it after breakfast," William said. His nickname was Grumpy for a reason.

"Maybe he will have run off by the time I finish my second cup of coffee," William said.

"I think you should go now," Doreen said as she poked her

head into the nook. "He might need looking after."

"Yeah, and he might have Ebola," Grumpy said, licking the frosting off his fingers.

"You know, a kid listening to you might think you were just a selfish old man," Doreen said.

Grumpy put on his overcoat and boots with ill grace, stomping around and muttering. It was a show, of course.

Doreen gave him a kiss. "I'll give you a new roll when you get back...with extra icing if you want."

Sure enough, there was a man sleeping in the hen house. He was on a pile of new straw.

Unless Grumpy missed his guess, the dude's clothing was top-end. Grumpy was not familiar with any of the brands but then Doreen did nearly all of his clothes shopping at Walmart and Tractor Supply Company.

The man was so skinny that Grumpy could see the sutures in his skull. There were a few, fading bruises on his head but nothing like the huge blood blisters the TV stations had shown before Ebola took them off line.

Grumpy also took in the bloody goose-down parka and the duct tape repair. Looking more closely at the man he found the source of the fecal odor, the back of the man's trousers were wet with diarrhea.

The man was breathing and Grumpy figured the man was not a total loser. At least he had the sense to shut the door behind him or Grumpy would have been chasing his chickens all the way to Archibold.

"Well, I reckon we better clean you up out here if you are going to be presentable to the ladies," Grumpy said talking to himself.

He walked the seventy-five feet back to the kitchen door.

"Sure enough, there is a man in the hen-house. Looks like he needs tending to," Grumpy announced like it had been his idea all along.

"He has been pretty short on vittles. Don't suppose you would whip up a mug of hot chocolate while I find him some clean clothes to change into," Grumpy said.

"Just bring him in here," Doreen commanded.

"Umm, I can't. He is...dirty," Grumpy said.

"I changed diapers before and we will make sure his private parts are covered before Rosie sees him," Doreen said. Then, after having second thoughts, "I will give you that mug of hot chocolate. He might need a few minutes to work up the strength to walk in here."

Doreen's Uncle Billy had been in Bataan during WWII. She had an inkling of what she might be getting into.

The man slowly sipped the cup of hot, sugary chocolate. Then he asked for another. An hour after Grumpy woke him, he was able to wobble his way to the kitchen door, leaning on Grumpy the whole way.

Helping Mark undress, Grumpy did not comment on the brown fleece wound around his trunk nor on the dozens of plastic grocery bags Mark had stuffed beneath his parka and down his trousers for insulation.

"Tsk, tsk, tsk," when he saw the bullet wound. It had mostly scabbed over but was still weeping fluid where it was deepest.

"Cop?" Grumpy asked.

"Nope. Muggers," Mark replied. Then Mark vomited up the hot chocolate.

Doreen figured out that Mark could hold down half-strength chicken noodle soup. After he had some liquid and some salt in him, he could hold down almost anything.

Outside, the iron grip of the most brutal winter in recent memory clamped down on the upper mid-West.

LP Gas

Jean Fect walked into Kate's store. She was slow in closing the outside door and everybody in the store noticed the frigid, early January wind.

Jean stumped up to the counter where Luke was standing and demanded "You need to sell me two hundred gallons of LP gas."

Luke said, "We don't sell LP gas."

"Yes you do. I seen your tanks outside," Jean contradicted.

Kate had been accepting partially filled LP tanks in payment for food and other necessary items. The tank's valves were turned off, the plumbing disconnected and then Kelly or Milo carted them to Kate's store. Kate had also contacted the families who had moved out of the neighborhood and got permission to "borrow" the LP and heating oil in the tanks.

The neighbors tolerated what would have been seen as heavy-handed if done by anybody else because Kate did not charge them for the fuel and she was rock-solid honest in how she metered it out.

"I think you need to talk to my mother," Luke said.

"MOM!" Luke called back.

Kate came out of a back room, discretely trailed by Ms Sheridan.

"Hello Jean," Kate said. "What can I do for you today?"

"You need to sell me a tank full of LP gas," Jean Fect said. She was happy to be dealing with the boss.

"I'm sorry," Kate said. "That gas is not for sale."

"They why do you have it?" Jean asked.

Kate said. "Cooking. We fill up five-gallon tanks and allow each family to have one every two months."

"Do you have a five-gallon tank?" Kate asked.

"Five gallons won't do me any good. I heat my house with LP," Jean said.

"Then you have a problem," Kate said. "Are your pipes freezing?" she asked.

"Not yet. We are all the way down to 67 degrees so it won't be long," Jean said, playing for pity.

Kate's eyes darted to the digital thermometer beside the cash register. It showed 61 degrees.

"What do you normally keep it at?" Kate asked. "...all the way down to 67..." implied they kept it toasty warm.

"We keep it at 77," Jean said. "As you know, Jerry is diabetic and has poor circulation."

Kate could not resist, "Didn't you notice there is an emergency going on and it might be hard to get fuel?"

"That is not my problem," Jean said. "Now, will you sell me the LP gas I need to keep Jerry alive?"

There were many things Jean and Jerry could have done. They could have kept one room warm. They could have put on warmer clothes. They could have heated up hot water bottles. But they did none of those things. Kate had little sympathy for them.

"The LP is not for space heating. There are mittens and

sweaters for sale in the consignment section," Kate said.

"You don't understand," Jean pleaded. "Jerry will die if he gets cold."

"I understand that," Kate said. "So, your job is to keep him warm. I can sell you mittens. I can sell you sweatshirts and vests and sweaters. I can sell you hats. I can sell you firewood.

"And I can give you information on how to deal with Type II Diabetes when medicine runs out," Kate said, pushing the sheet of paper across the counter.

"But I will not sell you LP gas for space heating," Kate said.

Jean balled up the sheet of paper and threw it at Kate. Then Jean stomped out of the store, muttering as she went.

Kate told Luke. "Follow her. Stop her if she heads toward the LP tanks."

"How?" Luke asked.

Kate opened the drawer beneath the cash register and pulled out a bottle of pepper spray. "Tell her to stop. If she doesn't, hose her down. Make sure you stay upwind," Kate said.

Jean veered away from the tank farm as Luke angled to cut her off. He had no idea what she planned on doing. Maybe she thought she could pull a 500-gallon tank home. More likely, she was mad and was going to open a valve and vent hundreds of gallons of LP to the atmosphere. If she couldn't use it then nobody would be able to.

A few hours after Jean left, Kate had a thought. She beckoned one of her "runners" as she thought of them.

"Hey kid," Kate said. "Don't suppose you would run over to Mike Kromitter and let him know I wanted to have a talk with him. Be worth a brownie to me."

Kate was no longer getting a steady supply of candy bars but most of the kids were very happy to run errands for a home-made brownie. Kate did not think the Health Department would be visiting any time soon.

An hour later Mike showed up. "You needed me?" he asked.

"Yeah. One of your neighbors was in. They ran out of LP and I don't think they are set up to heat with wood," Kate said.

"I don't suppose you could pay them a neighborly visit and check them out, could you?" Kate said.

Coming from Kate, that was almost a command.

"Yeah. I can pay them a visit." Mike was a fellow who truly cared for his fellow man. He was always willing to put his money where his mouth was. Or, these days, put sweat equity into helping the less fortunate. If there was a way to quickly convert Jean and Jerry's house to heating with wood, Mike would get it done. It certainly would not be the first he had converted in the last three months.

Mike came back the next day after lunch.

"I visited Jean and Jerry. You owe me," Mike said. "Big time."

"What happened?" Kate asked. The buzz in the rest of the store died down a little bit because entertainment was a scarce commodity.

"They called me everything but a human being," Mike said. "That woman can cuss like a sailor."

"They were all friendly until I said 'wood heat', then Jean lit into me," Mike said, shaking his head.

"That is not real bright, pissing off your neighbors," Kate said.

"I don't think they plan on being our neighbors for long. Eaton Rapids still has natural gas. They opened up the schools and churches for people to warm up. I think Jean and

Jerry plan on moving into town," Mike said.

"That is going to be a pretty neat trick, though," Mike said. "I hadn't seen Jerry in a while. He must weigh four hundred pounds."

The next day Kelly carted the Fect family to Eaton Rapids. They could not fit very much into the back of the truck and Kelly had better things to do than to move their household.

Seraph and Rick were still pounding out the details of the mutual reciprocity regarding clean vs. need to quarantine status. The Fects fell through the cracks and ended up in quarantine in the old school.

They were allocated four hundred square feet and the temperature was fifty-five.

For some reason nobody was motivated to respond to Jean's caterwauling that Jerry need to move back out to Kate's Store. Nobody had the time or energy for such nonsense.

Pray Church Store

"Mom," Luke said.

"What?" Kate said.

They were in the process of opening the store for the day.

"I listened to Mr. Hall's radio program the other day and I had a thought," Luke said.

"Hmm? What's that?" Kate asked. She was distracted as she re-arranged the clothing in the consignment area.

"I think I should open a store three or four miles north of here," Luke said.

Luke had all of Kate's attention, then.

"How did you get from Ed's program to wanting to open a store?" Kate said.

"Quarantines," Luke said. "About one in every seven customers is from outside of the neighborhood. Most of them are from north of here. If they had their own store it would cut way down on the traffic from there."

Then Luke said, "If we are serious about firewalling the various neighborhoods, we have to make them self-sufficient. That means each neighborhood needs its own store."

"And you want to be the guy that opens one?" Kate said.

"Yes," Luke said. "I worked in retail. I worked in a warehouse. I want to do this."

Luke felt hemmed in working for his mother. He was almost thirty. He had lived on his own. He had his own ideas.

"Just how would you go about that?" Kate asked. She was not challenging him. She wanted to know how his thoughts percolated through his brain.

"Pastor James came in yesterday. He was telling me about a pole barn and house that are available. They are exactly three miles north of here," Luke said, getting excited.

"The barn had cattle in it but one end of it has a concrete floor. It has a circular drive and is on the top of a hill, almost like here," Luke said.

Kate mentally measured out three miles in her head. "I know the property. It has a bunch of lilac bushes along the road," she said.

"Probably," Luke said.

Kate looked around at her store. She deliberately kept the shelves sparsely stocked. She would rather have less stock on the shelves and have it well displayed than to use her retail displays as warehousing. From a psychological standpoint, hinting at scarcity tended to prod buyers into purchasing "before supplies ran out."

"What would you need as far as stock to get started?" Kate asked.

Luke had a list. He pulled it out of his back pocket.

"I have been watching what the folk from Pray Church have been buying. It seems like they are buying things we were selling to our neighbors a month ago. Our neighbors were buying sleeping bags in early December and the folks from Pray Church are buying them now," Luke said.

Kate nodded. That made sense to her. It was easy for people living close by to purchase items and carry them home. Folks who lived farther away waited until they absolutely needed something before buying because transportation was a bitch.

Luke was a numbers guy. "I would love to see what we were selling last month and then take that as seed-stock to the new store," Luke said.

"How much?" Kate asked.

Luke knew that he was asking for a lot. "I think I could make it work if I took 1/3 of the merchandise we sold last month and then made arrangements to purchase more in the future."

Kate was not going to let him off easy. "What do the people in Pray Church have that folks in our neighborhood don't? They need to pay with something."

Luke looked at his mother like she was daft. "Mom, there is a dairy farm and a hog farm in that neighborhood. What would you pay for a young dairy cow? How about a sow that was about to farrow?"

Kate knew that Luke had thought this through. She had no objections. In fact, she had so many helpers that they tripped over each other.

“If I agree, when would you start?” Kate asked.

“No time like the present,” Luke said.

Kate pointed at the office computer. “Once we get going you will find daily summaries of what we sold on that computer. I hope you don’t mind if it is in Excel spreadsheets. It what your dad set up and it was easy to keep going.”

By noon, Luke had a detailed list of what he proposed taking.

Kate looked over the list and doubled most quantities. It would come close to wiping her out of some items but she stored most of her stock off-site. The grain was in Milo’s containerized cargo boxes and standing in the farmers’ fields. Ammo and firearms were at Tim’s. Beer and vodka were in Kelly’s barn and so on.

The one thing she really regretted sending was her last grain grinder. Gabriella had been quick to grab two of them. Kate understood Gabby (Grabby was a family nick-name) because she needed to grind grain for the still but Gabby had to explain the second one.

It did not take long for Gabby’s operation to exceed the two-gallon-a-day target for 180 proof spirits, primarily because Kelly sized everything for three gallons. Gabby looked around for another use for ethanol and she decided to start solvent extracting soybean oil. To extract the oil, she had to grind the beans.

The only thing she crossed off Luke’s list was firewood. She had twenty face-cords of “small” wood stacked up against the building. Her reasoning was that Luke would be swimming in firewood as soon as he opened for business so there was no sense shipping wood. It was heavy and bulky.

It took two long days for Milo to move Luke’s stock. Milo

gave him the family discount. That is, Milo did not charge Luke.

Luke was stumped for a name. He wanted to call it KSN for Kate's Store, North but that never took off. The locals all called it Pray Church Store.

Luke took in a lot of trade right from the very first day. Much of what he took for "money" in the beginning was shelving and tubs.

CHAPTER TWO

Duckworth Smirked

Dan Nestle knew he was a very lucky man.

He derived great satisfaction from his job. Other people considered him a "tool". Dan simply knew that most people were punished for bullying people. He got paid to do it.

Dan was in the lead vehicle of the convoy that was visiting hate-crime sites in the boonies. Dan's buddy, Norm Contrares was in the trailing vehicle. Between them was a bus and seven box trucks to "collect evidence."

Pulling into the third site of the day, Dan dismounted and served the warrant.

The woman was older than most of the folks he had been dealing with on this assignment. She blocked his entrance into the building while she read the warrant. That pissed him off. It was cold outside.

"This warrant was issued in Ingham County. This is Eaton County. I don't accept this warrant," and she handed it back.

Dan remained standing. He had not had that happen before.

"Look, ma-am, I got a job to do," Dan said.

"And what would that be?" the woman said.

"What it said in the warrant," Dan said. Fortunately, he had been paying attention when the suits at the Attorney General office had given the morning prep session.

The woman raised an eyebrow.

"There have been reports of hate crimes. I am here to 'confiscate materials used in the commission of hate crimes.' I am here to 'collect evidence of the crime of hoarding.' I am to give you a receipt for the materials and then I am to 'assess the site's potential to be an attractive nuisance and to take steps to remedy the risk'," Dan said.

"We have not committed any 'hate crimes' here" Kate said. "We have not been convicted of any 'hate crimes' so how can you claim we have materials used to commit hate crimes?"

Dan hated women, especially mouthy ones who challenged his authority and twisted his words. Dan was a simple straight-ahead kind of guy.

Norm had finished dismounting the crew. The crew consisted of Dan, Norm, twenty 'gunners' and ten strong backs.

"Ma-am. You can either move out of the way or we will move you," Dan said. He was sweating a little bit because the sound of the convoy's diesel engines had alerted the neighborhood that something unusual was up. The crowd pulled back as the 'gunners' came out of the bus.

The gunners were wearing Kevlar helmets, body armor and were carrying AR-15s with magazines inserted. Five of the gunners were so goofy that Dan insisted that the magazines be empty, but the rest were carrying live ammo.

Dan almost hoped there was an incident. Dan had buddies who were ready to edit any video evidence they collected from the cameras they wore on their body armor. His buddies guaranteed that gun-shots would be dubbed in before his crew raised their weapons.

Dan's concerns about an 'incident' was based on the fact that most of his gunners had been pressed into service from the Secretary of State and Department of the Treasury.

Most of the crowd from the neighborhood knew a thing or two about firearms. The lack of muzzle discipline gave them the heebie-jeebies. This was clearly a Keystone Kops operation and they had little confidence that there would not be an accidental discharge. The more prudent members of the community moved back a solid fifteen paces.

A few of the more foolish members, including Carson Duckworth, crowded closer even as most of the watchers moved back.

As soon as Dan had three of his more reliable gunners backing him up, Dan took great pleasure in grabbing the old lady by her forearm and giving it a big yank, causing her to tumble down the two steps leading up to the porch.

Then he and his three henchmen went inside the building and tossed out the remaining customers and employees.

Rick Salazar, Kate's husband, and Nyssa showed up about a minute after Dan went into the building.

Based on the crowd's response, Norm had half the gunners re-orient to low-ready to address Rick and Nyssa.

The last person pitched out of the front door was Ms Sheridan and she was as frenzied as a cat that had been dunked in ice water.

Kate brought Rick and Nyssa up-to-date with developments as the 'strong backs' started carrying the radio station equipment out of Kate's store.

The strong backs did not stop with the equipment. They carried out bags of grain, jugs of vegetable oil, 2-stroke oil for chainsaws, sleeping bags....and loaded the loot into the box trucks.

Nyssa had been watching the men working and something clicked in her head.

Nyssa had torn her ACL in her senior year of high school. Rather than sit on the bench and watch the varsity play soccer, Nyssa helped the JV coach with the younger athletes.

The JV coach had delegated the “subbing” to Nyssa so the coach could focus on strategy and tactics.

Because Nyssa studied the girls, she became very skilled at seeing which girls were gassed, which ones were ‘on strike’ and had stopped trying. Nyssa could see when a shoe need retying, a blister was forming or a strained muscle needed ice.

Then as she navigated through life she found she had a gift where she could watch somebody’s gait...even if they were one hundred yards away...and tell if there was something wrong with them.

Obviously, this trait is in every person because predators rely on it to select which member of the herd to chase. Nyssa had been gifted with the trait in a very high degree and then had reason to develop it.

Nyssa quickly sensed that at least three of the ‘strong backs’ were sick. Very, very sick. Looking more closely Nyssa saw that the skin beneath their collars was the color of raw meat. Blood blisters.

Looking at the ‘shooters’ Nyssa could tell that several of them seemed exceptionally listless, even as they had nothing to do but stand there.

Nyssa walked over to her dad as he was comforting Kate.

“Dad: I have the ping-pong paddles. Take mom inside and insist she take a hot shower with lots of soap,” Nyssa said.

I have the ping-pong paddles was family code alluding to the signal corpsman guiding pilots onto aircraft carriers. It was code for *I have better information than anybody else. Trust me.*

Then Nyssa walked over to Ms Sheridan who was about to get butt-stroked by a very frustrated Dan Nestle.

Nyssa whispered something into Ms Sheridan's ear.

Stacy Sheridan recoiled in distaste. She spat on Dan's boots, turned and stalked away.

The last thing Dan Nestle did was to have his strong backs break all of the windows in the structure, slosh ten gallons of gasoline on the floor and walls and to toss a lighted newspaper in through the front door.

Then they stood by to ensure the structure became fully engulfed before they left.

Nyssa asked Milo to move the closest spectators away from the fire. She did not want to have to treat any of them for burns or smoke inhalation.

Milo went around to the seven or so who did not have the brains to give the thugs and the fire a wide berth.

“OK, Duckworth, shows over. Time to move away,” Milo said.

“Not quite, Talon. In fact, I was thinking of getting marshmallows and weeners," Duckworth said with a smirk. “Too bad. It was a nice business. But that is what happens when you piss off the wrong people.”

Nestle and his crew got back into their vehicles. Nestle had done his job and had enjoyed it. He knew he was a very lucky man, especially when he had all the information he needed from the 1-888-462-3465 Report All Hoarding number.

Battle of Slocum Drain

Paul Seraph was just finishing up his meeting with the river development committee.

Eaton Rapids is blessed with two, very small hydro-electric plants. One is in the middle of town and the other is a mile-and-a-half southeast of downtown. One of the critical items in the development plan was to flesh out a plan to protect the power lines from the outlying hydro turbine.

The other developing issue was to have a plan in place to harvest the maximum amount of protein out of the Grand River as possible. There are twenty miles of open river downstream of Eaton Rapids. Fish that migrated upstream to spawn would stack-up at the State Street and Spring Brook dams. There had to be a fair way to give everybody access to the resource.

Paul's next meeting that morning involved "precincting" Eaton Rapids into self-policing sub-units. The leading citizens in East, North, Downtown, and Southwest were waiting outside the conference room when Paul got the call on his portable CB.

"Hey, Paul. Something is happening in Kate's Store. I think it might be important," the caller on the other end informed Paul.

Paul exited the meeting. The secretary would handle closing the meeting. It was not the first time Paul left a meeting early.

Paul retreated to a corner and tried to connect with Gladys in Kate's Store and was met with a barrage of calls and people stepping on each other. Remembering Kate's Store protocols, he tuned in to 37 and met another impenetrable thicket of jibber-jabber. That got his attention.

He dialed up to 41 and encountered moderately heavy traffic. He was able to cut in. "This is Paul Seraph in Eaton Rapids. Can somebody connect with me on channel 7 and give me a quick update?" Paul said.

Channel 7 was Paul's "native" channel.

One of the voices said. "Yup. Just give me a minute."

Paul turned the channel selector to channel seven and waited.

In a minute he got the call. "Hey Paul, got your ears on? This is Kelly Carney."

"Yeah. I hear you fine. What's going on?" Paul said.

"Bunch of thugs got the drop on us," Kelly said. "They showed up in Humvees and box trucks. They are wearing uniforms that look like Michigan State Police and Ingham County Sheriff uniforms. Said they were 'supplementary' troopers."

As a point of fact, Eaton Rapids is in Eaton County and warrants issued in Ingham County have no standing, even if the Lansing, the state capital happens to be in Ingham county.

"They are stripping Kate's store of everything that is not nailed down," Kelly said.

Paul looked at the clock. It read 2:15 in the afternoon. There were more than three hours of light left.

The geography around Kate's store was very defensible. That meant that there was little point in riding to the rescue if the bad guys already had possession of the high ground. Three hours of light meant that they would finish up at Kate's Store and then push into Eaton Rapids city. That was not something Paul would tolerate.

"Thanks for the heads up," Paul said. "I know you have a lot of balls you are keeping in the air, but if there is any chance you could tip me off if they turn south after leaving...the information will be very much appreciated.

“Is there anything else I ought to know?” Paul was effective because he knew there was ALWAYS more to the story.

"Yeah," Kelly said. “Word is going around that Nyssa saw blood blisters on at least three of the thugs. Sure-as-hell they are infected.”

That certainly changed the complexion of things.

Paul shooed the Water Resources board out and ushered in the next group.

“The shit is hitting the fan at Kate’s store, right now, even as we speak,” Paul said. “Sure as God made little green apples, they are going to come this way when they are done. That means we are going to meet them at Slocum’s drain.”

Then Paul started issuing directions.

◆ ◆ ◆

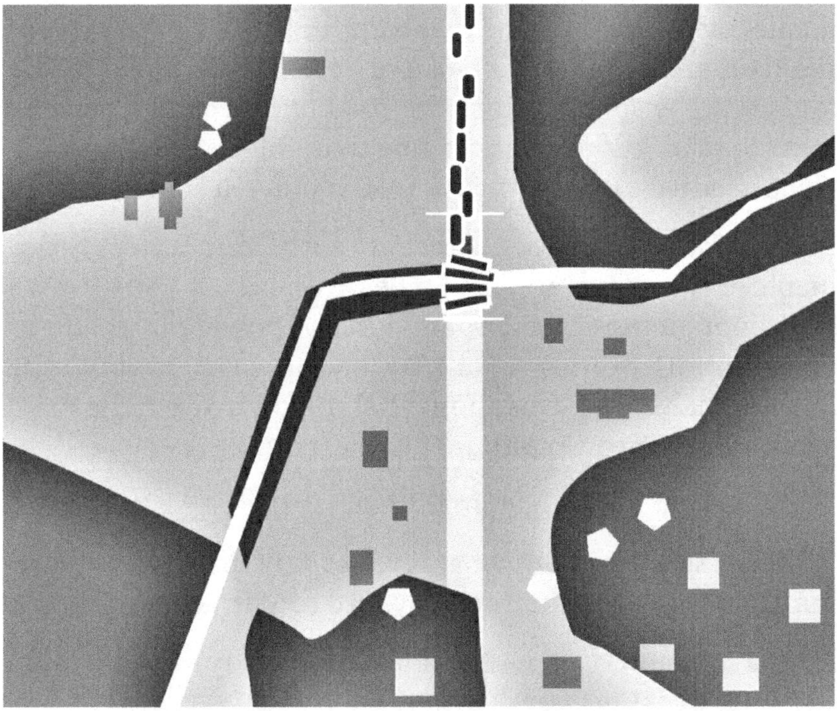

Thick vertical line is road, opposing forces coming from the north. Broad "S" line is drain. Light pentagons are shooters. Brackets beside road are guard rails on bridge over drain, not shown. Black 'sticks' across road at bridge are maple logs. Oblongs on road north of bridge are Humvees, the bus, and trucks, ten total. Distance from south shooters to trucks 270 yards. Distance from west shooters to trucks 100 yards.

"Ray, you have the list of shooters. Get a hold of them. I want at least two shooters west of the bridge over Slocum's Drain and as many shooters as you can stack on the ridge south of Slocum's Drain."

"Tell the shooters to bring a full load-out of ammo. Laser the ranges. I want full magazines and a round in the chamber and the weapon safed. We will use channel eleven to coordinate the shooters," Paul said. "Go!" and Paul gave Ray a brisk swat on the ass.

"Dale," Paul said. "We are going to see if your idea for spinning the logs works. Get it done."

Dale had come up with the idea of balancing large, straight

maple logs on blocks. The logs were aligned on both sides of the road and parallel with it. Dale claimed that the maple logs could be spun to close the road. When critics said the logs could be just as easily swung to un-block the road, Dale responded that logging chains would prevent that.

Dale demonstrated his concept with four, twenty-foot maple logs that averaged 24 inches in diameter. A single man could not swing them but any kind of powered vehicle or two men with pry-bars could. Oh, and he was right about the logging chains. Paul was about to shut down one of the main arteries into Eaton Rapids.

“Rachel, what am I forgetting?” Paul said.

“I am not sure, boss. But what is to stop them from just backing up and trying a different way into town?” Rachel asked.

After a moment of thought, Paul called Willy's Auto Repair. "Hey, Justin, is Chernovsky there with you?"

"Yah,” came back Justin's slow, laconic drawl. "No customers. We were just sitting here drinking stale coffee and countin' dead flies."

"Hey, Chernovsky, do you want a chance to prove you are as big a bad-ass as you tell everybody you are?" Paul asked.

"Beats being bored,” Chernovsky said. "Whatchya have in mind."

"Meet me on the ridge just above the water-plant,” Paul said. "Easier to show you than tell you."

An hour and a half later Paul was standing at the log barricade that made the bridge across Slocum’s Drain impassible. Soft mud to the east and west made bypassing the bridge unlikely for the Humvees and impossible for the trucks.

Paul waited as the convoy whined its way south. He had a ten-minute heads-up because Kelly had given him a call.

Paul used the time for a few last-minute tweaks to the plan.

The lead vehicle went right up to the barricade and tried to push through it. The vehicles behind the lead vehicle packed in tightly behind it. Paul thought that was particularly dumb move on the part of the convoy leadership.

A man got out of the passenger side of the lead Humvee.

"Clear this bridge," the man demanded from the other side of the maple logs.

Paul beckoned the man to the west side of the road. "Come here."

The man said, "You come here."

"I ain't moving. You wanna talk, you gotta come here," Paul said.

The man strutted to the logs, looked them over and realized it would be impossible for him to maintain his dignity climbing over the filthy logs.

The man had to negotiate the blockade by traversing the steep slope outside the guard-rail as the maple logs and logging chain also made the road impassible to humans. His shoes were not well suited for the task.

Paul met the man before he climbed back up to the level of the road grade. "State your business," Paul said.

"I have warrants to serve," the man said.

"Let me see them," Paul said.

The man handed the warrants to Paul. Paul was nonplussed to see that he was the subject of one of the warrants and the other warrant "impounded as evidence" all of the liquid petroleum fuel of the convenience store on the north end of town.

"I'll take care of it," Paul said. And then Paul very provocatively balled up the documents and pitched them into the drain.

"Waste of time, hay-seed," the man said. "I can always print up more. Now, you either move these trees out of my fucking way or I will jam them up your ass."

Being called a "hay-seed" shouldn't have irritated Paul, but it did. What the pompous ass could not know was that as a former police officer from Dearborn Heights, Paul spent most of his career patrolling neighborhoods less them five miles from the Brooks and Mackenzie neighborhoods of Detroit and exactly five miles from Dearborn, home of ISIS-North America. Evil does not respect invisible lines on a map.

"I suggest you turn your clown parade around and return to whatever hole you crawled out of," Paul said, icily.

"You and what army?" the man said.

Paul had been running his mic hot. The shooters were deployed in two-man teams. When they needed to communicate team-to-team, one of the team could easily switch to another channel.

"The army that is about to shoot out your hazard lamps," Paul said in a simple, conversational voice. "Men, on the third blink starting...NOW."

The cocky man could not help but turn and look. He was sure that the skinny, old man standing in front of him was bull shitting. Waiting another three seconds would not change the outcome in any material way.

In three seconds, thunder rolled across the north side of Eaton Rapids. The teams had been deployed along the brow of a ridge that gave them forty feet of elevation looking out over Slocum Drain. The laser range finders indicated that the "targets" were two-hundred, sixty-five yards from the shooter's positions.

Shooting from a bench-rest, most competent shooters with a modern, scoped rifle can turn in a two-inch group at a hundred yards more than half the time. Sure, every once in a while, they will luck into a one-inch group but realistically you cannot count on that.

Paul's defense group were not shooting off sand-bags and bench rests. They had hurried to the site and some of them were still huffing and puffing. Two inches in one hundred yards would be five inches at 260. The fire teams fell woefully short of that mark. Most of the first volley missed the hazard lamps, as did the most of the second, third, fourth and fifth volley. Cumulatively, though, most of the hazard lamps were disabled by the fifth volley.

What Paul had not anticipated were the effects of the high-powered bullets after they passed through the cheap plastic and thin metal on the front end of the trucks.

The hunters brought 30-06s and .270s and 7mm and .338 Magnums; rifles capable of taking moose, bison and brown bears. The bullets blew up automotive hardware near and behind the hazard lamps. They exploded batteries and punched through firewalls. In one case a bullet shattered the right kneecap of one of the drivers.

One hunter was careless with his trigger finger and launched a round that ricocheted off the pavement near Paul and whined off over the horizon.

The lack of expertise in execution was more than masked by the enthusiasm with which it was delivered.

The electronics on the vehicles with the damaged batteries started acting "weird". Motors raced. Dashboards burned out.

"I got thirty men in those trucks," the man sputtered. "What is to stop me from lighting your men up?"

The impact of the man's challenge was deflated by the shrieks of pain from the driver whose kneecap had been hit by a round from one of the magnums.

"Teams on the west, shoot out their side windows and rear tail lamps," Paul said.

The teams on the west were a scant 100 yards away and had thirty feet of elevation on the targets. They took care to ensure that the drivers were not immediately downrange when they aimed for the side windows.

Drivers were showered with glass splinters as side windows exploded. Bullets hit windshields from the inside and split them asunder. The men in the bus cowered as bullets ripped through the rear end after striking the tail .

"You know, I ought to..." was what the man intended to say but he found himself pushed up against the bridges guard rail with the muzzle of a pistol jammed up into the juncture of his chin and throat. The pain was breath-taking.

Paul never found out what the strutting peacock though he ought to do.

Many men carry handguns. Most of them carry semi-automatics. Most semi-automatics have a "rail" beneath the barrel to mount accessories. Most men mount lights or lasers on that rail. Paul Seraph had "Dilyeu's Dork" mounted on the rail of his SIG 229.

"Shut. The. Fuck. Up," Paul said, enunciating very carefully into his ear. "Get your sorry ass into your clown car and go back to whatever hole you crawled out of."

***

Paul's instructions to Chernovsky had been clear. "I want you to set up at the S-curves north of town. I want you to disable or kill the vehicles but I want you to do it in a way that gets them to get as far away from Eaton Rapids as possible before they puke. The last thing I want is for those infected to walk back here.

"That is why I picked you. You are a mechanic," Paul said.

"S" curves are common on north-south country roads. Some of them are due to the lack of precision in older surveying methods. Most of them are due to the fact that it is not possible to lay a grid of square-miles on a sphere. The curvature of the earth's surface adds up and it must be reconciled every 30 miles or so.

Paul had given Chernovsky his own, personal AR. Chernovsky slinged it up and rode his mountain bike the mile north of town to the S curve.

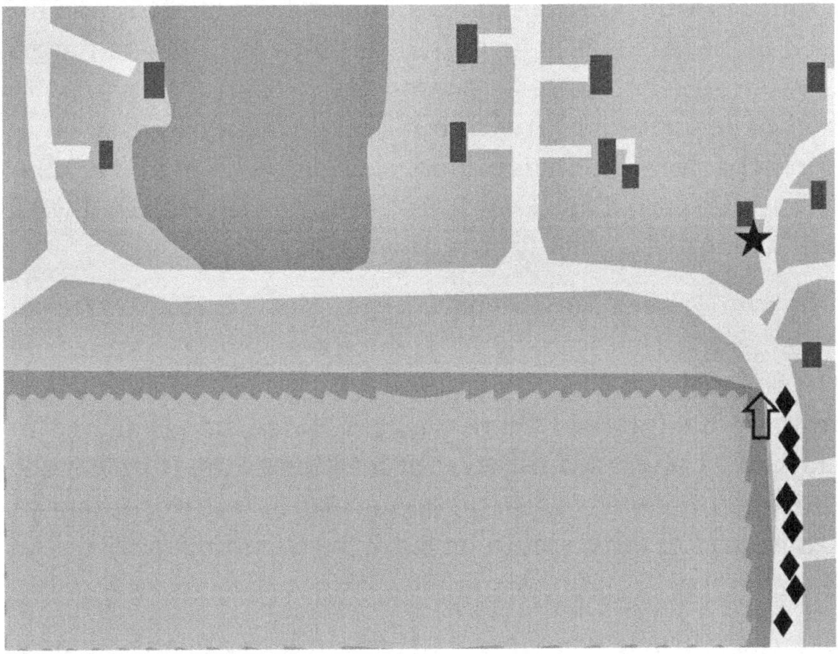

Chernovsky counted ten vehicles that passed his position as they headed into Eaton Rapids. Thirty rounds in the magazine. Even a gym-rat like Chernovsky could do that math. Paul had given him two magazines but Chernovsky didn't want to dick around with changing out magazines when he needed to be shooting.

The first driver heard the shots and saw the muzzle flashes as he entered the first S-curve.

The driver was not a soldier. He was a truck driver with the Department of Management and Budget. He delivered copy paper, carpet, desks and such. The closest he came to crime was when he trucked evidence to the vaults. He did what any bureaucrat motivated by forty easy hours a week and a pension that was almost within his grasp would have done. He floored the gas pedal.

The other drivers followed his lead.

Chernovsky put three rounds into each radiator. He kept the rounds low because Seraph said his rifle was dialed in to hit two inches high at fifty yards. Chernovsky hit the radiators low because he wanted to completely drain the engine. He had never done the math, but there was a one-chance in three that any one of his bullets would sever one of the tubes in the radiator. The other 2/3s of the space was filled with fins which did not carry coolant.

The two Tahoes did not have heavy-duty transmission oil coolers and there was a 70% chance of being disabled by the three shots. The box trucks and bus had discrete transmission coolers and there was a 90% chance that one of the three bullets would sever at least one tube in either the radiator or transmission oil cooler. Total loss of coolant or transmission fluid would be enough to immobilize the vehicle.

The first vehicle dropped out three miles after the S curve. The others vehicles stopped to render aid and puked in quick succession. The vehicles that suffered a catastrophic loss of tranny fluid lost the ability to "clutch up" into gear, that is they were stuck in Neutral. The vehicles that suffered catastrophic coolant loss were shut down by their computers. Vehicles with exploded batteries would not start once turned off.

Chernovsky had been following the caravan on foot. He saw great swaths of orange coolant and red transmission fluid in the dim light of the late afternoon. He knew that at least some of them were not going to make it back to Lansing. Looking up the road he saw the disabled vehicles.

Chernovsky radioed back to Seraph. "I got some of them. You might want to call Kate's Store because they stalled out almost where the road leads into there."

Paul got on the horn to Kelly Carney. Several of the young bucks grabbed their guns and hauled ass to keep an eye on things.

They were amused to watch the strong backs completely unload the one working box truck and then all of the men getting into it to ride back to Lansing.

By chance, the one working truck was the one carrying the radio equipment. Nestle had the men stomp on the delicate electronics, urinate on the bags of flour and shoot the jugs of oil to drain them.

Dan Nestle originally planned to ride in the cab of the truck but shards of glass were embedded in the fabric of the seat from the blown-out side window. That, and it would be as cold as hell.

The worst part of the ride back, for Nestle, was that the "strong back" next to him kept leaning against him and kept drooling down Nestle's arm and hand.

Somebody in the truck was wearing aftershave that made Nestle's eyes burned. He rubbed them.

Outside, the snow started falling.

Dilyea's Dork

Paul Seraph actually got to meet Doug Dilyea at a cop charity golf event in 2006. At that time Doug was a minor celebrity in Southeastern Michigan law enforcement circles.

Dilyea was in Paul's foursome. Like Paul and Dilyea, the other two in the foursome were also cops.

Since Dilyea was retired and more than seven years had passed since the dork was invented, it was not hard to convince Dilyea to tell the un-edited story. The fact that Doug had a few beers before teeing off didn't hurt.

The course was selling beer for $10 a can which is how they made money for the charity. Some cops are big drinkers. Dilyea was in a class of his own.

“This is the absolute, no-shit truth,” Dilyea started his story in time-honored fashion.

“I got a call about a domestic disturbance and it was a full-scale riot when I got there. The address was an unregistered “Little-bit club”. Little bit of moonshine, little bit of weed, little bit of numbers, little bit of pussy...you got the picture?”

“Anyway, I was young and stupid and thought I could dance with anybody. So, I didn't wait for back-up, I got out of the cruiser and started dancing.”

“Except I found myself dancing with a four-hundred-pound man, no shit. And he was kicking my ass. He was slippery as a seal with sweat and he was slammin' my ass.”

“Well, the one thing a cop can't do is lose control of the situation. Problem being I had lost my service piece somewhere along the way. That was before we had decent secondary retention holsters,” Dilyea said.

Dilyea's beer was empty and one of the guys handed him a full one.

"Anyway, this guy is batting me around like drunk Mexican hitting a pinata on Cinco de Mayo when I finally get twisted around enough to pull my back-up piece out of my ankle holster. He hits me two, three more times before I can untwist enough to stick it in his gut."

"Did I mention he was a big guy? I jammed the gat into his gut at least six inches and pulled the trigger."

"Nuthin happened. I pulled two, three more times and the piece won't go off."

"Well, finally back-up shows up and they have mace and batons and all kinds of other good stuff. They break up the fight. I find my issued service piece. And I am madder than hell. I had the guy and the gun didn't go off."

Dilyea need another beer and he got one.

"I talked to the department armorer. He asked me what I carried and I told him, an H&K P2000. Then he told me, 'Your slide was out of battery.' "

"I asks him, what can I do about that. He said 'Carry a wheel gun'.

"That wasn't going to do because I loved that gun. Shit, it was a .40 and it shot duty ammo. I haven't bought ammo in twenty years and I wasn't about to start."

"Soes I talks to my brother who worked at the tech center. He said he would help me out but I had to make sure he got credit for the invention. I say 'Sure. No problem.'"

Another beer.

"He shows up the next day and clamps this...THING on the rail of my piece. It is one of the pins they use in auto factories to locate parts. Said he had a couple of hundred of them at home."

"The guys at work, they ask me what it is and I tell them it is so my piece won't go out of battery. And they asks me, 'What's it called?'"

Dilyea's Dork, aka NAAMS APS122M, half inch diameter, 1 1/4" long. Stiffer than Bruce Lee's index finger and twice as painful when it is stuck in your ribs.

"Then one of the bastards points at my crotch and says, 'It looks like Dilyea's dork."

"Me and my brother were selling ten, maybe twenty of them a week. Charging $100 each, too. And my brother got them for free because the heat treat was wrong. Soes then he asks me, 'Did ya make sure I got credit for inventing it?'"

"An I told him, 'Sure, we named it after you.'"

"An he asks, 'How's that?' So I tells him, 'They named it after you, Dilyea the dork...and you are the only Dilyea who is a dork so it's gotta be you.'"

Paul bought one on-the-spot.

Chernovsky Unbound

Chernovsky was invited to Paul Seraph's house to discuss 'Lessons Learned' from the recent engagement.

Paul lived in a 1955 vintage ranch house on the south side of town, east of the big cemetery.

Chernovsky walked from his apartment above the dollar store. The snow was ten inches deep and still falling. The wind was brisk enough that the snow drifted as it fell.

A few hardy citizens were shoveling snow by hand but not a motorized vehicle could be heard running even though it was nine in the morning. That included snow plows.

Chernovsky plodded the half mile to Seraph's house and a gray-haired woman who Chernovsky pegged as Paul's wife let him into the enclosed front porch.

He stomped the snow off his boots. Seeing "outside boots" lined up next to the door, Chernovsky took his off and entered the home stocking footed.

The woman asked him if he would like a cup of coffee. Chernovsky said it would be a treat.

Seraph was in the sunroom on the southeast corner of his house. There was another man speaking with him, somebody Chernovsky thought of as being the same 'vintage' as Seraph. There was also a thirteen-year-old boy entertaining himself playing a game on a smartphone.

Paul introduced Chernovsky to Rick Salazar. Rick had cross-country skied into town.

Paul did not beat around the bush. "We were lucky. We were not prepared and we escaped getting whipped."

Rick started to object.

Paul bid him stop. "We can save a lot of time if we don't candy-coat things. Let's speak plainly. Rick, you had first crack the thugs. What has to change so you can turn back future raiders before they get to the city of Eaton Rapids."

"Wow. Throw us under the bus," Rick said. "By the way, how did you know they were thugs and not legit?"

"Did anybody show you a badge or any kind of credentials?" Paul asked. "Of course not. Because they did not have any." Paul was a former cop and a gaffe like that would be glaringly obvious to him.

"Look. We all have different missions. I don't want invaders bursting into the city. You don't want them rampaging over

Kate's Store. Our goals aren't identical but they do overlap," Paul said.

"You forget that I have to worry about gangs coming south on M-99 and north out of Jackson on M-50," Paul said.

Paul had large scale, topographical maps laminated to poster board. The maps were propped up against the now-useless, large screen TV.

"If you can plug the dike and keep gangs from Delta Township and Grand Ledge out of Kate's Store then I won't have to deal with them. That means I WANT you to be successful," Paul said.

"Well, for one thing, it would grand to have a few hours warning before we had to deal with raiders," Rick said.

Chernovsky let the older men talk. He had nothing to add.

"Don't forget it is not just Delta Township and Grand Ledge. We are going to get people marching out Old Lansing Road and turning left," Rick said. "That doubles the number of people we will have to fend off." Rick was pointing at the map that covered the terrain between the center of Eaton Rapids and Billwood Highway.

Chernovsky cleared his throat. "What kind of numbers are we talking about?"

Paul ticked the numbers off on his fingers. "Ten-thousand in Oneida Township, basically the City of Grand Ledge. Thirty-five thousand in Delta Township and maybe another twenty-thousand in Lansing who might scatter this way," Paul said.

"Roughly sixty thousand?" Chernovsky said. "No way can we stop them."

"It's not as bad as it sounds" Paul said. "I figure a third of the people fleeing Delta Township will come this way. The others will go north and west."

It remained unsaid that none of the people fleeing Delta Township would head east, that would take them into Lansing.

"So we are still talking ten thousand from Delta Township alone," Chernovsky said.

"We are talking a base population of ten-thousand. Realistically, gangs are young men and that is who we really need to worry about," Paul said.

"The question still stands, 'How many'?" Chernovsky pressed.

Paul looked over at Rick who was more of a numbers guy.

"Five percent," Rick said. "Males between ages fifteen-and-thirty are ten percent of the population. Figure half join gangs to survive."

"Call it a five-hundred-to-one-thousand," Rick concluded, the upper estimate adding in the numbers from outside Delta Township.

Chernovsky got up and looked at the maps. "Why wouldn't you try to shut them off here?" Chernovsky said pointing to three choke points that throttled north-south traffic in and out of Eaton Rapids.

The Grand River snaked back and forth as it traveled from south-to-north across Eaton County. Chernovsky splayed his right hand with a finger on each bridge and his index finger pointing at the first road that completely avoided the river. That road continued north through the heart of Delta Township in an unbroken line.

"You know how to read maps?" Rick asked, surprised.

"Sure. I had a crazy uncle who used to hide five-dollar bills when we camped as a family. He marked where they were on map and then cut us loose to find them," Chernovsky said. "I sure liked finding that money."

Paul regained control of the meeting. "That is where I was heading," Paul said.

"Rick, you would have a fighting chance of holding your own if you had advance warning. What do you think of putting observation posts where they can monitor incoming traffic? At least then we would have time to katy-bar-the-door," Paul said.

Chernovsky looked at the map. "How many people live between Eaton Rapids and Billwood Highway?" Chernovsky asked.

Paul shrugged and looked over at Rick. Rick said, "Maybe two thousand. Depends on how many went to the big city."

"What is five percent of two thousand?" Chernovsky asked.

"One hundred," Rick said.

Looking at Paul, Chernovsky said, "If you and the City of Eaton Rapids can hold the bridges on M-99 and Waverly, I can hold the roads west of that with 100 fighters."

"Well, get that out of your head," Paul said. "We are 99% sure that Kate's Store, Pray Church and the neighborhood north of Eaton Rapids city limits are clean. The other 1200 people, we don't know.

"If we are lucky you will get enough volunteers to man an observation post on the road west of M-99" Paul said. "OBSERVATION posts."

The rest of the After-Action-Report was even uglier.

Paul had grossly overestimated the ability of his shooters to physically move around. Paul was physically fit and could jog or bike five miles with no apparent effort. The same could not be said of the shooters at Slocum Drain.

The one-inch-at-one-hundred-yards marksmanship the shooters bragged about was pure fantasy.

The plan was OK but it put Paul too close to the line of fire.

The multiple layers of defense worked well. The barriers on the bridge turned the moving convoy into a line of stationary targets.

The siting of the ambush worked well. Clear fields of fire for the defenders and setting up at a higher elevation than the hostiles put the hostiles at a disadvantage.

Having advance warning so shooters could select positions with cover worked well as did having enough time to laser distances. In fact, if there was one single factor that allowed Seraph's men to succeed, it was the luxury of advance warning.

Having two groups of shooters who could work the hostiles over from right angles relative to the hostile's formation worked well in spite of the shooter's limitations.

Nobody could find fault with Chernovsky's performance although Paul would have preferred Chernovsky had used both magazines.

Chernovsky defended himself saying, "I would rather play within my limitations and do it very well rather than overreach and fail."

Then Chernovsky commented, "I had a few hummers fly overhead. I think you may have forgotten I was a mile downrange."

Paul winced. It had completely slipped his mind that he put a man downrange of firearms capable of killing men seven miles away. There was a long learning curve ahead of them and it was all steep.

This was the first time Rick had run into Chernovsky. If you didn't know a little bit about Chernovsky, he could be a little bit off-putting. For one thing, the man floated on a cloud of testosterone vapors like the Charlie Brown character Pigpen. Chernovsky didn't sit, he sprawled. Some of it was due to his size. The other part was character, he was going to claim as much floor-space as possible.

"You know," Rick said "I think this might be a good time for you to tell me a few things about yourself. Paul told me you played college ball..."

"I grew up playing football in a Sterling Heights, Michigan," Hunter Chernovsky said. As soon as I could carry a Nerf football, us kids played football. Tackle football, none of that sissy stuff.

"I tried all the positions. The one I loved the most was Linebacker," he said. "I got a scholarship to attend Grand Valley State over by Grand Rapids. As I got closer to graduating, I realized there was no way the pros were going to look at a linebacker from a Division II school. It just wasn't going to happen."

"What were some of the things you liked about football?" Rick asked.

Hunter thought for a minute. "I love the tempo: Make a plan, execute the plan, analyze the results. Do it again," Hunter said.

"What attracted you to the linebacker position?" Paul Seraph asked.

"Everything!" Hunter said with enthusiasm. "It is ironic that the players on defense are the hunters. We have more freedom of motion. The offense has to be in very precise locations at exactly the right time or their play falls apart. Most of the players on the offense are dedicated to protecting the few 'skill' players.

"On defense, I looked for seams that were going to open where I could slice my way to where the ball had to go. There were always a half dozen ways for me to break the play," Hunter said.

"I also loved the intellectual challenge of football," Hunter said. "I loved getting into the quaterback's head and noodling out the offense's intended play. I really loved it when the quarterback was spooked into calling an audible seconds before the snap because the QB knew, he FEARED that I had figured out the play.

"More than anything I was jazzed when I saw that fear in a quarterback or running back's eyes just before the hit. It was not that I am cruel or like to hurt people. It is because when I saw that fear I knew I had done my job. I had taken them out of their game. I loved that instant feed-back," Hunter said.

"Were you good?" Rick asked.

"I started every game for three years," Hunter said, modestly.

"Then what happened?" Paul asked.

"I graduated with a degree in exercise science. There weren't many jobs and they didn't pay much. I enrolled at Lansing Community College and took auto repair classes. I got a job after a week of class in an auto parts store. The best thing about auto repair was that it is counter-cyclic. The worse the economy gets the more folks are willing to spend on repairs if it kept them out of a new car payment. Another advantage of being a mechanic is that the skill is portable. I can get a job anywhere," Hunter said.

"Did you miss the physical parts of being a college athlete?" Rick asked.

"I found ways to scratch my itch for the physical by teaching power-lifting and conditioning classes at one of the local gyms. I had clients who participated in more than just football. I wasn't in a position to turn clients away just because of the sports they played. I found I had to pay more attention to those other sports to help my clients" Hunter said..

"What did you think of those other sports?" Paul asked, neutrally.

"As a football player I used to dismiss basketball and hockey as frenzied chaos but my views changed after as I watched a bunch of video. I pulled the video from the high school coaches so I could see what the demands were on the athlete's bodies," he explained.

"Of the sports you started following, were there any that stood out for you? Rick asked..

"I like hockey," Hunter said.

"Is that because it is so physical?" Rick asked.

"Partially," Hunter said. "What really turned me on is that hockey is a metaphor for life. It doesn't slow-down or stop. And when a player screws up and draws a penalty, he is pulled from the game. Hockey is the only sport where teams have to play in degrade. It was an eye opener to watch how teams instantly changed their style-of-play when they went down one or two players. Teams that cannot adapt, lose."

"You are hired," Rick said when Hunter slowed down.

"Beg your pardon?" Chernovsky said.

"You are hired," Rick said. "How would you like to lead the defense of Kate's Store?"

"On one condition," Chernovsky said.

"What is that?" Rick asked.

"That my men have freedom to engage the invaders in addition to 'OBSERVING' them," Chernovsky said.

Ed's After-Action Report

"Welcome to Mr. Ed's Coffee Hour. Transmitting on paper in 12-point font. Mr. Ed's Coffee Hour where you will read the news straight from the horse's mouth.

"I am dictating this show to Janella Salazar from beside the smoking foundation of Kate's Store, where the men are men and the women and children can shoot a flea off a hound's backside at two hundred paces.

"Most of you have already heard. We had visitors yesterday. They were dressed up like State Police and Ingham County Deputies but they did not act like police. Nope. They were Viking raiders intent on looting.

"There are two things I want to get off my chest.

"One is that everybody who came to witness the looting was smart. We saw thirty men with weapons and they had the drop on us. It was tempting to start something but nobody did.

"The second thing I want to say is that we were smart but not smart enough.

"If any one of them looters got twitchy there would have been thirty dead Ronnie Rubbernecks on the ground. This will happen again. Next time, go home, send the kids and your wife someplace safe, grab your gun and ammo and pick someplace defensible to post up and keep an eye on things.

"And that ain't standing in the open thirty feet from men who are wearing body armor and holding automatic rifles.

"Someplace defensible is a place that has elevation and clear fields of fire out to a couple of hundred yards -- even a quarter mile out Someplace defensible is a place that is visually cluttered which makes it harder for the bad guys to pick out where you are shooting from. Someplace defensible is a place where logs or sandbags are stacked or foxholes are dug and can shield the majority of your body from return fire. Finally, someplace defensible is a place you can retreat from when things get too hot so you can live to fight another day. Corpses can't fight."

Ed took a sip of coffee to sooth his throat.

“Today’s tipple is a stout cup of instant coffee. Today is not a day for weeping. Today is a day for rolling up our sleeves and getting on with it,” Ed said. “There is a time and place for caffeine. Now is the time and Kate's store is the place.”

"The day before yesterday we were fat, dumb and happy. We were sitting pretty. We have good, fertile land and sweet water. For the most part we have neighbors who truly care about other's well-being. And we could always run to Kate’s store for all of those little things we forgot.

"Yesterday was a wake-up call. Our innocence died yesterday. It reminded us that evil walks in the world and that it can strike at any time.

"Today we stop coasting. We will get this done but only if we bring our “A-Game” every day.

"And now a word from our sponsor, Kate’s store.

"If you are running a balance with Kate, she needs help sifting through the ashes for anything that can be salvaged. That is a good way to work down your balance.

"If sifting through ashes aren’t something you want to do, Kate is in the market for tool handles. For those of you who like to whittle, she is looking for straight ash poles about an inch-and-a-quarter in diameter and at least five feet long.

"Kate is also in the market for any tools with broken handles, so look around those barns and sheds for shovels, hoes, rakes and the like.

"Kate is also in the market for paint. The fire burned the paint off the metal siding and Kate wants to repaint it before re-using it. Color don't matter. It just needs to be exterior grade paint.

"Now I am going to let you in on a secret. Betsy Salazar brought a little bit of silver with her from New Hampshire. She is giving it to Kate so Kate can pay cash-money, $1.10 a day, for workers."

(In point of fact, the seventy-pound backpack that Mark slung into the back of the SUV held 1000 ounces of silver in "junk" US coin. At current exchange rates that was a thousand man-days of labor.)

"Kate plans to re-open but it will be a couple of months before Kate and Rick can rebuild the barn, and even then it will be smaller than it was.

"Regarding the cargo that was abandoned. Don't go near it. It is contaminated by Ebola. Dmitri thinks he has a way to rig up a solar panel, a battery and an ozone generator to sterilize the trucks but he can only guarantee one truck a day. Work with Dmitri regarding which trucks are cleared for salvage.

"The final thing I want to say is to the people who betrayed us.

"These thugs did not stumble on us by accident. They had inside information. They knew where to park. They knew how many trucks to bring. They knew what we had to steal.

"To the rats who betrayed us, you will rot in hell because people will die this winter because of your actions. In fact,

Mrs O'Connor had a heart attack last night and is probably not going to make it."

All In: Lock, Stock and Barrel

Luke sent his mom a note. "Let me know what you need. I will send it back."

Kate responded, "Think we will be OK. Thanks. Will let you know."

Mrs O'Conner died eight hours after her coronary event peaked.

Milo kept his mouth shut regarding Duckworth's smirky comment. To repeat it would be to give Duckworth more leverage. Still, he could not stand by and do nothing.

"You know they did you a favor," Nyssa said.

"Forgive me if fail to take joy in the favor they did me," Kate said. A rare note of bitterness crept into her voice.

"At least three of those men were oozing Ebola from open wounds and another three looked feverish and had no energy," Nyssa said. "Burning down the building and everything left in it was the only practical way to sanitizing it."

"Dmitri pulled a report off short-wave that said Michigan was reporting 2% Ebola. Based on what I saw it could be ten times that," Nyssa said.

"The other thing is that in two months most of those men will either be dead or blind," she continued. "We can rebuild but we should be patient and wait until spring."

"I can understand the radio, but why did they take everything else?" Kate wailed. She was still in denial and was struggling to come to grips with the violence that had been dealt her.

Rick said, "I guess that they were bunkering up. They took

stuff because they did not plan ahead."

That is when Dmitri walked up.

"I saw what happened," Dmitri said. "It was the same in Romania under Ceausescu."

"You were smart to get out of the way. Many unarmed people died in Romania when they tried to stop armed men," Dmitri said, trying to cheer Kate up.

"But the radio station? There is no way we can get more equipment. We are finished," Kate said.

Dmitri looked around. "Did they touch the antenna?" he asked.

"No. Why would they?" Rick said.

"Because good antennas are the hardest, most expensive thing to replace," Dmitri said.

"But the transmitters...Where would we get more of those?" Kate asked.

"Transmitters are everywhere," Dmitri said. "So are amplifiers. It is a simple matter to retune a transmitter. Of course, it is even easier if somebody had the foresight to purchase backup units ahead of time," Dmitri said.

"I take it that you never looked at the detailed receipt I gave you. The equipment we installed was three hundred dollars short of what you gave me. That was spent on spare parts," Dmitri said. "The only question is a matter of timing. When is the best time to go back on-line?"

A Quarter Mile to the West...

Janelle and Nyssa walked over to Kelly's shop after hanging the laundry. There was always something going on over at Kelly's.

Today was no exception. Kelly and Milo were having a

heated discussion about the best way to fabricate some shape.

Janelle helped herself from a cold beer from the cooler and sat down to listen while Nyssa went over to stand next to Milo. It was the best entertainment available.

From the sound of discussion, they were trying to go into production and make a hundred of something. That roused Janelle's interest because she had worked in various custom shops on the west coast that specialized in those size production runs.

The problem was that Milo and Kelly had very different ideas of how to make things. Both were masters of making one-of items but they didn't know diddly about making hundreds or thousands of pieces efficiently.

Carrying her bottle of beer over to the table, Janelle saw that they had a disassembled, single-shot 12-gauge shotgun on the table.

The barrel and the receiver were in the center of the table and those seemed to be the parts generating the heated discussion.

Kelly had a rack full of 0.75" ID, 0.125" wall steel tubing in stock and he wanted to ream the chambers. Milo argued that would make the walls too thin just where the stresses were the highest. He wanted to make a tapered spud and drive it in with a hammer to dilate the tubing. Kelly said they would never be able to pull the tapered spud back out.

Kelly was at a loss for the receiver. He did not have enough steel billet in stock to make a hundred of them and even if he did it would take forever to whittle one out on the milling machine. Milo wanted to weld them from plate. Kelly objected that the tolerances would not work.

Round and round they went.

"Why do you need a hundred of them?" Janelle asked.

"We want every adult in Kate's Store to have a weapon," Kelly said. "This is the simplest thing we could think of and it isn't so simple."

"How many times is the user gonna shoot it?" Janelle asked.

"Maybe never. Maybe a couple hundred times," Milo said. "It isn't a front-line weapon. These are last ditch weapons to shoot home intruders."

"Or woodchucks in the garden," Kelly added.

"Hmmm. Why don't you hydro-form the barrels?" Janelle asked. "Custom chopper shops out west do it all the time."

"That takes special equipment," Kelly said. "Equipment we don't have."

"Nope. That is not so. You have everything you need to do hydro-forming here," Janelle said.

"Ok, miss smarty-pants, how would you do it?" Nyssa asked.

"I would hydro-form the barrels two at a time, breech-to-breech and cut them apart afterward," Janelle said.

"How do you seal the hydraulic fluid so it doesn't spray all over creation?" Kelly asked. Kelly did know a little bit about production processes.

"You don't use hydraulic fluid for short production runs. Use a cylinder of rubber. Put a piece of tubing twice as long as a finished barrel into a die where the outer diameter is bigger in the middle...for maybe six inches where the chambers will be. Form them breech-to-breech...then a mandrel in one end of the tubing, then the rubber slug and then a ram in the other end. The rubber pushes out when you crush it and the tubing expands to fill the larger outer diameter," Janelle said. "Split the two pieces in the center after you are done."

“You just have to do a little bit of math to figure out how big the outer diameter of the chamber area needs to be to give you the right inner diameter.”

"That won't work,” Milo said. "We don't have any rubber like that."

Janella refrained from rolling her eyes. "You have to want to make this work, silly. If you don't have rubber then use bread dough."

“Have you seen this?” Kelly asked.

“Sure. Hundreds of times,” Janelle said. "I mean, not with bread dough, but I have seen it with the rubber slugs."

“Got any ideas about the receivers?” Milo asked.

“Out west they would have cast them from ZA-7 but we probably don’t have any of that. What about using your piece there,” she said pointing at the table, “As a pattern and casting them from melted down aluminum wheels. That has to be pretty good alloy. You might need to add some tape to thicken up the walls to account for shrinkage, but you would be close to your final shape,” Janelle said.

In spite of herself, Nyssa was proud of her older sister. Once Milo was in a shop surrounded by milling machines, lathes and welders he had a hard time listening. Janelle's knowing WAY more than he or Kelly did about production processes really rocked him back on his heels.

Janelle, you go, girl.

CHAPTER THREE

The Phoenix Arises from the Ashes

Bill Spackle walked up to Rick and Kate as they were raking through the ashes.

Bill was not entirely comfortable around women. He had come of age in rural Michigan in the mid-1960s and standards had changed. Behaviors that used to be acceptable, even funny back then were now almost criminalized.

Bill farmed onions, carrots and corn on muck ground before he retired and sold the business to a multi-state conglomerate.

They bought Bill's land. They bought Bill's customer list. They did not buy his tractors or his barn.

"Hi Bill," Kate said. "What's up?" she asked wearily.

"I ain't using my barn, much," Bill gruffly announced. "It would be OK if you used it until you were back on your feet," he said.

"That is very generous of you, Bill," Kate said.

It was, in fact, very generous. Bill's barn was in the exact center of the neighborhood and it was a beautiful barn with a concrete floor, running water and many doors.

"I am not sure I want to re-open the store," Kate said. "This happening..." she said, looking around..." has been a kick in the gut.

"And I am not sure I can, in good conscience, put your property at risk," Kate said.

"I think you earned the right to lick your wounds and recover," Bill said. "My wife has been getting in touch with nephews and grand-kids. They will be over tomorrow. Give them a list and they will start moving stuff."

"Bill, I don't feel heard," Kate said. "I. Can't. Do. This."

"Ma-am. With all due respect, this is bigger than you. Do what you gotta do. But this neighborhood NEEDS a store and you don't wanna piss off my wife," Bill said.

A hundred years from now anthropologists will sort through what defined "family" in the late 2000-teens and twenties. In some places, family is defined solely by the maternal-offspring bond. In other places "family" is defined with much more generous and expansive rules.

In Bill's "family", half-siblings and half-siblings of half-siblings were considered brothers and sisters. Cousins ran to the multiple hundreds.

When Bill's wife stepped up and said, "Bill, let Rick and Kate use the barn for a while," Kate instantly had an army and intelligence organization that spanned three counties and numbered over four hundred after Bill's line and his wife's line were combined.

Kate's decentralized style came to her rescue. While others might have insisted on control of inventory, Kate was perfectly happy to let the owner's warehouse their products and to let the price float based on conditions. She valued happily making their products available over squeezing the very lowest price out of suppliers. If demand went up, Kate thought it only proper that she pay more.

The warrant Dan Nestle handed Kate could have not been

more wrong. Kate did not hoard goods. Very much the opposite, her store pulled goods into active trading and helped them find people who needed them most. Nestle's warrant claimed she was a price gouger. Again, Kate priced goods to balance supply and demand. As shown by the limestone, letting prices float motived risk-seeking suppliers to find new supplies.

Nestle may have burned the physical facade of Kate's store but his actions had the effect of energizing the core idea of trading what you had a surplus of to others so you could get more of what you had in short supply.

Much to Kate's surprise, the consignment tables were the first space to fill up. Kate did not have a way to compensate the owners for the loss of the merchandise that had been on the tables when Dan Nestle burned the store. That mattered little to most of the people who filled the tables. Kate had always treated them well and there was no other outlet for the goods cluttering their attics, garages and barns.

Winter gripped Michigan. People would die without access to warm clothes, clothes that sellers had grown out of or whose kids had grown up and moved away.

Luke sent half of his merchandise back. He also sent old chainsaws, splitting wedges, axes, windows and boxes of copy paper. He had been taking them in as trade.

Janella and Ms Sheridan signed on for 24 hours a week. Nyssa signed on for 16 hours. Various other folks in the neighborhood signed up for four-to-twenty hours.

Kate did need a rest. She had run the good race. She had finished the fight. Now it was time for others to carry her while she healed.

Thy Rod and Thy Staff Comfort Me

Rick was sitting near the woodstove picking on a guitar.

He had always intended to pick up the skill but never had time. Now, after the sun set, there was nothing but time.

He was not working very hard at it.

Kate had been distant, cold even, after the store had been burned down. She grieved the loss. Rick didn't know how to deal with that.

Rick, for his part, had a raging need for intimacy with Kate.

A year earlier, that need for intimacy had been flagging. He attributed it to the inevitable effects of aging. That diminishing of libido had taken an abrupt reversal when Milo started working with Rick on physical conditioning. Rick felt like he was twenty-five again.

That made Kate's withdrawal particularly vexing.

One of the advantages of being sixty is that many learned patience.

Rick continued to pick at the guitar, slowly adding notes to the string he was working on.

"Wanna talk about it?" Rick asked.

" 'bout what?" Kate said.

"What do you miss the most?" Rick asked. "Was it meeting the people?"

Kate could talk about that. "Nope. I still get to see them."

Rick picked for a couple of more minutes then he tried again.

"Do you miss the old barn?" Rick asked.

"It does feel like a lost tooth, doesn't it?" Kate said. "I remember losing my teeth when I was five. I couldn't help but pushing and pulling at that tooth with my tongue. Then, after it was gone it just felt so strange. I kept running my tongue over that spot.

"But no, it is not the barn that I miss the most," Kate said.

Rick kept picking on the guitar. It was getting complicated and he had to slow down to get it right.

"What makes me mad," Rick said, "Is the shear waste of all they destroyed. The fire destroyed so much. They did it just to be mean."

"Hmm," Kate made a non-committal sound.

Rick shifted to another chunk of melody. He did not know if this was the best way to learn to play but it did fill up the time.

After a minute Kate spoke up. "The bullies think they won. That is what bothers me most. That, and there are hundreds of families huddled in their houses not knowing what is going on. At least I have the store and I get to hear what is happening," Kate said.

"The radio station?" Rick asked. That is not something he would have guessed, that Kate grieved the loss of the radio station more than anything else.

Kate nodded her affirmative.

"We have the hardware. We can restart it later," Rick said.

"People need the information now," Kate said.

"An entire family east of M-99 committed suicide. Times are hard. Times are much harder when you think you are totally alone," Kate said.

Rick thought that sounded just like Kate. Kate was an empath. She felt other people's pain. That is why she was hurting.

"The raid could have just been an extinction burst. We could start transmitting again and everything might be fine," Rick ventured.

"And it might not have been an extinction burst," Kate said. "I would be putting us all in danger."

Yup, Kate had a dilemma on her hands.

The next day, Rick sought out Dmitri.

"How hard would it be to restart the radio station?" Rick asked.

"Not hard. I have all the parts," Dmitri said.

"What if we wanted to do it clandestinely?" Rick asked. "Is there a way to do it that won't point right back to us?"

Dmitri said, "I wondered when you would ask."

"FM is easy. AM, almost impossible," Dmitri said.

"OK, what would it take for the FM station?" Rick asked.

"You just need a battery and a high place to mount the antenna. I can put the transmitter and amplifier on a board," Dmitri said. "You will want to shift around and transmit from different places each show.

"You want to pre-record the show...maybe put it on a smart phone and then just play it through the earphone jack," Dmitri said.

"Well, that made sense," Rick said. "Sometimes it gets real windy out there. Wind and mics don't get along."

"Anything else?" Rick asked. So far this looked like it was going to be a snap.

"You need a different announcer," Dmitri said. "As soon as they hear Mr. Ed, they will know it is you and then it will be game over."

Oh, yeah. Rick had not thought of that. Who could he find that had the time and skill set to host the radio show...?

***

“Good evening everybody!” the cheerful, well-modulated alto said with every phoneme roundly and precisely formed.

“I am Peppermint Candy Mandy recording on the banks of Peppermint Creek and transmitting at 104.3 on the FM dial.”

"This is my first broadcast and I don’t have much material prepared so I am going to steal from the best."

Among the books the Heilers left behind were a copy of the Bible and a 1937 reprinting of book of poetry compiled by James Mudge in 1907.

Peppermint Candy Mandy had been bored off her rocker in quarantine. She jumped at the chance to record a ‘dramatic reading’ on Uncle Rick’s phone. He passed a wireless mic to her when he brought the food and he stood with his phone on the other side of the window as she recorded.

Rick had batteries. Milo had no problem pitching a weight with 200 feet of 550 cord tied to it way up in a white pine growing two miles away

Dmitri expressed concern about National Guard 155mm cannon that can lob rounds fifteen miles based on EM emissions. Based on Dmitri's concerns, Milo decamped to an observation point a quarter mile distant before starting the timer. He gave himself fifteen minutes to evacuate.

Milo also remembered Dmitri telling him that antenna towers that conduct electricity are a problem. He knew that living trees conduct electricity so he took the precaution of turning up the gain-knob on the amplifier one more increment, plus a scootch.

Unbeknownst to Milo, the dial was log-scale. That is, each major hash mark increased the gain by a factor of ten. Instead of transmitting with one Watt of power, Milo had set the amplifier to transmit twenty Watts.

Since it was advisable to wait for a response, Milo programmed his smart phone to repeat the two minute-thirty second transmission four times on fifteen minute intervals.

Back at Casa Salazar...

Rick was picking at his guitar that evening when the timer on his phone went off.

He casually strolled over to the radio and turned it on before walking back to his chair.

Kate was mystified.

Then she heard Mandy's voice coming through the radio speaker.

Half a league, half a league,
Half a league onward,
All in the valley of Death
Rode the six hundred.
"Forward, the Light Brigade!
Charge for the guns!" he said.
Into the valley of Death
Rode the six hundred...

After The Charge of the Light Brigade, Peppermint Candy Mandy recited The Twenty-third Psalm. She added nothing. She took away nothing. She read it the way the authors intended it be recited.

"...The Lord is my shepherd; I shall not want.
He maketh me to lie down in green pastures: he leadeth me beside the still waters.
He restoreth my soul: he leadeth me in the paths of righteousness for his name's sake.
Yea, though I walk through the valley of the shadow of death, I will fear no evil: for thou art with me; thy rod and thy staff they

comfort me...."

After the transmission ended, Kate turned off the lights, extended her hands to Rick as he sat in the kitchen chair with the guitar, forgotten, on his lap.

She pulled him up, out of the chair and kissed him.

The Blast of War Summons, Dishonor Not Your Mothers

"Hello all! Peppermint Candy Mandy broadcasting on 104.3, your source of information in Kates Store, Pray Church and elsewhere.

"The big news today is that Hunter Chernovsky is looking for a few good men to move our first line of defense farther to the north. Folks, we are taking the battle to the enemy.

"Mr. Chernovsky is looking for men from sixteen-to-thirty years of age. He is looking for a four-month commitment starting now. If you are that man, or if you know that man, forward those names to Kate, Rick in Kates Store, Pastor James or Luke Salazar in Pray Church or Paul Seraph if you live in the area immediately north of Eaton Rapids.

"A few of you said you liked yesterday's reading, so that is how I will close this broadcast..."

KING HENRY V:
Once more unto the breach, dear friends, once more;
Or close the wall up with our English dead.
In peace there's nothing so becomes a man
As modest stillness and humility:
But when the blast of war blows in our ears,
Then imitate the action of the tiger;
Stiffen the sinews, summon up the blood,
Disguise fair nature with hard-favour'd rage;
Then lend the eye a terrible aspect...

Now set the teeth and stretch the nostril wide,
Hold hard the breath and bend up every spirit
To his full height. On, on, you noblest English.
Whose blood is fet from fathers of war-proof!
Fathers that, like so many Alexanders,
Have in these parts from morn till even fought
And sheathed their swords for lack of argument:
Dishonour not your mothers; now attest
That those whom you call'd fathers did beget you.
Be copy now to men of grosser blood,
And teach them how to war. And you, good yeoman,
Whose limbs were made in England, show us here
The mettle of your pasture; let us swear
That you are worth your breeding; which I doubt not;
For there is none of you so mean and base,
That hath not noble lustre in your eyes.
I see you stand like greyhounds in the slips,
Straining upon the start. The game's afoot:
Follow your spirit, and upon this charge
Cry 'God for Harry, England, and Saint George!'

She said, "From Ecclesiastes Chapter 3, King James Version..."

To every thing there is a season,
and a time to every purpose under the heaven:

A time to be born, and a time to die;
a time to plant, and a time to pluck up that which is planted;

A time to kill, and a time to heal;
a time to break down, and a time to build up;

A time to weep, and a time to laugh;
a time to mourn, and a time to dance;

A time to cast away stones, and a time to gather stones together;
a time to embrace, and a time to refrain from embracing;

A time to get, and a time to lose;

a time to keep, and a time to cast away;

A time to rend, and a time to sew;
a time to keep silence, and a time to speak;

A time to love, and a time to hate;
a time of war, and a time of peace.

What profit hath he that worketh in that wherein he laboureth?

I have seen the travail, which God hath given to the sons of men to be exercised in it.

God hath made every thing beautiful in His time:

And moreover I saw under the sun the place of judgment, that wickedness was there; and the place of righteousness, that iniquity was there.

I said in mine heart, God shall judge the righteous and the wicked: for there is a time there for every purpose and for every work.

***

A candle placed within a reflector made from a beverage can is visible from five miles when placed on the shores of a wilderness lake. That same candle is not visible from more than fifty feet when placed in a parking lot illuminated with sodium vapor lamps.

The difference is contrast.

If you place a package of cigarettes on the roof of a car, satellite imagery can discern the brand of cigarettes if anybody cares enough to look.

Twenty Watts of power at 104.3 megahertz was plenty of power to punch up to those same satellites.

The collapse of commercial media and the death of the power grid created the contrast.

The computer's algorithms had already identified 104.3 as a

frequency of interest.

The format of the last show, the same two minute segment repeated four times at set intervals, twigged more filters.

Voice-to-text, then keywords finally floated it up to actual human ears.

The young man who listened to the segment was instantly homesick. It had been too long since he heard a 'normal' girl talk. To him, a normal girl was one who did not out-rank him.

He parsed the station history and saw that the transmission site was different than yesterday's. From the map overlay, he saw that today's site was from a cemetery two miles east of the tall white pine.

Out of curiosity, the young man listened to the previous broadcast as well.

Then he bumped it upstairs. The food-chain upstairs would be interested in armies being raised in the continental United States. The term 'upstairs' was an aping of western idiom rather than literal fact. There were very few stairs in Zhenjiang.

Recruiting

Chernovsky's first morning of recruiting was turning into an exercise in frustration.

He showed up at Luke's store in Pray Church expecting to have a line of young men wanting to join the defense force.

Two hours after sunrise a fifteen-year-old boy showed up.

Chernovsky regretfully told him he was under-age and to not even fill out an application.

The second applicant showed up about an hour later. Chernovsky estimated him to be seventeen years old. The youth had spaghetti-thin arms, sallow complexion and a multitude of piercings and tats.

Scanning through the youth's application, which was barely legible, Chernovsky was surprised to see he was twenty-four. He also noticed the youth had lived in Lansing up until four months ago.

"Why did you move out here?" Chernovsky asked.

"Dude! I just moved in with my girl-friend," the young man said. "It's not like I wanted to move out here but my mom kicked me out."

"Twenty-four and still living with your mom? What's the story there?" Chernovsky asked.

"Dude! I am going to school. I gotta double-major," the young man said.

That was something Chernovsky could relate to. He figured that between his Bachelor's degree in Exercise Science and working-out/practice twenty hours a week, year-round for football he was pulling the equivalent of a double major.

"What are you majoring in?" Chernovsky asked.

"Mixology and Cannabis Blending," the young man said, happy to have found a common ground with Chernovsky.

"Why do you want to join the defense force?" Chernovsky asked.

"Dude! It's like my girlfriend is my baby-mama and she expects me to do stuff. I mean, she had to take me in because I am her baby-daddy but, shit, she keeps telling me to do stuff," the young man said.

"Like....?" Chernovsky asked

"You know, like house work or bring home money or something," the young man said. "I left my job back in Lansing and it is too far to walk every day."

Chernovsky felt some relief. The guy had a job. He couldn't be THAT bad. At least he had some skills.

"What was your job?" Chernovsky asked.

"Dude! I am a drummer in a band. Blue Clam Calculus. I am sure you have heard of us," the young man confided. "We played two Saturdays a month at the Slam-Dance club."

"So, let me get this straight. You want to join the defense force because you are tired of your baby-mama, who you didn't marry and because you think she is too demanding?" Chernovsky summarized.

"Yeah man, that's it exactly," the young man said.

Chernovsky slid the application in a drawer. "I am afraid I cannot use you."

"Dude! Why? I was counting on it. I already told Charlene I was moving out," the young man said. "Don't worry about that baby. It ain't like I owe it anything."

Chernovsky correctly interpreted that to mean that Charlene, the baby-mama had already kicked the slacker out.

"Let's just say that I don't have absolute confidence that you will be there when things get tough," Chernovsky said.

A couple more hours went by. Pastor James popped in to see how it was going. Then, because Pastor James' sermon was done for the weekend, he hung around to watch.

Shortly after Pastor James showed up, two young men walked into Luke's store.

The one who moved like an athlete filled out both applications. Then they both sat in chairs on the other side of the table.

"I want to interview you alone," Chernovsky said. To him it was a perfectly reasonable request.

"We come as a two-fer, Mr. Chernovsky, two-fer-the-price-of-one," the athletic one said. "My name is Quinn Spackle and this is my cousin Buddy."

"OK, Mr. Spackle. Why should I let you join the defense force?" Chernovsky asked.

The athlete was at a loss to explain why he would be an asset. Heck, everybody knew him. He thought Mr. Chernovsky would just KNOW why he was the man for the job.

"Well, I guess because I am a bow hunter. And I hunt sheds and mushrooms. I'm not much for schooling but anything outside, I am your man," Quinn said.

"And how about you?" Chernovsky asked the other young man.

"I want to be with Quinn," the man said, haltingly.

Chernovsky scanned the applications. The handwriting was painfully neat.

"I'll get back to you," Chernovsky said as he put the applications into the drawer.

After they left, Chernovsky said, "Hey, Pastor James, what is the story there?"

"Quinn and Buddy Spackle?" Pastor James said.

"Yup," Chernovsky said.

"You took them, right?" Pastor James said.

"No. Quinn looked OK but Buddy's lights are on and nobody is home," Chernovsky said.

Pastor James sat down across from Chernovsky.

“Here is the story,” Pastor James said.

“When Quinn was sixteen and Buddy was fifteen, they were staying with some of their cousins while their parents went to a Detroit Tigers baseball game.”

“The boys went to a bonfire. The older guys were doing some drinking and then offered to take Quinn ‘hood-surfing’,” Pastor James said. “You know what that is, right?”

“Where somebody stands on the hood of a car while it drives down the road,” Chernovsky guessed.

“In this case it was a truck that had been lifted,” Pastor James said.

“The thing is that Buddy wanted to go real bad so Quinn let him go first. Things happened. Buddy’s head hit the pavement. The cousins agreed to not tell the parents and hoped nobody would notice,” Pastor James said.

Chernovsky knew a little bit about concussions. “How bad?”

“Buddy will always be a ten-year-old,” Pastor James said. “That is why Quinn feels so responsible toward him. Quinn figures it should have been him and he would have landed on his feet, Quinn being athletic and all.”

“Well, then I definitely can’t use Buddy,” Chernovsky said, dismissively.

“You don’t know people or small towns very well, do you?" Pastor James said.

“You know Larry Tomanica, the guy Salazar lined up to train your recruits how to shoot ‘The Marine Corp way’?” Pastor James said. “Quinn calls him ‘Uncle Larry.’

“Do you know what a bow hunter is? He is a guy who sits out in rain and snow for four, six, even ten hours at a crack. Not moving. Not scratching his face. Barely blinking....and they do it for FUN. They brag when they are so still that a deer pees on them.

"Everybody around here looks up to Quinn, especially the ones who are a little bit younger than he is. You take Quinn and you will have five more just like him the next morning," Pastor James said.

Pastor James was wrong. It was fifteen young men. Buddy received a special assignment. He became Chernovsky's Executive Assistant.

With a core of Quinn and his near clones, Chernovsky didn't have any problems filling out the rest of the roster. He shut down recruiting when he had thirty-two, counting him and Buddy.

Firearms Training

The fire-teams were selected in the simplest possible way.

Milo snow-shoed a track around one of the sections to pack the snow.

Then groups of recruits were released in small groups to run the four miles.

The six fastest times were the six team leads...for now.

Then Chernovsky dealt the team-members from the bottom. The fastest leader got the slowest runner of the thirty. Buddy was exempt.

Then the second fastest leader to the second slowest...and so on.

Quinn was the second fastest runner around the block. He grumbled that it made more sense to group all the fast runners together.

Chernovsky interrupted the grumbling. "Each team can trade ONE member, and one member only with another team."

One of the leaders, who was a rabbit in personality as well as speed, volunteered to swap himself out with a team-member on another team who was a natural leader and almost as fast.

Chernovsky said, "This is your team. Own it. It moves no faster than the slowest person. If you don't like that, figure out a way to fix it."

Quinn looked at Donnie, his slowest guy. Donnie's dad was one of the drunks who moved to town. Quinn had played basketball with him and Quinn did not remember Donnie as being a particularly slow runner.

"How come you let Petie beat you? I know you are faster than he is," Quinn asked.

Donnie lifted up his right foot. "It's my damned boots."

Donnie was wearing an ancient pair of "Tims", a common brand of work boot. Donnie's boots were worn smooth on the bottom.

"What size do you wear?" Quinn asked.

"Size eleven-and-a-half," Donnie said.

"Lemme ask around. I think we can do better for you," Quinn said. Next chance he got he was going to ask Bill Spackle to shake the bushes and see if anybody had some decent footwear in size eleven-and-a-half or 12.

In Quinn's estimation, things were looking up.

Firearm training was an exercise in humility for Chernovsky.

He had enough maturity to not open his mouth when he didn't know the answer. That was the only thing that saved him.

Most of the kids, as he thought of them, could run circles around him with regard to marksmanship.

Larry Tomanica had been teaching neighbor kids to shoot ever since he mustered out of the Marines thirty-five years ago. There was not a lot of un-teaching that had to happen.

Quinn pushed back against the rifles they were issued. Like most people, he did not hold the .22LR in high regard.

Larry Tomanica changed the subject.

"Nice buck you got two years ago," Larry said. "Ten point, wasn't it?"

Quinn like talking about his big buck. "Yeah, I never had it officially scored but I taped it out as 150 class buck," Quinn said, modestly.

"Tell us again, what did you shoot it with? I am a little fuzzy on the details," Tomanica said. In fact, Uncle Larry remembered every detail with crystalline clarity.

"I shot it with my Hoyt compound bow," Quinn said. "It is an over-draw," he said by way of explanation.

"How far was the shot?" Tomanica asked.

"Twenty-seven yards," Quinn said. "I lasered it afterward."

"How far would you be comfortable shooting a deer with your bow?" Tomanica asked.

"Fifty yards. But it is dumb to take the long shot when you can be patient and take the shorter one," Quinn said.

This was all Bowhunting 101 to Quinn.

"Do you think deer are dumber in the woods than city people?" Tomanica asked.

Quinn snorted. "Hell no!"

"So, you are telling me that you shot a big buck at twenty-five yards and it never knew you were there but you don't think a rifle that can shoot two-hundred yards, eight times farther than twenty-five yards you shot a buck at, can kill zombies?" Tomanica asked.

"Bullshit," Quinn said.

The tight training timeline made the instillation of military discipline a touch-and-go thing at this point.

".22LRs are squirrel guns. They aren't any good past seventy yards," Quinn scoffed.

"Let's see," Tomanica said. He had anticipated push-back and was glad to get it out of the way.

Tomanica had a pile of DeNile delivery boxes in his garage. He said to Quinn "Put them out there," gesturing with his arm to indicate the weed field behind his house.

"Pick out six of them and put them anywhere between ten and two-hundred paces, then come back here," Tomanica said.

It was clear that Tomanica intended to shoot them so Quinn took the precaution of inspecting the six boxes to ensure they didn't already have bullet holes in them. A few did but the holes had been patched with masking tape.

The boxes were standard 12" by 6" by 24" boxes. There were already a couple of boxes out on "the range." Quinn faced the boxes so the target was 12" wide by 24" tall facing the shooter so they matched the boxes that were already up. He had to settle them four inches in the snow so they wouldn't tip over in the wind.

He put one at fifty paces, one at one hundred, one at one-twenty, one at one-fifty and the last two at two-hundred paces and then came back to the garage where Tomanica was holding his class.

Tomanica activated the range with the standard, “Ready on the right....”

He loaded a magazine into this .22LR, cycled the bolt and then threaded his left arm through the sling, raised it to the off-hand position and fired almost as fast as he could pull the trigger.

“Let’s all walk out there and look," was all Tomanica said. He picked up the roll of masking tape and put it in his pocket.

All of the shots were solid hits. Tomanica said, “You won't be shooting squirrels, so stop thinking of it as a squirrel gun.

“These are zombie-killing rifles. Everything about this weapon is tuned in to make it a zombie-killing machine.”

That is when Tomanica started walking them through the science of ballistics, the use of the sling and getting the most out of field expedient supports. He strongly advised that they carry a plastic grocery bag with them. It can be filled with leaves or the half-rotted duff that collects between rocks and then used as a "sand bag" in the field. Plastic bags weigh almost nothing and have a thousand other uses.

He focused very heavily on basic field positions.

After the recruits left, Tomanica had a heart-to-heart talk with Chernovsky. “Basically, you are screwed by your Rules-of-Engagement. Paul Seraph in Eaton Rapids is scared you will go ‘cowboy’ on him. He insisted that your primary weapons be .22LR because your primary mission is 'observing'," Tomanica said.

“He was also worried about stray rounds hitting civilians. He doesn’t want to have to explain giving a bunch of teen-aged boys high-powered rifles after things get back to normal.” Tomanica said. “You can be sure a bunch of Monday-morning quarterbacks will be all over anything that goes haywire."

Chernovsky was shaking his head. He was a novice at this Rules-of-Engagement bullshit. In football the rules were clear and they did not change. Don't clip. No late hits on the QB. Kill the guy with the ball. Disrupt play when you cannot kill the ball carrier.

"Another thing I don't get," Chernovsky said, "Is why so many team-leaders. I thought three squads, three leaders."

Chernovsky thought of team-leaders as management, that is, non-productive workers.

Tomanica gave Chernovsky's comment a few seconds thought before answering.

"Suppose you send a squad of ten on a mission," Tomanica said.

Chernovsky nodded his head. That was exactly how he planned to run things.

"The squad encounters the hostiles," Tomanica continued.

"What will work better? If they split up and one team creates a distraction while the other team hits their blind-side...or to have the one team take on the hostiles from a single direction?" Tomanica asked.

"Obviously splitting them up and hitting them from the blind-side," Chernovsky answered. That was a no-brainer in his book.

"How does the squad manage itself if it doesn't have two fire-team leaders?" Tomanica asked. "Are you going to do it by radio? In that case, why have any team-leaders at all?"

Then Tomanica drove the wooden stake into the heart. "Seraph agreed to let fire-team leaders carry AR-15s."

"Rick Salazar made the case that the team-leader needed to be able to project over the entire team's footprint, that the leader needed a weapon with a longer reach so he could support every person on his team," Tomanica said.

"Under your Rules-of-Engagement the only way you will get a reasonable number of AR-15s is if you run a little bit rich for fire-team leaders," Tomanica said.

Chernovsky grumbled but grudgingly agreed that ten-man squads composed of two, five-man teams were the only way to fly.

CHAPTER FOUR

Boot Camp

Quinn hated Chernovsky with an undying passion.

Chernovsky, for his part, killed Quinn at least three times a day.

Quinn was one of six fire-team leaders and the senior FTL in his squad.

Chernovsky ran training as a game, squad-on-squad. He also had them multi-task. They never just "ran". Rather, they would run cross country to become intimately familiar with it while dragging sleds filled with supplies to build forward observation posts.

Set-piece battles were only run once a week. That was their recovery day.

"Bounding" or "Broken Play" was run six days a week. One squad was in bounding retreat. Two were in advance.

The exercise was exceptionally demanding of the defense. They had to retreat away from their position so they were out-of-sight from the road. Then they had to haul ass south to get well ahead of the offensive forces. Then move to the road close enough to effectively ambush the offense.

Sometimes they gamed with snow-on-ground where a retreating squad leaving tracks visible from the road was instantly killed. Other times it was snow-not-on ground where fastest path was safest, provided the advancing force was far enough back not see them move.

The irony was that there was ALWAYS snow on the ground. It was one of the coldest and snowiest winters on record. With the huge increase of wood burning for warmth, there were far more 'particulate' matter in the atmosphere to trigger snow. Snow reflects sunlight back into space and does not turn it to heat. First it was snowy. Then it was COLD.

Quinn learned where the drifts were deepest and learned to avoid them when gaming S-N-O-G. Bounding offense used the road while defense did not. It was almost impossible for the defense to stay ahead of the offense. Staying out of deep snow was the only chance defense had to make speed. Consequently, they learned where the snow drifted.

They gamed north-to-south, which was the direction that they would be pushed if an overwhelming force rolled through their set-piece defense. But they also gamed south-to-north. South-to-north gamers carried max load-outs. It was also a way to move supplies up to the line.

The game was simple. The defenders had a head start arbitrarily announced by Chernovsky at the start of the bound.

The defenders had to bound back to the next defensible salient. Then they defended it with smartphone cameras. Chernovsky loaded apps that both time-dated and ranged the “shots” photos.

Chernovsky was totally ruthless. If you were carrying a .22LR and launched a shot that was more than 200 yards, he killed the whole squad. If you were carrying an AR and shot before it became clear the suppressed .22 LRs couldn’t handle it, he killed the whole squad. And yes, each squad member carried their personal weapon. They loaded the magazine, racked a cartridge and then put the weapons aside and continued the “game” with smartphones.

The sessions became more and more brutal.

Short bounds became a rarity. By the second week the typical bound was between one and three miles. Squads pulled sleds with hundred-fifty-pound loads. The loads were not just to build muscle. The logs and sandbags were strategically placed where elevation and field-of-fire were advantageous but cover was lacking.

Chernovsky demanded that every "hide" have a secondary. He also had them build forward hides that covered likely lines of advance toward the primary. Strong attackers always expect defenders to fall back. They are perpetually surprised when defenders 'retreated' forward and take the attackers off at the knees.

Quinn's squad was successful one-time-in-three on offense. They were killed the other two times. On defense they were killed seven-times-out-of-eight.

Quinn tried to point out that it was not logical when Chernovsky killed off both the advancing and the defending squads.

Chernovsky was unmoved. "You can have a tactical win but if you leave one survivor who is carrying Ebola and they get into Pray Church then you are still all dead, even if it takes the bullet four months to land."

Quinn had to admit that his squad was much sharper than when they started. They were at that magical age between fifteen and twenty-two when young muscles, clean air and obscene amounts of exercise grow muscle and lung capacity at a freakish rate.

Quinn's squad was able to pull three times as much, move three times farther and at twice the speed as when they started. More important, they could break-down and man defensive positions within three minutes of hitting the salient.

Quinn quickly learned to avoid salients where his squad were quickly wiped out.

One time he completely smoked the opposition. Chernovsky started them out on the west side of the road. The west side had very little in the way of favorable defensible terrain.

Quinn put the spurs to his men and was just barely able to cut across the road to the east side as the advancing group trudged up the opposite side of a hill. They crossed at a side road where other traffic masked their footprints.

Quinn's squad cut the advancing force to ribbons because the advancing force KNEW that the defenders were on the west side of the road. That was one of the few times when Chernovsky praised Quinn.

Another time Quinn saw birds flying around a small patch of cover growing on a rock pile near the middle of the field. His team gave it a wide berth. The force they were pursuing had left an ambush that was intended to whack Quinn in the back after they passed. That earned Quinn another atta-boy from Chernovsky.

Quinn learned when to concentrate forces. He learned when to leave a trailer to collect intelligence. He learned when to stretch out his forces to dilute the firing power of opposing forces. Every lesson was hard won.

They practiced "bounding" four hours a day. Then an hour of recovery. Then an hour of reviews where Chernovsky ripped them for their mistakes. Then the teams broke up for firewood detail.

As soon as the squads had mastered fixed defense, Chernovsky had them drop the trees that restricted visual access to the killing ground. They dropped the trees with chainsaws but bucked them up with cross-cut saws. Not only were the cross-cut saws quieter but no better tool has yet been invented to develop core strength. Chernovsky demanded that they alternate days sawing right-handed and left-handed. Get caught using the wrong "hand" and your fire-team had to do an additional 100 push-ups.

The firewood was distributed to the local families.

Quinn would have rebelled long ago but Chernovsky was a force to be reckoned with.

Quinn watched him rip branches four and five inches in diameter from the trunk of a cottonwood tree they had just dropped.

He wasn't mad or anything. He just got impatient waiting for the guy with an ax to show up. He gripped the branches in his hands and ripped them off the trunk as easily as a teenage boy ripped the wings and drumsticks off a roast chicken.

Later Quinn learned that Chernovsky regularly deadlifted and squatted 600 pounds in the gym. Quinn did not have a basis for comparison, but that sounded like a lot of weight.

Chernovsky effortlessly ran with the defenders to better critique them. The son-of-a-bitch weighed 270 and loped along like a marathon runner.

Quinn hated Chernovsky, but listened to him just the same. It was an alpha-male/alpha-male thing.

We Play on Saturday the Way We Practiced All Week

Chernovsky was chewing Quinn's ass. Again.

The squad had been running across a flat expanse when Chernovsky slipped on the surface and a string of obscenities escaped his lips. He had been surprised.

He scraped the snowy surface and uncovered ice.

He blew the whistle and beckoned the squad form up on him.

Then he got on the radio and informed the "offense" to stand down.

"Spackle! WTF is this?" Chernovsky demanded, pointing down at the ice.

Not knowing where Chernovsky was going with his question, Quinn honestly answered "Ice."

Chernovsky looked around and the snow was as flat as an airport runway for nearly a hundred yards in every direction.

"What is under all this snow? Chernovsky asked.

"More ice," Quinn answered.

"What does ice turn into when it melts?" Chernovsky asked.

"Water," Quinn answered.

"Did you know this was a swamp when you led us in here?" Chernovsky asked. He was giving Quinn the benefit of the doubt.

"Yes sir. Everybody knows it is a swamp," Quinn said.

"And how would they know that?" Chernovsky asked.

Quinn pointed to the trees. "Those are soft maple," Quinn said as if explaining to a six-year-old. "The only place they grow in solid stands like this is where it floods in the spring. The flooding kills everything else."

Chernovsky pinched the bridge of his nose as he got control of his temper.

"So, we are out here running exercises so we can overcome our enemies. These exercises are supposed to build our muscles and make our decisions automatic...AND YOU LED US INTO A FUCKING SWAMP!" Chernovsky ended up yelling.

"All of you," Chernovsky said, swinging his arm about, pointing. "You should all know better. You have a responsibility to speak up when you see something that risks the mission."

"Four-mile run," Chernovsky said.

And off the squad ran pulling their sleds.

Quinn and his squad were a major source of stress for Chernovsky. On paper, Quinn's fire-team should have been mopping up all of these exercises. Donnie, who Chernovsky expected to be a boat anchor, could suddenly run neck-and-neck with Quinn.

Quinn's fire-team had SO MUCH POTENTIAL and they muffed every exercise with screw-ball antics.

Chernovsky was much calmer when Quinn's squad came back.

"Teams play on game day the way they practice all week," Chernovsky said. "I want you to think about what you were doing. Is this something you would do if real hostiles were chasing you after the snow melts? The answer is no, you wouldn't try to run across a swamp. That means then you should not be doing it now."

That is when Quinn contradicted him.

"That is not quite right," Quinn said.

Chernovsky glared at Quinn. "OK, Spackle. Explain."

"This swamp is "Y" shaped. It has a finger sticking into it. With the right kind of bait, I bet we could get the hostiles to run out onto the finger and then be trapped and we could fire on them from right angles," Quinn said.

"Show me," Chernovsky said.

Quinn walked Chernovsky through the swamp. It was

formed by two drainage ditches coming together from the west and then draining out to the east. The finger that projected out into the flooded area was between the two ditches coming into the swamp. It also happened to be the side facing the road. While not pronounced it was clearly above the ice.

"How would you gull the bad-guys into the trap?" Chernovsky asked in a conversational voice.

"I dunno. Maybe tracks leading out, onto the finger. Put a guy on the far side and have him hollering that he'd broke his leg," Quinn said.

"We would have to put enough tracks onto the ground so it isn't obvious that the squad split off from the main set of tracks," Quinn added. "The squad would have to hunker down there, there, and there, where there is concealment."

"Set it up," Chernovsky said. "Your job, Spackle, is to make this work. If it does, we are going to call this the Pied Piper play."

At dinner that evening, Chernovsky announced that Quinn's squad would be the defense again. He also announced that the rule-set changed. The offense was now allowed to leave the road and pursue the defense.

The exercise was working like a champ when one of Quinn's guys blew the setup.

A loud "mutherfucker" was heard from the ambush as Quinn's guy stood bolt-upright.

The hostiles were not all within the kill-sack.

Quinn's fire-team was massacred while the other fire-team was still able to hold the line.

Chernovsky had Quinn's fire-team run four miles. As they were running, Quinn asked his guy "What the hell happened?"

His guy said, "Cameron threw a snowball that hit me in the face."

Cameron was the leader of the other fire-team on his squad and it was not the first time that Cameron had sabotaged Quinn's team.

Quinn decided it was time to have a talk with Cameron.

Bouncing Cameron

The talk with Cameron did not go well.

Cameron told him "Fuck off."

Quinn was not a people person. He did not have a vast repertoire of skills and was at a loss for the next step.

At the start of training, Chernovsky told the teams that a unanimous vote could remove a fire-team leader. Quinn went and discretely sounded out Cameron's team.

To a man they loathed and feared him. When Quinn asked if they would vote to remove him, they all said "No."

When Quinn asked them why, to a man they said that they feared the retribution they would have to endure if the vote was not unanimous.

Cameron had quietly been digging dirt on each one of his team members. He needled them until he got a reaction and from there he figured out what each young man was most ashamed of. Sometimes he weaseled it out of other team members. Other times he kept pounding until he made a logical deduction.

One team-member wet his bed until he was twelve.

Another team-member had an older brother who was in prison for molesting younger boys and Cameron made some lucky guesses about what the older brother had done to the team-member.

Everybody had a secret and Cameron was a master of worming it out.

Quinn went to Chernovsky.

“Can we talk, privately, sir?” Quinn asked.

“Sure, Spackle. Let’s take a walk,” Chernovsky said.

“You said that we should speak up if we knew something that jeopardized the mission,” Quinn said.

“Yup” Chernovsky said. “Whatchya got?”

“It is about one of the other team-leaders,” Quinn said. “He is setting us up to fail.”

“Which one?” Chernovsky asked.

“Cameron,” Quinn answered.

“I don’t play God” Chernovsky said. “There are only two rules, Win and to follow my direct orders.”

“Take care of it,” Chernovsky said.

“I’d like to kick his ass,” Quinn said, vehemently.

“What is stopping you?” Chernovsky asked.

“You would kick me off the squad,” Quinn answered.

Chernovsky stole a quick glance at Quinn. “Get kicked out of school much, Spackle?” Chernovsky asked.

“About once a year," Quinn admitted.

“This ain’t school. You guys are fighters. I expect some fights. I won’t kick you out but you will get disciplined,” Chernovsky said.

That was an intriguing thought. “Just the instigator?” Quinn asked.

"I don't play God. Both parties get the discipline," Chernovsky said.

The next evening, Quinn tackled Cameron as they were in the chow line. Quinn was pounding the snot out of him when they pried them apart.

Chernovsky did not even ask them what the altercation was about. "Ten-mile run. Billy, trot with them down to Vermontville highway. You two," he said pointing at the combatants, "Five trips out and back. You need to be running. If you walk you will run the full ten miles again."

Then to the chow line, "Save Billy some dinner."

And that was that.

For men the age of Cameron and Quinn, running ten miles got their attention. Missing chow REALLY grabbed their attention.

The next day Donnie tackled Cameron in the chow line and was beating the snot out of him. The two combatants were pried apart.

Chernovsky almost appeared bored. The ill-feelings that had been building for almost a month were coming to a head.

"You," he said, pointing at Donnie. "Run ten miles. Quinn, go with him to Vermontville to make sure both of these bozos run the entire leg."

Then Chernovsky said to the guy ladling out the chow, "Save a plate for Quinn."

Quinn and Donnie jogged out of camp.

"You," he said pointing at Cameron. "Run twenty miles."

"What the fuck!" Cameron said. "Why is he running ten and you are sticking me with twenty?"

"Because it is his first time and it is your second time. You obviously didn't learn your lesson. So, I am turning up the volume. Maybe you will hear the message better," Chernovsky said. "The distance doubles every time you are in a fight."

"But I didn't do anything," Cameron whined.

"Don't give me that shit. I ain't stupid. I played football. The guy who gets the whistle isn't the guy who started it. He is the guy who finished it," Chernovsky said.

"I can't run twenty miles tonight. It is not humanly possible," Cameron objected.

"You are right," Chernovsky said. "Ten miles tonight and the other ten tomorrow."

That is when Cameron noticed the other team-members standing behind Chernovsky, where Chernovsky could not see them. They had learned a little bit about 'sneaky' from Cameron himself.

Pepperoni, a brawler of note was blowing on the knuckles of his right hand and then rubbing them into the palm of his other hand in the universal sign of 'we are going to rumble'. Pepperoni was not intimidating because he was so much bigger than Cameron. He was scary because he had the wing-span-to-height ratio of a orangutan and the ropy muscle to match.

Dean, who had shoulders that looked like the front of a school bus, was cracking his knuckles.

"So what happens if somebody tackles me in the chow-line tomorrow?" Cameron asked.

"You run forty miles. Like I said. The distance doubles every time it happens," Chernovsky said in a voice that brooked no argument.

“Fuck that,” Cameron said. “I quit.”

Chernovsky shrugged. “Probably a good idea. Start walking. We will sort through your shit and drop off your personal gear the next time we swing through Kate’s Store."

After Cameron Duckworth started walking home, Chernovsky signaled ‘Gather in’.

“From now on, if you bozos want to cut somebody from the squads, all you have to do is find four men willing to miss dinner and run ten miles each. I don’t want you guys to be afraid to mix-it-up but I cannot afford to have anybody hurt,” Chernovsky said. “I want to remind you that we are now running short of men...so think it through before you go down that road.”

An hour and a half later Quinn and Donnie came jogging back into camp. "He did all five out-and-backs” Quinn said.

“We have one other order of business tonight. That is to find another team-leader for Squad 2. Do I have any nominations?” Chernovsky said.

To nobody’s surprise Donnie Galligan was selected as the new team-leader and Quinn volunteered to run a man short to free him up.

Later that evening, Donnie noticed that Quinn could not stop smiling. "Happy I am the other team leader on the squad?"

"Nah. I am just remembering how good it felt when I nailed Cameron in the head with an ice-ball as he went by me. That was a pay-back for when he blew the ambush,” Quinn said.

The Cost of Chaos

Innovation growth is “factorial” in nature since most innovation results from novel combinations of existing innovations.

That means innovation can grow even faster than compound interest. The time for new knowledge to be "created" shrinks as the amount of "known" knowledge increases.

Conversely, chaos is a tax on the principal. A chaos-tax that is sufficiently high results in a negative growth-rate as witnessed that fact that some demographics LOSE reading ability between grades nine and high school graduation.

The chaos sown by Cameron Duckworth caused the training to stall-out. With him gone the learning rate exploded.

The morning after Cameron left the pot of oatmeal did not burn nor did it tip and fall into the fire. Nobody woke up to find the damp laces of their boots knotted and frozen. Nobody found their socks knocked off the drying line and trampled into the snow.

The same number of spoons were in the drawer that had been washed and put away the night before. Nobody went the shooting range only to learn that some of the rounds were loaded into their magazines backwards.

Chernovsky was in an expansive mood. The squads were on the practice field a full hour earlier than they had ever managed before. An hour of daylight is not trivial when you only have eight to work with.

Not only that but they showed up ready to work. There were no arguments nor was there foot dragging or “forgotten” items.

Chernovsky started the exercise with a short treatise on screen passes and the draw play. “That is how we are going to run our set-piece battles,” Chernovsky said. “Draw them in. Have them hyper-focus where WE want them looking. Get them to over-commit. Then run the play from where they are not looking.”

As a linebacker he had unique insights into the toughest plays to break. He hated draw plays and screen passes.

They ran through the play a few times when Chernovsky had to tell the offense to "dumb down". "Our advantage is that we have seen this play and will have run it a hundred times before we do it for real. Their disadvantage is that they will have never seen these plays before.

"But to make it work, we gotta be perfect," Chernovsky lied. These plays even worked when people dropped assignments. In programming language, they were fault tolerant. That is why Chernovsky chose them for his set-piece engagements.

The offense had to slow down to about 1/4 speed before Chernovsky was satisfied.

"What has to happen next?" Chernovsky asked part-way into the slow-motion ambush.

"Everybody on the blind-side needs to start shooting," Quinn said.

"How are you going to communicate?" Chernovsky asked. "You are a leader, that means you need a way to command-and-control."

Chernovsky did not have any strong opinions. He was giving them the problem to unravel.

"I could start shooting," Quinn said. "Everybody would hear the AR."

"You could, but you would be tipping your hand. You would lose the advantage of surprise that the silenced .22LRs give you and all the hostiles would know where the second threat was coming from," Chernovsky observed.

After thrashing through the options the fire-teams decided

that radio clicks were the best option. But when it was windy or the radios were in-op then they would have the team-leader start the party with the AR -- with the caveat that that the team-leader was positioned well away from the body of the team; preferably biased toward the distraction so the hostiles would think it was part of the distraction.

Chernovsky then said "Those are reasonable proposals. Test them. Try to make them break. Make them earn their place in the play-book."

The young men threw themselves into the challenge of making the proposals fail. As they worked through those issues, they also solved issues with the optimum spacing between team members and optimum spacing from groups of hostiles when executing ambushes.

More was accomplished in one day than had been resolved in the two prior weeks.

After lunch a group of the young men were talking about Duckworth.

"Why?" Pepperoni asked. "I don't get it. Why do people act like that?"

Pepperoni's last name was Prestigiacomo, which was a mouthful. Everybody called him Pepperoni except for Chernovsky when he was really, really angry.

Donnie, who had been in counseling and knew a bit about psychology suggested "Maybe his head is filled with chaos and it just leaks out."

Quinn said, "You are WAY too kind. He is just a piece of shit."

Dean, the young man with shoulders that made him look like a school bus said, "I have a younger brother who is ADHD and he always stirs-the-pot. My mom things that chaos is normal to him and he is just leveling the playing field."

Quinn objected to that. "I think Cameron is just a mean-shit. I mean, maybe he keeps people off-balance and jacked-up because he can grab more of what he wants behind the smoke screen. But mostly I think he is just mean."

Walt Shaw was Shadrack's older brother. "Nope. It is because the devil is in him," Walt said.

Donnie scoffed. He believed in science; not folk tales written in a four-thousand-year-old book.

"I don't care what other names you give them," Walt said. "The Bible says 'Your name is legion' of demons. Whatever the name of the demon, it is going to make itself right at home as long as the sinner invites him into his soul."

That was tough thing to argue against. Nobody was likely to change if they didn't want to.

The afternoon was spent practicing retreating out of prepared positions.

"Suppose you tore off a bigger chunk than you could chew," Chernovsky said. "You are shooting it out with hostiles and reinforcements keep adding to their number."

"Who is going to decide it is time to pull the plug? How is it going to happen?" Chernovsky asked.

Then he let them walk through it. It quickly became apparent that the positions the defense chose to fight from became death-traps when they tried to retreat from them.

"So, what do you have to change to make the positions survivable?" Chernovsky asked. "Do you change where you position people? Do you change the playing field?"

Quinn was baffled. "What do you mean, 'change the playing field'?" Quinn asked.

Chernovsky rolled his eyes. "We have chainsaws. We have more than thirty people to cut and move brush, to open up lines-of-sight or create concealment. We have shovels. We can move logs. We can get sand-bags. Use your brains. How can we totally stack the deck against the hostiles?" Chernovsky asked. "We get to pick the fields of battle. Let's make it work to our advantage."

Sipping from the Pot of Resentment All Day Long

The training pace picked up during the second month.

Chernovsky had the squads repeat the bounding exercises along Vermontville Highway which ran east-west. He also ran two-on-one exercises. The exercises ran six hours a day. There was barely enough time to eat and dry sweaty clothing before hitting the rack and doing it all over again the next day.

It was early in the second month when MT, Mandy, and Dysen came out of quarantine.

While Mandy made good use of the time by recording broadcasts, Dysen had wiled away the days by brewing up a big pot of resentment every morning and sipping from it all day long.

Sure, she had been as freaked out by the home invader as her mom and sister. But she felt steam-rollered into moving out to the sticks. Her mom and sister were more compliant personalities than Dysen. They were not thrilled to move into the Heiler house for forty days of quarantine but they did it with a smile and a thank-you.

Dysen, for her part, felt she was made of sterner stuff. MT ripped into her the first time she was snappish to the people bringing food and firewood. MT reminded her that nobody was under any obligation to feed them, that they were doing it out of the goodness of their hearts. Dysen sulked for a week afterward.

One of the things that made life endurable was the daily delivery of the Mr. Ed newsletter. Mr. Ed enthused about the skills the squads were working on. He left out the areas-of-operation because there was no way to control where Mr. Ed's newsletter went after it was run off on the office printer.

Mr. Ed exercised journalistic license. Leaving out certain details made it sound like a jolly romp in the woods; Summer Camp without mosquitoes, if you will. He figured the folks in Kates Store and Pray Church needed something to lift their spirits.

Dysen determined that she was going to join one of the squads as soon as she got out of quarantine. She knew that anything a boy could do; she could do better.

Quinn's squad was tasked with swinging through Kate's Store three days after MT and family decanted from quarantine. Quinn's squad was picking up ammo, suppressors, booze, fabric bags to use for sandbags, provisions, etc.

MT and Dysen confronted Quinn and demanded that Dysen be allowed to join his squad.

Quinn punted. He called Chernovsky on the hand-held. After outlining the demands, Quinn asked for guidance.

Chernovsky told him to hang loose for a few minutes. Maybe let the squad go in the store for fifteen minutes after cautioning them to not break anything.

Chernovsky radioed Kate and Rick. Kate asked Chernovsky to give Dysen a "fair chance" otherwise it would disturb the harmony in the community.

Chernovsky reluctantly agreed but told Kate and Rick that Dysen would have to pull her own weight, literally. By then MT and Dysen had joined the conversation. Very little is private in the small spaces that are heated in the winter.

Everybody but Quinn agreed that Dysen could join Quinn's squad provided she proved she could pull her own weight and keep up.

Chernovsky told Dysen she had an hour to get her kit together.

Chernovsky then added to his order. He needed another utility sled. The sleds were vacuum formed from HDPE, a tough and slippery plastic. The sleds were four feet long, two feet wide and twelve inches deep.

He requested another eight quart cast iron Dutch oven. Another iron tripod. Ten pounds of corn meal. Three pounds of split peas. A gallon of vegetable oil. Salt....

Quinn loaded the extra sled with the additional gear. It looked like it weighed about sixty pounds. There was a lot of extra room and Quinn wondered how he was going to tie it down so it didn't slosh all around.

Dysen came out with her "kit". It barely fit into the spare room on the sled. Sloshing around was not going to be a problem.

Quinn had been livid when he learned that Dysen was joining his squad. At least he had the brains to get out of earshot before complaining to Chernovsky.

Chernovsky told him, "She is not on your squad until she shows up in camp. She has my permission to follow you but you are not to render any more aid to her than you would any other civilian."

That gave Quinn a glimmer of hope.

Dysen stood beside the sled wondering who was going to pull it. Her kit brought the weight to about ninety pounds. Quite by design that was very close to her body weight.

That was in contrast to the other sleds which weighed between one-twenty and one-ninety.

"OK, men. Let's go. We are burning daylight," Quinn said.

The squad was chomping at the bit. They knew dinner waited for them in camp. Tonight's camp was nine miles away and it would be dark before they reached it.

They each grabbed their sled-line and broke the sled free by first pulling to the right and then the left. Then they took off following Quinn at a fast shuffle. One of the keys to pulling sleds efficiently is to keep them moving. Otherwise they stick to the ground.

Another trick is to learn just how high to lift your feet. Too high and you are wasting energy. Too low and you are kicking through snow and wasting energy. It is not a teachable thing. It is learned by doing.

"What the hell!" Dysen said.

Mr. Ed broke the awkward silence. "You wanna run with the big dogs, you better grab that line and start pulling. Don't look like they are coming back to help you."

Dysen, being last had the easiest pull. The snow was packed and smooth. Frankly, she never had a chance. She had not been in great shape going into quarantine and forty days of inactivity not only reduced her muscle mass but tightened her muscles.

Her togs made her look like a model for LL Bean but the cute boots quickly gave her blisters and the snug jeans wet through the first time she slipped and fell.

To her credit, she made it a quarter mile before throwing in the towel. The first half of the quarter mile was not too bad. The second half was uphill.

Turning around she had the presence of mind to bring the sled back with her. She ditched it at the bottom of the hill, barely able to hobble due to the blisters.

"I'll get it tomorrow," she spat out at her mother answering the question MT was about to ask.

The next day Dysen was not fit for human company. MT was at the end of her rope. "Let's take a walk," MT said to Dysen. Refusal was not an option.

MT started out gently. "Do you remember when you were young, I used to read you a bedtime story called 'Who moved my Cheese'?"

Dysen snapped back. "Mom. I am not five."

MT responded in kind. "Then stop acting like a five-year-old."

Dysen recoiled. The fact that her mother was calling her to account was a new feeling.

"We are guests here," MT said. "We are eating their food. We are living in their house. The least we can do is ask how we can help rather than pouting and stamping our feet when things are not going our way."

"Maybe you haven't noticed. But nobody here is eating better than we are. Nobody is warmer. Nobody has been asked to do less that we have been asked to do. We did not earn this. This is a gift," MT said.

"What would you have me do?" Dysen asked. Even to herself it sounded petulant.

Dysen did not like what MT told her. It went against her very grain....

CHAPTER FIVE

Cupid Delivers an Arrow

A few days later Chernovsky and the squads were operating near the extreme southern end of their operations area. The pace of operations had been leisurely, a fact that tipped Quinn off that the other shoe was about to fall. The only time Chernovsky gave them a break was when he was planning to drop a big task on them.

Chernovsky announced that lunch would be delayed. This was met with a huge moan.

Chernovsky called out Quinn. "I need to have you pick the three fastest men. You can pick from all squads."

That was easy: Zak, Ngandu and Wolde. Quinn used last names for fighters who were not in his fire-team.

Chernovsky said, "I have intelligence that a person is heading north on the paved road. They are carrying materials that cannot fall into the enemy's hands. Time is of the essence. You are to proceed south down the paved road using all due precautions as quickly as you can. You are to intercept the courier and relieve them of their cargo. Then you are to return with all due haste back here. Do Not, I repeat, Do Not open the package and upon pain of death do not let it fall into hostile hands."

Even with boots and heavy winter clothing the young men churned out eight-minute miles with ease. They were helped by the fact that much of the snow had melted off the road.

Quinn spotted the courier three-quarter mile out. The runners left the road and angled into the woods. Half popped out in front of the courier and half behind.

To their eternal surprise, the courier was a young woman. She was pulling a sled behind her.

"Oh my," she exclaimed.

Cupid interposed. Neither Dysen or Quinn realized they had met before. It is ironic that popular culture has Cupid shooting his targets with arrows. It would be more accurate to picture him with blind-folds than a bow-and-arrow.

Dysen had a chest cooler in the sled.

"Son of a bitch! What is in this?" Zak exclaimed as he lifted it out.

Quinn said, "Watch your mouth. There is a lady present."

Except for the surly, spoiled child Quinn had seen three days earlier, none of the men had seen a young woman for a month and a half. Chernovsky ran a tight ship and nothing would lose support among the Dimondale natives quicker than his men dallying with their daughters. That, and it would break quarantine.

This young lady's eyes sparkled and her blushed cheeks dimpled when she smiled. Quinn was smitten.

"No worries," Dysen said. Every woman enjoys the attention of healthy, young men. And these four men were prime, if undernourished specimens.

The first two guys hoisted the cooler and started north toward Chernovsky and the camp. The best pace they could manage was a ten-minute mile. The other two spelled them after five minutes...

Staggering into camp, they found Chernovsky near the kitchen. “Here is your package,” Quinn said.

The rest of the crew had just finished eating. Chernovsky said he would open the package after Quinn, Zak, Ngandu and Wolde had eaten. They were famished and it took three minutes for them to vacuum down their stew.

With great ceremony, Chernovsky undid the ratchet straps holding the cover on the cooler. Popping open the cover, the three squads were met with the smell of fresh peanut butter cookies.

Chernovsky handed them out. They were still warm from the oven...thanks to the hot water bottles Dysen had placed beneath the cookies.

The cookies were technically more like frosted brownies than cookies. They were ¾ inch thick and generously frosted with peanut butter frosting. Each fighter received a five inch by six-inch slab. Dysen had tweaked Kate’s peanut butter cookie recipe.

Dysen had originally been VERY resistant when MT suggested she could make cookies to support the effort.

Dysen had worshipped Hillary Clinton ever since Senator Clinton had run for President. Dysen was 18 and a starry-eyed idealist. Dysen had been crushed when Senator Clinton lost to Trump. In her fervor, Dysen had memorized Hillary’s statement:

> "The work that I have done as a professional, a public advocate, has been aimed . . . to assure that women can make the choices whether it's full-time career, full-time motherhood, or some combination. I suppose you would have preferred that I could have stayed home,

baked cookies, and had teas."

Dysen had no idea what the future held but she knew two things to be facts, she would never make cookies or serve tea.

MT asked Dysen why Dysen thought Hillary Clinton was a hero. Dysen answered automatically, “Because she is a ball-buster.”

MT had winced at that and automatically said, "That will be a quarter for the swear jar."

Then MT said, “I think Hillary Clinton is heroic and a person to emulate because she was among the first to recognize that the rules for women had changed. She recognized that America had changed and needed women lawyers, women judges, women politicians. Then she threw her whole being into making that reality happen.”

Dysen was shaking her head “No.”

MT then added “Hillary recognized opportunity when it knocked on her door. If it hadn’t been for Hillary, Bill would have been a second-rate lawyer who boffed every real-estate agent in Little Rock.”

MT stuck to her guns. “You can look at the superficial things about Hillary, about her being a ball-buster and model that. Or you can look at the things that really made her heroic, that she had the clarity-of-vision to see what had changed from yesterday and that she had the intestinal fortitude to throw herself completely into the new reality.

“Your choice,” MT said.

It took Dysen two days to digest that information.

Two other things came together for Dysen in her cookie making venture. Gabby was extracting soy oil so there was no longer a shortage of edible oils.

The other thing she learned was that Chernovsky's guys were struggling to keep on body weight between the physical work and the cold. The answer was obvious. Dysen increased the shortening by 50%, as much as she could sneak in. She also bumped up the vanilla.

It took her a while to process that nobody had prevented her from joining the squad. It was simple physics and biology. She could, however, support the squads.

Her plan was to make and deliver a batch every three days...

First Slowly, then All at Once

You could ask ten people when the grid went down and you would get nine different answers.

At first, the grid died a little at a time.

The first inkling the people of Kates Store and Pray Church had that the grid was stressed were the rolling brown-outs.

It caused annoyance over Christmas when stoves did not come fully up to heat, cakes fell and those lucky enough to have meat were not able to get it fully cooked in time for dinner.

Even gas stoves were affected as the ignitor could not generate enough heat to open the gas valve.

The duration and severity of the brown-outs increased rapidly after Christmas.

Trains were no longer running because the cities were in chaos. Coal fired plants were starved for fuel.

Lack of key maintenance people took other power plants or power lines off-line.

The rolling brown-outs became rolling black-outs as utilities attempted to keep line voltage at acceptable levels by dropping parts of the grid. They tried to ensure at least thirty minutes of full power every day so people with battery backups for critical medical equipment could recharge, but even that became impossible.

Power was cut to cell phone towers just before it was rationed at hospitals. The natural gas-powered turbines (aka, surge capacity) were the last of the grid, other than nuclear and hydro, to remain running. It was not enough.

Carson Duckworth was insufferable. He smugly ran his natural gas-powered generator at full bore. He ran outdoor lights and lit up his house like a Christmas tree. He bragged to everybody he could collar how smart he was and how stupid everybody else was. For some reason, people started avoided Carson Duckworth.

People in rural areas adapted by sleeping more. Houses that had been abandoned were investigated for blankets, sleeping bags and other bedding. In most cases, IOUs were left with an inventory of materials that had been "borrowed" and who was using those blankets.

People in the city were more radically impacted. For the most part, they didn't have very many blankets and the warmest garments many owned were hooded sweatshirts. It had been inconceivable to most people, especially those who lived in apartments and managed properties, that the heat wouldn't come out of the ducts.

City folks saw no other choice than to sleep two, three or four to a bed to maximize the number of blankets and conserve body heat.

By the middle of January, the pressure in the natural gas pipelines fell off a cliff as key personnel did not show up and as the electricity required to run most of the pumps faded. Even when the electricity came back on, there were procedures that had to be followed to restart the system. It was not as easy as pushing a button.

Pumping stations from New Orleans to Maine went into bypass mode.

Carson Duckworth's generator sputtered and stalled. His lights went off. Without natural gas Duckworth's furnace did not go on.

His freezers filled with meat would have quickly thawed except the temperature inside his mansion quickly dropped into the upper thirties.

Without electricity the inserts in his handsome, fieldstone fireplaces sent the heat right up the chimney. The fans had no power to circulate air and push the heat out, into the rooms. Attempting to get SOME heat in the house, Duckworth piled the firewood high in the fireplace. He only succeeded in overheating the inserts and cracking the liners.

Duckworth, who had been charging his neighbors for water from his well, received little sympathy from the neighborhood.

Like Rick and Kate, he found that the static level of the water was forty feet below ground level. Attempts to pull the water from that depth with a cistern pump failed. Unlike Rick and Kate, he did not have a backup to the backup. He was reduced to dipping water out of a local pond and carrying it back home in two, five-gallon buckets.

He found out that getting water was not the only problem. Getting rid of it was also an issue.

Due to quirks in his soil composition, he had an above-ground drain field just like 65% of the houses that had been built in the last fifteen years.

The permitting people required that the system be sized for two people per bedroom (five bedrooms) and 200 gallons of waste water per person per day...then rounded up to the next thousand gallons. They also required redundant pumps and motors, each pump sized to run three thousand gallons a day up to the drain field.

The half-horsepower, single-phase induction motors pulled eight amps of 220 Volts at start-up. That is not a very easy power number to deliver with solar panels, windmills or even batteries.

Others, those who lived on a smaller footprint, found the transition easier.

A small economy developed. Zane pulled lead-acid batteries from the vehicles and attempted to recondition them. Primitive windmills were constructed and the wind power was used to turn alternators.

The first generation of windmills did not rotate to follow the breeze. Belts were used to step up the speed and turn the alternators. The power was used to recharge the batteries.

The tiny amounts of electricity forced people to set priorities. CPAP machines, clocks and two-way radios do not take much power. LED lights, and computers with small screens (smart phones, for example) used only a little bit more.

Using electricity for resistance heating was a non-starter as were most electric motor applications. In some cases, the mechanical "motor" applications did not require constant power. In those cases, users experimented with bypassing electricity and powering the device directly from the windmill. Examples included grinding grain.

As difficult as Duckworth's situation was, those in the city were far worse off. At least Duckworth could use a pick-ax and shovel to dig a trench to drain his septic tank overflow way from his house.

The food distribution centers in the cities manfully switched from passing out foods and reconfigured as soup kitchens. Instead of having one third of the population showing up on any given day, the kitchens were now serving the entire population three times a day.

Water bottles were handed out wholesale. As inconceivable as it seems, some people tried to use the water, a half-liter at a time, to flush the toilets.

The sewage situation in the cities was dire. Lift pumps stopped functioning.

The most common form of multi-family dwelling was the two-and-a-half story townhouse. The other half-story was a sub-grade first floor, thereby avoiding the code that mandated expensive automated fire suppression systems.

The sub-grade floors started with raw sewage. Once the spring thaws came many of the units would have four feet of raw sewage in their lowest floor and it would be flowing out over the threshold of their door.

Most of the storm drains had been separated from the sewage drains but a few connections had been missed. Without the lift stations to carry the storm water over the levees, the storm water crossed over into the sewage lines at the remaining connections and backed it up into basements everywhere.

By all reasonable medical metrics, modern US cities reverted to the status of medieval cities in three months.

Food Planning

The native Americans called the period from the snow's melting until the first baby rabbits were born and the first flush of greens "The Hungry Time". The grain and pumpkins had been eaten and the meadows and forests depleted of game by hunters, both human and animal.

Later in the spring fish would be spawning, water-fowl would be returning, birds would be laying eggs and greens, though low in calories, would be abundant.

The people of Kates Store and Pray Church were working on food security throughout the winter, long before the first greens poked their head above ground.

Old fruit trees that had been cursed for the mess they made of lawns were looked at in a different light.

The old timers trained the youngsters on the fine art of pruning fruit trees. Every old timer had a different method but they all seemed to work.

Wood cutters mapped out nut trees as they cruised the woods cutting firewood. In the first, frenzied rush to cut enough wood to keep citizens from freezing, there had been a natural tendency to cut everything within easy reach of the road. The farmers put a quick stop to that. They marked the walnuts, hickory and oak.

Any tree can be burned for heat but only a mature walnut tree can produce ten pounds of nut meats that are 65% fat and 15% protein. Ten pounds of nuts does not sound like much but ignoring them was like leaving money on the table. A few of the citizens who had lived in the south wished there were pecan trees because of their productivity and ease of cracking.

Flat areas with good sunlight were paced off and corners marked with hunks of firewood, the ground being too frozen to drive stakes. Sizes of gardens varied but twenty paces-by-forty paces was a common size.

Seed catalogs from previous years were unearthed and looked at for growing instructions.

Windows and doors and plastic were fabricated into cold frames to get the jump on the season.

Long debates were held over the merits of cabbage versus

broccoli and kale while others debated the merits of tomatoes versus cucumbers. In general, the less experienced the gardener the more vehemently they argued their opinion, certainty being inversely related to experience.

The more experienced gardeners quickly came to agreement on the "heavy lifters". They all planned to put large portions of their gardens into potatoes, brassicas and carrots. Green beans and tomatoes may be delicious but in the final analysis they are mostly water while potatoes, cabbage and carrots can be stored without the effort of canning them.

Milo and Kelly visited the farmers of Kates Store, Pray Church and North Eaton Rapids in turn. Kates Store and North Eaton Rapids had roughly three hundred souls each while Pray Church had about four hundred.

The farmers had little to go on regarding the yields they could expect with no commercial fertilizers and replanting seeds from hybrid plants.

They recalled stories told at Thanksgiving when grandparents spoke of forty bushels of corn to the acre being a good crop and fifty bushels to the acre was exceptional. That compared to the two-hundred plus bushels-to-the-acre they got as a matter of course now days.

Budgeting 2000 Calories per day per person came to about seven bushels of corn per person. Said another way, an acre of corn could produce enough calories to feed almost six people at forty bushels to the acre. Working the math that way, Milo figured he would need to till about 200 acres of ground to ensure there was enough corn to feed the thousand souls in NER, Kates Store and Pray Church.

Families would have gardens and cattle would graze pasture and provide milk, cheese and butter. There would be other sources of calories, but Milo banked on bad luck. He would rather have a surplus than a shortfall. In the back of his mind was the fact that somebody needed to grow the food the 3000 souls in Eaton Rapids needed to eat.

The other concern Milo and Kelly had was that they BURNED corn to run the gasifiers. They did not have enough experience to estimate how much corn they were going to need to till two hundred or more acres.

Each of the three commercial farmers in Kates Store volunteered to grow thirty acres. They nominated the thirty acres that were least likely to have weed problems and were favorably disposed for access to roads. They anticipated that they would be hiring people to hoe or cultivate those crops.

Milo suggested that they put in several, smaller plantings to be closer to the end-users but the farmers rejected the idea. They told him that the losses due to wildlife...birds, raccoon, squirrels and so on...are always highest at the edges of the fields. Planting several, smaller plantings would result in unacceptably high losses.

Farmer Don volunteered to grow twenty of corn, one of edible beans and nine of soybeans. Don would have grown more edible beans but there were just not enough seeds to plant more than one acre. He intended to keep a substantial amount of his harvest for future plantings.

Farmer Ken volunteered for twenty-five of corn and five of sugar beets.

Farmer Earl opted for twenty of corn, five each of oats and five of sunflowers. When Kate asked him why he wanted to grow so many sunflowers he told her, “My wife was saying we were going to run out of peanut butter. Seems like everybody is using a lot of it now. We figured that if we grew sunflowers we could make sun-butter and if we had enough of it, maybe it would be something that can be traded to other places for things we need.”

That was in addition to the ten acres each farmer had seeded with winter wheat the previous fall. At Milo's request they spun seed into standing soybeans before the leaves fell...soybeans that there was no market for.

The rains were favorable and the seed germinated well. In late winter, after a thaw reduced the snow cover to a few inches, Milo spun red clover seed into the young stands of wheat.

Farmer Don had several books by David Kline and Gene Logsdon, a couple of Ohio farmers who were proponents of "Amish farming". The farmers of Kates Store, having been severed from traditional ways of farming by seventy years of high-input farming were willing to START with the crop rotation of the Ohio Amish.

They would keep what worked and experiment with what needed improvement.

A typical "Amish rotation" started with:

- A year of hay. Feed the hay through the winter on the field it came from. Move the hay feeders around so the poop was spread across the field.

The farmers of Kates Store were about to find out if their soil had any viable grass seeds in it after more than a decade of growing Round-up Ready crops.

- A year of grass/clover pasture. The grass came in naturally as the red clover stand thinned.

- Plow-down the two-year-old pasture/hayfield and a year of corn (maize), a crop that demanded a great deal of nitrogen for high yields and tolerated a rough seed-bed.

- A year of spring-planted small grains like oats or barley or perhaps beans. Unbeknownst to Kelly, Farmer Ken managed to find a fifty-pound bag of two-row barley and planned to sneak in a half-acre field of it behind the corn field.

Barley, like many small grains yields roughly fifty times as much grain as the seed planted. Corn, or maize as the rest of the world calls it, is the champ at 600X return while potatoes at 12X is the laggard.

- In the early autumn of the fourth year, winter wheat spun into the standing crop of grain or beans. Mid-winter, an additional planting of Red Clover or alfalfa would be spun into the young wheat to take the cycle back to the starting point. Since Michigan does not have a climate suitable for harvesting alfalfa seed, locally harvested red clover seed would have to suffice.

The only trick, according to Logsdon was the hop-skippity-jump to get into the sequence.

The farmers in the other two areas agreed to similar plans.

The farmers, for their part, started scrounging up horse-drawn equipment. Primarily they were looking for mowing equipment. The vast majority of their land would be left fallow and the best way to control weeds is to mow them or to graze them.

Since there were not enough horses, sheep and cows to provide sufficient mowing power, the weeds would be mowed and baled as hay. Very mediocre hay to be sure, but far better than trying to feed an animal snow. The situation would correct itself in a few years as the farms converted to the H-P-C-SG-W rotation.

Another piece of equipment that was suddenly in high demand were the heads for harvesting clover seed.

The first greens were nettles, dock, and violets, garlic and nodding onions. Families shared recipes and tips for harvesting.

Chickens were allowed to free-range under the watchful eye of a responsible family member. More often than not the family member had a shotgun close at hand. The free protein provided by the wealth of bugs that had been living in the duff beneath the snow was not a bargain if a family lost even a few hens to predators.

Campfire Talk, Vlad the Impaler

"How many of you know Dmitri from Kates Store?" Chernovsky asked.

The sun sets early in the winter. It was full dark. Two sentries were posted up at the north gate but with the temperature at fifteen degrees and the southwest wind kicking along at 10 miles an hour, nobody was coming.

The eight hours of daylight were used in heavy, physical activities. The young men thrived on nine hours of sleep. That left seven hours to fill.

A gentle bed of coals burned in the steel truck wheel that served as a fire ring. The red light of coals does not diminish night vision nor is it likely to telegraph position.

Chernovsky had been jollied into telling stories. He used the opportunity to pass lessons on to his soldiers. Tonight, he was going to share one he heard from Dmitri.

About six young men raised their hands.

"Where did Dmitri come from?" Chernovsky asked.

"Russia", "Rome," various young men guessed. Finally, Walter Shaw said "Romania".

"Yup, that's right. Romania," Chernovsky said.

"Do you know where Romania is?" Chernovsky asked.

Everybody, even Walter Shaw was very fuzzy about the location of Romania.

“Have any of you ever heard of a place called Adrianople?” Chernovsky asked.

Walter said, "There is a town named Adrian down by the Ohio border."

"Yup," Chernovsky said. "It was probably named after Adrianople."

“Adrianople is the most fought over piece of real estate on earth. Sixteen times, epic, world-war scale battles were fought at Adrianople. There are no gold mines in Adrianople. There is no silver or gems. The weather sucks. No government ever set up a capital there. Why would anybody, much less thirty-two armies fight for control of Adrianople?”

Nobody knew.

“It is because geography rules. Adrianople is the single best place to defend against an army trying to get from Asia-to-Europe or from Europe-to-Asia,” Chernovsky said.

The young men were trying to figure out what this had to do with Romania.

“The second-best place to defend is in Romania,” Chernovsky said. “Armies from Asia have to move up the Danube river to reach the heart of Europe. The Danube river flows through Romania and then into the Black Sea. If the European army could not stop the barbarians at Adrianople, their next best chance was Romania.”

Chernovsky spit into the coals and thought about what he was going to say next.

“Fifty years before Columbus discovered America, a Turkish army invaded Europe. Europe was Christian. Turkey was Muslim. Muslims offered captured cities the opportunity to surrender and convert to Islam. If they refused, they killed everybody in the city. The Quaran, their holy book, told them to do that," Chernovsky said.

"In fact, one of the Turkish generals, one named Tamerlane, was famous for making pyramids of his enemies' skulls after killing everybody in the cities.

"The Turkish army crushed the main European army at Adrianople. The only thing between them and northern Europe was a minor Romanian warlord named Vlad," Chernovsky said.

"The Turkish army was almost a quarter of a million fighting men. Vlad's army was scattered through the hills and less than fifty thousand," Chernovsky said. "So, Vlad's army was outnumbered five-to-one.

"A fog covered the mountains in the first battle and twenty thousand Turkish soldiers were separated from their main force," Chernovsky said. "They surrendered to Vlad's army. Threw down their swords and surrendered.

"Vlad could not spare the food to feed them. He could not spare the soldiers to guard them. He could not turn them back over to his enemies because then he would face them on the battle field again," Chernovsky said.

Changing topics, Chernovsky said, "In those days they executed criminals by impaling them. They did not run them through with a nice, clean spear and have them bleed out in forty seconds. Nope, they made an example of them."

"They would find a young tree growing in the woods, a tree that was between one and two inches in diameter. They cut the tree at four feet using an ax so the tip was a sharp point," Chernovsky said. Then he was quiet while his audience visualized what he had described.

"Then, six strong men took the prisoner, who was all tied up or had been thumped on his head so he did not fight, and they pushed him down on the stake," Chernovsky said.

“Why would it take six men?” Walter Shaw asked.

“Because they rammed it up his ass,” Chernovsky said.

“When it was half way in, and there was no way he could wiggle off, they untied his legs. As long as he stayed on tippy-toes, the point of the stake would not pierce his heart,” Chernovsky said.

“Vlad’s army took the twenty thousand prisoners to a valley that the Turks had to move up to attack them. The young maple trees grew thicker than hairs on a dog’s back,” Chernovsky said.

The young men drew their collective breath. “NO!” they whispered in horror.

“Vlad had his men impale all twenty thousand prisoners. The men cut the maple saplings and sharpened the ends and they had at-it,” Chernovsky said.

"The other thing you need to know is that not all of the prisoners were soldiers. There were women...cooked and washed and did...ahem, other things," Chernovsky said, delicately. "And there were kids who followed the army. Vlad the Impaler had them all executed."

“When the Turks moved up the valley they came to the place where all the saplings had been cut and their squad-mates were stuck to the ground like twenty thousand lollipops.

"The Turkish soldiers recognized executed soldiers. Soldiers they had grown up with in the same villages. Cousins. Brothers. Fathers. Sons," Chernovsky said. "The amazing thing is that some of the prisoners were still alive, even after two days...they told the Turkish soldiers and generals what happened. And they begged the Turks to kill them out of mercy.

"Do you want to know what the two-hundred, thirty thousand Turks did?" Chernovtsy said. "They turned around and went home.

"The other thing you need to know about Vlad the Impaler is the name of the castle where he lived. The name of that castle is Castle Dracula, and consequently Vlad the Impaler is also known as Count Dracula," Chernovsky said.

"That is horrible," one of the younger men opined.

"That is easy to say when you are five hundred years from the event. If the Turks had conquered Europe, none of us would be here," Chernovsky said. "Our fore-fathers would have been executed and our female ancestors would have been sold into slavery."

"Vlad's treatment of those twenty thousand prisoners spared the twenty million people in Europe," Chernovsky said.

Campfire Talk: The Morality of Killing All Zombies

John Gault was troubled by the need to kill all of the raiders.

He asked Chernovsky "Why?" and Chernovsky decided it was a good topic for the campfire talk.

"How many of you have younger sisters?" Chernovsky started out by asking after the fighters who were not standing sentry got settled.

About a quarter of the young men raised their hands.

"Keep your hands up," Chernovsky said. "How many of you have girl friends?"

About three-quarters of the men had their hands in the air.

"How many of you have mothers?" Chernovsky asked.

Of course, all the rest of the men raised their hands.

“OK, you can lower your hands,” Chernovsky said.

“Do any of them DESERVE to get Ebola? Did any of them do anything to earn death?” Chernovsky asked.

After hearing nothing but gentle snapping from the bed of coals for ten seconds he said, “I didn’t think so.”

“How about the zombies?” Chernovsky asked. "Michigan is under martial law and has been for a month. Those zombies aren't supposed to be here. They are supposed to stay at their address-of-record.

“If you had to choose between one zombie dying and your girl-friend or younger sister dying, who would you choose? Would it be fairer for all of the innocent girls to die in Kates Store, Pray Church or for a raider to die in Windsor Township?” Chernovsky said.

Gault objected. “But it is not fair. The zombies aren’t any different than we are. They didn’t do anything that makes it fair to kill them.”

Chernovsky stared at Gault. “You did not listen to what I said. You were busy thinking of what you were going to say.”

“I didn’t say ‘fair’, I said ‘fairer’,” Chernovsky said. “We weren’t given any choices that are ‘fair’. All we can do is choose between the best of a bad lot.

“If we don’t kill the zombies, all the zombies, then everybody in Kates Store, Pray Church and points south dies. Not just us but the truly innocent. Not only does everybody in Kates Store die, but the zombies die anyway. Ebola is out there. Somebody said the infection is running at 10%, that means that in a group of ten zombies one of them is infected, guaranteed,” Chernovsky said.

Math and statistics were not Chernovsky's strong suit.

"If we kill all the zombies, then your younger sisters will have a chance to live to become adults. There will be a girlfriend to go back to," Chernovsky said.

"The choice is yours. Kill all zombies now, here in Windsor Township or let everybody back home die," Chernovsky said.

Everybody could see that Gault was wrestling with what Chernovsky had said.

He started to speak up when one of the other fighters told him to shut up.

"No. Let him speak," Chernovsky said. "It is beyond important that every one of you, every single one of you, squeeze the trigger when you have the target in front of you."

"I cannot have half of you going on a morality strike. I cannot have five of you on strike. I cannot afford to have a single one of you not drop-the-hammer when I, and your comrades in arms, are counting on you to stop the zombies," Chernovsky said "If you cannot pull the trigger, then we all get rolled over and die."

Then Chernovsky decided to take a big gamble.

"What do you think the raw odds are?" he asked. "How many zombies and how many of us?"

The high end of the count was five-to-one, just like Vlad the Impaler.

"You are all wrong. There will be at least thirty zombies for every fighter," Chernovsky let that sink in.

"That is why I have been a cast-iron bastard. The only way we have the slightest chance of completing our assignment is to take unfair advantage every chance we get," Chernovsky said. "And we have to be perfect in our execution. Not 90%, not 95%. PERFECT."

Most of these kids had not done well at school. Many of them scraped by with a D on the second test retake...for every single test. Perfection in the field was a challenge but they had seen short windows of perfection, unlike tests that asked about gerunds or igneous rocks.

"The other thing is that Gault is the canary-in-the-coal mine. I gotta believe that some of you have the same questions that Gault has but you don't have the balls to ask. Either that, or you figure you can count on Gault to ask," Chernovsky said.

There was some mumbled agreement.

Encouraged, John Gault said, "Christ said we are supposed to love our enemies. I don't see how to square executing potential hostiles that we got drunk with being a Christian."

Chernovsky was stuck. He was not a church goer, nor did he read the Bible. One thing Chernovsky was good at was thinking on his feet.

"I gotta admit that I am not the guy to ask those kinds of riddles," Chernovsky said.

"What I want to do is ask Walt Shaw what he is thinking," Chernovsky said.

Shaw frequently pulled out his battered Bible to study in moments of downtime. Not only did he read the Bible but he was one of the most enthusiastic fighters.

"Hey, Preacher...what is your thinking on what Gault said?" Chernovsky asked.

Walt Shaw was not used to being the center of attention. He looked across the bed of glowing coals at Gault and said, "I assume you mean Matthew 5:44 when you said we should love our enemies."

"Yeah, I am not sure what the chapter and verse is but I remember hearing it in church," Gault said.

"Chapter 5 is mostly short comparisons that highlight the dangers of the slippery-slope," Shaw said. "Swearing at your brother being the same as murdering him. Divorcing your wife being the same as making her a prostitute."

"Jesus did not tell us to not kill our enemies. He told us to pray for them," Shaw said.

"I have been combing through the Bible and I think Deuteronomy 20 speaks to your concerns," Shaw said.

Gault had to admit that he was not very familiar with the Old Testament.

"I am not going to read it, 'cause the light sucks. But in a nutshell, cities...and I think that can mean armies...that are in the Promised Land are to be destroyed to every last man, woman and child. Destroyed...killed.

"Cities that you have to attack for strategic reasons but are not in the Promised Land are to be offered a chance to surrender. If they don't, then every man is to be killed and the women and children allowed to live," Shaw said.

"Yeah, but that is the Old Testament," Gault said. "That cannot outweigh what Jesus said."

Shaw was almost hesitant to call Gault out. He really was a gentle soul. "That same chapter you were quoting earlier, Matthew 5, also has verse "I have not come to abolish the Law", meaning the Old Testament "but to fulfill it.

"You can't cherry pick," Shaw said. "It may be hard, but it is the mission we have been given."

Chernovsky took a poll. He determined that the person who

lived the farthest north was Gault, and he lived on Rossman Highway, two miles south of the fighter's current position.

"OK, everybody got it? Anybody gets close to Rossman Highway and they all go down. Between Bridge Street and Rossman, we put up a sign at Bridge Street telling them to turn back. We warn them that everybody who moves south of Bridge Street will be considered a hostile and will be treated as such," Chernovsky said. "We let families, women, and children walk because they might have somebody who will take them in. Any group that looks like an army ... it dies."

CHAPTER SIX

To Whom-ever it May Concern

Grumpy and Doreen Cowper, the couple who took Mark Salazar in before the iron grip of winter closed its grasp, died in the middle of February.

Grumpy and Mark had been bringing large rounds of wood in from the big barn to the woodshed. There, he and Mark would split and stack them prior to carrying them into the house for burning in the small woodstove in the kitchen.

Like many old men, Grumpy got caught up in the task and forgot he was not thirty years old any more. His hands got cold or the big chunk he was carrying had some ice on it...the exact cause did not matter.

Grumpy dropped it on his foot.

Even Doreen did not know that Grumpy had Type II diabetes. The laws surrounding medical privacy required that Grumpy's doctor not tell Doreen.

Grumpy decided that when it was time for him to die, he was going to die. Until that happened, he was going to enjoy his potatoes and cinnamon rolls and all the other good things in life.

He didn't even fill out his prescriptions when he had been diagnosed because there was no place to hide them from Doreen. He did not want her to treat him like an old man.

He might have changed his mind if he had seen a ward full of patients with complications from advanced diabetes.

The hunk of wood landed on the top of his foot and broke two metatarsals close to where they dovetail into the ankle. It was a big chunk of wood.

Grumpy was surprisingly cheerful after Doreen wrapped it with a compression bandage and set him next to the wood stove with a big cup of hot chocolate. Grumpy stretched out the injured leg and rested it on a footstool.

Mark had beefed up enough to do all the chores. They had been doing the chores together for companionship more than for the actual effort involved.

Except for hobbling to "the can" and to bed every night, Grumpy stayed on his "throne" beside the woodstove.

Mark was typically the first one up in the morning and the last one to bed in the evening. Grumpy took to keeping him company, probably to delay the discomfort of hobbling off to bed. Lately, Mark had been heading to bed up in the loft before Grumpy turned in.

Doreen and Rosie shared a bed for warmth.

Mark found Grumpy sprawled out dead in the middle of the kitchen floor when he went to stoke the stove with kindling in the morning. It was two weeks after the hunk of firewood had slipped out of Grumpy's hands.

Doreen was inconsolable. Even though they had not slept in the same bed for almost two decades, because Grumpy snored, they had not spent a night apart since they were married.

A week later, Doreen passed. She left a letter written in her distinctive, loopy, Palmer cursive. It was addressed primarily to Mark. She apologized for her weakness.

In the letter she called him “a God sent”. Doreen suffered from Seasonal Affective Disorder. The dim light of winter triggered depression. Much of Grumpy’s banter was his engaging her to keep her out of the funk. The loss of electricity made the disorder a hundred times worse. Doreen had hidden her depression to shield Rosie, but losing Grumpy was too much.

She also informed Mark, “and to whom-ever it may concern” that she had taken her life with rat poison and had not died by foul play.

She left all of the contents of the house to Rosie and appointed Mark the guardian of both Rosie and those contents.

Mark put Doreen’s body next to Grumpy’s out in the old granary next to the hen house. The granary was metal lined to keep out rodents and that was the safest place to put them while the ground was frozen.

Sometimes Life Just Sucks

Rosie and Mark spent a couple hours each day sorting through Grumpy and Doreen’s house.

The house stood on forty acres, the majority of which had been rented out to a farmer.

The actual lot the house and outbuildings stood on was a couple acres in size. There was a foundation from an old, gambrel-roofed barn that had fallen in half a century ago. There was the big pole barn and a smattering of smaller outbuildings.

In Mark’s poking around he determined that the old barn foundation was riddled with woodchuck holes. He figured that out from the vast numbers of rabbit and fox tracks weaving through the tall weeds that still grew in the soil that had been enriched by a hundred years of horse and cow poop-and-pee.

Mark would take Rosie when he set out toward Eaton Rapids in the spring. He had little hope that the house would not be pillaged, perhaps even burned down.

By shifting around rotted barn beams and judiciously arranging shocks of dried nettles and giant ragweed, Mark created several caches for the most important contents of the attic. Some of the contents had no intrinsic value...old letters and photos of Rosie's ancestors, for instance.

Other contents were nearly priceless: Aladdin lamps, charcoal fired food warmers, corn knives, hay saws, horse harnesses and books on how to make those and hundreds of other items needed in everyday life in the 1890s.

Mark also found that Grumpy had a sixteen gauge Browning semi-automatic shotgun and a GI .45 handgun.

The sorting was therapeutic for Rosie. Just as we all have different gifts; we all have different styles of grieving. There is no right or wrong way of grieving.

A surprising benefit of Mark's salesmanship was that he had developed a keenly honed sense of empathy.

Sales is one of the last bastions of self-made super-stars. Nearly every other endeavor has been analyzed, documented and turned into a college degree. Sales people often fall into their profession after a series of career pratfalls which tainted the status of the profession.

Mark came into sales early in life with few preconceptions. He knew he had to establish a bond with the potential customer, but other than that he had few things to un-learn.

One of the techniques he found particularly powerful, especially early in his career before he had other tools, was to mirror his customer's body language, sentence cadence and functional vocabulary. Not only did it establish rapport with his customer, he found that it actually worked backwards, it actually put him in the same emotional state-space as his customer.

At least one-person-in-ten who walked onto the lot was a distressed buyer. Perhaps it was a recently divorced person who lost the vehicle to the ex. Sometimes it was a working stiff living on the edge whose vehicle crapped out and they no longer had reliable transportation to their job. The reasons for a distressed buyer to walk onto the lot were myriad.

What they all had in common is that they tended to be "lookers" rather than "buyers." All the other sales people avoided them like the plague. The last thing they wanted was to be tied up with a loser when a real hot prospect walked onto the lot.

Mark had a phenomenal closing rate with the distressed buyers. He figured he made plenty of money on his regular commissions and he could help 'a brother in need' out.

Many of Mark's customers did not use a lot of words. Even though most of the other sales people were from New England, they were from URBAN New England and were much more voluble than the distressed buyers. Mark was rural. He was very comfortable with a slower speech cadence. He had also been in the Coast Guard and he was equally comfortable with the compact, information rich speech of mil-talk.

Even though Mark did not sound like he was from Baa-abba his distressed customers quickly trusted him more than they trusted Joe Isuzu.

Every distressed customer had a story to tell and nobody who wanted to listen.

Mark listened.

"She cheated on me. She burned through the bank accounts

and maxed out the credit cards. The judge gave her the Volvo."

Mark might say "That happened to my brother. It took him three years to get back on his feet."

"The dog got sick. The vet bills were $6000 and the dog died anyway. Then my truck died."

Mark might say "My dog died when I was 12. Worst day of my life."

None of what Mark said was made up. None of it sounded like one-upmanship. It was affirmation that Mark had some inkling of how much the distressed person's life sucked RIGHT NOW.

Mark would just nod. Many people cannot process words when stunned by grief. Even if they could hear the words, there are times when no words can ease the pain. Sometimes life just sucks.

Mark went into the conversation with no expectations. He just listened.

Sometimes it took the distressed customer fifteen minutes to spin down.

More often it took a bit more than an hour.

Sometimes it would go on for four hours.

Mark had never made a sale after a four-hour grief counseling session. But he had no expectations so that did not matter.

The irony is that if he had gone into the session with any kind of expectation, he would have fallen on his dupa in sales. Only true psychopaths can fake empathy that exquisitely.

Mark sold boat-loads of vehicles after the fifteen minute and one-hour counseling sessions. The fact that he had invested in an empathy-bond was only half the magic. The other half is that Mark gleaned information from the customer that helped him guide the customer to the vehicle that was going to meet his needs.

If they absolutely had to have a Volvo, Mark found them a Volvo.

If they needed a truck to drive to work, Mark would guide them to a reliable truck that was within their price range. They might kick about the lack of creature comforts but Mark would quell their objections with, "I would make a lot more commission selling you a fancier truck. Selling you this truck is taking money out of my pocket...but this truck is the truck you need right now. You can always sell it for what you put into it and buy a nicer one after you get back on your feet."

While Mark got into it for the crassest of reasons, to make more money by selling more vehicles, Mark found that the acorn had not fallen too far from the maternal tree. Like Kate, Mark found great satisfaction in easing the deepest aching pain in other people.

There was a screaming need for Mark back in Kates Store.

Depression

Modern science is successful because it is able to decouple phenomena into easy-to-study, stand-alone fields where relatively simple experiments can be designed and run to quantify cause-and-effect relationships.

Modern science fails when proponents ignore the fact that many phenomena are highly coupled.

Did Grumpy die because he was careless while handling firewood? Did he die because of his intrinsic personality? Did Grumpy die because of Doreen's to-die-for cinnamon rolls or because he did not move after breaking his foot or because a clot detached from a vein in his calf and lodged in his brain?

The deepest truth is that Grumpy died because of the intersection of all of these circumstances.

Delving too deeply into untangling the warp-and-weft of a tapestry is to destroy the tapestry but sometimes it is necessary to finding those deeper truth. So, it is with stories.

Most of the people who were dying in Kates Store were dying from shattered dreams.

Science would have us treat mental health as something separate from physical health, diet and exercise. The unfortunate intersection of those make it a practical impossibility for those who would minister to the people of Kates Store.

Take something as simple as one's diet.

As countless dieters who attempted super-low fat and heart-smart diets can attest, it is not hyperbole to say that for a while fat is the only thing that makes life seem worth living.

Buttressing this argument is the documentary Lorenzo's Oil. Lorenzo had a rare brain disease that suddenly manifested when his parents moved from the Comoro Islands to the United States. Through frantic experimentation his parents determined that his brain disease could be remedied by changing the fats in his diet to include oils that were rich in certain short-fatty acids that effectively healed his damaged myelin sheath (the insulator around nerves) tissue.

The people of Kates Store were no different than most Americans. They ate pizza, ice-cream, hot-pockets, pizza rolls, chicken nuggets and burritos. They ate fast food hamburgers and French fries. They ate foods drenched in mayonnaise and dripping ranch dressing.

The high-fat diet impacted their blood and neural chemistry directly. It also impacted their mental health in a myriad of indirect ways.

The "human microbiome" is a concept that attempts to comprehend the fact that the number of human cells in the organism that comprise "us" are outnumbered by non-human cells. This is due to the fact that mammalian cells are exceptionally large. They can be exceptionally large because our circulatory system is very effective at feeding, oxygenating and detoxifying our human cells. Thus, the constraints on cell surface area-to-volume ratios are eased relative to "wild" organisms.

While it is Freudian to fixate on our lower bowels, the microbiome in our large bowel is effectively a secondary central nervous organ. Those microbes digest materials we cannot. They synthesize vitamins and there is evidence that changes in the lower bowel's biosphere can dramatically impact mood and emotion.

The bowel's microbiome is no less an ecosystem than a river valley, an island, or a pond. While the temperature does not change, the transit times, the fineness of the incoming material and its chemical composition will cause huge shifts in the types of bacteria that dominate the realm. When the bacteria change, so do the neural-chemical interactions between the human-cell us and the macro/microbiome us.

The typical pre-Ebola diet for the people in Kates Store was very, very calorie dense. The transit times in the large bowel was very, very long and there was little selection pressure that favored the most quickly reproducing bacteria.

The human body is 'plastic', that is, it slowly attenuates organs that are little used and grows organs that are used a great deal. Digestive organs are no different. The super-rich pre-Ebola diet resulted in stomachs, upper bowels and lower bowels with very low interior volume.

The typical post-Ebola diet was higher in fiber and much,

much lower in fats. The higher carbs resulted in sharper blood-sugar spikes and the high fiber/lower fat ratio resulted in transit times that were much quicker. In many cases the higher calorie demands and higher fiber foods caused severe belly aches. People who defecated once every three days found themselves dashing to the outhouse six times a day.

The human body is not just plastic in the dimensional sense, it is also plastic (or adaptable) in the chemical pathway sense. If a certain neural transmitter, for instance, starts to accumulate due to a chemical imbalance, the brain compensates by creating parallel pathways. Like water rushing past a boulder, the boulder does not stop the water. The boulder may slow it or redirect the stream or force it to percolate...but in the end the water will win.

Looking at just the changes in diet, consider the change of composition and amounts of lipids, the loss of 'comfort foods', the wild swings in the human microbiome and the fact that many people ricocheted between raging hunger and severe stomach cramps and you will understand why most people were depressed.

And that is just looking at food.

Consider the demolition derby between former expectations and current realities. A successful working couple might have expected new vehicles every three or four years. The new reality was that their vehicles would never run again and they would never have another. They had to WALK everywhere.

Their retirements were nuked. There was no medical safety net. There was almost no medical anything.

People were tired because they were depressed. Many of them were depressed because they had to physically work for the first time in their lives. Many were depressed because of their diets. Many were depressed because of the lack of light. Primarily most of them were depressed because they had almost non-existent coping skills; the coping skills that functioned in the pre-Ebola world had little applicability in their new reality.

They could not binge watch Netflix. They could not binge eat chocolate ice-cream and potato chips. They could not pull up porn on the internet or lose themselves in video games or drink themselves silly or engage people on social media. They could not drive 90 miles to a factory outlet mall or a professional athletic event.

It is clearly suicide when somebody eats rat poison.

Is it suicide when somebody abuses alcohol or drugs and dies as a result?

Is it suicide when a depressed person cannot get out of bed to make a fire in the woodstove and the canned goods in the pantry freeze and the jars shatter?

Is it suicide when a depressed person takes stupid risks like breaking quarantine and going into large urban areas?

Is it suicide when somebody stops caring for themselves and does not take care of cuts or puncture wounds or stops taking medicines?

Seventy percent of the increased mortality in the post-Ebola, rural environment is a conservative estimate of the number of deaths in which depression and changes of diet played a significant role. It would have been even higher if Gabby hadn't explored finding other uses for ethanol...including the extraction of soybean oil.

Distress Tolerance

Nyssa and Milo were spending the evening with her parents, Kate and Rick.

Dinner was cornbread and chili served with shredded cabbage salad wilted in bacon grease with a spritz of vinegar on the side. Desert was apple pie. The chili was heavy on beans and very light on the meat.

After dinner the two couples sat down to play cards. Losers would wash the dishes. Tonight, they paired off boys against girls.

Conversation turned to the number of people dying in the communities surrounding Kates Store.

Nyssa, a nurse, was frustrated.

Most people have a suite or portfolio of coping skills. Many of those coping skills did not transition well to the new reality. That was not a surprise. What was a surprise was the lack of flexibility many people showed in developing new coping skills.

Nyssa talked about one patient, of course she did not mention names, who was completely incapacitated. "It was as if she didn't have a bone in her body. She was a puddle of sobbing flesh on the floor," Nyssa said.

"She did OK until the battery on her phone died," Nyssa said. "She had games she played.

"And this last week was cloudy and she didn't get up to the store to charge her phone and....BAM! She became completely non-functional," Nyssa said.

"What did you do?" Kate asked. "It is not like you have any antidepressant drugs."

"I asked her what her favorite games were," Nyssa said. "One of them was Solitaire."

"I looked around the room and found three decks of cards, THREE OF THEM. One of them was on a book shelf less than six feet from where she sat and played on her phone."

"It never occurred to her to look for a deck of cards," Nyssa said.

The boys weren't saying much. Nyssa and Kate were not the world's greatest cards players but nobody was any better at reading their partner's body language. The boys liked it when the girls were caught up in a riveting conversation.

Milo asked, "Is that really such a big deal, one person who is stressed out because the battery on their phone died?"

"It sure is," Nyssa said.

"Dad, do you remember teaching us the rule of threes? And the first rule is that three seconds of stupid can get you killed," Nyssa asked.

Rick nodded his head "Yes."

"People who are stressed are just plain daffy, Milo," Nyssa said. "They do stupid things. Some even try to kill themselves."

The couples played through the next hand with no conversation.

"A lotta guys use video games to unwind," Milo volunteered.

"Duh!" Nyssa said. She had two older brothers and one who was younger.

"Guys have to eat a lot of crow," Milo said. "Bad bosses. Customers who are dickheads.

"Seems like anything a guy does is automatically wrong. They might sort it out afterward but it is always too late to do the guy any good.

"Video games are a way for guys to deal with their aggression without having to do hard-time at Jackson State Prison,"

Milo said.

Rick was looking at his cards. Kate had turned up a ten-of-diamonds. He had the jack-of-hearts, ace and nine of diamonds. He looked up at Milo hoping for some hint regarding the hand Milo was holding. No luck. Milo had been sucked into the conversation.

"Back when I was a kid my dad would hand me a hoe or machete and point me at the nettles and thistles," Rick said. "That worked fine for me."

"God knows we need people cutting brush," Milo said. "Seems like they all want chainsaws when a sharp hatchet or billhook is faster."

"That, and it is a great way to get rid of anger," Rick agreed.

Kate turned over the ten-of-hearts and said "Pass.

"One thing I remember about my grandpa," Milo said, "Is that he whistled while he worked. You don't hear that anymore."

Nyssa, Kate and Rick perked up. Milo rarely talked about his family.

"Why did he do that?" Rick asked.

"He said it helped him think," Milo said. "I think it helped him tune out distractions."

The bid came back around to Kate. She called clubs. The girls made their point.

"Remember when Mark started drumming on everything?" Nyssa said. "It drove me nuts."

"Yup. I remember," Rick said.

Then Kate added, "It drove you nuts until you started drumming in self-defense. Then it was like listening to dueling banjos."

"Good times," Nyssa said.

Milo was shuffling.

"Another thing I remember about Parous is that he never missed a coffee break or lunch," Milo said.

"He was a millwright for the railroad, right?" Rick asked.

"A rigger. Almost the same thing," Milo said. "Unbelievably heavy work: digging, lifting, swinging hammers, carrying railroad ties."

"My guess is that taking breaks was the only way to keep his blood-sugar levels from going in-the-ditch," Kate observed. "If you wait until you feel it you will never catch back up."

Kate could see Rick's cards reflected in his glasses. He was holding a lot of red cards. Milo had turned up a spade.

"I wish my patients would get out of their houses and do something outside," Nyssa harrumphed. "The sunlight and moving around would do them a world of good.

"Fight or flight," Rick said. "Either deal with it or it will eat you up."

Nyssa told Milo to pick up the nine-of-spades.

Kate said, "Something I never got over as a Social Worker was the people who always thought it was somebody else's job to fix their problems."

Nyssa nodded emphatically in agreement. "I had patients who were cold and did not think it was "their job" to split some kindling or put on warmer clothes.

"I had another patient who handed me a piece of paper that he claimed was a prescription. Said his doctor prescribed a Paleo diet and I was supposed to supply him with meat because he couldn't eat grain or vegetables," Nyssa said.

"Sounds like Duckworth," Rick said to nobody in particular.

"Professional ethics require that I not divulge the names of my patients," Nyssa said, starchily.

That confirmed it was Duckworth.

"What did you do?" Kate asked.

"I told him that...I mean him-or-her... that Gabby had all kinds of defatted soy flour that was pure protein and she would be more than willing to sell it to him. He went stomping out in a huff," Nyssa said.

In a bid to distract the women, Rick observed "Some evolutionary biologists believe that anxiety is pro-survival."

Kate raised her eyebrows in the universal sign of an unverbalized question.

"Anxiety is like steam in a boiler. It is the pressure that gets work done," Rick pontificated.

"They even speculate that different environments caused families to evolve different, optimal anxiety relieving activities. An area with a lot of ticks and fleas, for instance, might favor families whose anxiety was reduced by mutual grooming," Rick said. "Climates that were cold might favor tactile activities like spinning and knitting. Environments with lots of hides might favor chewing which is how primitive people cured hides."

In spite of the distraction, the girls won another point.

Rick said to Nyssa and Milo, "I don't mean to be disrespectful of your generation, but one of the things we did to get closure was to write things down. Faced with a tough decision I would write all the reason TO do something on the left side of the page. Then I would write all the reasons TO NOT do something down the right side."

"Then I didn't have to keep all that crap in my head. I could always dig up that piece of paper and refresh my memory," Rick said.

Milo was nodding his head in agreement. "I did almost the same thing. Sometimes I would write down a dozen reasons why I shouldn't do something. I would look at the list the next morning and realize half the items I wrote were different ways of saying the same thing.

"Writing things on paper was a good way to clear my mind," Milo said.

"The bottom line," Nyssa said "is that things suck. They might get better but we will never return to 2019. It is still better to be alive than to be dead. We need to grow up, put our broken dreams behind us and move on."

The boys lost the game and had to do the dishes. They didn't mind. Kate and Nyssa had cooked the meal.

The couples had spent almost three hours together. Nyssa and Milo walked back home. It was eight-thirty in the evening.

Kate no longer had a paid job as a professional social worker but that did not prevent her from thinking like one. There had to be something she could do to make the situation better.

Winter Faire

"Hello! I am Peppermint Candy transmitting at 104.3 FM with your news from Eaton Rapids, Kates Store and Pray Church.

"The big news is that Kates Store and Pray Church will host Winter Faires.

"Kates Store will host their Winter Fair Thursday and Friday of next week. All entries will get a coupon for a free cookie from either Kate's store or Luke's store.

"The age categories are Under 11, Under 21 and Open.

"Competitions will be held for corn-rows hair braiding, whittling, penny pitching and whistling.

"Corn-rows will be two person teams. The team members are to braid each other's hair and parade around the faire. Other faire-goers are to vote for their favorites.

"Euchre, cribbage, and Egyptian Rat-screw tournaments will be held concurrently with the Winter Faire for those of you who are card players. The top four finishers will be invited to compete in the Pray Church Winter Faire which will be held two weeks after the one in Kates Store.

"A flea market and trade tables will be held outside. People from outside Kates Store will be allowed to participate in the trade fair as long as they abide by rules to be published later.

"Separately, a cooking contest will be held for the best cookie recipe that uses only locally produced ingredients, and a knitted scarf contest. The scarves are to be 42" long. After the contest, scarves will be sewn together to make baby blankets and given to expecting mothers."

The first day of the Winter Faire at Kates Store dawned with excitement. Nearly forty inches of snow was on the ground but faire goers were able to get there along pathways of beaten down snow that the people walked along.

There were fifteen entries in the corn-rows contest. Mandy and Dysen did not make the top three for their age group but they had enjoyed the time "practicing" for the contest.

The whittling contest was to make a willow whistle from rods Rick had cut and soaked beside the wood stove for a day. The foot-long willow rods, lulled into thinking spring had come early had bark that slipped. The test that the whistle was functional was to play first four notes of Beethoven's Fifth Symphony.

The card games were played in Spackle's barn. The euchre and cribbage tournaments were sedate but the adults had to tell the kids playing Egyptian Rat-screw to calm down several times.

The big excitement was when a couple of men from Charlotte, a nearby city, tried to ride their snow machines up to Spackle's barn.

Rick had the foresight to ask Chernovsky to send a security detail back to Kates Store for the fair. Chernovsky sent back one fire-team from Squad One and one fire-team from Squad Three.

Quinn Spackle was pissed. He thought his squad should have been the ones to guard the faire. Of course, it was because he wanted to spend time with Dysen.

Chernovsky could only roll his eyes. Spackle had volunteered for every detail to "intercept the courier" when Dysen was bringing cookies. Stevie Wonder could have seen the crush he had on her.

The two snow machines were coming up the roadbed because it was the smoothest way. Terry Lake, the fire-team leader from Squad Three stopped them a quarter mile from the Faire. He told them to park and walk the remaining quarter mile. They were pissy about it but the fact that he was carrying an AR was very persuasive.

The other excitement did not cause a big stir.

Paul Seraph came to the fair. Seeking out Rick, Paul did a little bit of prodding.

"You know we are starving in the city," Paul started with little preamble. “I think you should give us food.”

Rick said, “Let’s get out of the crowd so we can talk.”

Moving away from the hubbub of the fair, Paul repeated his demand. “You should give us food.”

“We aren’t doing so hot ourselves. Why should we give it to you?” Rick said.

“You know, we could just come and take it,” Paul said. “I have three thousand people in Eaton Rapids and what do you have, three or four hundred?”

“Are you threatening me?” Rick asked.

“Just pointing out certain realities," Paul said.

Rick thought for a moment. “I suppose you could. But what would you get? Even if you found every kernel of corn, how much would you have...maybe enough to feed the city for a month.”

"And you would lose your blocking force to the north,” Rick said.

Paul waved that argument aside. “The invasion of Ebola may never come.”

“I am not done,” Rick said. “The other thing is that nobody from the city would ever be able to enter Kates Store without an army to guard them. That is a pretty stiff price to pay.”

“That is why I was hoping you would just give us the food,” Paul said. “I am desperate.”

“It is not my food to give,” Rick said. “But I know for a fact that the three farmers around here have more corn standing in their fields than they will pick before spring. The problem is a lack of fuel and labor. They might work with you if the city sends work crews to pick the corn.”

Farmer Ken's farm was the one that was closest to the city. Paul Seraph went up to him and said, "I want to do some business with you."

"What is on your mind?" Ken asked.

"What would it take to make it worth your while for you to sell me corn," Paul said.

"I can't" Ken said.

"What if I supplied crews to pick it?" Paul said.

"That would be brutally hard work. They would need to pick from snow shoes and the snow is so high the ears will be down around their knees," Ken said.

"So, you are agreeable, at least in principle?" Paul pushed.

"Yeah, but you will still need to pay something," Ken said.

"Sure, no problem. I will write you a check," Paul said.

"You are joking, right?" Ken said.

"Of course I am joking," Paul said. "What do you need in trade?"

Ken scratched his stubble while he thought. He didn't want to make a bad deal.

"I have eighty acres of standing corn. I am willing to let your people pick five of it. That should be enough to last you for two weeks. Then we will renegotiate," Ken said. He was a whiz at math and did the calcs in his head.

"We can do it on shares, 50:50...but then the corn you take will only keep you for a week," Ken said. "Or I am willing to sell you a hundred pounds for an ounce of silver or for ten pounds of copper or four hundred pounds for a new car battery," Ken said.

"Where would we get copper?" Paul scoffed.

" 'bout ten pounds of copper in a car alternator. That would be close enough for me," Ken said.

"So, you think anybody is going to yank the alternator out of their car or truck and trade it for a hundred pounds of corn?" Paul said.

"That would be up to them," Ken said. "You can check with Farmer Earl or Farmer Don. Maybe they will give you a better deal.

"Oh, there is one other thing I would accept in trade," Farmer Ken said.

"What is that?" Seraph said.

"I would take an AR or AK and two hundred rounds of ammo," Farmer Ken said.

"When pigs fly," Paul Seraph said. "There aren't many of those around and the folks who have them don't want to give them up."

"Yup. I get that. That is why either one of those is worth forty ounces of silver...or two tons of corn," Ken said.

Of course, the other farmers didn't offer a better deal. Ken, Earl and Don were cousins and they had already talked through what a "fair deal" would be. They had also agreed to rotate whose fields the city people would be picking from so each cousin would get a share of the bounty.

Paul really had no choice. Every morning a crew of thirty fit men trudged from the City of Eaton Rapids to Kates Store pulling sleds. Every evening they trudged back dragging 120 pounds of corn back to the City of Eaton Rapids.

Within the week they hit upon the plan to bunk out in Kates Store and pay Di Carney to haul the picked corn to town. That saved fourteen miles of walking a day for the men and

Di's horses needed the exercise.

Winter Faire Part II

Steve Reynolds and Dave Matthews ran their Polaris snow machines into the commercial garage eight miles west of Kates Store.

After stripping out of their windproof suits, they walked up to the office on the second floor of the administrative building.

"What do you think?" the beefy man said behind the desk.

Reynolds, the more cerebral of the two regretfully shook his head. "They don't have a snowball's chance in hell."

Matthews nodded his head in agreement.

"We only saw one AR. Other than that, it looked like an Amish flea-market," Reynolds said.

Clearly, they missed the fire-team member who had been tracking them in his 4X scope from a hundred yards away. The even tan color of the work over coats and leggings had become mottled from the sun bleaching and the relentless grinding of firewood bark-dust and lichens into their surface.

They were also unaware of the landholders who hauled ass out of their houses and barns at the first sound of motors. They grabbed their weapons and posted up at the defensive positions they had dug-out since Dan Nestle's raid on Kate's store.

"A pity," the beefy man said. "No matter. We can flow in after the Ebola burns them out. It will be that much easier to take it over."

"What about Seraph?" Matthews asked.

"What about him?" the beefy man said.

"He was there checking things out," Matthews said.

"Eaton Rapids is on their ass. Got too many old people and too many approaches. The other thing you gotta remember is they are closer to Lansing than we are and they didn't see this coming," the beefy man said.

"If Paul Seraph is alive a year from now, he will be begging us to come into Eaton Rapids and restore order...that and to execute the blind zombies roaming the streets," the beefy man said.

***

The second day of the fair involved more trade than the first day. People learned what had the most trading value. They went back home and rummaged around in their garages and basements. They brought back reloading presses, bottles of smokeless powder and bricks of primers, transformers from defunct microwave ovens and so on.

The vendors kept a small supply of goods at their table. When large orders came in, they sent a "runner" with a sled to collect more goods. They operated out of a small display for several reasons. One was simple theft prevention. You immediately notice when somebody walks off with half your visible inventory. You might not notice if they took 1/20th. The other reason was operational security. Visitors came from outside Kates Store and they did not want to appear too wealthy.

Gabby did a VERY brisk business selling soybean oil. Most people had been monkey-hammered in the transition to a high-carb, high-fiber diet. They CRAVED oils and fats. As her supply diminished, the price rose. Some of the people who bought early succumbed to the temptation and resold what they had bought cheap.

Farmers took note of Gabby's prices. Clearly, there was now

a market for oil-seeds. It was a pity that so much of the crop had not been harvested and was now beneath a heavy blanket of snow.

The fire-teams from Squad One and Three had swapped out. The ones who been on guard took sentry duty on the northern frontier while the ones who had been on sentry duty guarded the faire.

Quinn Spackle continued to belly-ache.

To nobody's surprise Mrs Shaw, Shadrack and Walt's mother, won the cookie contest. The batch of cookies she entered in the contest had a shortbread base, a fruit-leather middle and an oatmeal-crumble top. She used honey for sweetening.

The other major change in the Faire was that the second day focused on "manly skills."

Particularly popular were skills of throwing. The weather was too cold for the snow to pack, so snow was mixed with water the night before and compressed into balls to freeze over-night.

The two most popular contests were hitting a target that was in a swinging, spinning tire and throwing "darts" with an atlatl. In both cases pictures of various political figures were offered as targets. It should not be surprising that the politicians who had most stridently demanded open borders were the most popular targets. The people of Kates Store clearly blamed them for Ebola being in the United States.

The third most popular contest was beheading a swinging dummy with an axe.

Battle axes would never be a viable weapon against Ebola carriers. Too much blood would spray on the defender. Battle axes did, however, make the wielder feel manly and taking the head off of a dummy was great fun.

Conspicuously absent were bows. Arrows were in very short supply and one problem with bows is the awkward transition to hand-to-hand combat. A well-designed atlatl transitions well to a light club or baton while a bow only tangles up the shooter.

CHAPTER SEVEN

Planning for Battle

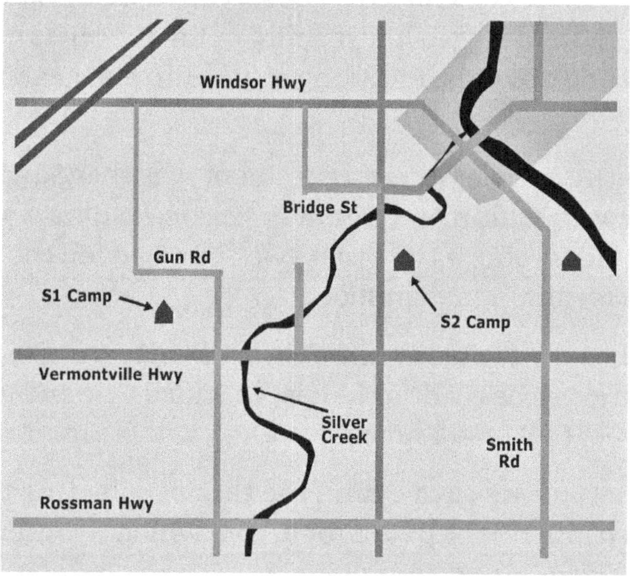

Scale of map is approximately three miles N-S and four miles E-W. Close-up is shown later in story is slightly north of Squad 2 Camp near center of image. People who live near Dimondale will notice slight liberties were taken.

There were three roads that Chernovsky had been tasked with "observing".

Only one of those roads was likely to have much zombie traffic. That was the paved road that started twelve miles north of Dimondale and ran south, straight as a laser south, into Eaton Rapids. Additionally, that paved road ran through the middle of Markle Estates Mobile Home Park a scant mile north of the northern frontier Chernovsky was tasked with "observing". Markle Estates hosted four-hundred units which meant twelve-hundred residents lived there before Ebola hit.

The other two roads, one a mile to the east and the other a mile to the west, were gravel. The one to the east started at the outskirts of Dimondale and meandered to the east a bit before making up its mind and turning south. The one to the west of the paved road started a mile north of the point where Chernovsky chose to "observe" it. The road to the west jiggled and jogged like it could not make up its mind before settling down and heading south into the heart of Pray Church.

Chernovsky's professional assessment was that Squad Two, the one with Quinn and Donnie as team-leaders was head-and-shoulders above the other two squads, even though the squad was running a man short.

So Chernovsky tasked Squad Two with observing the paved road and gave the road to the east to Squad One and the road to the west to Squad Three.

Then Chernovsky gave Quinn the task of selecting the four best positions on the paved road from which to observe, and attack, south-bound zombies.

Furthermore, Chernovsky required that Quinn pick at least two defensive positions within a mile of the northern frontier and two that were further back in the event that the zombies blew past the two primary defensive positions.

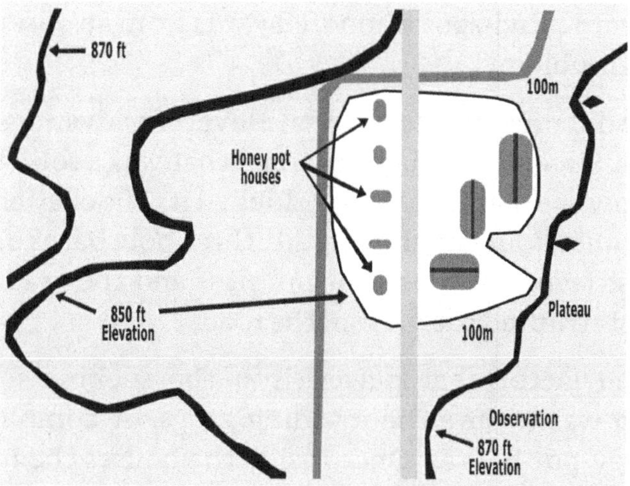

Arrows indicate approximately 100 yard distance. Dark grey oblongs are wooden-trussed pole barns. Smaller ones are houses. Approximate scale three hundred yards N-S and four hundred yards E-W. Again, real location with slight liberties taken.

Quinn and the team had just walked Chernovsky and the other four team-leaders through their choice for the northernmost post on the paved road.

"Spackle, that plan sucks," Chernovsky said.

Quinn was immediately defensive.

"The only other defensible place in the first mile is Observation Post #2," Quinn said.

"Your set-up has too many holes in it," Chernovsky said with the emotion of a man stating that a dropped set of car keys will fall to the ground. It was a simple statement of fact.

It stung all the more because Quinn knew that it was 100% true.

The only two positions that had a view of the road were separated by two hundred yards and there was a huge, gaping hole in the observer's fields of vision where hostiles could disappear. Forty yards might not sound like much but a forty yard blind-spot a hundred yards from an observation post is a problem.

The site did offer an exceptional elevation advantage. Over the eons, Silver Creek dug a channel that was a solid twenty feet below the plateau that overlooked it. The challenge was that an ambitious developer built three pole barns between the most favorable 'observation' sites and the road. Those barns interrupted the view of the road.

A second factor that played into the suckiness is that the plan was to lure the invading gangs, or zombies, into the honey-pot houses. Once inside the houses the invaders would find AMPLE supplies of booze and weed. Chernovsky's stated plan was to send in a team after dark and to...well...execute the incapacitated invaders.

That plan would crap-out if the observers could not identify exactly how many invaders went into exactly which houses. Hence the excruciating pain caused by the blind-spots.

An aspect of leadership that is rarely commented on is the element of theater. Oft times the leader will have a very precise picture in their head of the optimum solution.

Sometimes they are wrong, but often they are right.

The easy path is to simply direct the underlings to create the leader's vision. The easy path is not always the best path.

If the underlings do not OWN that plan, then they are not invested and will have little incentive in making the plan work. On the other hand, it is a well-known fact that people with investment in a plan can make a concrete canoe float.

"Suppose," Chernovsky said, primarily addressing Quinn and Donnie but also mindful that the other team-leads were listening. "That you were designing a video game and you were given this map," he said waving his hands at the landscape.

"Now suppose you are designing level 6999, the one that nobody ever gets to because it is way too hard," Chernovsky said. "How would you change the houses or the pole barns to make it so fiendishly difficult that the players...the invaders coming from the north...will all die and nobody will ever make it to level 7000?"

"I'd get rid of the pole barns," Donnie said without hesitation.

"No, I would make the pole barns holograms," said another team leader. "So, the observers could see through them and the hostiles could not."

"I would put bottomless-pits-to-hell in the pole barns so anybody who went into them would fall to their doom," said another.

Chernovsky let them thrash around for about ten minutes. He could not fault them in their enthusiasm for video games.

"OK, Spackle. From all of the ideas you heard, what would you do to make this the perfect killing field?" Chernovsky asked.

Collapsing the barn roofs allowed all potential observation sites to have unobstructed view of the road. Southernmost observation site is in near-enfilade position for columns advancing south on the road while the other two positions are in defilade positions.

"I would leave the pole barns standing but collapse the roofs so the observation posts had clear fields of vision. I would remove the door handles on the insides of the barns and put wire mesh over the windows. And I would fill them with barbed wire," Quinn said.

"Why not get rid of the barns?" Chernovsky asked. He had his own opinions but wanted to hear Spackle's.

“We might have to start shooting at the zombies. If we get rid of the barns then they will figure out the only place the shooting could come from is our observation posts. If we leave the shell of the barns standing then they will probably figure the shooters are in the barn,” Quinn said. “I would rather have them shooting into empty barns than have them shooting at an observation post where they might get lucky.”

“Is there anything else you would do?” Chernovsky asked.

“Yeah, I would put something outside the doors of the honey-pot houses so I would know if the doors had been opened. Maybe a two-liter pop bottle with some water in the bottom. It would get knocked over if somebody opened the door to the house,” Quinn added. “Then I could do a quick walk-by and would know if there might be zombies in the house.

Chernovsky was impressed. He had not thought of that.

"Your plan to let the hostiles into the barn sucks,” Chernovsky said. "Once they are in there you lose sight of them. You need to rethink that part of the plan.

“Is there anything that you need help with?” Chernovsky asked.

“Nope. I think my squad can handle this,” Quinn said. “We will cut the bottoms of the trusses and the snow load will take care of the rest.”

Duckworth

Orion and Fidelis moved slowly along the edge of the grassy marsh in the gathering gloom of evening. They moved east with the wind at their back, a nearly impenetrable scrum of thorny scrub to their left and the partially frozen bog to their right.

Fidelis was a great hunting dog and Orion was a very good hunter...for a human. But even a mediocre dog can turn a good human hunter into a great hunter if they can work as a team.

Rumors of deer sign had come to Kate's Store even as winter belatedly showed the first signs of loosing its jaws on the land. Orion was looking for rabbits or the elusive deer. Either would be a welcome addition to the pot.

Orion moved slowly and stopped often. Rabbits will hold tight if the hunter keeps moving but will bolt if they fear the predator is triangulating a fix for the pounce.

The rabbits along the edge of the marsh had not been hunted by humans much. They would run thirty yards and then freeze. That was a pay-day shot with either shotgun or .22. Orion carried the smaller gun, the .22 as the shells were far more plentiful and either were equally deadly when put in the right place.

The .22 was decidedly on the light end of weapons for deer but Orion had taken them before. Close shots between the eyes meant the deer dropped in its tracks. A shot to the heart or lungs took longer. The key was to wait an hour and let the deer bleed out. Consequently, Orion was dressed in expectation of a long wait in the gathering wind.

It felt like it was going to storm as the wind was coming in gusts and was slowly clocking from west to north.

A half mile from where the hunter started out, a rabbit scooted out from beneath a tent of cattails. It stopped thirty-five yards out, which was just a little farther than the hunter was comfortable shooting given the gusty wind. Edging forward, the rabbit darted another ten yards out.

A game of cat-and-mouse resulted in Orion investing twenty

minutes before harvesting the rabbit. Only then did Orion realize that Fidelis was missing.

Back-tracking, Orion found where their tracks diverged. Following the tracks Orion found Fidelis caught in a snare with unseeing eyes bugged out. The poacher had used a spring pole and a cam-lock. Fidelis never had a chance.

A smoldering rage grew in Orion. Somebody had been snaring deer and not sharing them or taking the excess to Kate's Store. That would account for the scarcity of deer. Orion knew that families were snaring deer on the north end of the neighborhood and sharing among themselves. Nobody hunted where they had their snares set.

Orion saw the trail stomped by boots leading northwest from the snare. Orion followed the trail the way a buck follows a scrape-line, walking parallel from the track, ten yards to the downwind.

It bee-lined to Carson Duckworth's property.

The smoldering rage became all consuming.

Liars lie. Thieves steal. Cheaters cheat. Duckworth had been a burr under everybody's saddle, including Orion's ever since Ebola hit Michigan.

Thinkers think. Planners plan. Hunters hunt.

Orion moved back toward the snare and made a small prayer to Fidelis's soul. Fidelis would understand. Fidelis was a hunter, too. Fidelis's body was bait in the great hunt.

Orion waited for two hours. It was beyond full dark when a flashlight came bobbing through the tangled brush toward the snare. Orion had his back turned to ensure that the flashlight did not cause night blindness. Nothing is more recognizable at night than a human face or eyes reflecting light back to the holder of a light.

When the poacher bent over to examine his catch, Orion shot him in the back of the head. The gentle cough of the .22 with the suppressor was swallowed up by the snow and wind. The poacher had been given just as much chance as the poacher had given Fidelis.

Looking at the poacher, Orion saw that it was Cameron, Carson's 19-year-old son. Cameron had been pulling a sled.

Orion set up in another concealed position. It seemed likely that Carson would come looking for his son when he did not return, either to help drag the deer or to see what the problem was. Orion did not want to be surprised disposing of Cameron's corpse.

Ninety minutes later, another flashlight came bobbing down the track. That confirmed in Orion's mind that poaching was a family project and that both were culpable for Fidelis's death and for poaching.

Orion killed the second Duckworth from a range of fifteen feet as the senior Duckworth slowed to push aside some thorny canes Orion had woven across the track at belt and head height.

Orion had a long night but nobody was waiting at home for Orion's return.

Orion dragged the two Duckworths, one at a time into the marsh and deposited them into an old drainage ditch. A fringe of brush grew along the cusp of the ditch. The coming storm would fill the ditch with snowdrift driven by the north wind. The snow would not melt until April.

Then Orion took Fidelis back home and placed him in a plum thicket that grew on a rise in the marsh. There was no way to secure Fidelis's body from scavengers but Orion knew that Fidelis would not mind.

Finally, Orion scrubbed the blood out of the sled and dragged it back to Duckworth's property. Orion left the sled on the west side of the property beneath some spruce trees.

Then Orion walked home as the snow fell thickly and covered the story that had unfolded that night.

Brittany Duckworth

Gladys called Kate a little before midnight. Mrs Duckworth was frantic with worry.

Kate got the details. Cameron and Carson had gone out shortly after dark and had not made it back.

Mrs Duckworth put the two other children to bed and waited up.

Mrs Duckworth apologized as Kate and Rick were ushered into the Duckworth living room. "I always get like this when I am pregnant," Mrs Duckworth said. "I am a worrier by nature and the closer I get to my due date the worse I get."

She was due in a month and it was very apparent that she was "in the family way."

Kate had not seen her for several months and her being pregnant was news to her. "Have you seen Nyssa? She is a nurse," Kate asked.

Mrs Duckworth hung her head. "Carson said we couldn't afford it."

Kate silently fumed. Nyssa never charged a fee for a visit. She could not officially diagnose or prescribe; she could only advise. Carson had never asked anybody about fees. He just decided.

Kate would have called Nyssa that very night but the wind was whipping along at twenty miles per hour with gusts to forty and the snow was falling furiously, the way only moist, heavy spring snowfalls can.

"Do you know which way they went?" Rick asked.

"You can't go out looking for them," Mrs Duckworth objected. She could hear the wind shrieking in the eves.

"Maybe not, but we can put lights in the windows on that side of the house," Rick said.

After hearing that Carson and Cameron had disappeared south of the house, Rick went to the upper story and put LED flashlights and candles in the windows looking out over the muck bog.

Rick did not have a very good feeling about Carson and Cameron's chances. Either they had picked tonight to get-out-of-Dodge or they had gotten tangled up in the bog. Wet clothing, thirty-degree temperatures and high winds are quickly lethal. But of course, he would not share his fears with Mrs Duckworth.

When Rick came back downstairs, he learned that Mrs Duckworth's first name was Brittany. He also learned that Cameron was Carson's child by a previous relationship. That made sense to him. He had never spent any time close to Brittany without Carson getting in his face. Now that he had a little bit of time Rick saw that she was not be much older than twenty-five.

Rick and Kate were up at seven in the morning. It was before sunrise and the storm was abating in fits and starts. They made breakfast for the Duckworth family and found themselves promoted to Uncle Rick and Aunt Kate.

As soon as Rick could see his shoelaces when he was outside, Rick started calling up a search crew.

Six neighbors showed up to help Rick search. The late winter storm had dumped seventeen inches of new snow.

Rick laid out a search pattern that not only covered the ground between the house and the bog, but he added generous wings to either side.

The crew did a quick search with searchers fifty yards apart. If either Carson or Cameron were conscious and in the search area, they should be able to hear the searchers as they hailed each other to stay properly spaced. If they were conscious then they should be able to get the searchers attention.

The searchers pushed as far south as they could. They turned around when their boots started sinking into the bog.

After the first, non-productive search Rick tightened up the search grid and they swept the search area on fifty-foot intervals. They were looking for melted snow where living-but-unconscious bodies may have created hot-spots.

That sweep failed as well.

They had done what they could. Rick called Gladys and asked her to put out word to the surrounding communities. Perhaps Carson and Cameron had become disoriented and ended up in North Eaton Rapids or the cluster of houses east of Kates Store.

Frankly, Rick did not have a very good feeling about Carson and Cameron's chances.

After eating a late lunch Rick and Kate held an impromptu huddle. There was no way Brittany could keep the huge house warm and parent her two, small children without another adult to help.

Rick and Kate did not have fancy. They had something better. They had "enough", enough to be generous.

Coming back into the Duckworth house which was already starting to become gloomy as the sun slowly lowered itself in the cloud-screened sky, Kate told Brittany, "We want you to stay with us while we continue to look for Carson and Cameron. We will leave a note right here," Kate said while pointing at the door of the refrigerator, "So they know where to find you when they come back."

Brittany "lost it" when she realized that she did not need to be strong, to be the only one looking out for her children.

"I really shouldn't be weepy like this," she said, wiping her eyes. "It's the damned hormones."

Rick emptied the dresser drawers in the kid's bedrooms into plastic trash bags. He pressed a couple of the neighbors who were still hanging around into helping him carry the luggage back to Casa Salazar.

Kate, for her part, called Nyssa and told her that Brittany was close to giving birth and would benefit from an exam. Nyssa quickly accessed her midwifing textbooks. It looked like she was going to need to use those skills sooner rather than later.

Nyssa sent Milo on, ahead of her. The Salazar house was undoubtedly cold and Milo could stoke the woodstoves and start to take the chill out of the house. Milo looked through the cold-box and found a pot of beans. He put it on the back of the stove to start warming up.

Working on Mysteries Without Any Clues

"Tell me again what we are looking for?" Milo asked.

Nyssa said, "We are looking for any clues about where Carson and Cameron went."

"And if we cannot turn up any clues, we are looking for anything the kids can wear or that Brittany can sell so she can be self-supporting," Nyssa said.

"Everything about this guy creeps me out," Milo said.

That was so out of character that Nyssa stopped and looked at him. That had the unfortunate effect of blinding him.

Even though it was mid-day and the curtains were open, it was so dark in the cavernous house that they were both wearing head lights.

“You are over-reacting,” Nyssa said. “Just because you don’t like somebody doesn’t mean they are bad people.”

“You didn’t hear me,” Milo said. “Nothing about this guy rings true.”

“Like what?” Nyssa challenged.

“Did you see the tools when we walked through his garage?” Milo asked.

“Yeah. So?” Nyssa said as she returned to sweeping the room with the beam of her headlight.

“They were all new,” Milo said.

“New tools are nice,” Nyssa said. “You told me that you wished you had newer tools.”

“Not ‘newer’. His tools are new...still in the box,” Milo said. “Every one of them.”

“He is supposed to be some kind of hot-shot pipe-fitter and all of his tools are still in the box,” Milo said.

“Maybe he just stores them in the box?” Nyssa offered.

“Still got the factory tape sealing the flaps of the boxes,” Milo said.

“What else bugs you?” Nyssa asked.

“His truck is too clean,” Milo said.

“Maybe he is just an inherently clean person,” Nyssa said.

Milo snorted. “You go to new construction you get mud on your truck. It gets splashed up into the frame. His truck looks like it came off the show-room floor. Not a single scratch in the bed, either.”

Nyssa was willing to chalk that off as "men" stuff.

"Anything else?" she asked sweetly.

"Have you seen any pictures of his family? Any diplomas or certificates? Any pictures of Cameron playing sports or doing anything?" Milo asked.

That started to get Nyssa's attention. "Now that you mention it, I haven't seen a single picture on the walls. Maybe they just aren't picture people."

"Every guy has an "I Love Me" wall, even if it is just a couple of pictures of fish he caught," Milo said.

"Look at the décor," Milo said. "I am not an interior decorator, but this place looks like a Hollywood stage set for the inside of a 1955 Memphis whorehouse."

Up until then, Nyssa had been pushing away that same thought. She liked Brittany and was ignoring the ugliness in an attempt to be kind...perhaps Brittany was one of those poor unfortunates who simply could not harmonize interiors.

"I bet Carson picked all of this stuff out," Milo said.

"No," Nyssa said.

"Flocked wallpaper? Gold tassels on the curtains? A naked cherub lamp stands? Brass spittoons?" Milo pointed out.

"I'll ask when we get back," Nyssa said.

For all of the baroque splendor of the rooms, there was very little that was usable.

They had finally worked their way through all of the rooms in the house except for Carson's "man cave." It was locked.

"I guess we will have to ask Brittany for the key," Nyssa said.

"I bet you a month's worth of doing the dishes that she

doesn't have a key to the man-cave," Milo said.

Thinking of mousy, brow-beaten Brittany, Nyssa declined that bet.

"So, what do we do?" Nyssa asked.

"Wait here while I go back to the garage and pick up a couple of skeleton keys," Milo said.

He came back a minute later with a three-foot wrecking bar and an eight-pound sledge. He also brought along a brand-new pair of gloves, still joined with the zip-tie. The wrecking bar was still sticky with cosmoline as shipped from China.

Nyssa held her tongue.

It is a common shortcoming of people to use the screws supplied with the door and frame. Carson was no different. The $500 heavy duty, steel, exterior grade door was no better than the screws attaching the hinges to the door frame.

"The problem with brute force" Milo said with lofty assurance "is that people rarely use enough of it."

He had been prepared to chisel his way through the stud-wall and was pleased that he didn't have to break a sweat.

The man-cave was starkly utilitarian. In contrast to the parts of the house that somebody might see, it was nearly bare. The only thing of interest was the 14-gun, gun safe.

A strong man, well versed in the use of large hammers and cold chisels can un-zipper an exposed piano hinge in about the time it takes to read this sentence. Milo was that man.

There were no guns in the safe but there were ten boxes. The top box was open and revealed six, bottles filled with white tablets.

Milo opened one and shook out a handful of tablets. He inspected them in the bright light of his headlamp. It was a white scored tablet that was slightly longer than a half inch with M367 impressed into the side.

Nyssa whistled. "That is hydrocodone. Well, hydrocodone and Tylenol," Nyssa said using the name of a common, brand name for acetaminophen.

"Hydrocodone?" Milo asked.

"Norco. Vicodin," Nyssa said. "When I was working up in Saginaw it had a street value of $10 a pill. It is probably counterfeit because I can't imagine this much product disappearing out of the supply line without huge alarms being raised. Even so, it is still be worth $10 a pill."

Milo hefted the bottle. "Feels like it is about a pound."

"At 400 mg to the pill, that would be more than a thou

sand to the pound," Nyssa said.

Doing some quick math, Nyssa said "A thousand pills to the bottle. If all of those boxes hold six bottles the we are looking at sixty thousand pills."

"Holy shit. That is over half million dollars' worth of street drugs!" Milo said. "Duckworth sure-as-hell didn't walk away and leave this. Something happened to him."

Making Evidence Disappear

"It raises the question, what are we going to do?" Milo said as he looked at the ten boxes of pills, each worth $60k at pre-Ebola street prices.

Nyssa looked at the boxes of pills speculatively. "You know, it might be decades before civilization gets back on its feet. That means no more pain meds for surgery or broken bones."

"This stash is incredibly valuable," Nyssa said.

"If it is counterfeit, how do you know it is any good?" Milo asked.

"The problem is that it tends to be too good," Nyssa said. "People over-dose on the counterfeit pills. By the time it is smuggled into the States, fentanyl or carfentanil is cheaper than hydrocodone as far as bang-for-the-buck. The trade articles I read said that most of the counterfeit pills were either made with Fentanyl or some other souped-up, synthetic opioid. Most of the counterfeits have more zip than the real ones."

"Well, we can't just start passing them around like candy," Milo said. "Somebody has to know that Duckworth had this kind of stash. With these kinds of quantities, he was a wholesaler. He had suppliers and he had customers and none of them are nice people."

"Let me think about this for a few minutes," Nyssa said.

"You know, there is another problem," Nyssa said. "Brittany and the kids can't come back here. Ever."

"It would be even better if she changed her name and left Kates Store. As long as somebody named Duckworth lives anywhere near here, they will be a lightning rod," Milo said in agreement.

"Hmmm," Nyssa said thoughtfully. "I wonder if she could move in with Luke up in Pray Church and pretend to be his girlfriend, at least until we sort things out and come up with a better plan."

"That would work but what if Luke already has a girlfriend. She might object," Milo said.

"Can you keep a secret?" Nyssa asked. "Seriously?"

"Well, I should hope so," Milo said, offended that Nyssa had to ask.

"Luke is gay," Nyssa said. "Dad does not know. Mom suspects. There is no girlfriend to worry about."

In fact, Luke was bisexual but there were not that many girls who found Luke all that interesting. It has just been far, far easier to tell Nyssa that he was gay so she would stop setting him up with all of her fellow nursing students.

Thinking through Luke's living arrangements, "He has enough room. Do you think he will go for it?" Milo asked.

"Luke is a very private person. He will jump at the chance to shift the focus off himself," Nyssa said. "Having a girlfriend with a ready-made family will be a lot easier for the people in Pray Church to understand than finding out that he is gay."

"Besides, he will have forty days while Brittany and the kids are in quarantine. They have to go into quarantine if we want to convince anybody they are from somewhere else," Nyssa said.

"OK, let's say Brittany and family moves in with Luke and she takes her maiden name. That still doesn't help us get rid of the drugs." Milo said.

"And that is why our next stop is Christine Cherrystone," Nyssa said. "Put one of those bottles in your pocket. We are going to take a walk."

Christine Cherrystone was a witch.

She lived in a stone-faced cottage nestled in a hollow just east of a ridge. In the summer her house was a riot of flowers in the style of a Thomas Kinkade painting. In the winter the yard was a dreary, stick-filled space with cats beneath every bush.

Mobiles with every manner of Wicca paraphernalia dangled from the branches of every tree: crystals, pyramids, runes and effigies.

Widow Cherrystone was a mousy looking woman with naturally gray hair tied back in a bun. Surprised to have visitors, she invited her guests in.

Her house was festooned with bundles of herbs hanging from the rafters. Every horizontal surface was covered with antique, colored bottles or arcane jade carvings.

After the normal pleasantries, Nyssa came to the point. “The drug companies are not able to distribute drugs. I know that you have a garden of medical plants. Would you consider expanding it ‘for the duration’?”

“What kinds of plants are you thinking of?” Widow Cherrystone asked, timidly.

“Well, I know you grow poppies. What do you think of making tinctures for pain?” Nyssa asked. “And you grow fabulous foxgloves...maybe digitalis for heart medicine?”

“Oh, dear,” Mrs Cherrystone said. “Growing and harvesting poppies on that scale is a serious Federal crime! I am not sure I am willing to do that?”

“I have people who are not healing,” Nyssa said. “I have people ripping out their stitches because they are in pain.”

“I am not into Wicca, but I have talked to a few witches. If you are a white Wiccan, then you pledged to heal. I am a nurse and I need drugs to heal with. It is push-comes-to-shove time,” Nyssa said.

“I can get kids to help with the weeding. I can get a flat, fertile piece of ground tilled up for you. I don’t have the time, expertise or seeds to do what you can,” Nyssa said. “You can always plant the seeds and if things flip right-side-up in the meantime then we don’t have to harvest them.”

“You make some valid points, but I only have a little bit stored up until we can harvest in August. What would you have me do until then?" Mrs Cherrystone asked.

"I am glad you asked," Nyssa said. "Would you consider making tinctures with what you have and enhancing it with other herbs?

Mrs Cherrystone mulled over the proposal. "I suppose I can synergize it with capsaicin and catnip, but it will still be pretty weak."

"What if you added some Tylenol?" Nyssa asked. "We brought a bottle just in case you agreed to the proposal."

Nyssa gestured to Milo to hand her the bottle.

Mrs Cherrystone opened the bottle and shook out some pills. She looked at them carefully and crushed one of the tablets between her molars and chewed it.

Then she looked at Nyssa accusingly. "These aren't Tylenol, are they?" In the 1960s Mrs Cherrystone had a more-than-casual relationship with some very hard drugs.

"They have Tylenol in them. They also have synthetic codeine in them," Nyssa said.

"Why did you lie to me?" Mrs Cherrystone asked. "That is not a good way to treat your business partners."

Milo answered. It was the first time he spoke. "There are still drug users and drug dealers around. That bottle you are holding has a street value of $10,000."

"Nyssa thought...we thought that you could help us. We need the drugs for legitimate patients but we also don't want to alert every bad person in central Michigan that we have them," Milo said.

"We thought that if you dissolved it into a tincture you could standardize the strength and mask the source...killing two birds with one stone."

"You would just give me this bottle?" Mrs Cherrystone asked.

Nyssa and Milo nodded their heads.

"And you would expect me to just give away my tinctures?" she asked.

"Well, no. Actually, we want you to charge what the market will bear," Nyssa said. "If you gave it away for free then we would have a drug problem when everybody needs to be on their toes and able to put in a full day's work. In fact, it would be a good thing if you priced your tinctures on the high side."

"Let me think about it," Mrs Cherrystone said. "May I keep this bottle until I make up my mind?"

Nyssa knew she had made the sale. "Absolutely," Nyssa said.

Flooding

Ah-fula Shi-Thead was livid with rage. The meals-on-wheels delivery was late.

Unlike most residents of Lansing, Mz Shi-Thead had her meals delivered to her because of her three children under the age of five. It was deemed too difficult for a single mother to shepherd three, pre-school children to the soup-kitchens three times a day. Consequently, she had her meals delivered.

While she could have walked to the nearest kitchen, three blocks away Mz Shi-Thead was not inclined to do so. It had been raining for three days straight. The intensity varied between steady to monsoon-like. Furthermore, the temperatures had risen into the mid-forties to the mid-fifties. The higher temperatures compacted the packed snow on the sidewalks and streets into glare ice.

Mz Shi-Thead was not athletic and despite her low center-of-gravity she was prone to falling. She had weak ankles and knees and her unique physiology resulted in an impaired view of the ground in the vicinity of her feet.

She knew her rights. When the driver showed up, she was going to give him a piece of her mind.

Had she looked out the window she would have been praying for a boat rather than a meals-on-wheels truck. The corner of Francis Street and Kalamazoo Avenue was under three feet of water and rising fast.

The extensive snow-pack changed the albedo of the eastern half of North America. Most years the increasing day length and intensity of the sun would have resulted in gradual warming of the surface and a slow, progressive melting of any lingering snow.

The snow reflected the radiant energy of the sun back into space without converting it to heat. There was a crisp break between bare ground and snow-covered ground. Even through the cloud cover the bare ground absorbed heat and the difference in temperature drove violent storms where the two met.

Adding to the storm was the warm moist air generated in the Gulf of Mexico.

Most years the air would have pushed into eastern Texas and headed north, gradually curving to the east. This year the cold dense air over the snow-pack fought to move south just as hard as the less dense Gulf air tried to move north.

The stalemate resulted in the spring rains arriving to the mid-West four weeks later than usual. Eventually, old Sol pumped enough heat into the Gulf and the warm air was able to win the arm-wrestling match with the cold, stationary air and a jet of hot, super-saturated air knifed upward into the nation's underbelly.

It pushed the cold air to the east and the super-heated air

bulled its way north and quickly chilled as it passed over the snow, dumping its water in a ceaseless deluge.

Rivers that drained to the south were less impacted with flooding than the ones that flowed north.

The Wabash river, for instance, drained into the Ohio and encountered little in the way of ice-dams and the surge was long and drawn out over several weeks.

Rivers that flowed north, like Minnesota's Red River and Michigan's Grand River upstream of Lansing were monkey hammered with flooding. The northward roll of melting added water to the river in synch with the flood surge. Furthermore, the leading edge of the surge was impeded by the thick ice that had built up on the rivers.

Within the cities the storm drains were overwhelmed. The leaves that would have been hauled away by the city workers were washed down the streets and clogged the grating of the storm drains.

Downtown Eaton Rapids was underwater from Canal Street to Elizabeth Street.

Nothing is unique in history but the last time Lansing saw such flooding was before the 1600s.

Portions of the Red Cedar Floodplain were under twenty-five feet of water.

The path of the Grand River through Lansing is much like a sickle or Question mark. The river flows in from the south, hooks to the east for more than a mile, then a mile to the north and then it turns west toward Lake Michigan ninety miles to the west.

The portion of the river where it turned west was both narrow and high banked. It was a natural choke-point.

The geographic evidence suggests that at various times the

flooding on the Grand River has been high enough to flood most of Lansing and East Lansing east of Martin Luther King. There was also evidence that the river cut across the west side of Lansing east of Dibble and short-circuited by diverting through the Carrier Creek channel turning the portions of Lansing that were not submerged into an island surrounded by raging torrents of ice-cold water.

Those people who had sufficient situational awareness and mobility quickly retreated to the high-points in Lansing and the tops of multi-story buildings.

The flooding destroyed the soup kitchens.

The hundreds of thousands of bushels of grain that had been moved into Lansing had all been stored on the ground floor. Grain is heavy and the people who moved it dropped the bags as soon as they were out of the boss's sight. The grain was all destroyed. Worse, what grain appeared to be sound was infested with vomitoria and other fungal toxins.

If there was an upside it was that the vast volumes of water diluted the fecal matter that citizens had been pitching out their doors and into their front yards. In most cases the level of typhoid, cholera, E. coli bacteria was such that most cases of dysentery were not fatal.

The biggest downside of the high water was that the rats were flooded out of the sewers and millions of rats comingled with the soaked refugees.... refugee being the most appropriate term for somebody who had been evicted from their home.

Shotgun Start

The change in weather purely sucked for Chernovsky's forces.

Chernovsky made it a practice to move camp at least once a week. Sometimes it was after a four-day interval. Sometimes it went a full seven days.

During the cold of the winter, the young men became adept at cutting brush and driving the stems into the wind packed drifts. They salvaged brush from the old site and wove them into the new.

The soldiers, for they were soldiers now, slept two-to-a-tent. They erected the tents on wooden pallets and piled straw into them before unrolling their sleeping gear. Wet is the enemy of warm. Body heat will melt snow if there is not separation between the warm, sleeping bodies and the snow. The pallets, straw and sleeping bags did just that.

While they were not exactly comfortable, they all survived a night of -14F without the loss of any fingers or toes.

Moving camp was a full squad evolution. One fire-team held over-watch while the other team moved a single tent. Wooden pallets are heavy and the fire-team alternated moving heavy and light parts.

Quinn Spackle thought the constant moving was a waste of energy. When Quinn pushed Chernovsky he simply replied, “Best practice.”

Later, after the relationships had developed, Chernovsky pointed out that they went through a lot of firewood. He also pointed out the fact that they could not dig proper privies given the deep snow and frozen ground. That was not a problem now but would be when the spring thaws came.

Finally, Chernovsky pointed out that permanent camps were magnets for attacks. Moving the camp on a frequent, semi-random basis was one way of denying attackers solid intelligence.

Quinn regretted calling this to Chernovsky's attention because Chernovsky immediately started drilling them on how to respond if/when the camp was attacked. If a human can imagine it, Murphy will make it happen someday

The relentless rain made hot meals almost impossible. The tents shed the rain and thus ended up teetering on two-foot tall plateaus of melting slush.

Needless to say, "Cookie Girl" did not make any deliveries which added to Quinn's misery.

Chernovsky blew the whistle and they moved camp during the heaviest of downpours.

They moved to the ridges and knobs of a played-out hay field where the exposure to wind and rains had melted off all of the snow. They threw the pallets on bare, mineral dirt for the first time...ever. Ok, not dirt.... mud.

Chernovsky barely thought about the breach in “best practice.” His soldiers’ tents were in the open and sky-lined from 360 degrees of approach. If he thought about it at all, it was that NOBODY was going to be pushing through the rain and flooding for weeks.

The water in Silver Creek backed up and flooded the ground floor of the honey-pot houses and the de-roofed pole barns.

The approach to the bridge in Dimondale was under water.

And while 24 inches of water does not sound like much to wade through, it must be remembered that the water was snow-melt, that is, as cold as ice. The water was flowing swiftly and with the grid down there was no easy way to dry out wet clothing and footwear. Furthermore, famine depletes a body's resources and there is not enough fat to shiver-more-heat. Hypothermia is a mortal risk to a hungry person.

The young men in Lansing were less organized than Chernovsky’s soldiers.

More often than not, a gang of young men forcibly evicted a

family from their home shortly after sunset only to wake up at mid-morning to find their new home was surrounded by three or four-foot-deep water.

No food. Rats. Fleas. Cold. As often as not one of the gang members had some Shithole-i-stan form of the cooties. Miserable.

But they were alive, which might not have been the case if all of the gangs had crowded into the small bits of old Lansing that had not flooded.

As the flood waters receded, the first bits that were opened up were the roads and bridges upstream in Eaton Rapids and Dimondale.

Then the roads that crossed Carrier Creek became passable. Then land-bridges formed over the Dibble Street flooding.

The receding waters also made the gangs escaping the flooded houses a progressive thing.

From the perspective of Chernovsky's soldiers, they would see the tide of refugees and gangs as a shotgun start rather than a Le Mans, standing start.

Janelle Gets a Bee in Her Bonnet

Janelle sat, staring at the table covered with the parts of a disassembled rifle.

Kelly was not the kind of man to fill the air with senseless chatter. He let her stare.

After five days of watching her spend virtually every spare moment just staring at the parts, Kelly "What are you thinking?" he asked.

"I am thinking the shotguns were a piece of cake," Janelle said. "I think it is time to reach a little bit."

They agreed to build the shotguns in "batches" of ten. That

would give them some efficiencies of scale but would also give them opportunities to make changes.

The first batch was a struggle. The second batch of ten was hard. The next two were built with no issues. Even though they had planned on building 100, the demand slacked off after thirty-five. They stopped building at fifty preferring to conserve resources. The fifteen extras were in the vault.

Kelly got a cold chill down his spine. Janelle was looking at a disassembled AR-15, a very sophisticated weapon that used high-tech processes.

"You aren't thinking of making AR-15s, are you?" Kelly asked.

"Nope," Janelle said.

Kelly's relief was short-lived.

"We are going to have to make a lot of changes if they are going to work with black powder," Janelle said.

That is when the hackles went up on the back of Kelly's neck.

A bit of history is in order to make sense of what Janelle said.

The AR-15 was a space-aged weapon made from forged, aircraft grade aluminum and made with exquisitely tight tolerances.

When first deployed in Vietnam, the weapon was subject to jamming after relatively few rounds were fired. The cause of the problem was quickly traced to the chemicals added to the smokeless powder to buffer the acid products that accelerate the deterioration of smokeless powder in hot, humid climates.

The other factor that made the AR-15 exquisitely sensitive to powder residue is that the design is a "direct impingement" design. A small hole was drilled in the barrel and a tube carried the high pressure, contaminated, gasses directly into the upper receiver where a small piston/cylinder arrangement harvested the energy of the gasses...and then indiscriminately spewed the ash contamination into the upper receiver where all the small, moving, closely fitted parts lived.

Other chemical buffers were found that did not leave solid residues and the problem, mostly, went away.

Approximately 1% of the original smokeless powder became solid residue that gummed up the lock-works. By contrast, black powder leaves almost 50% of its original mass as solid residue.

Had it been anybody other than Janelle, Kelly would have harshly rebuked them for the stupidity of the idea.

"Why black powder?" he asked.

"Someday we are going to run out of components for reloading AR ammo. I am trying to stay ahead of the game," Janelle said.

"You know that you picked about the worst action in the world for running black powder, don't you?" Kelly said.

"Yup. That is why it has to be changed," Janelle agreed as if that was not a big deal.

Poking the gas key on the bolt carrier, "Why does that have to be in the upper receiver?" Janelle asked. "Why can't the gas key be longer and have the gas tube end in the handguard?"

Kelly had never thought about that.

"And since the gas is still under pressure when the gas key moves away from the gas tube, why not have a reed valve close as the gas key moves aft and we could cut the end of the gas tube on the diagonal so it biases the gas to the right and out of the handguard or route it around and vent it out the bottom?" Janelle asked.

"Those guys who build two-stroke racing motorcycles know a lot about using pressure and momentum to move air and fuel where they want it," Janelle said. "I don't see why we can't use tuning to kick most of the gas out, away from the upper receiver and action."

"You know black powder cartridges won't have nearly the power of smokeless ones, right?" Kelly asked.

"Yeah, I get that. But everybody else will be running out of smokeless powder ammo. too," Janelle said. "It is like the old joke; I don't have to be able to out-run the grizzly bear. I just need to be able to out-run the guy I am fishing with."

"I looked up the ballistics of the old 25-20 Winchester. It has a case volume similar to the 5.56mm round," Janelle said. "1500 feet per second for an 85-grain bullet is a lot more impressive than a .22LR pushing a 40-grain bullet at 1200 feet per second."

"The other thing I was thinking was to see how much potassium nitrate we could replace with ammonium nitrate. Ammonium nitrate won't leave the residue that saltpeter does," Janelle said.

"So what are you going to do about receivers?" Kelly asked. "It is not like we have a forging press for 7075 aluminum."

"You are right. We don't," Janelle said. "The lower receivers don't need to be that good. Heck, you can buy them..." then she corrected herself, "..You used to be able to buy them made of polymers."

"Did you know that we have a neighbor who worked in a small shop making investment castings for a company that sold custom jewelry?" Janelle asked.

"You mean Bob?" Kelly asked.

"Yeah, Bob," Janelle said. "I bet Bob could design and make the patterns in his sleep."

"I thought investment casting used wax pieces that were melted out of the mold," Kelly said. "Why would we need molds?"

"I was thinking it would be more 'production' if we used steel molds for the exterior surfaces, and sand or plaster cores interior surfaces that aren't undercut. Then use Bob's wax pieces for the most detailed areas," Janelle said.

"I still don't think you will be able to hold the tolerances the AR demands," Kelly said.

"That is what shims are for," Janelle said.

Northward Bound

Mark Salazar and eight-year-old Rosie Cowper started north a week after the rain stopped. Mark expected that they would have to hole up a few times along the way to wait for flooded bridges but he had a bad feeling about staying with the buildings.

The day before they left Mark filled the most isolated outbuilding on the east side of the property half full of firewood. He did not stack it, he left it jumbled. He wanted to have a good draft into it.

Then he brought Grumpy and Doreen's bodies and gently laid them on the pile with about a one-foot gap between them. Then he arranged them so they were holding hands.

Mark read from Isaiah 35 and John 14.

He asked Rosie if she wanted to say good-bye. She did.

"I don't know how to pray," Rosie said.

"What would you say to God if he was standing right here in front of us?" Mark said.

"Do I have to say it out-loud or can I say it in my head?" Rosie asked.

"Either way works," Mark said. "But my mom always said that saying it out-loud was to pray twice. That, and it feels more like you were praying."

Rosie had a heart-to-heart conversation with God as she leaned into Mark.

Rosie wanted to know why God made the plague.

Rosie wanted God to keep her parents safe, where ever they were.

Rosie asked God to buy a stove like the one Doreen had cooked and baked on for fifty years. She asked that Grumpy have plenty of dead ash to split, cinnamon rolls to eat and coffee to drink.

"It is probably better if you don't watch the next part," Mark said.

Rosie went back to the house and stood by the two backpacks on the porch. Old Shep waited there with her as Mark started the fire on the windward side at the bottom of the woodpile.

He waited to ensure that the wood was catching before turning away.

"Fair winds, Grumpy and Doreen. Fair winds," he said out-loud as he walked away.

They shouldered their backpacks and Mark opened the door to the chicken coop on the way by. He blocked the door open. Maybe they could make it as feral chickens. Maybe not. But at least they would have a chance.

They made it five miles the first day. Rosie lacked suitable shoes. Everything she owned was 'fashionable'. They sparkled and had heels. Mark had to dig through the attic and find some of Doreen's old shoes. For now, they were too big but extra socks helped with that.

Mark and Rosie camped beneath some red cedar trees two hundred yards from the road they were following. He dipped water from the swollen stream that had served as the water source for the old pasture they were in.

Dinner was rice and chunked summer sausage.

It took three days to make it to the Michigan line. Mark breathed a sigh of relief.

A consequence of high school sports is that residents of the Upper Peninsula, four hundred miles away were more likely to have heard of 'Eaton Rapids' than Ohio residents a mere seventy-five miles south of Eaton Rapids. Eaton Rapids rarely had a winning football season but they were widely known for their wrestling and softball program.

The first challenge was at the East Branch of the St Joseph River.

The man had his gun trained on Mark and Rosie from fifty yards away. He had them stop five paces away and demanded that Mark give up his gun.

Mark said, "I don't think so." He had it hanging from a loose, tac-sling across his chest. The 16-gauge shells were loaded with #6 shot, a shot size typically used to shoot rabbits and squirrels. At five yards it would act like a solid slug.

"All we ask is safe passage. We are heading north," Mark said.

"Where are you going?" the man asked, keeping his own weapon at low ready.

"I have family in Eaton Rapids," Mark said. "My daughter and I are going to rejoin them. My name is Mark and this is Rosie."

Mark and Rosie decided that it would be far easier to explain away Rosie as being Mark's daughter.

"That is a mighty long walk," the man observed. Then as an afterthought said, "My name is Dean."

"Well, Dean, we would have taken the bus but it seems as though they stopped running," Mark observed, wryly.

"How far do you think you are going to go today?" Dean asked.

"We have been averaging about ten miles a day," Mark said. "We are still toughening up after doing nothing all winter."

"Where did you start?" Dean asked. Dean and all of his neighbors were hungry for information.

"About three miles south of here," Mark said. "Can you recommend a high place for us to camp a couple hours north of here? That would be about six or seven miles."

"Yeah, you might try the Pittsford State Game Area," Dean suggested.

Mark winced. "Probably crawling with a bunch of city dudes that 'bugged out' thinking they are going to hunt for a living. Any other suggestions?" Mark asked.

Dean frowned a little bit. He did not know it but Mark had turned him into a friend by the simple expedient of asking for advice.

"A couple of miles east of the State Game Area there are a couple of lakes. As far as I know, there aren't any people living in them right now. Might be 'OK' if you were tidy and didn't make a mess of the place. Most of them leave a spare key under the mat or a garden gnome," Dean offered.

"Sounds perfect," Mark said. Where there were lakes there were likely to be ducks. A northbound duck would be a welcome change from the summer sausage. Who knows? They might even be able to turn up some vittles in one of the cabins that the locals missed. Either one of them would be a welcome change from spaghetti, rice, Spam and summer sausage.

CHAPTER EIGHT

Battle of Bridge Street

The call came in as Chernovsky was picking the shreds of breakfast from between his teeth. He picked up the mic and asked, "Whaddya need?"

The soldiers could not make out the exact words but the speaker was clearly excitable.

Chernovsky asked "When?"

"Gotchya," Chernovsky replied. "We are on it."

"OK, boys. Game time. Spackle, take your squad and set-up. That call came from the bank by the corner of Creyts and East Road. Said there are a hundred hostiles coming our way," Chernovsky said. "You got about five minutes. Make it count."

"A hundred hostiles? We need everybody and we will still be outnumbered three-to-one," Spackle responded.

"I don't see a problem. You each carry ninety rounds. I ought to be able to send two of you and have eighty rounds to spare," Chernovsky almost sounded bored, as if they had done this a thousand times before. "Just remember to aim before you stroke the trigger."

In fact, it was Chernovsky's forces first, hard contact with hostiles. Chernovsky was more nervous than he had been before his first college game. Football is physical but it is not a matter of life-and-death. That, and he was sending others into harm's way. He would not have the release of physical activity to burn off the adrenaline and deplete the fight-or-flight impulse.

For all that, he was channeling the best coaches he had ever worked under. In a sense they had done it hundreds of times before. Every exercise, every time they flipped off the safety and changed magazines faster than conscious thought. The best pep-talks don't challenge athletes to rise above their true ability. The best pep-talks call athletes to reach within themselves and tap the mastery they gained through countless repetitions.

Pep-talks that demand athletes play above their ability invariably result in the athlete "shitting the bed". Pep-talks that tap mastery result in top 10% performances time-after-time-after-time. Mastery plus a healthy level of adrenaline do that.

"What is our mission?" Quinn asked.

"Same as always. Kill them. Kill them all," Chernovsky responded.

After five seconds of staring at Chernovsky to see if he was making some strange kind of joke, Quinn said, "OK, men. Time to saddle up. Grab your guns and spare magazines. We have four minutes to get into position."

That was a bit of an exaggeration. If the hostiles were lollygagging then they might have as much as ten minutes. The downside was that the camp was as exposed as balls on a goose, perched on knobs in a hayfield where the vegetation had been beaten down by the crusty snow as it melted.

This was about a week sooner than they expected and had caught everybody off guard.

Fortunately, the men knew the southwest side of Dimondale

like the backs of their hands. They had walked it countless times, dragging firewood and such.

As they double-timed to set-up, Quinn said to Donnie "Wait here while I get the rest of the crew planted."

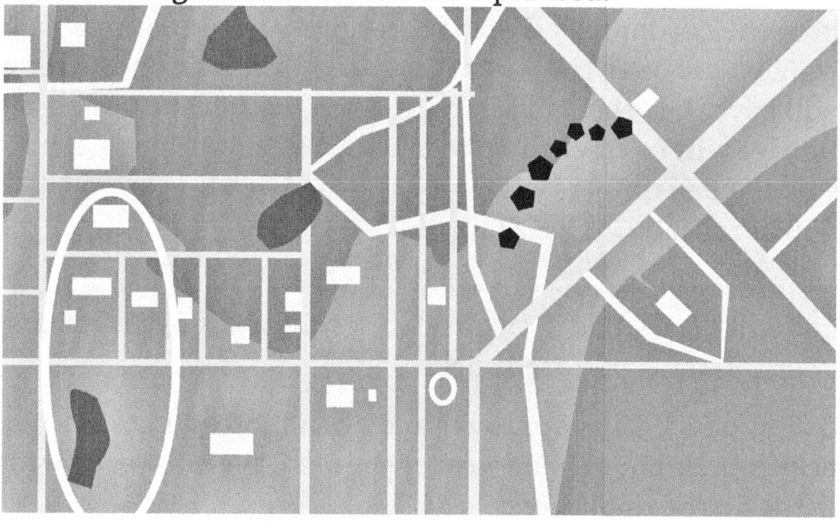

From upper right down diagonal road is the assumed direction of hostile advance. Oval on left side of image is location of Chernovsky's camp. "O" in the low center is position of Donnie. Pentagon keystones are the ambushing force. Southmost keystone is Quinn's position. Northmost keystone is Jason Weide's position. Light jagged s-shape line from central top to central bottom is Windsor Drain.

Quinn told his fighters to align parallel to Bridge Street about 80 yards from the road. By now the fighters realized that Quinn's directions were general guidelines. If the lay of the land demanded that the fighter be 100 yards from the road then that is where they would be. If there was a gap in cover then they would make adjustments.

Quinn picked Jason to be the gate-keeper. Jason was notable for his clear and deliberate diction. "Post up on Caruss Drive. You are my eyes-and-ears. Use the radio to let us know what is happening."

Then Quinn trotted back to Donnie. Even though they were

both Team Leaders Quinn was the senior leader. It was the simple recognition that Quinn could collect and process information quicker and with more surety than Donnie could.

"I want you to set up so you are looking up Bridge Street. You have the unsuppressed AR. When I give you the command, I want you to open the party. Then, a couple of seconds later I will have the other guys open up from the side. Just remember, we will be stacked up to the west of your targets. Don't shoot at any runners who leave the road heading west. That will be my job. Got it?" Quinn said.

"I start the party on your command. Everything in the road and east of the road is my meat. Anything west of the road is yours," Donnie parroted back.

Quinn nodded his approval and then trotted back to his position. He chose to be west of the road, the most southern in the line of ambushers.

He looked to the north and saw his men with their backs to the road. They were on their knees or crouched down, hands and weapons in front of them. They picked positions that put tree trunks and rolls of earth between them and the road.

As a group they were running with a 150 yard zero on their suppressed, .22LR semi-automatics. That meant that that their rounds would be hitting nine inches above the point-of-aim according to the second cheat-sheet Quinn had taped to the buttstock of his AR. "Just a reminder. Belly-button point-of-aim to compensate for the range. Donnie will be starting the party. After his third shot, we join the party. By then nobody will be looking our way."

Then there was nothing to do but wait. Quinn reached down with his left hand and grabbed a handful of mud and smeared it on his face. He had to watch the hostiles and had not thought to grab his balaclava.

Jason came on-line with a play-by-play description of the approaching hostiles. “They just broke the windows of the ice-cream shop and three of them went in.”

“I see a couple of them running up onto Granny Rollin’s porch and they are looking in her front windows.”

“I gotta kid on a bike riding out in front of them. Make sure you are down.”

In a couple of minutes, the kid, maybe twelve, became visible. The ankle-deep water on the south side of the bridge did not deter him. He was on a trick bike. Because he could move much more quickly than the group of hostiles, he kept riding fifty, seventy yards ahead of them, turning around and then riding back.

Jason came back on-line. “I count thirty, maybe thirty-five of them.” Jason had counted the first group of ten and then estimated based on the length and density of the group.

Quinn thought "Better than a hundred but still outnumbered three-to-one."

In two more minutes, Quinn was able to see for himself. Other than the bike rider the hostiles were bunched up into a group about twenty yards long. The biggest knot of people was about twenty feet back from the leading edge.

The bike rider rode up the bend in Bridge Street within ten yards of Donnie and turned around. Donnie’s clothes were tattered and had lichens, moss and tree bark ground into them. It was a natural ghillie suit. Donnie picked a position beneath an isolated evergreen that had branches all the way down to the ground.

Jason said "There are a few stragglers who had become separated from the main group and won't be in the kill sack."

Quinn waited until the leading element, less the bike rider, were directly in front of him. Then he signaled Donnie. By previous arrangement the signal for *fire at will* was three clicks on the mic.

Donnie had heard Chernovsky's rebuke to Quinn, ""Just remember to aim before you stroke the trigger," and thought it had been directed at him.

Donnie picked a target near the front of the swarm, the one that the others seemed to be orbiting around. He knew that Quinn's direction to aim for the belly button was directed at the guys carrying the .22LRs. His AR shot much flatter than their weapons. Donnie settled the cross hairs of the Burris MTAC on the center of the dude's chest and willed the AR to go off.

The target was 160 yards from Donnie's position and Donnie was fully capable of hitting a golf ball at that range. The target appeared to trip and sag.

The person behind his target became visible. Donnie caressed the trigger again. Then he shifted to the right and fired again. Then again....

At the first shot Quinn's fighters slowly spun around to face the road. For the first time they saw the opposing force. Quinn's fighters on the south end of the "fan" had five-to-eight hostiles in the zone they were responsible for. The fighter on the north end had far fewer.

The suppressed semi-automatic .22LRs made little more noise than a person snapping their fingers when firing. The hostile forces hyper-focused on the booming AR directly in front of them and remained oblivious to the threat from their side.

After five seconds of confusion and hesitation, the mob turned and started running north on Bridge Street. That is when the ambushers on the north end of the fan had a target rich environment.

One of the hostiles had an AR and seemed to have more situational awareness than his fellow hostiles. Quinn thought, “We can’t have that,” and he dumped him with a head shot. Other than that, Quinn kept over-watch. He knew from experience that his guys would be blinded by tunnel vision and were incapable of seeing targets that were not in their focal plane. Those threats were his to take care of.

In what seemed like both an eternity and a scant second, Bridge Street was free of standing targets.

After waiting in position for an agonizingly long ten minutes...Quinn used his watch because he did not trust his body clock...Quinn left his troops in position and went to examine the battle field.

There were seven bodies on the road. Donnie had emptied his thirty-round magazine. The eight team members had emptied their twenty-five round magazines and Quinn had fired once.

Nobody had targeted the boy on the bike.

The Battle of Bridge Street, First AARs

There were three post-mortems after the Battle of Bridge Street.

The first was between Quinn and his Squad. The only major criticism was for Donnie. He did not have an egress route from his position and he would have been toast if things had gone sideways.

The second was delivered by Quinn to the other fire-team leaders and Chernovsky. Chernovsky was a big believer in sharing lessons-learned.

The third was between Quinn and Chernovsky, in private.

“The .22s aren’t worth a shit,” Quinn said. “We had zombies

with multiple, solid hits who ran off."

Chernovsky asked the obvious question. "If they ran off, how do you know you hit them?"

"Locals told me they had dead gomers in the street as far as a half mile away from the ambush site. Some of them with six, count them, six pass-throughs," Quinn said.

"I can only imagine how far some of the hostiles with one or two hits went," Quinn said. "Thing is, the next time they could keep fighting and we would be up shit-creek."

Chernovsky nodded. This was not unexpected. Several of the fighters spoke disparagingly of the .22s. One of them told of shooting a raccoon, a fifteen-pound animal with a .22 and it was still alive and hissing...ready to fight twenty minutes later.

The slow-moving bullets did not destroy much tissue as they passed through the body. They tended to push blood vessels aside rather than tear them and cause quick bleed-out.

"Anything else?" Chernovsky asked. There was not an iota of sarcasm in his voice. He really wanted to know.

"The AR had the same problem," Quinn said. "It just didn't slap the bad guys down."

"What are you looking for me to do?" Chernovsky asked.

"Can we up-grade?" Quinn asked. "Maybe to 12-gauge shotguns or Ought-Sixes?"

Chernovsky shook his head "No."

"Seraph was very clear, .22s except for the fire-team leaders," Chernovsky said.

"Maybe you can call Salazar and Carney. Maybe they can think of ways to make the .22s more lethal," Quinn suggested.

"Good leadership always throws the problem back on the person who brings it," Chernovsky said.

Quinn knew that was coming. It was not the first time he had heard Chernovsky say it.

"What is under your control? What can YOU change?" Chernovsky asked.

"We are using a double-tap," Quinn said. "I want to change it to a triple-tap."

"The other thing I want to try is to shoot for the head first, then the body shots to anchor."

"Why go for the head first?" Chernovsky asked.

"The silencers work great with the standard speed, target ammo," Quinn said. "A lot of the hostiles did not even know they were under fire from the side. But they sure-as-hell did after one of the guys nailed them center-of-mass with a .22."

"Hell of a lot easier to hit them in the head BEFORE we hit them with a body shot. Then, when they are moving, the body shot is a bigger target and we are more likely to hit it then to be able to hit them in the head," Quinn said.

"I officially approve your plan. Triple taps and attempt the head-shot first. I want you to roll that out to the other Team Leads. Make sure you give your reasons," Chernovsky said.

The conversations that Chernovsky had with Rick Salazar, Larry Tomanica, and Kelly Carney were not very productive.

There is not much that can be done with the .22. Adding more speed took the round super-sonic and negated much of the advantage of the silencers. Super-sonic bullets create a sonic-boom. While the "boom" can mislead the hostiles regarding the exact location of the blue force, it is close and does inform them that they are under fire.

Even the high-velocity rounds from the .22 LR don't expand reliably so using them provided little advantage and much disadvantage.

Using hyper-velocity .22 LR like Velocitors not only lost the advantage of silence, but often resulted in the spent brass sticking in the chambers and necessitating the use of a cleaning rod to expel it. While the hyper-velocity rounds did expand, the cost in terms of reliability was way, way too high. Furthermore, the change in trajectory complicated long-range accuracy.

Like many things in life, the solution with the fewest drawbacks was a compromise.

Kelly suggested magazines with the first ten rounds being sub-sonic, target ammo and the last fifteen being high-velocity rounds. His reasoning is that by the time every fighter had fired ten rounds the hostiles HAD to know something was up.

Tomanica suggested that the high velocity rounds be hollow-points. There was always the possibility that some of them might expand. He also suggested a blue magazine and red magazine system. The blue magazines would have the first ten rounds sub-sonic and the last fifteen high-velocity. The red magazines would be all high-velocity.

Engagements would always start with one blue magazine. All magazines after that would be red.

Quinn and Donnie were only slightly impressed when Chernovsky shared the red/blue magazine solution. They halfway expected that answer. They both knew for a fact that there at least twenty times more "high velocity" ammo around than "sub-sonic" ammo in people's gun safes.

Then next time Quinn went to pick up cookies from Dysen,

he asked her to take a letter to his great uncle Bill.

The easiest item for Bill Spackle to find were the 5.56mm loaded with expanding bullets. Bill had a shirttail relative who got damage control permits to cull white tail deer. He killed hundreds of them a year.

The relative had five hundred 5.56mm already loaded up with 60 grain Hornady soft-points bullets. It was his round of choice for culling whitetail deer. He also used them to 'discourage' dogs who were running livestock. They would not be the projectile of choice if the zombies wore body armor or if they weighed three hundred pounds. As it was, the zombies were wearing tattered clothing and most were as skinny as scarecrows.

Two days later Dysen brought another care package. This one had taken longer to assemble.

Bill and his wife Judy sought out Christine Cherrystone and asked her for "something that will kill rats."

Cherrystone was put into something of a dither. As a "white" Wiccan she rarely thought in terms of toxins. However, she had just pressed the oil from the seeds of a certain, tropical plant. She used the oil to treat constipation and as a base for certain kinds of topical ointments. The spent seed flour was very, very toxic.

Bill did not have enough powder to treat all of the bullets so he stretched it with pig filth from the stall where he had lost a litter of new born piglets to the scours. If the toxin did not get them maybe gangrene would.

Bill first tried dipping the tips of the bullets into melted wax from a toilet seat ring but the wax was too hard and not sticky enough to get any of the powder to stick. It worked much better after Bill mixed it 50:50 with melted lard.

Bill and Judy spent several nights dipping the points of .22

ammo first into melted wax:lard and then into the small pile of powder. A long time ago Bill had worked with an insecticide called Guthion and he had a very healthy respect for toxic materials. Both Bill and Judy wore disposable nitrile gloves, goggles, and N-95 masks.

Chernovsky's hands might be tied but that did not mean Quinn's were. And if Quinn didn't ask Chernovsky for permission, then Chernovsky wasn't going to say "NO!"

Hindsight

Paul Seraph's rage was palpable even through the clipped frequency of the CB radio. Rick Salazar held the speaker/mic away from his face as the volcanic anger radiated outward.

According to Seraph, Chernovsky and his men had murdered more than two dozen "harmless civilians out for a springtime stroll." An additional twenty "hostiles" had suffered mortal wounds during the engagement. However, the deep and narrow wound channel, though mortal, had allowed them to retain mobility for ten, even twenty minutes after being shot.

Seraph informed Salazar that Chernovsky's role was to provide intelligence, to be a listening post.

Rick, for his part, kept his silence. That is not the charter they had given Chernovsky. Yes, one of Chernovsky's missions was to inform the second line of defense when a group of refugees was heading south on any of the three roads he was tasked with watching.

When Chernovsky pressed the point, they gave him permission to defend his group with lethal force when under attack and to engage potentially hostile forces when the majority of the evidence indicated that the force were invaders, not refugees.

Rick had to take a half hour walk after getting off the horn with Paul Seraph to cool down. Paul had given him a thorough and expert ass-chewing. Rick wanted to be calm when he called Chernovsky.

Rick asked Chernovsky to find a private place and call him back. Chernovsky, guessing that it related to the recent engagement asked if he could bring Quinn Spackle with him in case there were questions he, Chernovsky, could not answer.

Rick agreed.

Ten minutes later Chernovsky and Spackle were on a hill a five-minute walk from the camp.

Chernovsky used his best "talking to the ref" voice. "What is up?"

"I got a call from Seraph. I am not going to go into details but he expressed concern that your actions poisoned the relationship between Eaton Rapids and Dimondale," Rick said.

"You got me there boss. I don't know what you are talking about," Chernovsky admitted.

"The kids you killed were Dimondale natives," Rick said. "According to Seraph, most of the natives are about to give you a visit carrying torches and pitchforks."

The wheels turned in Chernovsky's head. Somebody --obviously a parent of one of the hostiles they had killed -- had gotten ahold of Seraph and lit him up.

"Hang on a second," Chernovsky said. He dangled the mic from the cord so it was very, very clear that he did not have a hot mic and he asked, "Spackle, are you comfortable talking about this, what you saw and did not see?"

As long as Chernovsky wanted him to talk about what he saw, Quinn was fine.

"Sure," Quinn said.

“Hey, Mr. Salazar, I want to put Quinn Spackle on the horn. He ran the operation.”

“Hello Mr. Salazar. This is Quinn,” Rick Salazar had known Quinn since Quinn was eleven and Rick spotted him a couple of bucks so Quinn could participate in Open Swim at the Eaton Rapids Middle School.

“Hi Quinn. I need to know. Why did you think the group was hostile?” Rick asked.

Quinn thought for a few seconds before answering.

“The first thing was that the person who informed us of the group identified them as hostiles. That was a person who lives in Dimondale,” Quinn said.

“After we set-up, I had Jason Weide act as eyes-and-ears. Jason reported that members of the group were breaking into buildings as they walked through town,” Quinn said.

“The final thing is that they were all men. Not a single family,” Quinn said.

The unhappy sigh was felt through the speaker. “But you didn’t see any guns or other weapons?”

“It happened pretty fast,” Quinn said. “One of the hostiles was carrying an AR. I definitely saw that.”

“Wait...you saw one of <quote> harmless civilians out for a spring-time stroll. <unquote> with an AR?” Rick asked.

“That is what I saw,” Quinn said. “Thirty or thirty-five young men, breaking into houses and vandalizing property. No families. At least one of them had an AR.” At that point Quinn would have walked across hot coals before admitting that he had not seen the AR until after they had fired upon the hostiles.

Quinn did not think it was necessary to add that if the group were hostiles and had not been stopped, they would have seen Chernovsky's camp and the momentum would have swung in favor of the hostiles. In retrospect, Chernovsky's choice of camping places was ill-considered even if it was the only dry place within a quarter mile.

"I have one more question," Rick said. "Did you take their wallets or anything else?"

"No sir!" Quinn said. "Chernovsky was very clear. Don't touch them. Don't take anything. They might have Ebola. In fact, he says we cannot get closer than ten feet from them."

"So if wallets were missing..." Rick started out.

"Somebody else took them. Not us. I can vouch for every one of my men," Quinn finished for him.

Rick said he would have to think about things before getting back to them.

Events accelerated and Rick did not have to think about events for long. A similar group of "harmless civilians out for a spring-time stroll" approached the Eaton Rapids men guarding the M-99 bridge across the Grand River. Unlike Chernovsky's men, all of the Eaton Rapids men were in plain sight, standing in the middle of the bridge.

The "harmless citizens" ignored the guards' demands that they halt. Then the "harmless citizens" bashed the guards' heads with aluminum baseball bats and several dozens of them dashed southward up the road toward Eaton Rapids.

Roger Greenberg, one of Paul Seraph's long-term coffee-drinking buddies was on the bridge. He died of a cerebral hemorrhage shortly after one of the twenty-year-old "harmless citizens" hit him just below his left ear with a 31", aluminum Easton Typhoon baseball bat. Roger was in his mid-seventies and a former Marine. The Rules-of-Engagement that Paul had given the group did not authorize lethal force to address pilgrims who were not compliant with orders.

Paul never called Rick back to follow-up on Rick's investigation.

Moving Day

The first order of business after the initial debriefing was to confirm the sighting in of all weapons. Chernovsky assumed that the scopes had been bumped or something had happened. He had seen his men shoot and it was inconceivable to him that they missed so much.

Most of the arms were .22 LR semi-automatics and the most common model was the Ruger 10/22, a model Larry Tomanica thought very highly of due to its extremely robust magazines. Most of the .22 LRs carried fixed 4x 32mm scopes like the Simmons 22 Mag Rimfire scope.

To Chernovsky and Quinn's surprise, only one of the rifles needed adjustment.

The second order of business was to move camp. The current location was both indefensible and glaringly visible. It was past time to "get off the X".

Squad One was tasked with moving a little more than one mile to the west and "observing" southbound traffic on Gunn Road and eastbound traffic on Vermontville road. They had already scouted the area and prepositioned some of their supplies. They chose to camp immediately east of an old gravel pit. The property was owned by a man who had played on the 1959 Eaton Rapids Varsity football team and he was more than willing to let them set-up out-of-sight from the house.

Squad Three was tasked with moving a mile to the east and "observing" southbound traffic on Smith Road and West bound traffic on Vermontville. They expected zero traffic on Vermontville because Eaton Rapids had the bridges clamped down at M-99. They did not yet know that Eaton Rapids allowed a group of fighters through.

Squad Two, Quinn's squad, was tasked with the paved road that was expected to see the lion's share of traffic. That is also where Chernovsky hung out so he could efficiently support the other two squads.

The move was an all-day evolution. You don't just throw all your stuff in the back of a truck and move it, nor was there any snow so sleds could not be used. It has to be carried and the people who are doing the carrying need over-watch.

One squad carried for a quarter mile while the other did over-watch. Then they switched. After dropping off the goods from the first trip, each fire-team left one member to guard the goods while the remainder went back for more goods.

Quinn's squad had it much easier. They still had to move but they only moved a ¼ mile. They followed the same protocol.

Life became less fun with the squads broken up. Each squad had to do its own cooking and cleaning. Each squad had to come up with an observation rotation AND they had to have one fire-team on-call to support the other squads in the event the number of hostiles was overwhelming.

The operation of Quinn's squad was typical.

They had a primary observation post that was pushed as far north as was defensible. In the case of Quinn's squad, it was where the paved road crossed over Silver Creek. That is where they set up the honey-pot houses and dropped the roofs of the pole barns.

Water creates natural boundaries. "Real" armies avoid bridges because they are choke-points. Their institutional knowledge informs them that bridges are death-traps and it is better to wade through mud, slide down steep banks, swim through water even if you have to steady yourself with a guide-rope than it is to saunter across a bridge where there might be opposing forces watching you.

Chernovsky was betting that none of the hostile forces that were expected to explode out of Lansing had any institutional memory of such things.

The second ambush point was half a mile south of that. The west side of the road was a very steep embankment that had been carved out by Silver Creek and the east side was a knotted, thorny mess.

The third ambush point was a full mile south of the second ambush. That was the one that support teams from Squads One and Three were expected to boogie to when Squad Two went into the ditch. It was a mile-and-a-half run from their camp to the third ambush point.

A half mile south of the third ambush point was the refugee in-processing station at the northern limits of Pray Church.

Chernovsky's plan was simple.

He expected the hostiles to check out the honey-pot houses, get drunk and pass out.

Then a force would go in during the night and execute them as they slept. They would drag the bodies out of the houses and back up the road. There they would stack the bodies as a deterrent to any hostiles who might think of heading south toward Pray Church.

Chernovsky had a few cards he was holding close to his chest but he couldn't see any holes in the plan. In his mind it was a play guaranteed to generate a first down every time it was run.

Chernovsky's Campfire Talk on Animal Zombies

Chernovsky was picking up the vibe that Loren, one of his younger fighters, was as nervous as a whore in church.

"What's biting your ass?" he asked, not unkindly.

As an athlete, Chernovsky had observed his coaches subtly changing their approach for individual athletes. Some athletes needed encouragement. Some needed pep talks. Others needed harsh correction. Chernovsky watched and Chernovsky remembered.

He was still working on the subtle part. He often dropped into the hyper-testosterone mode of weight rooms when he was interacting with "his guys".

"Them birds. I think they are zombies," Loren said.

Most of the fighters called the potentially Ebola infected raiders as "zombies". It was a way of emotionally distancing themselves from young men who were really not that different from themselves.

Chernovsky looked up at the flock of starlings in the trees. "Why do you think that?" Chernovsky asked.

"I seen them pecking at the corpses in the road and they ain't afraid of us," Loren said.

That helped explain the skittishness of many of his younger fighters. It was starting to effect operations so Chernovsky knew it was time to address the issue.

He ended up making several long calls back to Kates Store. He talked to Nyssa because she was a nurse. She called him back after looking at various books in her family's library.

It took several conversations before he could explain the dynamics of virus reproduction in his own words.

At the evening's campfire Chernovsky broached the topic in his own delicate way. "I've been hearing that some of you pussies are worried about catching Ebola from animals. I'm gonna talk about that tonight."

That got the fighter's attention. Not because he called them pussies. That was an everyday thing. It was the topic of catching the zombie disease from animals, an issue that every watcher of zombie movies knew to be "fact".

"I ain't gonna say there is no risk. But I am gonna say that it is a very, very low risk," Chernovsky said. "But you ain't gonna believe me unless you know a little bit about how virus make baby virus.

"A virus ain't much more than a shoe-lace made of protein. It isn't sophisticated enough to make itself. It steals bits and pieces from the host and sticks them together to make a copy of itself."

"It drills into the animal's cell and find DNA or RNA or other strings of protein. It starts at one end and looks for patterns of protein. Once it finds a string that looks like what the next piece needs to be, it cuts that chunk of protein...think of it as being like beads on a string...out of the host's string and sticks it on the end of the baby it is making."

"Simple, right?" Chernovsky asked.

Several of the fighters were nodding.

"It is like cutting words out of a magazine to make an anonymous letter you are sending to the police. Don't ask me how I know," Chernovsky said.

It was intended as a joke but only a few of the fighters laughed, nervously.

"The problem is that the virus is stupid and cannot check its work. It might be looking for the word "Then", it sees a "T" and an “n” in the right places and cuts out the word. But what if the word is Than or Thin or Thing or Tennis. The virus don’t care. It cuts it out and slaps it on the end, close enough for government work,” Chernovsky said.

“That is not much of an issue for the virus if it stays within a species. The chances of it finding ‘Then’ when it is looking for ‘Then’ is almost 100%.”

“The problem for the virus is when it is not working in its home species. That is when it cannot find ‘Then’ when it is looking for ‘Then’. Almost all the time, the substitute word makes the virus less capable.”

“Think about it, this virus has been mutating for brazillions of generations, evolving. The weak die. The strong survive. The chances of a random mutation making the virus running the table stronger is almost zero because the random mutation really isn’t random. The virus already tried that word the last six million times it infected a blackbird or crow or buzzard and it hasn’t worked yet.

“Almost,” Chernovsky said.

“Suppose you shot a couple of blackbirds so you could have some meat for lunch. You still have to worry about the blood on the birds’ beaks or feet. And there is a very, very, very small chance that the virus got stronger when it cooked in that bird and made babies.”

"Fact of the matter is," Chernovsky said, "Scientists still are not sure what species Ebola lives in between outbreaks. Some scientists think it might be bats. Others are not so sure."

"The biggest risk is from human blood. That is why you have to tell me or your Team Leader if you have a cut on your hands or your face. That is why we leave the bodies. We don't take ANYTHING!" Chernovsky said.

"If the locals want to sell us something, they have to be boiling it in a kettle of water when we get it. I don't care if they picked it off a dead hostile or pulled it out of their basement. It has to be boiled. We bring our own stick to fish it out of the pot. They take the risks," Chernovsky said. "We don't."

CHAPTER NINE

The Heavy Lifting Starts

Collin and Brandon were in the observation post on the bluff behind the metal pole barn that fronted the paved road leading south out of Dimondale.

The post was sandbagged in with grungy, mud smeared sandbags. They could just see over the standing walls of the barn and see the crown of the road. They could see for more than a quarter mile to the north since it was early spring and the trees were not carrying any leaves.

They had been watching columns of smoke from burning buildings to the north and saw their first band of "yutes" at mid-afternoon. "Yutes" was a made-up word. It was something between "youth" and " 'yotes", local slang for coyotes or worthless vermin.

They rang up Quinn and Donnie when the band of yutes came into view. There were eight of them. Brandon had the spotting scope and he estimated they ranged in age from fourteen to nineteen. Their orders were to get a count and to flag the house they went into to raid. There were no houses on the close side of the road but there were five large, ritzy, abandoned houses where both Collin and Brandon could clearly see both front and side entrances.

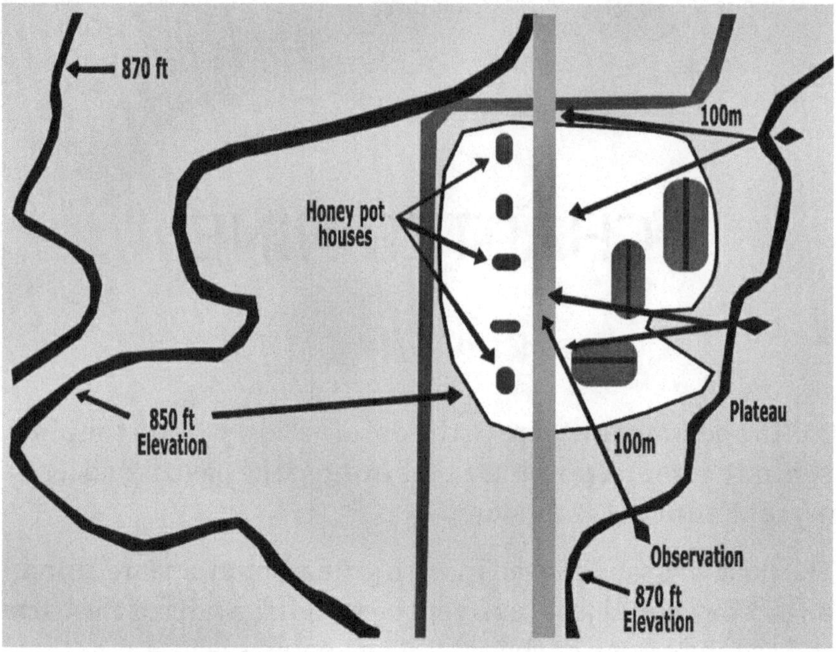

Hostile forces traveling north-to-south on paved road. Collin and Brandon in the southmost observation post. Bridge Street approximately 1/4 mile north of where Silver Creek passes beneath the road.

Everybody had assumed that the first band of yutes would go into the first house they came to.

Everybody was wrong. This band of yutes continued walking south on the road and would soon be south of Collin and Brandon and they would lose sight of them. That would pose a major problem.

"What are we going to do?" Brandon asked.

Collin was set up over the sandbag with his bolt action .22LR. Collin was a slightly better shot than Brandon so Brandon had the semi-automatic which was slightly less accurate. Collin was eyeing the yutes through his 4-power scope which was far less capable than the 20X spotting scope that Brandon had been using.

"Who is the leader?" Collin asked.

"The short guy in the U-of-M hoodie" Brandon said. The short guy was in the middle of the swarm and the other kids kept looking back at him as they played grab-ass. For his part, he stayed stone-faced and gave nothing away, letting them guess how he was feeling.

Collin frowned. He really wanted them to not be moving and, ideally, looking away when he took the shot.

"Can you hit that dead elm?" Collin asked, referring to the dead elm tree 120 yards away and on the far side of the paved road.

"In my sleep," Brandon said.

"Hit it about six feet up when they are just past it," Collin requested.

Both firearms had suppressors on them.

"You better duck down after you take the shot," Collin said.

Brandon pulled the shot and hit the trunk a foot higher than he intended. They had not done much target practice shooting over the over-stuffed sandbags.

When the group turned to parse the sound of Brandon's bullet hitting the punky wood of the trunk, Collin drilled the leader of the yutes in the left ass-cheek.

Then Collin quietly slid down, out of sight behind the sandbags.

The leader was thrashing around in the middle of the road making inarticulate sounds ranged from squeals to moans.

The other yutes pulled out their weapons and poured full magazines into the empty pole building. Some of those bullets skipped across the floor and went whining up, over Collin and Brandon's hide.

When the shooting suddenly died Brandon risked a peek over the sandbags. He saw the yutes inexpertly attempting to reload their weapons. They were all carrying handguns and in some cases were trying to jam magazines that did not fit into the weapon's magazine well.

The leader was getting a grip on his pain and barked commands at his troops. He was still thrashing back-and-forth like a freshly caught fish but he seemed to be regaining the reins of control.

One of the larger yutes helped him get up and the yutes went into the closest house.

"Damned good timing," Brandon said.

He was looking through the spotting scope again and he saw another band of yutes coming up the road. The new band of yutes seemed unphased by the massive amount of shooting they must have heard.

This group was smaller and only had six members.

"Do you still have that laser range finder?" Collin asked.

"Yeah," Brandon said.

"How far away is that road sign?" Collin asked.

"It says one hundred sixty-five yards," Brandon said.

"Same game plan," Collin said. "When they are even with the road sign, ring it like a gong, but not before you tell me who you think the leader is."

Brandon and Collin stayed in position until dark.

Chernovsky, Quinn and the rest of the Squad came after full dark.

Collin and Brandon's strategy had parked two different bands of yutes in houses, fifty yards apart.

Chernovsky told them to relax. The houses had been liberally seeded with 80 proof vodka and high potency weed. There were also candles and lighters in the house. "Time is our friend if we let it be," he cautioned.

After about four hours, when the candles had started to burn out, Chernovsky told them to wait while he checked out the houses. He came back a half hour later.

“Now the work starts,” Chernovsky said. “You young bucks gotta haul the bodies out and put them into the middle of the road up by Bridge Street.”

“Bodies?” one of the younger boys asked.

“You don’t think I was just looking at them do you?” Chernovsky snapped back.

“Now stop jerking off,” Chernovsky said. "I dragged them out to the porch. Now it is your turn to sweat."

Then to Collin and Brandon. “Good job, especially on the counts of the yutes that went in. I had to hunt a while to find one of them. Would have sucked if I hadn’t found him.”

Then to Collin, “I don’t know if you want put any notches in your stock, but one of the guys you tagged didn’t make it. He was dead when I got there.”

Lions and Tigers and Bears, Oh-my

Chernovsky and Tomanica had experimented on pumpkins back home. They found that if they pressed the opening of the suppressor firmly against the pumpkin just before pulling the trigger that the sound was that of the bolt slapping back and forth, only slightly louder than the shuffling of cards.

By Chernovsky’s count, he had more than 1500 rounds of Federal ammo that his Marlin 60 seemed to prefer. He rather hoped he would not go through all of it.

As the crew started dragging the bodies off the porches and arranging them the way Chernovsky told them to, Chernovsky found Collin and Brandon. He had them tell him the story again. He really did not like the part about the groups walking past the first honey-pot houses.

Afterward, he connected with Gladys and asked her to contact the hunters in the community. Surely some of them had electronic predator calls. Pushing the button on a remote would be stealthier than shooting.

Gladys called back and told Chernovsky she had one in hand with fresh batteries installed. Chernovsky dispatched Buddy on a bike to go pick it up.

Buddy showed up with the call at first light.

Buddy was not the most reliable person in the world. He had been riding with one of his cousins when he was twelve when his cousins convinced him to go "hood surfing". The cousins had been drinking. They hit the brakes. Buddy went tumbling and suffered a closed-head injury.

It is possible that aggressive intervention and therapy afterward could have negated most of the damage but Buddy's parents did not find out about it for two days. Even if they had learned about it, they had neither the financial resources or knowledge of the medical system to have been a good advocate for Buddy.

Buddy was doomed to spend the rest of his life functioning at the level of a nine-year-old.

Chernovsky told Brandon to keep an over-watch with the spotting scope. He wanted to know if ANYBODY was coming down the road.

Then he coached Buddy on what he wanted him to do with the corpses that neatly lined the road, face down.

While Buddy was doing what Chernovsky was instructing him to do, Quinn set the predator call to Coyote Howl and placed it in the brush where there was a clear line of sight to the primary observation post but where the call was screened from the road.

"What the hell are they doing down there?" Collin asked. He had been trained to not 'scope' friendlies.

Brandon was watching through the spotting scope. "You wouldn't believe me if I told you," Brandon said.

Brandon moved over so Collin could watch. While Collin was watching, Brandon had his rifle at low ready, just in case.

"Son of a bitch! Buddy is hitting them in the back of the head with a pick-axe," Collin marveled.

Buddy lined up on each corpse and hit them in the back of the head and nape of their neck with the broad bladed end of a mattock. Then he moved to the other side of them and smucked the other side of their head.

Chernovsky had to work with Buddy to ensure that the two cuts lined up so they looked like a bite mark.

After Buddy had desecrated all of the corpses, Chernovsky and Buddy walked back to the hide.

Chernovsky asked, "Do you have some place we can store this?" pointing to the mattock.

The wide blade of the mattock had a couple of 3/4" bolts welded to each side and it had "teeth" ground into the blade.

Seeing the boy's quizzical expressions, Chernovsky said "Buddy. Take a walk. I need to talk to these men privately."

Buddy very biddably walked out of sight.

"I don't get it," Collin said.

“Ever hear of were-wolves?” Chernovsky asked.

“Yeah. But they ain’t real,” Brandon said.

“You know that and I know that. But I have yet to meet a teenager who will go out after dark after watching a were-wolf movie” Chernovsky said. “Hell, my little brother still won’t walk around the back end of the truck when it is in the garage and it is after dark. And Jimmie is twenty.”

***

Peppermint Candy hinted very darkly during her next broadcast about Len Stuttman’s recent demise.

According to Peppermint, "The late Leonard Stuttman had been intimately involved in resurrecting extinct carnivores using DNA found on Siberian islands and from corpses found as glaciers retreated due to global warming.

"Authorities claim that Mr. Stuttman had been breeding for size and intelligence. In the margins of his notes, Mr. Stuttman wondered if some human DNA might have polluted the DNA of American Lions, Siberian Sabre-toothed Tigers, Neolithic Cave Bears and Alaskan Dire Wolves as they were far, far smarter than expected.

"Sadly, Mr. Stuttman’s mangled corpse was found outside the high-fence compound on West Windsor Highway just south of Dimondale three days ago. The gate was open and no animals were recovered. The most notable thing about Mr. Stuttman’s corpse was that the entire back of his skull had been cleanly sheared away.

"Since then there have been multiple reports of neighborhood horses and cattle disappearing. They were not killed and eaten. Nope. They were CARRIED OFF.

"I advise you in the strongest possible terms, people of Dimondale and Eaton Rapids never go outside alone and to never, NEVER go outside after dark,” Peppermint said. "Evil that has been extinct for ten-thousand years now roams the earth."

Chernovsky had written the piece and asked Dysen to carry it back to her sister, Peppermint Patty, to read on air. Dmitri got wind of the project and thought it warranted a boost in the signal.

The transmissions were pumped up to thirty Watts and repeated on the hour.

You damned betchya the yutes looked when the coyote howler lit up.

And Leonard Stuttman? Everybody in Dimondale and Eaton Rapids knew he died in 2012. And to repeat the tag-line he ended every Michigan Out-of-Doors TV show with: *Khudā Hāfiz*

The Plan Blows Up

“There is just one thing I am curious about,” Rick said into the mic after Chernovsky had given his daily report. “How did the 14 enemy KIA get to the corner of Bridge street? Didn’t you say they were killed a quarter mile south of there?”

“We dragged them,” Chernovsky said. “We tied rope loops and Columbus drilled them. I had two guys pulling each KIA.”

Contrary to what you might think given Chernovsky’s background in football, the Columbus drill has nothing to do with football conditioning. Rather, it is a way of securing an unconscious body with rope to pull it through a hole cut in the ceiling above the victim. It is still the best and fastest way to move bodies if you have enough people to pull.

Rick furrowed his brows in consternation. Something was not adding up.

"Fourteen enemy KIA. No casualties on our side. All KIA shot in the head. How does that happen?" Rick asked.

That is when Chernovsky spilled the beans about the honey-pot houses.

"So, a team went into the houses and executed them as they slept?" Rick asked, aghast...but not for the reasons Chernovsky assumed.

"Actually, I was the one who went into the houses and shot them," Chernovsky admitted.

Chernovsky was defensive. He expected praise, not Rick recoiling in horror.

"Look, you said yourself that we might have a thousand hostiles to deal with. I cannot put my men at risk. Even if I only lose one for every thirty we kill, we still lose," Chernovsky said. "You said we were going to see hostiles on an industrial scale. This is an industrial way to kill them."

"Hang on," Rick said. "I need to get a few more people to help me think this through. I will call you back in about twenty minutes.

Rick called back in a half hour. It took longer to find Nyssa than he had anticipated.

"OK, roll through what you told me before. I have Nyssa here," Rick said.

Chernovsky was mystified why Nyssa was there but he gave a quick synopsis of how they were using the honey-pot houses to efficiently kill hostiles.

"So, who went into the houses?" Nyssa asked.

"I did," Chernovsky said. "I don't ask my guys to do anything I won't do and going into a dark house to shoot sleeping zombies freaks most of them out. It don't bother me."

"What are you wearing for personal protective gear?" Nyssa asked.

"You know. The usual. Disposable gloves, tactical shooting glasses and an N-95 facemask," Chernovsky said.

"You are probably a dead-man-walking" Nyssa said.

"What?" Chernovsky said. "I was wearing PPE."

Nyssa said "I am going to explain this very simply. One Ebola virus can give you Ebola. If one of them gets into your body...through the corner of your eye, breathed in through your nose or after you lick your lips...and that virus finds a T-cell or B-cell...you are dead."

"And if you interact with anybody you will probably spread it to them too, maybe even before you have any symptoms," Nyssa said.

"But I was wearing a mask," Chernovsky said.

"N-95 means it stops 95% of microbes. Only one needs to get through to kill you," Nyssa drilled in. "And the number of microbes that get through is even higher if the mask did not fit perfectly."

"Did you burn your clothes after using them?" Nyssa asked. "If not, then rubbing your nose with your sleeve can push Ebola virus into your nasal membranes.

"Going into a house with Ebola patients and shooting them is the single dumbest thing I have ever heard," Nyssa said.

"But I didn't touch any blood," Chernovsky said.

"You didn't have to. Did you ever throw a rock into a puddle?" Nyssa asked.

Of course Chernovsky had.

"Wounds back-splash. Tiny particles of blood and tissue

back-splash out of the wound and fill the air with mist," Nyssa said.

Chernovsky was a little bit freaked out.

"What are the chances they didn't have Ebola?" Chernovsky asked.

"Not very good," Rick said. "The infection rate is somewhere around 10%, give or take, in Lansing. It is almost impossible to get a solid number."

"I think these zombies were from Dimondale," Chernovsky admitted. "They were wearing Holt and Potterville jerseys. Would that be any better?"

Rick did not activate the mic and turned to Nyssa. "That would make sense. Most of Lansing's roads are still flooded. There is a possibility that none of the fourteen were infected. What do you think we should do?"

"Quarantine," Nyssa said. "And compartmentalize. Chernovsky has to move out of camp and Squad One and Squad Three need to have zero interaction with Squad Two."

"OK, Chernovsky. This is what has to happen. You have to burn or boil everything you used when you went into the honey-pot houses. If you boil them you have to boil them for half an hour."

Far less time would have probably been plenty but Rick wanted it to be a little bit painful. That, and a few bubbles coming from the bottom of the pot was not a boil. Demanding a full thirty minutes virtually guaranteed that all of the material would be exposed to +200-degree water.

"You need to boil or burn your sleeping bag and everything you touched. You need to disinfect the mic you are holding in your hand. Then you need to move your tent at least a hundred yards from the rest of Squad 2," Rick said.

"You also need to isolate Squads One and Three so they are not exposed," Rick said. "Do you have any questions?"

Chernovsky could have lied by keeping his mouth shut, but he was not that kind of guy. If he was going to take an ass-whipping he wanted it up-front and without compound interest.

"Buddy Spackle helped me," Chernovsky said. "I gotta move him, too."

That was new information to Rick.

"What did you have Buddy do? I thought you said that you were the only one to go into the house," Rick said.

"I was the only one to go into the house when I was shooting them. But Buddy replaced the bottles of booze and weed. And I had Buddy hit the hostiles in the back of the head with a modified pick-ax," Chernovsky said.

"What?" Rick said.

"I had a pick-ax modified so it looked like a bite mark from a 400 pound were-wolf," Chernovsky said. "I directed Buddy to make it look like the hostiles had died after a were-wolf bit them in the back of their skulls. The hostile KIAs were stacked face down so anybody coming south on Canal had to see them.

"I figured it was worth the effort even if only one-in-twenty hostiles turned around and decided to pillage elsewhere," Chernovsky said.

Making Plans on the Fly

The atmosphere around the three Squad camps was distinctly tense.

First, Chernovsky said that they could not use the honey-pot houses the way they intended. In fact, nobody could touch a hostile, dead or alive.

He did soften the prohibition a little bit. He said that the honey-pot houses were to be reserved for the most threatening gangs. They were to be shuttled into the houses and then the house was to be burned down with the passed-out hostiles inside. The key point being that they were to not touch or come within ten yards of any hostile.

That triggered a much more aerobic style of defending the frontier. Hostile groups of five or fewer were rare but the two observers were able to take them out. One of the huge advantages of the .22s was that the mortally wounded tended to run off and not die on the road. The last thing the defenders wanted was for the invading forces to leave the road. Too many dead stacked up at any one place in the road would likely do that.

Another advantage was that the wounded NEVER tried to run up the bluff the observation post was perched on. Wounded almost always ran back the way they had come, assuming it was safe. Either that, or they ran downhill toward Silver Creek.

It became necessary to inform the homes downstream of Silver Creek that the water was polluted as many of the corpses were found half in and half out of the water.

Forces between five and ten were easily handled as long as the observer with the spotting scope saw them soon enough. Most hostile forces fell into this size category. Fighters from Squad Two would quickly move to the observation posts one hundred and two hundred yards north of the primary observation post. On cue the three fighting positions would open up on the group with each position having their own primary targets. Six shooters, ten targets; it was not much of a challenge to get at least one solid body hit on each target.

Forces almost always topped out at fifteen hostiles. That

seemed to be the maximum that a leader could command by force of personality. It was also beyond what Quinn's squad could attrit to zero from one position.

The first really large group, actually two groups that were working together that passed through the kill trap surprised Quinn by running through the kill-sack and out the other side.

Quinn called Squads One and Three and the reaction teams ran flat-out to the third ambush position. They got there just in time but were uncertain if any of the hostile force had peeled off from the main group. That caused additional tension, not knowing if you had hostile forces at your back.

The next large group was handled differently in part because Kelly and Janelle were able to whip up a weapon that adapted well to shooting large crowds of densely packed targets. Quinn's observers let them slip through unmolested. They called Quinn. Quinn called the quick reaction force.

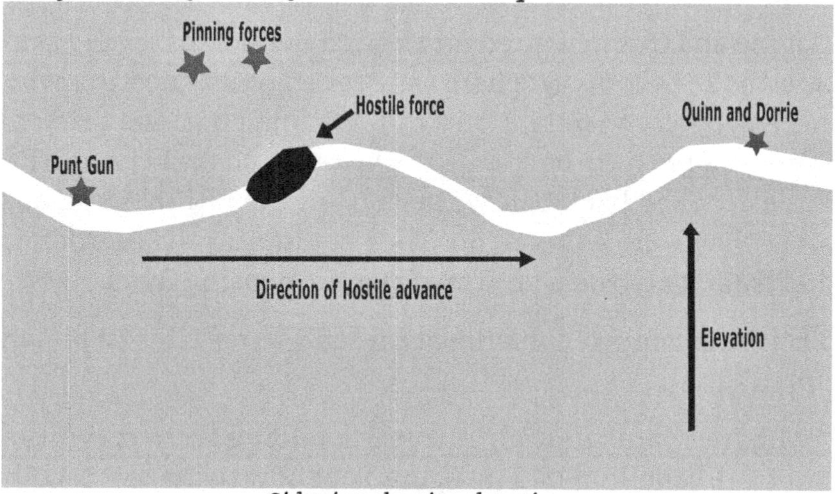

Side view showing elevation

Quinn and Donnie hauled ass to get out in front of the large group. They set-up on the military crest on the second rise in the road (the south slope) at the third ambush site. Their job was to pin the hostiles down on the north slope of the first rise in the road.

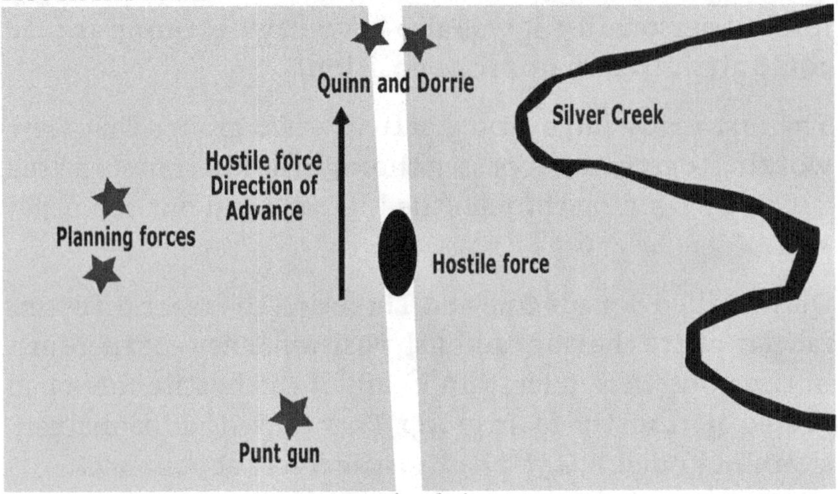

Overhead view

Another fire-team set up fifty-to-seventy east of the road to act as a pinning and clean-up force while a second fire-team a hundred yards north of the concentrated mass of hostiles. That is, they were behind the hostile forces.

Donnie and Quinn waited for the first person to be fully sky-lined before shooting. There were several other hostiles who were partially visible. Donnie and Quinn continued shooting as long as they had targets. The remainder of the hostile force dropped back below the crest of the hill to figure out what they were going to do. They could hear the AR rounds and could only guess how many were opposing them.

Their impromptu conference caused the hostiles to bunch up.

A hundred yards to their rear was a full fire team crewing a punt gun. Janelle and Kelly figured out how to make it recoil-less. The gun was a six-foot length of three-inch drill pipe. The shell launched five pounds of payload downrange and a fifteen-pound hunk of concrete aft ward. You did not want to be standing behind the punt gun when it fired.

The gun was operated by stuffing a long shell into the breach and positioning it with small wooden piece, actually a paint stir stick, as a sliding breach lock. The crew chief jammed a bloat trocar through the ignition hole to punch a hole through the side of the shell into the black powder charge. Then he positioned a .45 ACP shell primed with a magnum rifle primer over the ignition nipple. He tripped the hammer with a hood latch and cable Janelle had salvaged from an old pickup truck.

The twenty-ounce charge of black powder propelled the load of chopped rebar at a sedate 1100 feet per second. The projectiles lost even more velocity as they bounced off the pavement. The three-quarter inch long by three-eights diameter pieces weighed about 180 grains and impacted hostiles at about 800 feet per second.

The few practice shots the fire team had taken quickly showed them that the pattern was far too tight to effectively cover the road from edge-of-pavement-to-edge-of-pavement at a hundred yards. The solution was to bounce the pattern off the pavement in front of the hostiles.

The downside from Donnie and Quinn's standpoint is that bouncing the pattern off the pavement imparted a top-spin to each of the 320 projectiles and that caused them to curve it down into their position another hundred yards downrange. Donnie and Quinn had sandbagged revetments prepared for when the punt gun crew fired.

The punt gun crew fired two rounds and the +600 projectiles chopped the large group of hostiles to pieces.

Most of the projectiles caused leg, thigh and lower abdomen wounds. Given the medical situation the wounded would die in three-to-ten days. The two pinning forces did not relish the job of finishing off the wounded hostiles. To minimize actually having to look at the hostiles, they performed the task from their positions seventy yards back.

Better five minutes of pain before losing consciousness than to be in agony for ten days.

Chernovsky Catches the Gay

The other factor that was twisting Quinn's squad around the axle was the fact that many of the fighters decided that Chernovsky was gay.

Young, rural men are extremely puritanical about some-things. Being intimate with an unmarried, young woman? Most wouldn't bat an eyelash.

But gay sex? Totally repulsive. Reactions ranged from shud-ders to vomiting.

The evidence was in front of them. Chernovsky and his in-separable aide, Buddy, moved their tent seventy yards away from the main group. What other reason could there be?

Chernovsky's force of personality was such that nobody wanted to ask. They still obeyed direct orders. He was a force of nature and what he told them to do made sense.

But he had caught the gay.

Those kinds of swamp rumors happen when you stick a bunch of active people close together and then tell them to do nothing. Unlike the training through the winter when the young men were running ten miles a day through snow, actual guard duty was looking through spotting scopes and waiting and waiting and waiting.

The troops were never in the observation post alone. It was always a primary and a secondary with the two switching places on the hour. They had nothing else to do...except speculate and talk.

Then there was the fact that Chernovsky became extremely standoffish. He never came closer than ten feet from the people he was talking to...except for when he was talking with Buddy. If you tried to get closer, he looked extremely uncomfortable and edged away.

Chernovsky and Buddy waited until after everybody else had taken food from the kettle before they dished out food for themselves.

The only five people who were not read-into the debate were Chernovsky, Buddy, Quinn, Walt Shaw and John Gault. To their credit, neither Walt or John had any tolerance for gossip. They saw it as "...bearing false witness..." so nobody bothered to tell John or Walt about the issue.

Quinn was never clued in. Everybody knew that Buddy was Quinn's cousin and that Quinn was very protective of him.

Unfortunately, that turned the small-minded in the direction of thinking that maybe Quinn and Buddy's relationship was something more than just being cousins.

The rest of the guys were deeply conflicted.

There was no doubt that Chernovsky was still the boss. Nobody disputed that he was as masculine as a bag full of twenty-two-ounce framing hammers. Nope. Nobody dared ask.

Rather, they started avoiding him and told him less. They saw it as turn-around being fair play. If he avoided them, pitching his tent outside the compound and being very standoffish when talking to them, they would be gentlemen and return the favor.

Communication suffered.

Chernovsky noticed and attributed it to the stress of continuous operations. Everybody was on-duty 24/7. What troubled him as that the pace of operations had lulls and surges and the lack of communication and eye-contact remained constant.

The situation could have caused a catastrophe.

What floated it up to the surface was that Squad One and Three were making several runs to Ambush Site Three every day. It was pounding them to a pulp.

After a spate of rainy weather, the sun came out and temperatures rose even as the water isolating Lansing dropped.

The floodgates for both refugees and hostiles opened and Chernovsky's guys became very, very busy.

The fact that they no longer had to dispose of the bodies made the pace of operations doable, barely.

The gangs came through so close together that the first ambush site had to "burp" some groups through for the other fire-teams to take on. The entire business model was to ambush hostiles. It would not do to have a group under fire with another group immediately behind them to reinforce them and suss out where the defenders were firing from.

The pace of operation for the back-up teams was torrid. Unlike Squad Two who could remain in place waiting for the next set of targets, fighters from Squad One and Three were expected to flow back to their primary site afterward as expeditiously as possible. Often times they had not even made it back to camp before they had to turn around and run back to Ambush Site Three.

Events came to a head when Chernovsky walked into Squad One's camp and found several of his fighters soaking their legs in a pond. That is, a pond filled with 40-degree water.

"What the hell are you guys doing? You look like shit," Chernovsky said.

One of the fighters lost his cool and may have called Chernovsky a dumb-ass. Chernovsky may have lost his temper and forgotten he was supposed to stay at least ten feet away from his guys and may have pitched the fighter into deep water.

It took a bit for things to settle down.

Then Chernovsky asked, "If the run is beating the crap out of you why didn't you suggest we change? If it makes sense to temporarily pull a fire-team from a Squad and park them at Ambush Site Three, then your team-leaders should have made the pitch to me and the other team-leaders."

That caused a bunch of them to look down and kicking at dirt clods. Finally, one of the braver guys said, "We thought you were too busy doing other things to pay attention to our problems."

Chernovsky shook his head in frustration and disbelief. "What else would I be doing? Killing zombies is my only reason for being here."

Then one of the team-leaders decided to earn his pay. "I ain't saying I believe this. I am just saying that I might have heard some guys talking about this," he said.

"There are some people who think you and Buddy are buddies, you know, doing the wild-thang." The team-leader gulped. "I don't believe it but that is what I heard.

"That, and whenever we walk up to you to talk about something you walk away," he said. "That kind of made us think you had other things on your mind."

Up until then Chernovsky had been very careful to not to talk about his and Buddy's exposure to Ebola. That is when he decided to come clean.

"Yeah, you are right. I did move away when you guys got close. And I did move my tent so Buddy and I are away from the rest of Squad 2. But there is a reason that I wasn't telling you. I see now that was a mistake," Chernovsky said.

"Buddy and I were exposed to Ebola the first night we used the honey-pot houses. Rick Salazar was going to yank both me and Buddy out and throw us into quarantine. I BEGGED him to leave me in place and I promised both Buddy and I were never in a position where we could infect any of you," Chernovsky said

"I made a mistake...a really big mistake. I thought that because I enforced the rules that I OWNED the rules. But I don't own them. Salazar and Tomanica don't own them. The rules are Mother Nature's rules or God's rules. They are not mine to enforce or not-enforce," Chernovsky said.

"Salazar agreed to let me stay but only if all of us are under quarantine. Buddy and I are in a separate quarantine from the rest of you and each squad is separated from the others and from the civilians of Pray Church and Kates Store for forty days," Chernovsky said.

That certainly changed the complexion of things. Suddenly they could see why Chernovsky arranged the intricate dance to ensure that fighters from Squad One and Squad Three never intermingled at Ambush Site Three.

Given the distance between the camps and the ambush site, Squads One and Three agreed that they would alternate weeks of supporting the site. That would fulfill the compartmentalization requirement.

They would leave one fire-team on-site for the week and if they got slammed at their primary sites, Squad Two would flow a fire team over but not intermingle. If things heated up at Squad Two then the other odd-Squad would flow a team over to support Squad Two.

In a rare moment of introspection Chernovsky realized that he had made a rookie coaching mistake. New coaches are prone to stacking their team with players who were exactly like them.

A new basketball coach who was a guard in college will field five guards because he knows guards are the most important player. New soccer coaches will stack the pitch with six midfielders if that was the position they played, and so on... Chernovsky had been a linebacker. The linebacker position is a flex position. A team needs a few flex players but can disintegrate into chaos when every player is a "linebacker".

In Chernovsky's mind the squads had evolved. They could now defend against the run, the pass and the sweep and not destroy themselves while doing it.

CHAPTER TEN

The Gatekeeper

Sheila Gault stood behind the barricade across Canal Road, the main paved road connecting Pray Church to Dimondale and Lansing. Behind her and to the side were a couple of men. One was her husband. Both men held short barreled, pump shotguns. The guns were not for show. They were loaded with slugs.

They stood wide, one to either side of her so if they needed to shoot, one of them would have a shot where she was not in the line of fire.

The spokesperson for the refugee family in front of her was far too glib for her liking. The man was smarmy and the woman seemed spaced out.

“You cannot enter Pray Church unless you can find a sponsor family, either somebody who lives in Pray Church, Kates Store or Eaton Rapids. Otherwise you will have to go around,” Sheila repeated. "Also, you cannot enter if any of your party have a fever."

"Close your eyes,” Sheila commanded as she took temperature readings with an IR thermometer from three feet away.

After many shifty and evasive answers the man said, “OK, I know Bob Smith. He said we could stay at his place.”

“That is not good enough. They have to be willing to sponsor your quarantine. They have to be willing to put you up in a separate building and feed you for forty days," Sheila said. There was no "bend" in Sheila. She had seen pictures of people who died from Ebola. She had seen pictures of their families a month later.

"Yeah, like I said, Bob Smith is willing to sponsor us," the man said with assurance.

"Give me a minute," Sheila said.

She keyed the mic and spoke into it, then turned down the voice so the refugee family could not hear the responses.

Sheila asked the person on the other end of the radio where Bob Smith lived. She had to put her ear to the portable CB to hear the response.

"There are two Bob Smiths who live around here. Do you know the Bob Smith on Royston Road or the Bob Smith on Long Highway?" Sheila asked.

"The Bob Smith that lives on Long Highway," the man said.

"Are you absolutely sure?" Sheila asked.

"Of course I am sure," the man said, puffing up with umbrage.

"I ask because there is nobody named 'Bob Smith' living on Long Highway," Sheila said.

"This is when you turn around and walk away," Sheila said.

With that the men spread out more and there was a subtle change in their posture.

The man looked at the two guards. "You wouldn't dare."

Sheila said, "You might want to look behind you. There are a couple of corpses about fifteen yards behind you in the weeds. If we have to kill you and your family, we just move the barricade another ten yards down the road."

"Your call," Sheila said. "Each shotgun has five shells in it.

There are only four of you. Not good odds."

Sheila was a pillar in the local Church of the United Brethren. She was also almost an unbeatable poker player. In this case she held the cards and was not bluffing. The bullshit artist knew he was beaten. He had played against some of the best poker players in his time. He knew.

The man used language that, had her children used it, she would have washed their mouths out with soap.

"And where would you have us go, bitch?" The man spat.

"Not my call," Sheila said. "But there is more open space west of here than east. North will take you back into the city. South is not an option."

The man looked longingly at Rossman Highway. "You will let us travel on Rossman."

"Nope," Sheila said. "Rossman is in Pray Church. You will have to backtrack a mile north before you turn west."

"My children are hungry," the woman spoke up for the first time.

"I can give you water. We don't have food to spare. Life is hard, here," Sheila said. She put four bottles of water on the pavement and backed up.

The man kicked them. "Fuck you," he said and he flipped her the bird.

Sheila's husband started to shoulder his Remington 870. Sheila stopped him with a slight movement of her hand. She had taken care to back up far enough that she was out of spitting range.

"You have two minutes to get a hundred yards up the road. Otherwise we start shooting," Sheila said. "If we ever see you again, we will shoot you on sight. This is your first, last and only warning."

"The clock starts.... NOW," Sheila said.

It took them little more than a minute to get a hundred yards up the road, a distance that Sheila's husband had marked by tying a red rag to a tree branch.

As the first group was leaving Sheila got a call from Quinn Spackle that another group of refugees was inbound with an ETA of twenty minutes.

Sheila and the two men decided to wait. They chafed at being away from their homes and gardens but the ground was still too wet and too cold to work and plant.

The next group was a group of six. The family looked middle-Eastern.

"You cannot enter Pray Church unless you can find a sponsor family, either somebody who lives in Pray Church, Kates Store or Eaton Rapids. Otherwise you will have to go around," Sheila said. She had had a lot of practice.

"My name is Prakash Shah. I am Satish Shah's brother," the man said. "He invited us."

One of the children started to act up. The man turned and made a small motion with his hand and the child quieted.

Sheila had heard of Satish Shah but had never met him.

"They have to be willing to sponsor your quarantine. They have to be willing to put you up in a separate building and feed you for forty days," Sheila said.

"My brother has a garage he will put us in," Mr. Shah said. "I understand the cell towers are not working and it will take a while to confirm that. Do you mind if we rest over in that yard?" Mr. Shah asked as he pointed to an overgrown yard to the side of the barricade.

Sheila offered water bottles which the family gratefully accepted.

It took about twenty minutes for somebody on the other end of the CB radio to chase down Satish, who Sheila finally figured out was a neighbor she knew as “Steve”, and confirm that he had a brother named Prakash, four nephews/nieces and that he committed to supporting them through the quarantine.

Sheila handed him a laminated copy of the decontamination protocol. "Can you read?" she asked.

The man glared at her.

"I have to ask,” Sheila said, undeterred. "You have to take off your shoes, socks and any clothing that may have touched the ground and become contaminated. That includes your trousers."

Sheila was thinking about reports of numbers of KIA hostiles Chernovsky reported each day. She visualized the roads wet with blood and gore. There was no reason to track that gore into her nice, clean community.

She had already looked at their footwear and they looked clean. If there had been any visible 'ickyness' on them she would have demanded that they leave them on the hot side of the barricade and made them wear flip-flops on the clean side.

"We decontaminate them in an ozone chamber,” Sheila said.

"Then each one of you have to stand in bucket of bleach-and-water for five minutes,” Sheila said, pointing to a kiddie wading pool with water in it. "You will use the wash-cloths to wet your legs up to above your knees and you will continue to do so until the timer goes off. Then you will do the same for your children."

"It takes fifteen minutes to decontaminate your clothing so there is no reason to try to hurry through the leg washing," Sheila said.

"Is that clear?" Sheila asked.

After they had completed the rough decontamination Sheila gave him a map to Satish's home on the west side of Kates Store.

He nodded wearily. He knew where Satish lived but things looked different when walking and, obviously, they did not have GPS.

"I need to remind you. No touching other people. No interactions except for with your brother, who you may not touch. That goes for your children and wife, too," Sheila said.

"You will be in quarantine for forty days, not a minute less," Sheila said. She looked at her watch and said, "If all goes well your quarantine ends at 1:30 PM on May 3." She wrote that down on a form and handed it to him. Sheila kept a copy.

"Inshallah," Prakash said as his family trudged away.

Rounding Third Base

Mark and Rosie's travels were slowed by weather and flooded bridges. Even when they could travel Rosie's footwear limited them to ten-to-fifteen miles a day.

Mark followed his intuition and his compass. He stayed off paved roads correctly assuming that is where the most conflict would be. He did not want to be on the wrong side of a gun when the person carrying it had an itchy trigger finger.

As they headed north and were confronted with a fork in the road, Mark always chose the left fork. He knew they were too far east to hit Eaton Rapids.

Mark and Rosie took pains to be as invisible as possible.

They traveled in the earliest morning hours and left the road when they heard people approaching. You can't shoot a ghost.

They had an unusual encounter with a native guarding a bridge over the north branch of the St Joseph River. He asked for their names and where they were headed.

Mark replied "My name is Mark Salazar and I am heading to Eaton Rapids. I have family there."

The guard scratched his head and said, "Seems like I have heard of Eaton Rapids. Isn't that near Kates Store?"

Mark ruefully acknowledged that he had never heard of a community called Kates Store.

Another encounter in Amboy Township was similar. That encounter occurred just south of the bridge across the south branch of the Kalamazoo River. The situation was almost surreal.

On a hunch Mark followed signage a mile west to an Amish store. It was still in business. The proprietor would not let him in the building but negotiated prices from the front porch. Mark had some old silver coins he had found in Grumpy's attic. He had given them to Rosie and she handed them right back.

She could not be bothered to carry coins. She knew that wasn't 'real' money.

The proprietor was more than happy to sell corn nuts (deep fat fried kernels of corn), peanuts and other food for real silver.

Heading back to 29 Mile Road Mark ran into another person guarding a bridge. The guard knew exactly where Eaton Rapids was and knew somebody who had radio communication with somebody in that town.

Mark decided this was a good time to take a break.

Things got a little bit tense when Paul Seraph said that the Mark Salazar from Eaton Rapids was dead and his one daughter was accounted for. It took the better part of an hour to play twenty questions to assure Seraph that he was the real Mark Salazar and that the young woman Mark was with was his adopted daughter.

With Ebola, Cholera, Typhus and fraternal violence running rampant, there had been a great deal of familial re-arrangements. Even Bubonic Plague had made a roaring a comeback as Yersinia pestis had crept out of the desert and infected the rats of El Paso, Albuquerque, Sante Fe, Flagstaff and Pueblo. From there, the diaspora of Ebola panicked people carried it to every major city in the United States, even Lansing, Michigan.

Seraph apologized for not being able to send transportation. His people were stretched too thin. Paul said he would inform Kate and Rick that he was alive and well and four days hard travel from home, weather permitting. Seraph also said he would do what he could to have "care packages" of food available at 10-mile intervals. It would not be much...some oatmeal or hardtack or whatever could be spared by the locals.

Mark had never cared much for Paul Seraph. Paul had only been in Eaton Rapids for a few years before Mark joined the Coast Guard. Mark had a bit of a chip on his shoulder. Paul was much, much older and from "the big city." Mark was sure that Paul looked down on all the country mice.

Having been away for a decade, Mark never had a reason to reassess his biases.

Mark was almost undone by Paul's efficient kindness. The worst of the fighting was over. Mark was almost home.

The Population Increases

Sheila Gault looked up at the man and his extended family. If he was a grandfather, he was an exceptionally young one. He only looked to be in his mid-forties, although his driver's license confirmed he was fifty-five.

"Let me repeat myself, you cannot come into this area unless you have been invited by a family who lives here and they agree to sponsor your quarantine for forty days," Sheila said.

She was getting frustrated. The man was polite and courteous and not taking "No" for an answer.

"I have property here. We won't be a burden," John Wilder repeated. "I am sure if you check you will let us in."

There were things about the party that set off alarms in Sheila's head. They were too well dressed and too fat. They looked healthy. They were pushing their goods in wheeled carts. How did they not get mugged by the zombies?

Sheila's husband discretely nudged her. "Let's you and me talk. Billy can keep an eye on them."

They stepped away from the barricade.

Sheila's husband said, "The piece of property just up the road from us...the eighty acres on the corner...is owned by a man named Doc Wilder. I wonder if it is his. Doc Wilder owns several other parcels around here. Big ones. Guess he needed the tax break."

"Do any of Doc Wilder's properties have houses? Even if it is him, he can't live in a field. Somebody has to feed him. And how are we going to figure out if it is him?" Sheila responded.

"One thing at a time, honey. That is why God gives us time, so we can sort through things," her husband said.

"Do what you are good at. Just talk to him," he finished.

Doc Wilder was a semi-mythical figure in the neighborhood. They knew his family favored Ford pickup trucks because that is what showed up during hunting season. They knew he and his boys favored deer stands that were a full 12' off the ground and they knew that he bid more than the prevailing rate to purchase property that was contiguous to other property he owned.

They also knew that he favored large, well-drained fields that had a history of growing good crops of corn. Unlike some land-buyers, he continued to rent out the properties to the last farmer who had worked the land and he did not squeeze them for rent, preferring to have a business that ran on autopilot rather than one where his renters went out of business and he would be left scrambling to find somebody to rent the property the next year.

Learning that the refugees might not be grifters did wonders to improve Sheila's disposition. She had dealt with too many people who had no business coming into Pray Church or Kates Store. Some of them had violently stormed the barricade and it had been necessary to kill them.

Sheila carried a handgun in a small-of-back holster. She had used it and did not relish that she would likely have to do so again.

Sheila favored the group with a small smile. "You understand we have to be careful about who comes into our community."

The man obviously had people skills. He quickly agreed. "That is why we decided to come here. We had other options."

"How would you know that?" Sheila asked.

"Peppermint Patty is one of our must-listen-to shows," the woman volunteered. "Both John and I were news junkies. We were bunkered up and bored to tears. Peppermint Patty kept us sane."

The man nodded in agreement. "Reading between the lines, you still have the rule-of-law. Heck," John said, pointing at the barricade, "The fact that you control your borders is proof of that. Another thing that was attractive is that you have a curfew."

"Another thing we picked up from Peppermint Candy's broadcasts is that you still have working infrastructure and division-of-labor," John said.

"There are still a few things I need to do before I can let you in," Sheila said. "I need to contact Pastor James and Rick Salazar and tell them about the circumstances. I need their blessing before I can let you in.

"You also need to verify who you are. Can the rest of you put some ID on the table and specifically identify the property you own?" Sheila said.

The other five adults laid drivers licenses on the plywood top of the barricade and stepped back. John also put several envelopes on the table and shuffled through them until one that said "Eaton County" rested on top.

"What are those?" Sheila asked, pointing at the envelopes.

"Tax bills," John said. "Property taxes."

"Can you open them and lay the contents on the table? You can use some rocks to hold them down against the breeze," Sheila said.

Sheila would have whistled had she been a less disciplined woman. Looking at the tax bills, it was clear that the Wilder family was one of the top three land owners in the area...that is, if they were the Wilder family.

"Just out of curiosity, how many parcels do you own in Eaton

County?" Sheila asked.

The woman piped up. "About twenty, a bit more than two-and-a-half square miles in Eaton County."

"Which one of these will you be staying in?" Sheila asked.

"The hunting camp on Canfield Road," John said without hesitation. "It has a pantry and should have plenty of food to hold us for a couple of months to get us through quarantine."

Sheila cocked an eyebrow. "Would you also be known as 'Doc Wilder'?"

The woman spoke up. "That would be me. 'Doc' as in Ph.D. My name is Samantha and friends call me Sam or Doc."

"John was an insurance executive and I did research on drugs for chemo-therapy," Mrs 'Doc' Wilder clarified. "The thing about insurance executives, they are risk adverse."

Sheila offered them bottles of water, which they graciously accepted and then placed some calls to Pastor James and Rick Salazar. She strongly recommended that the Wilder family be allowed in despite the lack of a sponsoring family. She saw that as a formality. If the Wilder family could be believed, they did not require one.

Their arrival was going to cause some issues. Several families had started to infringe on their land for gardens and other chunks had been involved in Salazar's scheme to reforest unclaimed land for firewood.

Issues are different than problems. Sheila had the sense that the Wilder family would be easy to work with.

Two Pounds of Bacon

Perhaps the shit-storm would not have happened if Squad One had not been given a gift of two pounds of bacon.

Or perhaps it would not have happened if the wind had not

been the gentlest of zephyrs from the south.

Trying to make sense of the attack, Chernovsky concluded that the hostile force was one of the less skilled who had survived by adopting the tactic of staying off the roads and staying out of the way of the more aggressive and more competent gangs.

That was Squad One's undoing.

The notable thing about Squad One is that they had been tasked with observing a piss-ant gravel road that meandered in a southerly direction in the most indirect and leisurely of ways. They also observed Vermontville Highway, a paved road that ran east-west and connected with the freeway some five miles to the west of the observation post.

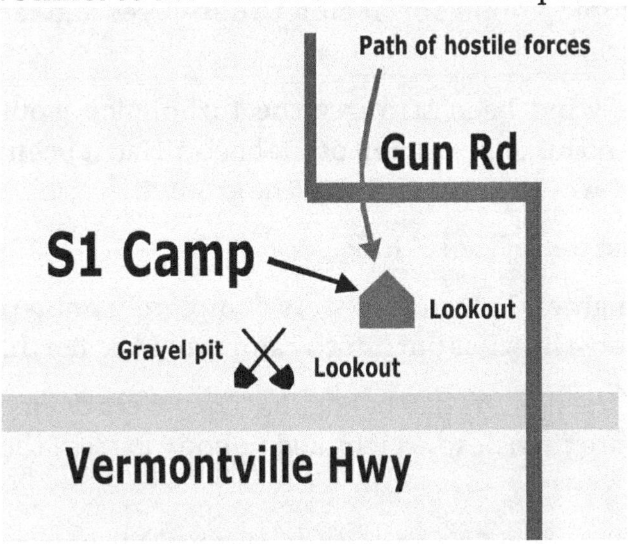

"Lookouts" depict observation posts.

Neither road saw much traffic and perhaps that served to lull the fire-teams in Squad One into a complacency that proved fatal.

Six fighters of the ten squad members were in camp shortly after breakfast had been eaten. Two fighters were in the Vermontville Highway observation post that was a quarter mile southwest of the camp and nestled into the gravel pit that overlooked the road. Two more fighters were in the other observation post that was a quarter mile to the east of the camp.

Unlike the camps of Squad Two and Squad Three, Squad One's camp was west of the north-south road so the camp was equidistant from, and could support both observation posts with equal ease.

Chernovsky concluded that the group of hostiles had been picking their way overland when they smelled the frying bacon. Nothing improves a person's sense of smell more than deep hunger and nothing throws a scent farther than frying bacon as each exploding sputter launches hundreds of microscopic globules of fat aloft to be buoyed and carried by the breeze.

Had the wind been stronger the turbulence would have baffled and mixed the smell of the bacon. Had it been weaker the scent would have settled to the ground.

It was just one of those things.

The six fighters in the camp were completely unprepared to have twelve hostiles burst into camp from the north.

None of the fighters had handguns. They were deemed to be little more than dead weight and nobody carried them anymore.

Terry Lake, John Gault's team-leader had his hands deep in hot, sudsy wash water.

John Gault was closest to the tents. His instincts were good. He secured his personal weapon, inserted a magazine, cycled the bolt and shouldered his weapon.

But then he froze. Almost half of the hostiles were young women.

Terry threw the tub of hot water into the face of the first hostile. The steam prevented him from seeing one of the women rushing at him with a knife.

Gault saw it from a different angle. He could see the woman carrying the butcher knife. He saw it happen but could not process the presence of the knife + woman quickly enough to do Terry any good. The woman jammed the knife into Terry's gut, angling upward until it had been run in all the way to the hilt.

The other four fighters were throwing off the lighter hostiles and trying to work their way to their weapons.

Finally, the screaming of one of them drilled into Gault's consciousness, "Shoot them. Shoot them."

Belatedly, something clicked in Gault's brain and he began servicing targets. The targets were so close that their heads were fuzzy in his scope. No matter, at this range he could not miss.

The last one he shot had dreadlocks. The hostile was twenty yards out and fleeing. Gault was numb. He did not care if it was a man or a woman. He shot "dreadlocks" in the back of his head.

***

Gault never figured out who called Chernovsky.

In addition to Terry, the other Team-Lead was a casualty. Although not fatal, the deep slice from one of the attacker's knives had severed several of the tendons in the TL's right forearm. He would not be able to function as a fighter.

Squad One did not have a functioning Team-Lead

After listening to the stories of the surviving fighters and getting the OK from Salazar and Tomanica, Chernovsky moved Donnie from Team-Leader of Squad Two to be the sole Team-leader of Squad One and left Quinn as the sole Team-Leader of Squad Two. Chernovsky needed Salazar's buy-in because Squad Two still had eight days left on their forty-day quarantine.

Chernovsky cycled Gault, the guy who froze from Squad One to Squad Two.

Chernovsky also had Squad One move their camp from west of the N-S road to east of the road so prevailing winds would be less likely to carry smells and sounds to the road. He left the observation posts where they were. "Ease of servicing" suddenly became a very, very low priority.

“I shouldn’t be a fighter anymore,” Gault said as a shell-shocked Gault and Chernovsky walked back to Squad Two's camp.

Chernovsky’s response was short and direct. “Bullshit.”

“I failed,” Gault said. “You should send me home.”

Counseling was not Chernovsky’s strong suit. Never-the-less, that is what he had to do.

“I already lost two fighters. I cannot afford to lose another,” Chernovsky said.

“I screwed up,” Gault said.

“Did I ever tell you about Matty Norton?” Chernovsky said as they walked east toward Squad Two.

“Who was Matty Norton?” Gault asked, in spite of himself.

“Matty was a football player in my home town,” Chernovsky said. “The thing is that he was way better than I was. I went to college on a football scholarship and he never went to college. Do you know why?”

“No,” Gault said. Of course, he did not know why.

"Because every time he would miss a tackle or not sack the quarterback, he would put on this big show about how mad he was," Chernovsky said.

"It was as if he expected the crowd to applaud his high standards rather than his football ability," Chernovsky said. "I would miss tackles, too. But I put the past behind me. I learned from my mistakes...but I did not let it poison me. Matty couldn't do that."

"Who is going to trust me after the story gets out?" Gault asked, voice heavy with misery.

"Stop being Matty. Lose the cry-baby voice," Chernovsky commanded.

"I trust you. I bunk with Squad Two. If I thought you were a loser, I would send you home," Chernovsky said. "Lose the pity. Stuff it in a box. Do whatever you have to do but keep putting one foot in front of the other."

Gault never did find out that Chernovsky had never played football with, or against a player named Matty Norton. But that did not matter. Matty was a composite of all the cry-babies Chernovsky ever met.

Loose Ends

Mark's homecoming was a tremendous surprise.

Paul Seraph had handed off the task of resupplying Mark to a minion who had connections in Albion and points south. Then Paul was distracted by a pressing problem and spaced the fact that he had promised to tell Kate and Rick that Mark was alive. That is one of the hazards of being a micro-manager.

Paul rode his bike out to Eaton Rapid's southern frontier after the guards radioed that a man-and-daughter named

Mark and Rosie requested safe passage. Paul recognized Mark as soon as he laid eyes on him.

Then he apologized profusely for dropping the ball. He said he would make it right.

He called Di Carney on the CB and requested priority service. He needed her to hook up her fastest horses to her lightest buggy. He had two people who needed to be carted back to Kates Store.

Then he whistled up Rick and Kate and told them that Mark was alive and to expect him on their doorstep in two hours.

It took closer to three but that is a damned good speed for a twenty-four-mile round trip.

Unfortunately, Mark and Rosie had to go into quarantine but there was plenty of room in the Duckworth mansion.

The celebration was muted. Every family was waiting for somebody like Mark to show up. Most of them were disappointed.

***

Chernovsky's forces requested that their sub-sonic (i.e. quiet ammo) be enhanced the way their high-speed hollow points were. Quinn was more than happy to help. Bill and Judy spent another couple of days collecting material and dipping the tips in melted wax/lard and powder.

The results were staggering. Zombies started dropping as if hit with .357 magnums. They worked almost too well. Many of the bodies barely crawled off the pavement.

Confident shooters make good shooters. The most vigorous hostiles were still shot in the heart-lung area but the ones that seemed less vigorous were tagged with liver-kidney shots.

What Chernovsky's fighters did not know was that they

were seeing the results of Ebola, Bubonic Plague and extreme dehydration brought on by prolonged diarrhea.

The toxin in the tropical seeds impaired protein synthesis and while lethal in very, very small doses it took five-to-ten days to kill. The time-frame for the strain of *Clostridium perfringens* that came from the swine filth was slightly shorter with death usually occurring three-to-six days after being shot.

The huge increase in knock-down power was not due to magic ammo. It was due to the fact that the hostiles were infected with a rogue's gallery of infectious diseases and were barely able to remain vertical before they were shot...the very reason the hostiles were being repelled. It did not take much trauma to push them into the abyss.

***

The disaster that Squad One experienced drove a host of changes.

Chernovsky informed Salazar that all Team-Leads needed handguns and appropriate holsters. Salazar authorized the purchase of handguns and holsters from the Dimondale population. They were awash in Glocks and Smith & Wessons and Hi-Points etc. taken from dead zombies. A Glock 19 with two magazines could be had for a hundred pounds of corn, the consequence of the implacable laws of supply-and-demand.

Salazar reiterated that the goods had to be in a pot of boiling water when Chernovsky purchased them.

Tomanica's advice was to purchase 9mm. Everybody knew that 9mm had less stopping power than a 40 or a 45 but the ammo was everywhere and Tomanica's advice was to shoot the magazine dry and to carry multiple magazines. Warfare is different than peace-time

Tomanica had several friends who had been active in IDPA. They hand loaded 9mm ammo and, in the spirit of Defensive Pistol shooting, they eschewed cheap, full metal jacket ammo and shot the same type of hollow points they carried for defense. Hearing of the circumstances they both volunteered a thousand rounds. That put a dent in their supplies but it was for a good cause.

Tomanica also advised Chernovsky to let any fighter who was willing to carry the extra weight to carry a handgun. Murphy's law dictated that the next time you needed somebody with a handgun the designated carrier would be in the shitter.

Tomanica also advised that the troops be drilled on handling and dry-firing but not accuracy. His reasoning was that any target far enough away to require careful aim was far enough away that the troops could get a rifle.

Other changes included putting up alarms. The simplest alarms were installed before nightfall. Those alarms were fish line strung through the trees at knee height and tied to cans filled with rocks.

Within a week, each camp had a dog. The dogs were trained to be on the alert for anybody entering camp. Barking was optional. The training was easy. Each person who came into camp asked, "Did he go on alert?" If the answer was "Yes" the dog got at least one kibble. Since that was the dog's only source of nutrition, the dog became highly motivated. It is true what they say, hunger doubles a dog's intelligence.

Dmitri worked on electronic alarms but did not get them perfected in time. Even the cheapest smartphones have microphones and accelerometers embedded within them. There was no physical reason they could not be attached to a wooden stake that had been driven into the ground and trigger an alarm via WIFI.

Chernovsky also outlawed fried food. It just smelled too good and hungry people can smell the tiny fat particles from half a mile away if the wind was right.

The troops grumbled even more when he required “cold camp” on the rare days when the wind blew toward the road. At least he still allowed Cookie Girl to visit.

***

Chernovsky was walking past Quinn when something caught his eye. "What the hell is that?" he asked.

Quinn followed Chernovsky's pointing finger to the web gear on his chest. He mentally looked in the mirror and found nothing amiss. "With all due respect, what are you pointing at?"

"Your magazines," Chernovsky said.

Quinn was carrying three, duplexed, 30 round AR magazines for a load-out of 180 rounds. The magazines were taped together, with the second one upside down.

Quinn pulled one out. "What’s wrong with it?"

"It’s not 'factory'," Chernovsky said.

"Yes it is," Quinn untaped them and snapped them apart. Then he snapped them back together. "They are designed to do this."

"Lose it anyway," Chernovsky growled.

"Why?" Quinn asked.

Chernovsky was tempted to say "Because I told you to," but checked his tongue. He was not entirely clear why he had a visceral, negative reaction to the magazines.

"I'll get back to you on that. But for now, I want you to carry your magazines as singles," Chernovsky said.

Quinn understood this to be the collective "you" and so he directed his fighters to breakdown their duplexed magazines into singles. There was much grumbling.

That night, at the campfire talk Chernovsky talked about his directive.

"Why do you duplex the magazines?" Chernovsky asked.

"Because it is faster to reload," one of the fighters responded.

"What happens when you are under stress?" Chernovsky asked.

This was a tough question to answer. There had not been many engagements where the fighters were effectively being fired at. The prepared positions were solid. The surprise was nearly complete. The marksmanship was good. It was a slaughterhouse for the hostiles.

Chernovsky did not get a response.

"I will tell you what happens. You go into tunnel vision. All you see is the target in front of you and all you do is pull the trigger. You have to work to remember to move," Chernovsky said. There had been many times he had not heard the whistle on the football field that signaled the end of play but stopped because his target stopped.

"What happens if you are in a hot fire-fight and you forget you already switched to the second magazine? I guarantee it will happen."

"You will switch to a dry magazine. And you will yank on the trigger. And you might not even notice that your rifle is not firing," Chernovsky said.

"Then you are fucked and so is your buddy next to you.

"Lose the duplexed magazines and practice dropping empty magazines and grabbing and loading full ones...with your eyes closed," Chernovsky ordered.

CHAPTER ELEVEN

Hard Times Make Hard Men

Wade Hawk eased down the gravel road through the humid darkness.

In a month the extensive flooding would bring forth a plague of mosquitoes. But for now, all he heard were spring peepers and barking dogs.

Wade was investigating a couple of barking dogs. It was telling that the dogs had barked sequentially and from different houses. Wade was pretty much on a first name basis with most of the dogs in the neighborhood.

Wade was one of the older men tasked with enforcing the curfew that everybody hoped would squelch the plague.

Yes, Ebola and the Black Death had penetrated Kates Store. Perhaps it was inevitable given the abundance of refugees percolating through the countryside and the number of ground squirrels and other rodents.

The horror of Ebola and the Black Death was that it was a virtual death sentence for the entire family when the first family member showed symptoms. The diseases did not care; man, woman, old, young, toddler, infants.

The protocol was to drop off prepared foods as the family fought the losing battle with either disease. Then, after the last member died...to burn the house.

The disease popped up seemingly without rhyme or reason.

***

The pestilence hit the east end of the neighborhood particularly hard. That was expected given the population density and the refugee traffic on the paved, north-south road. Curiously, the pestilence had only hit one home in the northwest corner of the neighborhood.

Wade had his own ideas about the spread of the disease. By his own calculations, nearly all of the families that had experienced the plagues either had teenagers or young men in their twenties.

Wade had been among the first to insist on a curfew and had been the very first to insist that the roads be policed and the curfew enforced.

That cause huge amounts of agony within the political elite of Kates Store. Enforcing rules meant that there needed to be consequences. The consensus was that miscreants who were caught breaking the curfew would first be warned and then be evicted from Kates Store if caught a second time.

Wade came to a stretch of road that had a ditch lined out along the east side. Unlike all of the other ditches, the spring frogs were not making any noise.

"Who goes there?" Wade called out.

Nobody answered.

Wade pulled out his four D cell flash light, turned it on and slowly and methodically swept the ditch. It would cream his night vision for the next half hour but he had a premonition that he had stumbled across what he had been looking for.

Wade searched with his ears as much as with his eyes. Perhaps more so. He slowly looked close then lifted the torch so he could see down at water level then lifted it even higher so he could look up and over the opposite ditch bank.

Then he shifted the beam half the beam's width and repeated. Every fifteen feet he silently crabbed sideways. In a month the brush would be all leafed out and even the thousand foot-candle Maglite would not be able to penetrate. But for now, the only green was the random honeysuckle and the ubiquitous garlic mustard. The native shrubbery had pessimistic genes.

He found his quarry thirty yards further down the ditch. The young man was attempting to hide by crouching behind a dense stand of naked elderberry bushes on the far side of the ditch.

"Andy! Is that you?" Wade called out.

"Turn the damned light off. I can't see a damned thing," the voice called out.

Wade did not turn the light off but he shifted it to his left hand and lowered the beam so the 1000 foot-candles were not directly in Andy's eyes.

"Come out here so we can talk like civilized men," Wade said.

"You come down her," Andy said. "I like it here a lot better."

Wade was not surprised. Andy always made things difficult.

"Whatchya doing out?" Wade said. "You know you are violating curfew."

"Cornbread gives me gas. I stepped out so I didn't stink up the house," Andy said.

"Bullshit," Wade said. "Nobody walks a half-mile from their house and hides in a ditch just to fart."

"Try again," Wade said.

"I was going to visit a friend," Andy said.

"Which one?" Wade asked. "I don't recall you having any friends in the neighborhood...Unless you were referring to your customers," Hawk finished.

"Whaddya mean, 'customers'?" Andy asked.

"Anybody with a brain knows you deal drugs," Wade said. "Not too many kids working part-time, minimum wage jobs can afford a brand new, four-wheel-drive truck."

"Dammit all, Wade," Andy said. "A business man has to make a living. My customers have needs."

Wade Hawk was old school. He didn't cotton to teenagers, even if they were nineteen, treating him as a peer and calling him by his first name.

"I ain't asking you, I am telling you," Wade said. "You can't be breaking curfew. You cannot be out after dark."

"OK, I won't let you catch me again," Andy said. Wade could hear the smarmy tones.

"You ain't listening," Wade said. "It is not a matter of 'catching'. It is a matter of you doing what you are supposed to be doing."

"Well, Wade old buddy, that ain't how I see it. I will do what I gotta do and it is your job to try and catch me," Andy said.

Wade lifted the flashlight slightly so it was directly in Andy's eyes.

The 158-grain hollow point entered Andy's sternum directly between his nipples and shattered his spine on the way out.

Andy's body started to slump into the ditchwater but the dense stand of elderberries arrested his slide.

Wade extinguished the flashlight and moved down the road a bit. Then he waited for the ringing in his ears to abate and for the bright, lavender spots in his eyes to fade.

"I guess I won't have too much trouble catching you now," Wade said to Andy as Andy's consciousness faded.

Wade slept late every morning because he stayed out late every night on curfew enforcement duty.

He was drinking his first cup of coffee when Connie, his wife, came into the breakfast nook. She was as excitable as Wade was phlegmatic. She was clearly busting with news.

"What's up?" Wade asked.

"Heather Miller went in to wake up Andy this morning and he was gone," Connie said.

"Shit happens," Wade said. "Especially to pieces of garbage like Andy Martin."

"I don't know why you are so hard on him. After all, he IS your nephew," Connie said.

"Hard times make hard men," Wade said.

Little Wedgie Stubert

Richard "Wedgie" Stubert had an IQ in the low 80s and fancied himself "a player". He was the poster child for every negative stereotype that urban dwellers have of "rednecks".

Some people assumed Wedgie's low IQ was due to the fact that his mother "liked to have fun" as one of her friends charitably phrased it. Even though his mother was sixteen when she became pregnant, she had no problems getting her hands on copious amounts of alcohol. Something about older boyfriends who liked young girls who "liked to have fun".

Others pointed out that Wedgie was a low birth-weight baby and his mother was barely seventeen when he was born and both of those are statistically related to lower intelligence.

Few observers had any energy for the Stubert family but those rare few decided it did not matter whether Wedgie was stupid because of genetics, pre-natal conditions or childhood environment. The entire Stubert family was stupid and the variables were knotted together and could not be separated.

Wedgie thought everybody else was an idiot because they all nodded when he told a big windy, that is, an outrageous fabrication.

Frankly, nobody cared about his miscreant behaviors and nobody saw an upside to pointing out that everybody knew when he was lying. On the rare occasions he told the truth, he stopped licking the corners of his mouth and stopped batted his eyelids every half second. When he was lying, he alternated licking the corners of his lips reminiscent of the Tin Man pumping the oil-can to unstick his lips and Wedgie batted his eyelids like a metronome. That, and when he was lying he stuck "I swear to God!" in about every third sentence.

Another habit Wedgie had was that he spit everywhere. He was sure it made him look manly and it was a way of showing his dominance and disdain for everybody around him. Marking his territory, if you will.

The first four years of Wedgie's academic career were unremarkable. He was lost in the herd.

By the beginning of fourth grade little Wedgie started to stand out. The social worker said he had Oppositional Defiant Disorder. His teachers said he was just being a Stubert. Wedgie did not complete assignments. His teachers passed him hoping the herd effect would pull him along. Besides, having him in the classroom was exhausting and the teachers the next grade up might be able to do something with him.

He graduated with a solid D- GPA. He was happy. He considered school to be a waste of life's energy and in his mind there was no benefit to getting a D when a D- was good enough. It must be noted in passing that he graduated with lower reading ability and math skills than when he left third grade.

The economy was hot when Wedgie graduated and he drifted from job-to-job, getting "released" for an enterprising range of bad behaviors. Sometimes he was caught rifling through a co-worker's purse. Sometimes it was taking fast-food home that he had not paid for. Sometimes it was for dealing a little bit of weed out the back door.

Once he was caught removing safety shields from mowing equipment. The boss told him to put them back on. Later that day the boss saw the mower had all the safety shielding removed. When challenged, Wedgie said it was like that when he picked it up in the morning.

Of course he was fired and, of course, the employer could not find the missing parts because Wedgie was smart enough to hide the evidence by throwing them into tall weeds. The employer lost the use of the mower for most of the season because the replacement parts were back-ordered. There are many, many Wedgie Stubert clones in every community and represented a profitable business segment for the mower's manufacturer.

Wedgie was not the least bit conflicted by authority. He expected to get screwed by them so he always made sure he got in his licks in preemptively.

Wedgie knew that everything authority figures wanted him to do was going to be to his disadvantage and he automatically did everything in his power to derail their efforts. It was a stupid-simple optimization strategy.

Nothing changed for Wedgie with Ebola.

The first time he was entrusted to use the chainsaw Wedgie deliberately bent the bar so the crew could go home early.

He lost steel wedges every day.

He broke sledge handles.

Within a week the only job he was trusted with was to hump firewood, and even then he had to stack it on his own, personal pile because the straw-boss could see Wedgie was malingering and not carrying his fair share.

Wedgie was booted from woodcutting the second week when the straw-boss caught him pitching chunks of wood from the main pile into his own personal pile.

Deprived of gainful employment, Wedgie sponged off his mother, who still “liked to have a good time” even though she looked fifty when she was only thirty-five. There were always guys who didn’t care what she looked like as long as she turned off the lights.

Initially the oldest profession did well, post-Ebola. Families were shattered. Lives were stressful. Men sought solace where they could find it and paid for it with whatever they could.

One of Ms Stubert’s customers paid her with a fake Rolex watch and left her with a whacking big dose of Ebola virus.

Ms Stubert shared the virus with her entire family, including Wedgie.

It was a point of pride for Wedgie that he violated the curfew. He and his buds would pillage vacant home looking for money, food and drugs. Some of his friends had girlfriends and they weren’t very discriminating after they passed out.

It was party-time every night of the week.

Like a comedy sketch of a bowling ball that knocked down every pin in the bowling alley, Wedgie's sloven habits, indiscriminate mating and exuberant and juicy expectorating not only infected all of his "buds" but resulted in the near extinction of their extended families.

For the most part the families that met their demise did not contribute much to the economy, either before or after Ebola. There were a few exceptions. One family had the misfortune of having their daughter going through a phase where she flirted with the bad-boys; her therapist called it the 'Leader of the Pack' stage of life. Unfortunately, the phase happened EXACTLY when Ebola hit Wedgie's posse like a torpedo.

But for the most part Wedgie's gift took out the grifters, the drunks, the slatterns, the lazy and stupid.

By the time Ebola burned out in Kates Store and Pray Church they had both lost another third of their population. The net effect was to raise the average IQ by five points and wiped out the sub-90 skirt of the bell curve.

The people who Ebola culled from the gene pool were the same people who sowed the seeds of chaos and discord due to their insatiable envy, inherent suspicions and their instinctive opposition to every rule.

John Wilder

John Wilder was not the typical middle manager in a large, American corporation.

His dad was a cop in a medium-sized town. John went to a second-tier state university and majored in history. Even then there were many academic advisers who gave the rotten advice "Follow your passions."

Graduating with student debt the equivalent of a new car, John found that his degree gave him exactly zero incremental hiring advantage over a new high-school graduate.

Determined to not make the same mistake twice, he did some research and chose a Master's program where jobs were both abundant and lucrative. His research suggested that the straightest line between where he was and where he wanted to be was to get a Master's degree in Business Administration. His belated research also revealed that graduates with an MBA from any state's flagship university commanded starting wages 50% higher than graduates from any of the me-too universities.

As the son of a city employee, he had almost no idea what "Business" meant. He knew "Finance" had something to do with accounting and he didn't want to sit behind a computer all day and do other people's taxes. He remembered his dad going nuts on April 14th every year and he wanted nothing to do with "Finance".

He opted for Marketing. He thought his flair for writing bullshit would make that a cake-walk.

And it was a cake-walk until the section of Statistics for Business Majors he was scheduled for was cancelled and the other sections had already filled up. He had a choice, take a different statistics class or spend another half year in school. He opted for Statistics for STEM Majors.

The class thoroughly kicked his ass. He would have failed except for the Chem major he sat next to. She was cute and quiet. Her name was Sam.

She dragged him kicking and screaming through that class. And then the next one. Sometime during John's academic Bataan Death March, a switch flipped in his head. He saw the power of statistics and he fell in love with Sam.

He graduated in the upper-middle of his class. He thought that his chances for a job were decent. He was surprised to find that his services were avidly sought by insurance companies. They were impressed that he took "real" statistics classes rather than the watered-down pap most MBAs took. Who knew?

His love of history informed him that Black Swan events are about a once-a-century events for the dominant culture. After a hundred years, all of the people who experienced the previous Black Swan were dead. Dominant cultures are a lightning rod for envy and chaos.

John had little success convincing his company to pad the rates for those Black Swan events. They would point to the paucity of wars and pandemics and famines and debauched currencies and say that the statistics did not work for sparse data. His argument that Black Swans could be aggregated and then there were enough data points was met with silence. He was informed, "Things are different now."

John and Sam found themselves swimming in money.

Sam's needs were simple. She did not crave cruises or spending time in all-inclusive resorts. Nor did she want a fancy BMW or a prestige house address. She bought a two-year-old Impala and drove it for five years before buying another. They had lived in the same blue-collar neighborhood for the last twenty-five years. She could have bought any or all of the prestige artifacts that define affluent people on her salary and bonuses. Her team had hit a home-run with a single drug a decade ago and had several Chemotherapy synergizing drugs that had come within one trial of being approved

She could have bought those things but felt no need.

John created his own insurance plan for the dreaded Black Swan event.

He rejected the billionaire plan of jetting to Fiji or Australia or Alaska. Moving is always a shock and why would people in Fiji want another mouth to feed, especially when that mouth was not family? And Australia or Alaska, he never understood the attraction of moving to an austere environment where the deer had to have legs that were six feet long to move through the snow or where every snake, bug and plant was toxic and could kill you.

Rather, he started buying farmland in Eaton and Ingham counties.

Ebola bankrupted his company. Life insurance is predicated on the idea that there will never be more than 1.4% of the population dying any given year.

The family bunkered up.

While holed up, John made an intensive study of England before, during and after the Black Death wiped out a third of the population. John chose England because the event had been extensively documented. History does not repeat itself but John was convinced that history rhymed.

John's take away was that labor would be in short supply, wages would go up and that the price of most commodities would deflate.

Another thing John gleaned before the internet went down was that livestock became the crop-of-choice after depopulating events. Growing grain and other food crops is labor intensive. A single man and a dog can manage a flock of six hundred sheep, about the number that a quarter of a square-mile of prime, mid-Western corn land could support. Without tractors or domesticated animals to pull implements, it would take eighty adults to farm that same amount of land.

Furthermore, it takes thirty years to double the number of "workers" in the population. Under ideal conditions the population doubles in twenty years but the majority of the increase is under ten years of age and not able to do heavy, ag work.

On the other hand, a flock of sheep can increase by 60%-to-70% every year. A flock of six ewes can grow to sixty in five years and 600 in ten, 6000 in fourteen and 6,000,000 in twenty-three years.

Unless John was willing to let his farmland revert to brush, the only real option was to become a shepherd.

The other thing pushing John in that direction was that fabric made from synthetic fibers was soon going to become nothing but a mythic memory. Cotton does not grow in Michigan which left hemp and wool as the only two options.

Fortunately, John had often worked from his home office. It was well stocked with toner cartridges for the laser printer and 24-pound, acid-free paper. John downloaded books on agriculture, animal breeding and sheep. Not trusting that his laptop would run forever, John printed them out and put them in three ring binders.

The first challenge for John was going to be to find seed-stock. Few commercial sheep farmers in Michigan raised "wool" sheep because the market had placed a large premium on "meat" breeds.

Agents and Managers

The quarantine was screwing with John's long-term plan. If he could not get things rolling he would lose a year.

John Wilder sent word via Gladys to Mr. Ed that he wished to have conversation with him.

Things were slow so Mr. Ed strolled over to the Wilder's hunting camp. Ed was not in a hurry. It was not like John would not be there. The Wilder family was in quarantine.

Ed stood a good twenty-five feet crosswind from the porch and tossed some pebbles at the window.

John and Sam came out. "Thanks for coming," John said.

"What's on your mind?" Ed asked. He was in a good mood. He was carrying a plastic grocery bag, the kind that used to be considered disposable. He had been picking greens on his way over to Wilder's and had even scored a few morel mushrooms.

"What does this community need most?" John asked.

"Everything," Ed said.

"What do we need most?" John asked. John had his own ideas but he was a Marketing man to the core. It never hurt to dip a toe into the water one more time before jumping in and most people were flattered if you asked for their opinion.

"Food," Ed said. "Machines. Gas and Diesel. Horses," Ed said. "We have all kinds of land but we don't have a good way to work it. We need all kinds of things but no way to buy them."

John and Sam knew where Ed was coming from. They held lots of land but did not have a way to turn it into wealth.

"I heard you say horses," Sam said. "What kind?"

"Draft horses," Ed said. "If you could only get one then get a stallion, a Belgium or a Percheron. If we had a stallion then we could breed the mares we have to it."

That got John to thinking about more traditional forms of agriculture and the Amish. "Seems like the Amish have a lot of pasture and a lot of animals," he observed. "Pasture doesn't take much equipment or fuel."

"Nope, they don't," Ed agreed. "We have dairy and beef cattle and hogs but are really hurting for sheep. If things don't get better...well, let's just say we can't grow cotton up here."

"Nobody has sheep?" Sam asked.

"Well, a few people have them as pets," Ed said "but they are dwarf breeds like Finn sheep and Icelandic sheep. They have wool but not very much of it."

"So where would we go to buy wool sheep?" Sam said.

Ed said. "There is a lady in Charlotte, Pat Treadwell, who raises sheep. She is a commercial farmer who raises sheep that put money in your pocket, not a hobby farmer raising pets. But what are you going to pay her with? It is not like dollars mean anything anymore."

"Ed, you raised some interesting points but we cannot get out of here for five more weeks. We need an agent and farm manager. Do you want the job?" John asked.

"No sir. I do not. I don't mind giving you my opinions but you are gonna get those whether you pay for them or not. I don't have the git-up-and-go to manage a farm," Ed said.

"Can you ask around and find somebody who you think would make a good farm manager and agent?" John asked. "Assuming we don't go Tango Uniform in the next month or so, we would provide room, board and a percentage of the harvest."

"What is the difference between a manager and an agent?" Ed asked.

"The farm manager manages the farm. The agent is authorized to buy and sell on our behalf," Sam said.

"Let me noodle around and see who I can find," Ed said.

"Given my druthers," John said "I want you to find three of them so we can check them out back-to-back."

Ed found three candidates and they were interviewed from the Wilder's deck in the following order.

Seth McGinty was the son of a local dairy farmer.

BJ Bennington had gone to Michigan State and gotten a degree in Agricultural Technology.

Mortimer Patch had a degree in Ag Science from a university in New Zealand. His wife had been going to grad school at Michigan State when the shit hit the fan. Mortimer was in his mid-to-late twenties, tall and prematurely balding.

Seth's knowledge was an inch wide and a mile deep. If you had tractors and diesel and wanted to run a confinement dairy then Seth was your man.

BJ's expertise was primarily construction related.

Mortimer, or Mo, seemed to have everything Bob and Sam were looking for but he came across as abrupt and abrasive. He had little good to say about US agriculture. At first Bob attributed it to sour-grapes. Mo had looked for a job in ag but had been repeatedly rebuffed.

When John tickled him on his dismissive opinion of US agriculture Mo was more than willing to talk.

"Look at your milking parlors," Mo said. "The top US suppliers brag that farmers will be able to milk 120 cows per man-hour. What a joke! In New Zealand only drunks and old men milk 120 cows per man-hour."

"Then, when you look closer at the numbers you find out that they only count the guy in the pit putting the machines on the cow titties. The New Zealand numbers count every person on the property and every activity associated with milking."

"So why do you think New Zealand leap-frogged the US?" John asked.

"Because we don't hyper-focus. We always keep the over-all goal foremost in our minds. What is the point of having a man in the pit processing 200 cows an hour if you need three men moving the cows?" Mo said. "The other thing is we count the guy who mucks the barn out after the milking is done. You Americans don't include him in your numbers."

That is when Sam whispered "We are hiring this guy," into John's ear.

"How long do you think it will take to buy a flock of sheep?" John asked.

"I dunno. I haven't looked into it," Mo said.

"How soon can you start?" John asked.

"Now."

"You are hired," John said. "Mostly I am going to trust you until you screw up and we find the limits of where you can be trusted.

"I want wool sheep. I want prolific, long lived mothers. The focus is not having the very finest wool but to have lots of pounds of wool with bulk and easy-to-handle fibers," John said.

"I also want a couple of different rams," John said.

"You know a single ram can cover forty ewes, right?" Mo asked.

"Yup. But I don't want to tip into in-breeding depression," John said.

"How many ewes do you have in mind?" Mo asked.

"As many quality ewes as you can get your hands on," John said.

"Basically, you are screwed for this year," Mo said. "Most of the lambs have already been born and the males castrated and the older ewes culled."

"I am hiring you to solve problems, not to tell me why something can't be done. Figure it out. See what you can do," John said. "Now, let's talk about wages...."

Long Term Vision

"So what is the long-term goal?" Mortimer Patch asked. Talking about long-term goals did not strike him as strange, given the fact that they were in the middle of an Ebola pandemic that would reduce the population by 80%. That, and the loss of modern healthcare and social order and other, ancillary epidemics would knock half of the Ebola survivors into the grave. To his way of thinking you were not lost if you knew where you were going.

"I want to have a fiber and fabric industry in ten years with sufficient capacity to make clothing and bedding for a million people," John said.

"Beg pardon?" Mo said.

"There are enough clothes in storage facilities for the next five years even if you figure the ones that burned or leaked. After ten years the clothing will be too tattered to mend," John said. "In case you didn't notice, it gets cold in Michigan. People will freeze to death wholesale unless there is a source of durable, warm clothing and quilts."

"But a million people?" Mo observed, skeptically.

"A million people. That is probably a half million sheep's worth of wool...so there is not time to waste," John said.

"How much land do you have?" Mo asked.

"We own six sections of land...maybe enough for ten or fifteen thousand sheep," John said. "But there will be all kinds of underutilized land vacant for the asking."

"In fact, that is a big reason for wanting to keep our property utilized. People will claim it if it is not under the plow or hoof," John said.

"The plan is to develop products and processes."

"Eaton Rapids has water power and a little bit of solar. They will be the manufacturing base," John said.

"To get the pipeline started, we need raw materials. It is a basic pump-priming exercise. Good products create demand. Demand pulls resources."

"I will need to travel," Mo said, still a bit stunned by John's long-term vision.

"For that you will need to talk to Mr. Ed or to Salazar. Remember, you get a percentage, so you really are working for yourself," John said.

Nyssa agreed that Mo could travel to the surrounding area as long as he stayed out of urban areas and the two parties talked outside. It had become a major faux pas to go inside somebody's house.

John had a scooter and a supply of canned gas.

Mrs Treadwell was surprised to have a visitor with a down-under accent inquiring about the purchase of ewes and ewe lambs.

"I am not sure I am doing you a favor by selling you sheep," she said.

" 'n why is that?" Mo asked.

" 'Cause you will have to feed them in the winter. Without fuel to run tractors it is impossible to put up hay or farm corn," Pat Treadwell said.

"Mmmm," Mo said in agreement as he looked out over the sheep. They were well cared for but clearly not pets. The first thing he looked at were the hooves of the oldest animals.

Trimming hooves is hot, dirty, back-breaking work. That was the first thing that slackers let slide.

"Assuming we could find a way to pay you, how many ewes and ewe lambs are you willing to part with?" Mo asked.

"I usually keep a quarter of my ewe lambs for replacements" Pat said. "I am willing to sell you all of the ewes I cull and ¾ of my ewe lambs...but again, I am not sure I am doing you any favors."

"Do they come with breeding records?" Mo asked.

"Some do. Some don't," Pat said.

"My first offer for the lot is to provide tractor power to put up your hay for the year," Mo said. "What will you need on top of that to make it worth your while?"

"That scooter would be nice," Pat said. "Put up my hay and my neighbors. There is a big market for hay. Throw in your scooter and five ounces of silver for every animal."

"My counter offer is to put up your hay and an equal amount of your neighbor's hay. I will find you a scooter that is as like mine, payable upon delivery. I throw in an ounce of silver for every ewe lamb but no silver for the ewes you were going to cull anyway...." Mo said.

Fifteen minutes later they had a deal. It would have taken a lot longer but Mrs Treadwell did not have any other buyers in sight, at least none who were in a position to pay anything for her animals.

***

"You are now the proud owner of 120 cross-bred, white faced, ewe lambs, 30 cull ewes and four ram lambs," Mo told John.

"Two of the ram lambs will be at least 7/8 Columbia and have fine wool. The other two will be about ¾ Romney and have long, coarse, strong wool. The only reason you are getting the rams is that she had some first-year ewes that bred late, otherwise the ram lambs are castrated within a day of lambing," Mo said.

"We have some time. She will have them driven over in the middle of August after they are weaned," Mo said. "All we have to do is convince Kelly Carney to harvest her hay and find a scooter and 150 ounces of silver and...." Mo mentioned a few other items including the fact that he had committed John Wilder to buying Pat Treadwell's wool clip for 10% over market price for the next five years. More than anything that would flush out whether John was a bull-shit artist or had convictions behind his dreams.

"Great job!" John said. "I would have been OK with ten ewes and happy with twenty. The only thing I want you to change is I want to take possession of the sheep the same week we cut the hay. You are something of an over-achiever, aren't you?"

John had always found legitimate praise to be a highly cost-effective motivator.

"Are we going to need a tractor for our operation?" John asked.

"Probably. We wouldn't in New Zealand but it is snowier here. There will be days where the sheep cannot dig for their grazing," Mo admitted.

"Why don't you see what you can do about having Kelly convert a tractor over with a gasifier?" John said. "Don't try to chisel down the price. We are going to need him to build equipment for the yarn and weaving operation."

***

Kelly was highly resistant to building a gasifier for John Wilder. First of all, he did not know Wilder. Second, he thought Mo's NZ accent was an affected, second-rate imitation of a British accent.

Mo did not push too hard, heedful of John wanting to stay on the good side of Kelly.

"So, I take it that your primary concern is that somebody will steal the design?" Mo said.

"Nailed it," Kelly said.

"What if we pay you a commission to build another gasifier tractor? You own it. You supply the drivers. You park and maintain it. We get first dibs on renting it and you give us a deep discount on the rental?" Mo said.

Kelly squinted at Mo. "Don't sound like you are getting much out of the deal," Kelly observed.

"We will get enough. Got to make hay while the sun shines," Mo said.

"Is that what you are going to use it for? Making hay?" Kelly asked.

"Mostly," Mo agreed.

Suddenly that sounded like a fabulous idea. Hay season does not compete with plowing, planting, harvesting or wood-cutting season. Kelly would have another tractor to rent out in those seasons and he would not have to put any money out-of-pocket to have a tractor to back-up Milo's.

"Deal," Kelly said, sticking out his hand.

Why Didn't the Government Do Anything?

Mr. Ed became the Wilders' go-to guy to run and fetch. Whether it be small creature comforts or information, Mr. Ed seemed to be able to find anything.

Mr. Ed, for his part, basked in being in the presence of wealth. He did not think he would like "rich people". He hadn't been exposed to very many. He saw that he had been hasty in his judgments. John and Sam were as comfortable as a pair of old shoes.

He might have reached a different conclusion if he had encountered John while he was a high-powered executive working seventy hours a week. After work, there were times when John barely had enough psychic energy left to be civil to his family much less random, old guys who liked the sound of their own voice.

Sam helped John reframe the time they spent with Ed. It was an investment in the future. If Mr. Ed liked you, then the rest of the community liked you by default.

And they needed Ed or somebody like him. They were confined to the house. Ed always had time to pop over. He even found himself a patio chair that he parked in a sunny, protected spot the mandatory distance away from the deck.

Ed could leave items and the Wilders could pick them up after Ed left. Exchanges could not go the other way until after the quarantine was lifted. Ed was in no hurry.

"I don't know if you know this," he started out after clearing his throat, "But I used to run the radio show before Peppermint Patty."

John wondered if he detected a bit of professional jealousy.

"I am thinking of getting back into it," Ed continued. "The one question I keep hearing is 'Why didn't the government do something?' "

"In talking to you all, I picked up on the fact that Mrs Wilder used to work in medical research," Ed said. He may have been sharper than he first appeared.

"I would like to be able to tell the folks of Kates Store what happened in language they can understand," Ed said. "Can you help me out?"

Samantha slowly nodded her head. She had worked in cancer research but everybody's attention had been pulled to the Ebola crisis. She had followed the story as raptly as any of the scientists in her community.

"You know they had a vaccine that worked?" Sam said. "At least, it worked in the Congo."

Mr. Ed nodded his head. "That's what folks are saying. Why couldn't we get that?"

"By my figuring, there were two big problems with that vaccine," Sam said. "The production could not scale up as quickly as we needed. We needed a vaccine based on recombinant technology. Recombinant technology is where yeast or other easy-to-farm microbes are genetically modified so their cell walls have the same patterns of proteins that the virus does. Then Anheuser-Busch or Coors could have been pressed into service and we could have produced vaccine by the oil-tanker load."

"The other main problem is that Ebola is an RNA based virus like the HIV that causes AIDS. It mutates quickly. Over the course of twenty thousand victims it changed 3% of its protein sequences. It was a moving target," Sam said.

"That caused the government to change direction. They cut loose funding for medical teams to develop new vaccines, not wanting to understand how long it takes to move from concept to approved product."

"There were other problems. According to early trial data and numerical simulations, the best US recombinant vaccines had a five percent fatality rate when administered and only conferred 95% immunity," Sam said.

"The politicians puked. They refused to start production when ten percent of the population was going to die anyway," Sam said.

"So, you are saying the government could have done something but they hemmed-and-hawed until it was too late," Ed said.

"The government did do something. They threw mountains of money at the problem. I am pretty sure the military got immunized with the 95% vaccine. They were pretty pissed off cowboys, though, because they could not get it for their families after the shit hit the fan."

"Oh, and another problem is that it took two shots, a primer and a booster and the shots needed to be at least three weeks apart," Sam said. "Things came unglued way faster than anybody anticipated."

"It was a case of trying to shut the barn door after the horse ran away...and the barn was on fire," Sam said.

"So, we had a vaccine..." Ed asked.

"We had a half dozen vaccines in trial," Sam said. "Think back a year ago. If somebody came up to you and suggested that you get two shots for a disease that was not officially recognized as being in North America and they told you there was a one-in-twenty chance the shots would kill you, would you vote for that person?"

Ed grumbled a little bit. "No. I woulda said they were crazy."

"That is the downside of a democracy," Sam said. "China is busy vaccinating their population with 90% vaccine. That is how effective the preliminary trials showed their vaccine to be before they pulled the trigger and went production.

"Their population was not given a choice. Everybody is getting vaccinated. They are going to lose at least 10% of their population. That is assuming that the virus does not mutate, which we know that it will," Sam said.

"They lost us and India and most of Europe as customers and their economy is going to collapse. They are going to lose a minimum of 10% of their population and I suspect their government is still going to have to deal with a revolution," Sam said.

"You know, I like to leave people with a ray of hope," Ed said. "You said there is a vaccine out there...a kind of yeast that even a home beer brewer could reproduce."

Sam had to admit ignorance. "Maybe. There was once. They made enough to vaccinate the military and most of the D.C. Beltway."

"I don't know if that strain escaped to the wild or how to get a sample of it. But in the strictly technical sense, yes, everything you said is true," Sam said.

"Just out of curiosity," Ed said "where did they make that vaccine?"

"That was confidential, but if I were a betting woman I would bet on Ames, Iowa. That is where the research team that was out-front was located," Sam said.

"People being people, do you suppose any of those folks might have taken a sample home, just in case?" Ed mused.

Quinn's Romance

Chernovsky's fighters dared to hope.

The pace of operations suddenly slowed to a crawl. It was as if somebody flipped a switch.

The number of refugees picked up. It was as if they suddenly realized that the dissolution of the social contract was the new normal. FEMA and the National Guard were not going to save them. No miracle drugs were going to magically appear.

Refugees from the south fled north. Refugees from the north fled south. East went west. West went east.

Even Chernovsky was baffled by the flood of refugees. "Probably going to bunk-up with family," he guessed. "When the chips are down, family has to take you in."

The fighters in the observation post placed wagers on who was going to make it and who wasn't, not that would ever know and be able to collect.

Some you looked at and knew. They had "VICTIM" plastered all over them in bright, blinking, neon signs. Zero situational awareness. Stupid clothing. Lots of bling or valuable goods clearly visible. Pretty girls dressed in slut-du-jour, look-at-me clothing.

Others projected the vibe that they would be a much tougher nut to crack. One group of six adults and a handful of kids were pushing two-wheeled gardening carts. Half the adults were carrying firearms on slings at low-ready. Close examination of the carts revealed that the tarps were untied in the back, right corner and the buttstock of a firearm was ready-at-hand. Even the kids were heads-up.

The flow of hostiles almost stopped. Where Quinn's squad may have tangled with six-to-ten groups of hostiles on a sunny day, that dropped down to one-or-two.

Quinn assumed that word had gotten around that the forces south of Dimondale were not to be trifled with. Another change was that the groups of hostiles were not bunched up like they had been in the beginning. It was impossible to sweep them all into the kill sack. Inevitably, the hostiles bring up the rear rabbited back to safety at the first hint of gunfire.

Chernovsky shared the old Finnish joke. "So many targets. Where will we bury them?" He did not tell his fighters that Russians were the targets in the original version of the joke.

There was more than a grain of truth in the joke. There were some north-slopes on Canal Road where it was hard to see the pavement for all the corpses. The punt gun had mowed down several large groups in exactly the same kill sack. Peak temperatures barely kissed fifty-five degrees Fahrenheit and other than some bloating and the blood drying, the corpses looked like they could have died yesterday.

Quinn shook his head. The ground littered with dead should be a sign to even the most obtuse that it was not a healthy place to enter. And the hostiles kept coming...until they didn't.

Chernovsky's fighters started talking about "after".

They dared to hope that they would go back home and re-start their lives.

Quinn looked forward to being able to date Dysen. All the fighters wanted to date her but they figured Quinn had dibs. For the healthy, women-deprived men—for the events of the last three-and-a-half months forged the boys Chernovsky had recruited in January into men---to the men of Squads One, Two and Three, Dysen personified everything that was good and worth sacrificing to save "back home."

Every two or three days she personally delivered warm cookies to the three squads. She came down Gunn Road, the westernmost road that had seen little traffic from the hostiles. She had a bike and cart parked on the "hot side" of the barrier that she transferred her cooler of cookies over to.

She came down Gunn Road because "Berfa" the punt gun had never been used on Gunn Road and the few hostiles who had been terminated had been shot with .22 LR and had run off before bleeding on to the surface of the road.

Then she delivered to Squad One before heading east on Vermontville Highway to Squad Two and Squad Three.

If the other fighters noticed that Quinn was often missing

from camp about the time Dysen would be retracing her path and moving westward on Vermontville Highway, they had the good grace to hold their tongues.

It was deemed unlikely that any "funny business" would occur in broad daylight in the middle of Vermontville Highway. The other thing was that Quinn's ephemeral romance, chaste though it was, gave the other men a solid foundation for their own dreams.

The most common description of Dysen among Chernovsky's fighters was "Classy chick." And she was. Pre-Ebola, Dysen would have bristled at the description but now she took it in the best possible light. She saw the sacrifice and privation "her guys" were enduring.

Pre-Ebola, most of Chernovsky's men would have been very defensive around the Dysen's of the world. Pre-Ebola, girls like Dysen moved out of town and went to college. They drove Hondas, liked "girly" boys and got jobs in payroll. When they married, they had 2.3 babies, a girl, a boy and a Shih-Tzu or Yorkie. Not every marriage went the distance, but many of them did.

The Quinns and Donnies of Eaton Rapids went to work after high school. They worked a series of short-duration, manual labor jobs. If they were lucky, they picked up a trade that paid a little more. They drove twenty-year-old, four-wheel-drive trucks that got fifteen miles to the gallon on a good day.

They never learned about the time value of money. They took on too much credit. They got chewed out by the girls in the office, girls like Dysen, because their 5s looked like their 6s and sometimes their 2s.

Girls? The Donnies and Quinns hooked up with girls with "issues" much like their own. Both parties were settling for the best they could get. Usually they could not afford to marry so they lived together, made babies, fought...sometimes they stayed together. Sometimes they did not.

Quinn and Dysen? That was like grabbing the brass ring on the carousel at the county fair.

The Game is Afoot

Word came into camp that hundreds of "zombies" were sighted three miles west of Squad One's camp. The reports claimed that the zombies were heading east on Vermontville Highway toward the buffer zone that Chernovsky's fighters controlled.

That was at the extreme western edge of their area-of-operation and even though reports of "a hundred" invariably meant twenty-five or thirty actual, Chernovsky deemed it advisable to send two squads to deal with the issue.

Chernovsky counter-measured the soon-to-be-empty camp and observation post in the center of his area-of-responsibility by directing Squad 3 to send one of the two fire teams over to support.

Quinn decided to travel due west out of camp and avoid Vermontville Highway. Being off the road meant they could bound west with almost no risk of being seen. Vermontville Highway was hilly and would have required a point unit being one rise ahead of the main group assessing the risk of encountering eastbound unfriendlies.

Everybody was pissy because it was an hour before lunch and they knew it was going to be at least a three-hour operation. Lunch would have to wait.

The operation went in the ditch for Quinn, personally, when he was crossing Silver Creek. Quinn slipped on a rock and severely twisted his left ankle, enough so that further walking on it was not possible. His footwear was battered by three continuous months of operation and the lack of support undoubtedly contributed to the mishap.

Quinn volunteered to guard the backdoor while the remainder of the squad continued west to hook up with Squad 1 and then, under the direction of Donnie, to continue west until contacting the enemy. It is not like he had a choice.

After they left, Quinn hobbled his way up the widening basin of Silver Creek. The vegetation was an unusual mix of Red Cedar and Catalpa and boulders...all three items being rare in Eaton County.

Setting up behind a rock pile with a good view of Vermontville Highway two hundred yards to the south, Quinn expected a boring day.

Quinn's first assumption when he saw the riflemen moving west on Vermontville was that Chernovsky had sent out the remainder of the third squad to support. Glassing them with his compact binoculars, Quinn realized that the riflemen were not from Chernovsky's group. They were wearing camo and they were all carrying AR clones.

His concern spiked when he saw them slipping into the brush at twenty-five-yard intervals. They were clearly setting up an ambush and they clearly expected their targets to be coming from the west. Five of the ambushers set up on the south side of the road and one of them set up on Quinn's side of Vermontville Highway a scant hundred yards to the southwest of him.

Chernovsky's squads had run enough games so that Quinn was able to make a few unpleasant deductions.

Quinn toggled his hand-held CB and alerted Donnie, the squad member who was next-in-line to cover him when he went down.

"Yeah Quinn, whatchya got. Run out of sunscreen?" Donnie asked.

“Listen you bastard! You used my deodorant. Where the hell did you put it?” Quinn said. Suddenly, Quinn was glad about Chernovsky's paranoia. That was the signal to switch to the alternate channel.

"Fuck you!" Donnie replied indicating, "Roger, will comply."

Donnie stopped his squad with a hand signal. When his squad stopped, so did the other squad. The fighters who had been walking along the edge of a field automatically blended into the bushes and scrub growing along the fence line. They also took a knee to break up the distinctive outline of a standing human. They did it without thinking because that is what training does, short-circuits the need to think of the appropriate response.

Chernovsky set the primary channel every morning by throwing two dice, one red and one white. All of the Team Leads had a laminated index card that translated the number thrown by Chernovsky into the primary channel for the day. Of the forty possible channels, the four most used were skipped over as there are thirty-six possible throws of the two dice. Then Chernovsky repeated the exercise for the day's secondary channel and then called out the four numbers: Red 1, White 1. Red 2, White 2.

Donnie switched channels. “Sounds serious.”

“I think you are walking into a trap,” Quinn said.

Suddenly, Donnie the perpetual screwball was all business. “Evidence?” he asked.

Back at camp Chernovsky was all ears. He had switched to the alternate channel after Quinn used the "..bastard...deodorant" code phrase. He could hear Quinn’s end of the conversation but not Donnie’s responses.

“I saw six fighters set up an ambush. They were setting up for when you come back. They are between Olive's Cemetery and Gunn Road," Quinn said.

That was a head-scratcher.

"Any clue where they came from?" Donnie asked.

"All I can figure is they cut cross-country from West Windsor Highway to Parez Road and then moved south to Vermontville Highway. That is the only way I can figure they would get in without our guys seeing them," Quinn said.

That was alarming because in four weeks of daily operations they had never run into those kinds of behavior: Rifles, ambushes, traveling cross country.

The fact that the strange riflemen were setting up an ambush suggested that they had intelligence about their operation.

Miscellaneous facts started to crystallize for Quinn. He had been involved in several engagements in the past ten days where the raiders had a trailing element that never engaged. The trailing element hung back a quarter mile and beat-feet as soon as Quinn's squad rolled up the raiders.

"I think we are out of range of the camp. Can you ping Chernovsky and ask for guidance?" Donnie said.

If the bad guys were setting up an ambush there was no point in rushing into it. Donnie and the squads were masters of waiting. "He who waits best, wins," was a Chernovsky saying.

Quinn relayed Donnie's request. "Hostiles sighted. Deployed behind our main force like ambushers. Suspect mission is compromised. Request guidance."

Back at Camp

Chernovsky rubbed the stubble on his chin, deep in thought. Then he responded "Forewarned is forearmed. Approach primary target with caution. Suspect they are bait. Use your resources to turn tables on them."

Quinn relayed the message to Donnie.

"What the hell does that mean?" Donnie wanted to know. Then he radioed back, "Clarification?"

Chernovsky replied "Probably a trap. Reported hostiles are bait. Real fighters will whack you when you are focused on bait. Ambushers are clean-up. Your mission has not changed. Kill all of them."

After getting off the radio, Chernovsky signaled that it was time to run "Play #47."

Chernovsky was fastidious in everything he did. The signal was not shouting or raising a flag or anything obvious.

Chernovsky urinated into the firepit. The eyebrows of the team that had flowed over from Squad 3 to backfill Squad 2's nearly empty camp shot up but the message was understood. Those who were too far away from the firepit to see the signal were quietly informed by others as they filtered out of camp in ones and twos with their weapons.

After settling down into a comfortable firing position that overlooked paths into camp, the Team Leader from Squad 3 realized that his counterpart, the Team Leader who led Squad 3's other fire team, probably did not hear the switch to the alternate channel. He changed back to the primary channel and gave his opposite a bump. "Hey Bernie?"

"Yeah," Bernie replied.

"I got 47 bullets left. 47. Copy?"

Bernie replied, "Copy. 47."

Then the Team Leader who had shifted over from Squad 3 to cover Quinn's departure switched back to the alternate channel and settled down to wait. He had done what he could to pass the word along.

A mile-and-a-half west of Quinn:

"Well, that was clear," Donnie said after Quinn relayed Chernovsky's message.

Donnie made the "Huddle up" hand signal and the two squads moved in for an impromptu planning session. It was not a hurried rush. It was two fighters doing over-watch while one moved...then a thirty second observation pause before the next 1-of-3 moved. During the thirty second pauses the entire squad scanned 360 degrees in narrow pie-wedges. It was like watching paint dry.

This was a scenario Chernovsky's fighters had practiced countless times. The second man moving before the full thirty seconds elapsed resulted in a three-mile run for the entire squad. Better to be slow than to run...or be dead.

Even as his men were moving silently toward him, Donnie was pulling up maps of the terrain to psych out where opposing force would deploy for the primary ambush.

When Plans Meet the Enemy

At the rock pile beside Silver Creek

After passing Chernovsky's instructions to Donnie, Quinn thought he was done for a while. With zero mobility he could not participate in mopping up the ambushers in front of him. He could however, precisely identify where they were. Using his binoculars he was able to sort through the cover and identify their precise locations relative to more visible surroundings.

On the odd chance he might be called upon to provide long-range fire support, Quinn pulled the disposable, plastic grocery bag out of his backpack and filled it with the loose duff on the ground. Larry Tomanica, the shooting instructor Quinn had during "boot camp" had impressed upon his guys that you did not want to use your pack for a steady rest because you might find yourself moving in a hurry and you did not want to lose your drinking water and other necessities. Hence the grocery bag. You would not feel bad if you had to leave it behind.

Quinn was impressed. These guys were as good as his guys. Whoever had recruited this group had obviously recruited ex-military. There was almost no head scratching and mosquito slapping even though he knew they were probably being eaten alive by the first hatch. It did not occur to him that they might have bug spray.

Everything was jolly until he saw Dysen riding east down Vermontville toward camp, directly toward the ambush. She was on a bike and pulling her cookie cart.

"Fuck, fuck, fuck, fuck," was all that ran through Quinn's mind.

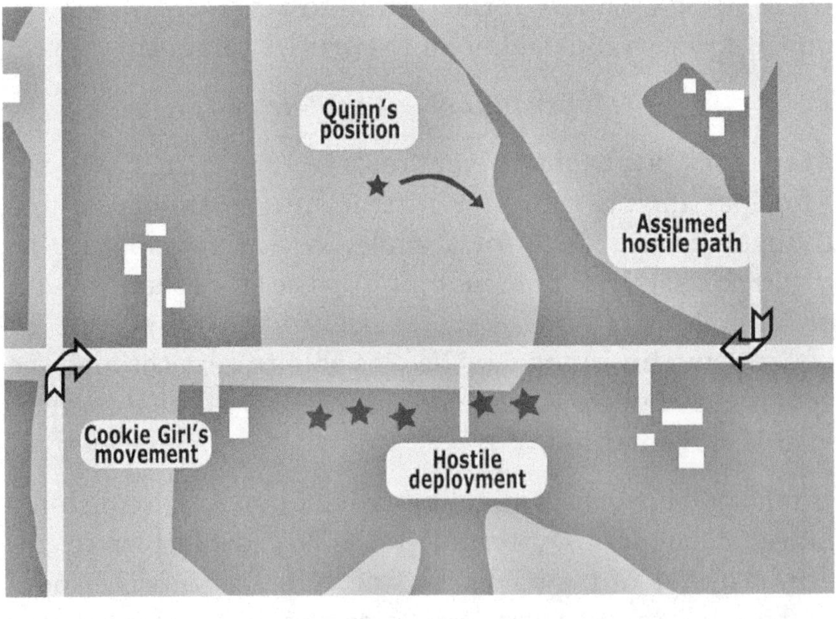

Being professionals, he hoped that they would let her ride

through. Quinn's squad had passed on shooting the kid on the bike in their first engagement because they had bigger fish to fry. Surely the hostiles would not want a dead body in plain sight where it would tip off Donnie's squad.

Quinn had almost breathed a sigh of relief as Dysen was passing the sixth ambusher when Quinn saw her somersault off the bike quickly followed by the report of a high-powered rifle. Quinn had seen enough limp rag-doll cartwheels to recognize a head-shot when he saw one.

"You rotten mother-fuckers!" he said as he flipped his AR's safety to the fire position.

Then the professionalism Chernovsky had been hammering into him for three months took hold.

"Spackle to everybody on the net. Be advised. Situation deteriorated. Repeat: Situation deteriorated. I will be starting the party."

Donnie radioed back. "Give me thirty seconds to button up the troops. Repeat, do not start the party for another thirty seconds."

Donnie transmitted to the two squads. "Did you catch that? Party starts in twenty seconds. Get cover. Get a sight picture and wait," Donnie had a thought that this might work out to his advantage as long as his guys didn't start shooting too soon.

At camp, Chernovsky thought "WTF!"

The thing is that Chernovsky had transitioned to coach and the coach is not on the field. He had to trust the guys out there. Trusting people he had trained was the hardest thing he had ever done.

After a slow count to thirty, Quinn started hammering the ambushers. He had dialed his 1.5-6X MTAC scope to six power. He shot the westernmost ambusher (the one who was closest to him) square between the shoulder blades. Then he transitioned to the most eastern ambusher because he was the one most likely to close with him due to the cover. From there he worked west, servicing each target with a double-tap.

At two hundred yards he could hit a pop-can with boring regularity. The problem was that the targets were not completely visible and were moving to get more concealment.

He had four probable kills and was working on the fifth. In a gun battle between a fighter with concealment and a fighter with cover, always bet on the fighter with cover. However, there were two fighters firing back at him and they were becoming way too accurate. Quinn knew the game would be over if he got stone chips in his eyes. Quinn decided it was time to abandon his hide.

Two miles west of Silver Creek

The two squads had just enough time to ease into cover at Quinn's unexpected radio call. One squad member was caught in the middle of an opening. He dropped to a knee and tipped his head so his face was not visible. The months of carrying firewood and living in the mud paid off. He looked like a rotten, moss covered stump.

The squads had been moving into position. The squads had no problem finding the bait before Quinn opened the party. They could hear the bait from half a mile away and were not moving east on the highway.

A quick look at the terrain, terrain they had gamed over many times, made it pretty obvious where the kill sack was and where the gunners had to be situated.

Surrounding the gunners had taken a long time because it required a lot of walking. The squads were a half mile north-east of the trap when they determined the exact location of the bait. One of the squads had to drop back farther east so they could get to the other side without being seen by hostiles. Donnie's fighters were within two-hundred yards of where he assumed the primary ambushers were when they heard the shot from the east and Quinn announced he was going to start the party.

Donnie had been getting ready to start the show when the first, distinctive "BOOM" of the AR came rolling in from the east. Then Quinn's call came. Then the sounds of a hot fire-fight.

The squads sat tight waiting for Donnie's word to light up hostiles.

Then the firing stopped.

The hostile gunners who were lying in wait to ambush who-ever came to the bait must have assumed that the ambush to the east had wiped out the squads Chernovsky was expected to send. The ambushers who were using the "bait" left their positions when the rash of shooting to the east stopped. They gathered in the open to confer. Donnie was embar-rassed to see that two gunners had been positioned in places he had not anticipated.

Donnie radioed the group. "Start with the gunners. Then the bait. Kill them all."

At Squad 2's camp

Hostiles who had been infiltrating the brush heard the shooting and assumed it was game-time and rushed the camp.

Finding the camp empty, they milled around in the center of the opening. Just because somebody they had once been in the Army, Navy or Air Force didn't mean they had retained any tactical sense. Many had been cooks and truck drivers and other, non-combat occupations.

Squad 3, the Squad that had seen almost no action cut them to ribbons. Three of the hostiles were wearing body armor but that made little difference as Squad 3 concentrated on head shots to compensate for the puny .22s they were using. In the chaos one of the hostiles shot Buddy in the short-ribs. Chernovsky had never run Play #47 as a live fire exercise and Buddy stood up to see what was happening

The two fighters who were in the observation post were shot when the hostiles stumbled upon them as the hostiles retreated. The .22 LR were very poorly suited for close range fire-fights.

Beside the rock pile at Silver Creek

Quinn dumped the empty magazine even as he crawled backwards with his swollen ankle smacking into every willow trunk and rock behind him. It was almost as if a magnet was pulling his ankle into hard objects. Quinn jammed in another magazine and slapped the bolt release to chamber a live round.

Quinn assumed he was screwed. He had not put in hearing protection before shooting and he would not be able to hear anybody rushing his position.

He had managed about seven yards of backward travel when two men vaulted over the rock pile, the man on the Quinn's right slightly before the man on the left. They hesitated for a fraction of a second as their vision homed in on the flesh colored grocery bag that had tumbled to the base of the rock pile and been dragged about ten feet as Quinn crawled backwards.

Quinn drilled the first man through the head. The second man was moving. Quinn nailed him in the chest and then another through his head, but not before the man was able to get off a shot. Quinn was not as smooth or as fast when traversing from right-to-left as he was when traversing from left-to-right. Perversely, he heard Chernovsky's gravelly voice in his head "Write that down: Training opportunity."

The bullet hit Quinn in his right butt-cheek and angled down across the outside of this thigh before burying itself in the dirt.

That is when time began to get funny for Quinn.

To Catch a Falling Knife

Kelly hauled ass down the road as fast as the frost shattered surface would carrying him. One of the lessons-learned from the Bacon Incident was that Chernovsky did not have a plan to care for casualties. That led to the Kelly Carney ambulance service.

Kelly was driving the truck and running pedal-to-the-metal. One of the lessons was that when you needed an ambulance on the battlefield you needed it NOW.

Kelly started taking gasoline in payment for plowing gardens. His plan was to use gasoline instead of taking thirty minutes to get the gasifier up to full speed.

The call came in that he had five casualties, two deceased and three alive although severely injured. Hence Kelly putting the hammer down.

A group was waiting as he paused at the turn-off to Kates Store on the way back. He paused just long enough for them to pull the litter holding Quinn out of the back of the truck. Quinn would probably survive.

Then Kelly floored it and was rolling toward the city of Eaton Rapids.

Somewhere between Kates Store and Eaton Rapids, Buddy breathed his last.

Kelly found out that Dysen was the least of Eaton Rapids'

problems and was way down the list for receiving medical care.

An organized, armed force hit the M-99 bridge the same time Squads One and Two encountered the ambush. Unlike Chernovsky's force, the Eaton Rapids men guarding the M-99 bridge had been unlucky. They were gulled into rushing to the aid of a woman who appeared to be assaulted by a couple of thugs. The men were mowed down by hidden snipers and two trucks with an unknown number of hostiles bashed through the token resistance on the bridge and were somewhere behind the lines and were unaccounted for.

Some of the Eaton Rapids fighters were still alive and were being tended to by the tattered remnants of the Eaton Rapids medical community.

Kelly refused to take no for an answer. He kept drilling for information until he found SOMEBODY with expertise to care for Dysen.

Fortunately for Dysen, Eaton Rapids still had two dentists. Neither one of them was pulled into caring for the Eaton Rapids men. It took both of them, working in shifts, six hours to stitch Dysen's face back together. The bullet blew out her lower, right canine and four left molars. The shattered teeth and bullet tore a huge gash in her left cheek.

The impact simultaneously knocked her unconscious and flipped her off her bike.

The work was tedious and there was little available in the way of pain killers. Tiny shreds of skin were stretched and mated with other shreds of skin and then joined with minute stitches. The dentists had not practiced this kind of work since Dental school. They knew how to do it but it was a skill they had not practiced in thirty-five years.

After the surgery, they loaded Dysen up with Cherrystone

laudanum and penicillin and sent her back to Kates Store to recover.

Will Janelle ever find True Love's Kiss?

What venomous beast has eight arms, eight legs, 108 teeth, half a brain and a shriveled, skanky heart?

A posse of mean-girls.

Janelle Bozer (A corruption of the French name Beaux Yeux) entered the Salazar household as a foster child the summer before she entered ninth grade. Janelle had been shuffled from foster family-to-foster family through no fault of her own. She did her best to fit in and be invisible.

As a ninth grader she came under the unpleasant scrutiny of four "mean-girls" in the tenth grade who resolved to make Janelle's life a living hell. The mean-girls were in the bottom tier, socially. They were neither beautiful, skinny, talented, athletic or smart. They compensated by being unpleasant, gifted in that regard by both intrinsic personality and motivation to achieve in-group status.

They possessed one other gift in abundance, the ability to sniff out the one person who just wanted to be invisible, the one person they could bully and belittle and thereby elevate themselves above the level of "total loser".

The mean-girls hounded Janelle. Particularly galling to Janelle was their pet nickname: "Princess Fiona".

Princess Fiona was a character in a popular animated movie. Fiona was a beautiful, Celtic princess by day...voluptuous of curve, a stunningly beautiful face and lilting voice.

By night Princess Fiona was an ogre and possessed a face that was distinctively porcine in nature.

Sadly, for Janelle, her face was not the austere assembly of concavities and angular planes much loved by magazine covers. Nope. Janelle did not look like the Celtic Princess Fiona.

Janelle's face was broad and fleshy. Her bulbous nose short and turned upward. her cheeks round apples, lips puffy and full. Her hair was rusty steel wool. Once the comparison was made it was impossible to ignore it.

Janelle stoically bore the insults, hoping they would get bored and find another victim. It did not happen.

Janelle snapped when they deduced which boy she was sweet on. He, too, was one who wished to remain invisible. The four mean-girls "outed" them in the cruelest of ways.

What venomous beast has eight arms, eight legs, 104 teeth, one brain and a shriveled, skanky heart?

The posse of mean-girls, Eaton Rapids Class of 2009.

Janelle had learned a few things about defending herself as she had sailed through the foster-care system. She used those lessons to good effect when she caved in the dentition of the leader of the mean-girl posse.

Janelle was completely shocked when Kate and Rick went to bat for her. It was to no avail. The high school administrators were Hear, See, and Say no evil kool-aid drinkers. It was IMPOSSIBLE that the four, sweet, native-born sophomores were the satan-spawn Janelle said they were.

Both Janelle and the school district administration jumped on Rick's proposal that Janelle opt out of traditional high school for the parallel, "electronic" curriculum.

The school district administration was far more flexible than the building administrators. They granted Janelle a great deal of flexibility in planning her curriculum. As long as the material was at least ninth grade level and it could be hammered into a box on the list of required courses they were more than willing to accept it as a valid course.

By the time Janelle was a senior, she was reading and critiquing Masters theses in Manufacturing Technology from Carnegie-Mellon, Michigan Tech, University of Cincinnati and University of Illinois.

Word got around. If you wanted to avoid getting blind-sided during your "Thesis Defense" examination, you sent a draft of your thesis to Janelle.Bozer@Mjail.com

They did not know or care if she was a high school kid or that she had a porky face. They saw her as a peer who had an uncanny ability to point out the land mines and "soft spots" in their research that unfriendly professors would home in on.

After graduating from high school, Janelle felt nothing binding her to Eaton Rapids. Kate and Rick had adopted her and given her a new last name. They also had to wisdom to see that they needed to let her go, that she needed to measure herself against the larger world.

The larger world was a cruel place. To men, she was invisible until thirty minutes after last-call at the bar. Or, in the workplace, men assumed that she was so starved for male attention that she would leap at the chance to bed even the most sloven and unhygienic of men. Women assumed she was a bull-dyke.

Janelle loaded up on tatts and piercings, hoping it would scare away the bottom-feeder men. Unfortunately, there is no kryptonite known that will deter a self-professed Don Juan at 1:30 in the morning after consuming too much strong drink. The ink and hardware only convinced the women that she was definitely a bull-dyke and she had to fend off clingy women and physically beat up lesbians who assumed she was infringing on their turf.

In spite of the hassles, Janelle loved the west coast. There were so many social niches and the population was so dynamic and mobile that she felt completely at home as she glided along the interstices between the niches. If the shoe started to chafe, she simply moved fifty miles and started over.

Ebola bit that in the ass.

She moved back to Eaton Rapids because she had a deep and profound faith that Rick and Kate would survive ANYTHING. In some ways she found them touchingly naive. In others she had them pegged as Resilience-R-Us.

Settling in, she found that she liked her siblings better as adults than she ever had as teenagers. Well, maybe except for Gabby. Gabby still was bossy.

Not only did she like her siblings, but she liked their mates and she especially liked Kelly Carney. He treated her as a peer.

What she did not like about Eaton Rapids, post-Ebola, was that she was doomed to be a spinster. Out west, she had been able to push the probability out of the top layers of her mind. Out west, everything seemed possible.

It wasn't just the close horizons of Eaton Rapids. It was Ebola.

Whether programmed by God or by Darwinian selection, it is a fact that men suffer much higher mortality during famines and epidemics than women. The ability for a population to rebound from a near-extinction event is bottlenecked by the number of viable uteruses, not the number of viable testes. It is highly desirable from a biological-evolutionary standpoint that mortality be highly skewed to spare girls at the expense of boys.

Everything about boys contributes to that mortality. Boys are more impulsive. Boys have shorter attention spans. Boys are more kinetic. Boys are much more risk seeking.

Everything that makes modern education difficult for boys are artifacts from the pro-uterus selection embedded within our genes so the species will survive extreme events. "I bet that sabre-tooth tiger got bored and went away. Let me check."

Not only had Ebola wiped out many of the young men...thank-you Wedgie...but the defense of the community had sponged up a good many of those that were left.

The few young men who were available were younger, spineless specimens who lacked ambition. If the continuation of the species demanded it, she would find an older DNA donor (Dmitri came to mind) and pop out a couple of pups, social conventions be damned.

Hope springs eternal, nevertheless. Because she liked Kelly and because she liked the energy that pubs created, she agreed to work in the bar that Kelly and Gabby cobbled together and ran on a part-time basis. Who knew, maybe a tall, dark stranger would walk into her life and sweep her away. Maybe Princess Fiona would find her Shrek.

Well Played

A storm system with temperatures in the mid-forties and twenty mph winds swept into the area.

Chernovsky left a skeleton crew pulled from the team in Squad Three that had seen no action. He had the rest of his men stand-down. They needed to lick their wounds and recover.

They went to Kates Store. Chernovsky had been called back to discuss redeployment closer to home. Clearly the aggression-profile of the hostiles was evolving.

Chernovsky gave them permission to visit Gabby's Bar in turns. He did not want all of his fighters incapacitated at the same time. He figured they had earned a chance to blow off a little bit of steam. Their weapons were locked up and he read them the riot act about behaving themselves.

He decided he could use a bit of snake-bite medicine himself before he had to do an unpleasant task. He had yet to inform Spackle that Buddy had passed away. He reminded himself to go easy on the sauce. He hadn't had a snort in four months and had lost fifty pounds while on deployment. He was not the man Rick Salazar and Paul Seraph had recruited in January.

Chernovsky heard scuffling, grunts and the sound of falling furniture even as he rounded the corner.

His fighters were under an overhang attached to the barn. Walt “Preacher” Shaw had a larger man in an arm-lock. The man's left arm was behind his back and Walt had the elbow torqued as far up and forward as it would go. It looked like Walt was trying to unscrew the man's arm and intended to stuff the man's fingers into his right ear canal.

The man’s face was mashed into the spilled beer and wind-blown rain on the table top. Shaw's feet were skittering on the wet floor as he sought to gain purchase.

This was not a "for show" fight. Shaw was doing everything in his power to rip the man's arm off.

Looking at the other fighters, Chernovsky deduced that any one of them would gladly have taken Shaw’s place. Whatever the man had said or done, it lit-off every one of his guys, including “Preacher.”

Chernovsky decided it was time to use a little bit of humor to defuse the conflict.

“Preacher, that is not normally how you are supposed to baptize somebody. Generally, it is supposed to be voluntary,” Chernovsky said.

The man took advantage of the distraction and struggled to break free but that only gave Walt the chance to lock one of his legs into the seat of the picnic table and exert even more pressure.

"What's the story?" Chernovsky asked. One of the other fighters started to pipe up but Chernovsky silenced him. "I wanna hear what they have to say, first."

The larger man whined "I was only joking. Fucking idiots don't know a joke when you hear one?" The man's voice was muffled because his face was mashed into the table top.

By now, Gabby and Janelle had come out the door and were watching. They seemed entirely willing to let Chernovsky handle it. The last thing they needed was to have ten fighters come unglued.

"Don't matter," Preacher said. "There are some things you don't joke about."

"What was the joke?" Chernovsky asked. He could not imagine anything that would have made his calmest and most religious fighter go bananas.

"I said 'she would make a great girlfriend.'" the man said.

Chernovsky gestured with his hand to continue. There had to be more. "Who would make a great girlfriend?"

"Dysen," the man said.

Chernovsky had time to look at the man. He was young enough to have been a fighter but had never interviewed for a position.

Further, the man looked...soft. Times were hard. People were working hard physical work and this guy looked like a grub, soft and white.

Chernovsky raised an eyebrow.

“That wasn’t all he said,” Preacher said as his free foot continued to scrape and slip on the wet floor.

“What else did you say?” Chernovsky asked.

The man was running out of breath and Chernovsky had to lean in to hear what he said.

“It was a joke. I said she would be a great girlfriend because she had three pussies,” the man said.

Chernovsky frowned. What the man said made no sense at all.

“I don’t get the joke," Chernovsky said.

“Yeah, she has the one between her legs and two on her face; one where the bullet went in and one where the bullet came out,” the man said.

Chernovsky considered himself a thoughtful man. He was as surprised as anybody when his hand came up and smashed the asshole’s elbow upward with the heel of his beefy right hand, dislocating the man’s arm. The man screamed and Walt stepped back in surprise.

“Get out of here and don’t come back,” Chernovsky’s voice was cold enough to freeze helium.

Things could have gotten ugly except Janelle heard what the loser said about her cousin.

Something in Chernovsky's unmodulated, atavistic defense of her cousin's honor thawed a part of Janelle's heart that had long been frozen.

Janelle felt as much as saw Gabby start forward.

"I got this," Janelle said. "Go back to your office and play with a spreadsheet or whatever it is you do in there."

Gabby was struggling to deal with her younger siblings as

full adults but there was something in Janelle's voice that advised her to let Janelle handle the situation. Gabby walked away.

“Will there be any more trouble?” Janelle asked.

“Not as long as that jerk stays away,” Walt said.

Looking at the Preacher’s nine squad mates Chernovsky said “I don’t think there is much risk of him coming back.”

"Ordinarily I would have to ask you to leave” Janelle said. "But considering the circumstances I think the next round is on me."

After Janelle had served the men, Chernovsky asked 'Preacher', "Who is she?"

Walt told Chernovsky that Janelle was Dysen's cousin.

Chernovsky was enchanted. Some men are "breast" men. Others are "face" or "leg" men. Chernovsky was into the entire package. He favored healthy, aerobic dancers with muscle definition over ornamental girls with spaghetti-thin legs and painted on faces.

"Wow!" Chernovsky said. "She has a great set of legs."

It didn't hurt Janelle that she had lost so much weight that she was wearing the clothes that no longer fit Gabby. Gabby had the taste, budget and inclination to buy clothes that flattered a woman's figure, far more than Janelle ever had.

***

Dysen woke up later that afternoon with a bloated, throbbing head. She could tell by the wall paper and curtains that she was in Kate and Rick’s house. She assumed Nyssa was caring for her.

From the next room she heard voices she recognized. Chernovsky was ripping Quinn a new asshole.

"Can you give me one good reason why you blew the operation for a civilian?" Chernovsky said.

Chernovsky felt he had failed; the squads had failed because of Buddy's death and the deaths of the two fighters who had been in the observation post.

"Sir," Quinn started. "I finally figured out that Dysen was the girl that you said would be a member of my squad if she made it back to camp and pulled her own weight."

Unseen by Dysen, Chernovsky made a hurry up gesture with his hands.

"I helped carry that first cooler full of cookies," Quinn said. "By my figuring, Dysen hauled 90 pounds of cookies to camp in the first two weeks she was bringing us cookies. By that accounting she pulled her own weight back to camp."

"It is my mission, as squad leader, to respond to threats to my squad members," Quinn concluded.

"And sir, with all due respect, let me remind you that you never rescinded your command to protect Cookie Girl's cargo and to take all steps required to never, EVER let it fall in enemy hands."

Quinn, and Dysen in the next room, waited in silence for Chernovsky's response.

Finally, "Well played, Quinn. Well played." It was the first time Chernovsky had ever used Spackle's first name.

Dysen then heard the sound of Chernovsky's footsteps leaving the room.

This is the end of Seven Cows.

Did you enjoy this book? How about a little sample of the next book in the series.....

The Shrewd King

...a new king rose to power. He said to his people, "See! The people multiply and become numerous! Let us deal shrewdly with them to stop their increase lest they join our enemies to fight against us." Accordingly, the king's men oppressed the people with forced labor.

-Adapted from Exodus 1:8-11

Chapter One

Derious was feeling pretty good about life as he dumped the Escalade into drive and stomped on the accelerator. The shock troops had demolished the Eaton Rapids defenses on the M-99 bridge. The operation was now a "GO" for Derious's portion of the raid.

Life could have been better. A couple of his riders were skin-head wannabes who he suspected had never been in the military. That was one of the risks of offering a month's supply of drugs as payment for theft and a kidnapping. Derious insisted on the skin-heads riding in the middle of the back seats with a couple of his trusted, nigga, street-soldiers sitting to either side of them.

At least Mr Heavy (a corruption of *el jefe*) hadn't assigned any spics to his team. Everybody hated skin-heads equally. They were barely tolerated by all the more "diverse" elements of Mr Heavy's organization. On the other hand, the diverse elements hated each other passionately and rarely worked together. Mr Heavy used skin-heads the way a baker uses frosting to "fix" a cosmetically challenged cake. The frosting is used to fill the holes.

The mission was simple. Blast through the defense. Drive fifteen miles, most of the way on a divided, state highway then another six miles on back roads. Break into the target's house. Torture him until he coughed up the drugs. Bringing back the target alive was optional. Derious hoped there was resistance. He wanted to see what the RPGs would do.

Derious, of course, was not going to be paid in drugs. Mr Heavy did not trust druggies and Derious was one of his trusted lieutenants. That didn't mean Derious didn't enjoy a few lines of blow on the weekend. He just didn't talk about it or put it on Facebook. There were some things Mr Heavy didn't need to know about.

The other thing that had Derious feeling good was that the team he was competing against got all tangled up south of Dimondale and couldn't seem to pin-down and destroy the defense. That had him smiling. Mr Benecio believed in healthy competition. Only the winning team was going to be compensated. Derious was looking forward to a $30k payday.

Derious surprised when the first sprinkling of small-arms fire started putting craters into the windshield directly in front of him. The glancing blows were not penetrating the windshield but were marking it with craters directly in his line of sight and sugar-fine glass was spalling off the inside surface. He would have been blinded if he had not been wearing his Serengeti Mondellos.

His first thought was "What the FUCK?" Nobody shot at his ride.

His Escalade was lifted, had heavily tinted windows, super low-profile tires, custom paint job and gold-plated spinners.

Everybody knew who owned this truck and no sane person allowed his dog to piddle within fifty feet of it. That would be disrespectful.

It did not occur to Derious that he was not on Lansing's near westside anymore. The people who lived along M-99 heard the fire-fight at the bridge and had run into their homes and come back with whatever gun they had on hand. Bird shot and .22 Long Rifle rounds don't have much ability to penetrate windshields or body metal unless the range is close and the impact is nearly perpendicular to the glass.

The story of Chernovsky disabling a half dozen trucks and Hummers by shooting at the radiators had been making the rounds. The smarter of the residents taking pot-shots at the two-vehicle caravan were aiming for the radiator opening. They could see that there were many people in the vehicles and the cooler heads thought that having the Cadillac Escalade and Lincoln Navigator making it a few mile down the road before they puked and the "soldiers" dismounted was a prudent thing.

Even the shooters aiming for the greenhouse started having effect. Though aiming for the windshield, the flight time for the slow moving rounds meant that the projectiles impacted the vehicles behind the point-of-aim. The effect became most pronounced as the vehicles were passing. Rounds aimed at the windshield impacted side windows.

Not only were the side windows nearly vertical but unlike the windshield which was made of laminated glass, the side glass was made from tempered glass that shattered into a thousand pebbles.

Derious lost two soldiers within seconds of each other; one to a blast of #6 shot to the head, the other to a .22 round in his right ear.

Everybody else ducked down. Derious could barely see over the dashboard and that contributed to his over-reaction as the tires of the SUV hit the rumble-strips at the side of the road.

Then the Escalade started picking up rapid fire from a heavier weapon. The shooter was clearly practiced and just as clearly knew what he was doing.

Derious responded by hammering the throttle, quickly increasing the vehicles speed to 85 miles per hour. Subsequent over-corrections sent the Escalade fishtailing as the top-heavy vehicle revealed itself as the evil handling pig that it was. It went off the road, slewing sideways. The tires sank into the soft, rain soaked sod and sent the Escalade into a roll.

'Gimp' Sullivan watched the brush bend beneath the Escalade and spring back afterward. The vehicle rolled through a heavy draping of wild vines and the vines swished back after the vehicle passed. There was almost no trace of the big SUV's passing, just some broken, red plastic from the tail lamps and the sparkle of glass shards.

Gimp had no intention of investigating. The SKS he had inherited from his dad was empty, the ten 7.62X39mm rounds simply pulverizing body metal and window glass where the .22s and birdshot had ineffectually bounced off. Not only was he on empty, but he did not have much mobility. He had earned his nickname 'Gimp' by virtue of blowing out an ankle when rolling out of a moving HUMMER with a full battle-rattle of 110 pounds. Cobblestones can be a bitch.

None of the passengers were wearing seat belts. Derious and

the skin-head who was sitting in back were the only two survivors. They crawled deeper into the brush. He was fucking pissed. He loved his Escalade and there was no chance he was going to collect his $30k.

Derious watched the Lincoln continue up the road before turning to the west. They were fucked. Derious was the only one with the GPS coordinates. The driver of the Lincoln had a paper map but Derious knew that none of the idiots in the Lincoln knew how to read it.

Derious knew that he had a long, six mile walk to get back to the other side of the M-99 bridge and the other survivor was getting hinky. It was clear that he was suffering from withdraw symptoms.

“Dude, my stash is in the Escalade in the glove box. Can you get it? I think I busted my leg,” Derious said to the other survivor.

Derious capped him in the back of the head as soon as he stood up and turned away. Derious didn’t need any witnesses who would tell Mr Heavy that Derious had screwed the pooch on the drive in. Without witnesses, Derious could say they ran into a two squads of twenty fighters that nobody knew was there.

Derious needed to get back and tell the boss that penetrating the rural areas was not like cracking an egg. Rather, it was like hitting a hornet nest with a stick.

***

Follow the evolving story and our able storyteller at
http://eatonrapidsjoe.blogspot.com

Also, check the www.auctoritaspublishing.org site for updates on future books and publications.

ABOUT THE AUTHOR

Born in Lansing, Michigan in 1959. He graduated from Michigan State University with an engineering degree in 1981. Three decades of experience in the automotive industry with areas of expertise in design, engineering, manufacturing. Special interest in improving quality and increasing throughput with minimal capital investment. In his retirement Eaton Rapids Joe blogs, gardens, cares for aging parents and offends people.

◆ ◆ ◆

Eaton Rapids Joe's short story, "The Farm" is featured in the collection: *Calexit - The Anthology*, edited by JL Curtis. Available on Amazon in both ebook and paperback formats.

Made in the USA
Coppell, TX
03 July 2020

30085300R00322